My Father's Keeper
Andrew Potok

Fomite
Burlington, VT

Excerpts from "Five Men" and "Mr. Cogito on the Need for Precision" from THE COLLECTED POEMS:1956-1998 by ZBIGNIEW HERBERT. Edited by Alissa Valles. Copyright (c) 2007 The Estate of Zbigniew Herbert. Reprinted by permission of HarperCollins Publishers.

ISBN-13: 978-1-937677-45-9
Library of Congress Control Number: 2013945952

Fomite
58 Peru Street
Burlington, VT 05401
www.fomitepress.com

Cover painting - Mytilini #3, 1970, Andrew Potok

For Anna, Nickie and Rachel

Other Books by Andrew Potok

Ordinary Daylight, 1980, Holt Rinehart & Winston, Bantam (non-fiction)

My Life With Goya, 1986, Arbor House (fiction)

A Matter of Dignity, 2002, Bantam/Random House (non-fiction)

My Father's Keeper

1.

My mother yells from the front seat.

"They are coming again."

Stunned and terror-stricken, we scramble out of the van and run into ditches on either side of the road. I land in the gritty mud on my belly, my father behind me, his weight pressing me into the muck. My breath is knocked out of me and my legs are bloodied by the stony earth. Tears begin to form in my eyes, but then an awful stench rises from the grime. I squint and cough and throw up the little bit of food in my belly. In front of me lies a well-dressed man in a brown suit and vest, his gold pocket-watch beside him in the mud. My father pulls himself up a little to cover more of my body. I can't see farther than the still man who is just far enough so I couldn't reach him with my hand if I tried.

Suddenly, my ears are deafened by the shriek of dive bombers and the thwack-thwack of bullets spraying the ground. I lift my head a little and see lines of brown grass swept as if a wind were blowing them.

"Get down," my father yells from behind me.

I can hardly hear his voice above the explosions and the cries and screams coming from everywhere. A bomb explodes very close and clods of earth nearly bury me.

"Tatush!" I yell. "Tatush, I can't breathe!"

I thrash until I get a mouthful of air. I turn toward him. We are both nearly covered with dirt. His hand struggles to move the earth off me. He has moved up and is almost on top of me. The man in the brown suit is motionless, his face turned away. A few pale fingers poke out of the sleeve of his suit jacket. Below his vest, a dark spot is growing, discoloring his pants. My tongue is coarse with mud and I spit and spit but can't get it all out. Another bomb explodes near us and the earth shakes. I hear nothing, so I scream. The head of the man in the brown suit shifts and his face turns toward me. It is torn apart. His shattered jaw hangs loose, almost on his shoulder. I retch and nothing comes up. My father crawls further up my back. I stare at the horrible face in front of me, more horrible than the walking skeletons my governess, Fela, once dangled in front of my face. Yet, I stare so hard that it loses all meaning, stops being a face and, looking down, in its place I see only the gold watch peeking out of the mud, still attached to the man's vest.

I am dazzled by the bits of shiny gold, by its perfect roundness. I pull its dirty, bloody chain toward me. I tug until the watch slides into my hands. It is thick and heavy, warm as a freshly laid egg, like eggs my grandmother plucked from under her hens in Bendzin. The rays of a shining sun are engraved on the lid of the watch and, as I open it, the horror all around me fades and the only thing I hear is the ticking of the watch. Its porcelain face has Arabic and Roman numerals in red and black all around its edge. In school, I learned the Roman numbers. This year is MCMXXXIX. The second-hand is making its rounds, never stopping, while the filigree gold hand clicks softly as it travels from number to number.

The roar above us becomes quiet again and, down by my feet now, my father starts wiping me clean. I twist my head around and look at his eyes, which are gray and focused on me, not, I hope, on the watch. Above us, the sky has cleared, as if nothing had happened. I begin to breathe regularly and stuff the gold watch inside the pocket of my short pants that are caked with mud. My father takes my hand and pulls me out of the ditch. He says nothing about the watch, so I'm pretty sure he never saw it. We climb back inside the Citroen van with my mother and Emilia, her mother Helena and Uncle Bolek, Aunt Eva and Uncle Lolek.

All around us, hundreds of other people are climbing out of ditches into cars and wagons reaching as far back as I can see. The screaming and shouting has almost died down. Doors are opening and slamming shut. I crawl to the back of the van, away from everyone, to examine my prize again. Emilia (little Mila) crawls to my side. She is muddy like me and her dress is torn. We are both on top of the pile of furs in the back. Everyone else is in their place, filthy but alive. No one speaks. No one is kissing anyone else.

The Citronka's motor starts and we inch slowly forward toward the border again. After a few minutes, Bolek slumps a little at the steering wheel and says, almost in a whisper, that he wants to go back to Warsaw. My mother says, her voice as always quiet but very, very firm, "You are being foolish. We cannot go back. We must go on."

Uncle Bolek looks like he is about to cry and says he can't go on. My mother strokes the back of her brother's head. She then turns around and yells at my father.

"And you, Zyga," she begins.

She is very angry and the way she looks at him scares me. "You have no energy. It is time you stopped sitting there with your head in your hands. Be a man."

I want to shout at my mother. I have never raised my voice to her except, they tell me, when I first came out of her screaming.

As usual, I say nothing, but in the way-back of the van, nestled in the furs, I reach into my pocket and my fingers make circles around the lid of the watch. It feels better even than the smooth, shiny horse chestnuts I collect from the park and love to hold in my hands. Round and round my fingers trace its outline. The feel of the metal and its perfect round-ness sends everything else into a peaceful background. Mila breathes softly a few inches from my face. I close my eyes and try to remember why we are here, how we got to wherever in Poland we are.

A DAY OR TWO BEFORE—I"m not really sure how long ago—I play with my soldiers under the dining room table. Everyone is there, aunts, uncles, cousins and grandparents, talking of war. It is almost two months since my eighth birthday. For days, funny Hitler songs on the radio made me laugh and dance. Attack Poland? People snort through their noses because it's a joke. If all of them think it's a joke, then I do, too, but tonight it's different.

It is very late at night and the faces at the table are long and sad, tears plentiful, arguments and insults serious and frightening. They talk of leaving, of airplanes and tanks. I sit on the plush carpet moving whole columns of soldiers from border to border demarcated by colorful boundaries in the carpet design. Little Mila, two years younger than me, is lying on the floor and watches my every move. I like her watching me. We play together a lot, in her house or mine.

Now, under the table, we are surrounded by dozens of shoes: my father's and Uncle Stash's covered with gray spats, Uncle Bolek's shiny as glass. Aunt Zosia's are the highest heels of all. Feet shuffle, cross one in front of the other, tap nervously. Chairs empty as an uncle or aunt gets up to squabble and pace. I can barely see my father on the other side of a momentarily emptied chair, opening the glass doors of the grandfather clock and, after looking carefully at his gold pocket watch, winding the weights which whir softly. The tall grandfather clock strikes twelve times.

Above me, the talk is loud, then my grandfather's deep voice commands attention.

"They are on the border," Grandfather Solomon says.

I love his voice and the way everyone pays attention to him.

"They are strong, very strong," says Cousin Henio.

"Ha!" says Uncle Stash. "We will destroy them."

Uncle Stash is a lawyer so he must be right. But then everyone speaks at once. My mother's voice, calm but firm, rises above the rest. She says that men and children must leave immediately.

"I don't want to go," I blurt from under the table, and Mila cries that she doesn't either.

Uncle Bolek yells furiously at his sister and, under the table, I watch as my father and mother kick each other, each of them yelling insults. Above me, spoons stir, tea and cakes are passed around, forks and knives clash. Someone bangs the table and all the cups and saucers bounce. On the radio, a chorus is singing the national anthem. I want to stand at attention. I always do when hearing these words accompanied by this music, but I am much too tall to stand under the table. I don't think that anyone else is standing now, not Aunt Eva, Uncle Stash or Lolek, not Helena or Bolek, not my parents or Grandfather Solomon, Grandmother Paulina or Inka my governess, not Cousin Henio or Pola.

"Poland is not yet lost," the radio chorus sings.

Though I know these words well, it feels like I am hearing them for the first time. But I am frightened. If Poland disappears, what will happen to me?

"Not while we live," they sing. "Poland is not yet lost while we live. What those others take from us, we will take back with our swords."

I arrange my soldiers, each one small and heavy, so cool in my hand, cool and alive with straps, buckles, rifles and helmets. Then Inka crawls under the table and whisks me away to bed.

I can hardly sleep and wake up while it is still dark outside. In the living room, my mother, Uncle Bolek, and Bolek's friend Helena with her little Mila asleep on her lap, are all talking quietly. Mila's grown-up name is Emilia, but everyone calls her Mila. Sometimes I call her Mishka, then she is Mishka and I am Mishek, two little mice, like the mice we saw in a Walt Disney movie. I walk in bleary-eyed.

"I can't sleep," I tell them.

"Of course you can't," Helena says.

She is just a friend, especially a friend of Uncle Bolek's, but I like her better than any other of their friends. She takes Mila and me to the movies and to the beautiful Warsaw parks on the governesses' days off.

"I must go to close up the house in Wieliszew," Uncle Bolek says. "Why don't I take Mishek with me?"

"At a time like this?" my mother says.

I don't really understand why this time is different from other times.

"Oh yes, please," I beg, awake now.

I love going places with Uncle Bolek. My father is quiet and comforts me when I have bad dreams. Uncle Bolek is loud, laughs a lot, and showers me with presents.

"We will be back in a few hours," Uncle Bolek assures them.

I get dressed, Uncle Bolek takes my hand, and we walk in the dark streets to his beautiful, blue Packard with red-white-and-silver hubcaps. The streets are empty and distant thunder is the only noise I hear. It is spooky and wonderful.

"Is it war? Is war coming?" I ask as we drive through the damp, eerie streets.

"Yes, it is coming, but it won't last long," Uncle Bolek says.

"Why is it war?"

"I don't know," Uncle Bolek says.

"You don't know? Who does know?"

Bolek says nothing.

"Are we going away?"

"Maybe for a little while."

"Where will we go?"

"Just play," Uncle Bolek says and leans over to the glove compartment to pull out a ball-bearing in a small leather case.

I forget all about war as I twirl this magical silver ring and spin the steel band around the tiny balls of the ball-bearing. I have no idea why the little nuggets do not fall out of the inner circle. Bolek says that the faint, gray light of dawn means that today will be another cloudy day.

"Maybe even rain," he says.

I have never seen Warsaw before dawn. All Warsaw is sleeping except for a few neighing horses as droshkies are beginning to line up at important corners. As Bolek drives over the Vistula, he is biting his lip and his hands grip the steering wheel with such force that his knuckles turn white.

"We'll be back in Warsaw for lunch," he says.

Bolek's nearly finished country house is still dark. As he talks to the cook and gardener who emerge from the kitchen looking worried, I race to my new bicycle leaning against the garden fence. A week before, Uncle Bolek brought it all the way from London. I've never had a full-size bike before. It's sleek and black, the most beautiful thing I've ever seen. Soon I am flying through the field across the road, laughing like a crazy boy. The speed is exhilarating, the air rushing through my hair, my whole body. I yelp and throw my head back as I fly over the bumps and stones. I try removing my hands from the handle-bars and laugh when I can't. I scream with joy, as loud as I can, then close my eyes for moments at a time. And still, I am flying. My whole body trembles with joy, a whooping, crazy, total joy.

And then, three airplanes appear just over the treetops. So much happiness and all at once. They are Polish planes, probably flying to war. They fly so low that I can see the pilots' faces in their hoods and masks. My heart beats faster. Their wings shine silver against the dark sky, the red and white checkerboard insignia as beautiful as ever. What a morning this is! I drop the bicycle at my feet, puff out my chest, and salute. And then the planes begin to scream, a horrible wailing sound, and bombs slip out from each of them, exploding all over the field. The stones and clods of earth and fire that hit me change me. I don't recognize myself. There is no myself. Trees are exploding and the air is filled with stones. The planes drone on as if nothing happened. The house is on fire. I see no one and keep running into the burning woods, screaming for my father. I run to my owl, Koko, hanging in his cage from a low branch inside a clump of pines. I flick the cage open and Koko flies off into the sky, high over the burning trees. Choking on smoke, I run and fall again. Lech, the gardener, finds me and carries me into a shelter, a hole he'd dug in the garden. Shaking with fright, my mouth opens wide and I scream, "Tatush, tatush, tatush!"

I want my father. My throat burns. In my head, stars and planets collide. The world has ended. They make me drink an awful tasting liquid and I fall asleep. When I wake up, I'm in the car on the way back to Warsaw, my head on the cook's lap in the back seat. Uncle Bolek is driving and Olga and Lech are weeping. My head is still ringing. My mind is black as night. My old self is looking down at the boy in Olga's lap. I don't know who he is, maybe a boy who is dead or nearly dead. I'm glad I'm not him.

Later that day, or maybe in two days, I am Miszek again. I don't like being touched. I can hardly hear what is being said. When it is dark outside again, I curl up in Inka's lap and listen to her read from one of my favorite books, about a locomotive which pulls cars full of everything I can think of, including a thousand athletes who have eaten a thousand cutlets. I can picture them flexing their muscles and opening their mouths, but then I squeeze my eyelids hard and see only bursts of light, like stars exploding.

In the morning, airplanes come again. The sound is louder and louder until they are roaring above my head. I lose myself inside the noise. I cover my ears and scream. The room shakes, buildings must be crumbling, falling to the ground. My father paces, in and out of my room, into his bedroom, around the dining room table, into the kitchen. He puts his hands on my ears and holds my head.

"This will soon stop," he says, almost as if he were asking me if it really would stop. "The English are coming," he says. "They will chase the barbarians from Poland."

His words, as always, comfort me, but in spite of what he says, the next day the barbarians come back. The noise lasts all day and I hide, cuddled under the table as the adults listen to the radio.

"The bombing is mostly across the river in Praga," my father reports. "Only a few planes crossed the Vistula and dropped bombs around the synagogue."

But I know that is not true, even though I don't know where the synagogue is and I have never seen it. I know for sure that the bombs are falling on me. I cannot breathe and my father takes my face in his hands again. He checks my forehead for fever, which he does whenever I cough or my nose is stuffed. If I am sick, the doctor will walk down Moniuszki Street, the cups clinking in his bag, cups he will lay on my back which make beautiful blue circles. I can picture those circles now.

Very early the next morning, Mila, her mother Helena, my father and I get into the white Citronka van, the name Mandelbaum's printed in large letters on both sides. The back of the van is stuffed with fur coats! I have seen many fur coats in my life but never so many in one pile. The driver Twardowski gets behind the wheel, while Uncle Bolek slides into the front seat of the Packard. My mother, Aunt Eva, and Uncle Lolek drive with Bolek. Half of Marszalkowska, which my father calls the Champs-Elysees of Warsaw, is rubble, but Mandelbaum Furs is as yet untouched. Trolley cars are lying on their sides or standing still between stops, as if they were my toy trolley cars or army trucks or ambulances. It is as scary and impossible as a bad dream. I blink my eyes and try to make everything right again.

The road leaving the city, heading south, is packed with honking cars and trucks. I grab my father's arm. He is slumping in a middle seat. I have seen him sad before but never like this. When he takes my hand to comfort me, his hand is cold and trembles a little.

"Where are we going?" I ask him.

"Rumania," he says.

Helena then says that the king and queen of Rumania bought furs from Bolek. I try to imagine Rumania where we will be greeted by the king and queen, invited to stay in the royal palace.

"Tatush, are we coming back?" I ask my father.

"Soon," he says, almost in a whisper.

In Lublin, the sound of tanks which, my father says, are coming from Russia, turns us back to where we came from. The Citronka stinks of the dead animal skins sewn into fur coats. Mila quietly sings a pretty song. I make a funny face to make her laugh. Mila is almost family. Though she is only six, she is very smart. Like me, she loves to count, loves words and numbers. We have been at each other's birthday parties all our lives.

"Tatush, where are we going now?" I ask my father.

"Lithuania," he says, not looking at me.

I can hardly hear him.

"Is it far?"

"Not too far."

We drive past the outskirts of Warsaw again, now on our way to Lithuania. Twardowski leads us over unfamiliar dirt roads. After a day or so, we stop in front of a country house.

"We need gasoline," Helena says.

Bolek and another man drive off and when they return they transfer large metal cans from the man's car to our van, which begins to smell of gas. I watch through the window as my mother gives the man one of her rings.

"Oh my God," Helena cries. "It's her diamond."

She pulls Mila to her chest.

"Bolek knows everyone," Helena says, looking a bit shaken.

Then we get back into the long line of cars and horse-drawn wagons, all of us racing to get out of Poland. I look out the back window of the van and I see a cage with chickens on top of a small car. People have chairs and tables tied on their roofs. Noisy little trucks are carrying goats and sheep. We drive across a long, flat plain and begin to hear airplanes in the distance. The thud of bombs moves closer. I squeeze my body into the smallest ball I can manage, my arms hugging my chest, clinging hard, my head down, my hands frozen into fists. I look plead-ingly at my father. His head is in his hands and he does not notice me. Mila cries for a piece of chocolate. Her mother takes two small squares out of her handbag and hands one to each of us. I love chocolate, but now I taste only gasoline.

The next day, we pull out of line again and drive into the yard of a ramshackle farmhouse, partly shaded by trees. A few cows graze not far from it. Through the mud-flecked back window of the van I can see a woman in a dirty dress standing by the farmhouse door, leaning on a scythe. At the wheel of our van, Twardowski is smoking a cigarette. My father sits still in the back seat. I don't think he even knows that we are no longer on the road. Uncle Bolek, my mother, Eva, and Lolek get out of the Packard. Helena rolls down the window and tells Bolek that the children are very hungry.

The woman with the scythe yells, "Jews!"

"Please Madam," Uncle Bolek says with the smile he reserves for his best customers. "Can I buy some food from you?"

She is wearing a shredded dress; Bolek a pinstripe suit, a white handkerchief peeking out of his breast pocket. I don't understand why she calls us Jews. Maybe Jews should be ashamed of being Jews. Fela, the governess before Inka, told me that Jews killed God. If they did, that could be the reason Jews should be ashamed. But I don't think we are Jewish. And I don't know how anyone can kill God. Uncle Bolek bows down, places his hand just inside his suit jacket. He looks like Napoleon in one of my school books.

"Esteemed Madame," he says, "we want nothing without paying."

He opens the van doors. Afraid of what is about to happen, the woman's scythe still in her hands, Emilia and I sneak away from the pile of furs. The woman comes closer, her eyes open wide. The furs are piled almost to the van's ceiling. The woman licks her lips. My father covers his face with his hands. An old stooped man comes in from the field.

"Jews from Warsaw," the woman shouts over her shoulder.

I slide out of the van's open door and walk over to the Packard. My mother is again sitting in the front seat, her face motionless.

"What are Jews?" I whisper into her ear.

"Jews?" she says. "It's nothing."

She opens her door and walks toward the van.

"Zyga, take him," she says to my father.

He does not respond and my mother pushes me back into the van.

A few minutes later, with a mink coat slung over her dirty dress, the peasant woman strangles three chickens, rips their feathers out, and cooks them in a large black pot. We are standing outside the farmhouse kitchen, and the smell brings saliva to my lips. I have never experienced hunger before. When the chickens are cooked, we pass the pieces around. It feels funny to be eating standing up, especially eating with my hands. I look at my mother, but she doesn't look back at me as she picks delicately on a chicken wing with her beautiful painted fingers. My father sucks on a chicken foot and passes another to me. Never having done so before, I suck on the coarse skin of the chicken foot and actually like it. Helena makes sure Mila and I get enough. Everyone seems satisfied. Darkness comes and we climb back into the vehicles, but we don't leave. Mila and I sleep on the fur coats, holding hands.

In the morning, with the farmer and his wife somewhere in the fields, we say goodbye to Twardowski and the Packard.

"Not enough gasoline," my father explains.

Twardowski shakes everyone's hand and wishes us well. He pats my head. "I know I will see the families Mandelbaum and Mendelssohn soon. I will meet you back in Warsaw."

A few hours later, creeping through the crowded streets of Wilno, the last city before the border, a bullet crashes through the windshield and lodges in the front seat next to Uncle Bolek. Everybody starts yelling and crying. I feel numb. Uncle Bolek again says he wants to turn back to Warsaw, to his apartment overlooking the Vistula, to his beautiful salon with its perfect little French elevator. My mother, sobbing, puts her head on his shoulder and says nothing. Then Bolek shrieks dirty words, much worse than "blood of a dog," the worst curse I know. Mila is crying in Helena's lap. My father hides his head in a white handkerchief. Everyone is wailing. The van keeps inching forward, following the cars in front of it, sometimes so slowly that Lolek and my father push it to save gasoline. Other people are doing the same. Dead horses and overturned carts litter both sides of the road. Children dressed in rags stare at us as we pass.

We move slowly all night. When I wake up, the landscape has not changed much. We are back in the countryside, farmland spreading out around us. It feels like we have been driving forever. Uncle Bolek says the border must be close, and that's when we hear more planes. My mother yells from the front seat, "They're coming again."

That is how we got here, why I am holding a gold watch in my hand. I wish I could be back sitting under the dining room table, playing with my soldiers, thinking that war was like a Charlie Chaplin movie, that we will kick Hitler in the dupa. I wonder if my English bicycle is still in the field. I don't even know if it was hit by a bomb. I hear Mila breathing softly next to me. We are breathing each other's breath. I also smell the filthy mud still on our clothes. I try not to think about the man whose watch this was. I stop thinking about where we are going, or where we have come from. I just keep running my finger in circles over the polished surface of the lid of my watch.

Around noon, the red-and-white-striped barrier of the border crossing appears. The mood inside the van changes. My father comes back to life, but looks worried. Helena sits up, and my mother, who has been humming to herself, falls silent. Bolek taps his fingers on the steering wheel. I shove the watch deep into my pocket. Mila and I press our faces to the window. We can see that, one by one, cars are being examined by the border guards. Some are allowed through, some pushed to the side. The people whose cars have been pushed to the side drop to their knees and weep. Our Citronka is, I think, ten cars from the painted wooden barrier which goes up and down with each car's crossing. We are hardly moving. Polish soldiers hobble past us and throw their rifles into a growing pile before getting in line to cross the border. Two of them peer into the Citronka and spit on the windshield, hissing, "Jews."

I think it's my fault. They spit on us because I stole a gold watch. I begin to cry.

"Don't cry," my mother commands.

"Let him cry," my father says, sitting up straight.

Then he pushes his way to the door of the van and climbs out, slamming it behind him. I want him to grab one of the rifles and shoot the soldiers, but instead he paces outside the van. I squirm forward, try to get out to be with him.

"Just stay," my mother yells from the front seat.

So I hide in the furs again, but a moment later, Uncle Bolek explodes in anger.

"Where's Zyga going? What's that swine up to?" he yells, peering over the steering wheel.

I sit up and look for my father, but he has disappeared from sight. No one answers Uncle Bolek.

"Coward!" Uncle Bolek yells out the side window. "Blood of a dog, smear of shit, son of a whore, may cholera take you!" His teeth are bared, his smooth, bald head all shades of purple.

Blood rushes to my ears and my body shakes.

"Don't listen to him," I whisper to Mila and cover her ears with my hands.

I want to hit Bolek, stupefied that I can even think such a thing. I know that my father is planning something good, something that will save us all. Come back Tatush, I think with my face all scrunched up, for who, if not him, will protect me if the planes come back?

My Uncle Lolek, who still has all of his thick brown hair, speaks up and says to Bolek, "What is the matter with you? Why do you hate him so?"

"Don't talk to me!" Uncle Bolek shouts.

"Let it be," my mother commands.

Uncle Bolek has never liked my father. When they are together in a room, I run away. They always look so angry that it scares me. The truth hits me like a slap in my face and brings burning tears to my eyes. Both Bolek and my mother really hate my father. I have never seen my parents kiss or hug. They don't joke and cuddle. They don't smile at each other or speak in soft tones. When I played at my friend Tadzik's house, I saw his mother and father kissing, so I know. My mother only shouts at my tatush and he shouts back. Sometimes she throws things. Some of the words that are now flying around inside the Citronka I have never heard, not really. Why does she hate him? Has she always hated him? Does she hate me, too? I shrink into the seat and try to cover my ears as she says, "Those Mendelssohns think they're so smart, always on the right side of everything. How does he dare to look down his nose at the business, the only reason he can live as he does. He knows nothing of the world. All he and his friends are capable of is talk."

"Ha!" she says. "They think they will change the world. Ha! War comes and they don't know what to do."

But now, my father is gone. Maybe he is never coming back. I begin to cry and Aunt Eva holds me close.

"Where is he?" my mother suddenly asks.

Bolek raises his eyebrows. "He ran."

"You saw it?"

Bolek stabs the windshield in front of him with his finger.

"On the running board of a Mercedes. I am sure it was Zyga."

Helena says that Zyga would never abandon his son.

"You know nothing," Uncle Bolek yells.

I close my eyes and bury my face in the furs. Voices argue, yell, and whisper. Soldiers shout. It is all muffled by the soft fur, now wet from my tears. When I stop crying and sit up again, the red-and-white-striped border has disappeared behind us. We are in Lithuania. Everyone is talking quietly. I take my gold watch from my pocket and listen hard to its ticking. Mila tries to pull the watch from my hand and I tuck it under my body.

"What is it?" Mila asks.

"It's a beautiful gold watch," I tell her.

"Show it to me," she begs and, shielding it carefully from everyone else, I pull it out to show her.

"It's a secret," I say. "Only you know, no one else."

The Citronka suddenly stops. We are a few kilometers inside Lithuania. I sit up and see my father at the side of the road.

"Tatush," I yell.

I push past Mila, throw the van door open, and run into his arms.

"Tatush," I say to him.

He is white as a ghost and his arms seem too weak to hold me. No one else gets out of the van. I take his hand and lead him back across the road. I get in first and sit down, still holding his hand. He keeps his eyes down as he climbs in. It is as if I am his father and he is the eight-year-old. No one says a word and Helena reaches over and closes the van door. Mila is staring at my father. My hands close into fists. My whole body clenches.

The trees and fields we are passing are ugly. We stop and Helena buys apples from a cart at the side of the bumpy road. Farmers are plowing the fields with large cows that Helena says are not cows but oxen. I bite into the apple but it is mealy and dry. We drive forever. My father remains as pale and silent as a ghost. Helena whispers to me and Mila that we are driving straight through Lithuania into Latvia, another country altogether. I wake and sleep and wake again. Each time before I am fully awake I think I am back in Warsaw, then I see the faces of the adults, cold and hard, feel the movement of the van, and my stomach shrinks again. Sometimes my mother chats with Uncle Bolek about what is on the road or where they should stop for gas. No one talks to my father, who never looks up from his shoes.

At the airport in Latvia, we leave the Citronka, our home for days though it feels like months. Time is so slow now. It feels like Mila and I have always slept on furs in the back of a van, like I have always had a gold watch I stole from a dead man, like my mother has always hated my father. When I get out of the van, my father reaches for my hand. We get on an airplane, my first time ever. Helena says we are flying to Sweden.

Bolek, my parents, and I move into an apartment in Stockholm that smells like rye bread and fish.

"Where is Emilia?" I ask.

"They are in another apartment," my mother says.

I wake up screaming every night in a small bed in a corner of the living room. Blackness makes me scream and screaming brings me blackness. The black is as heavy as all of space. It is a vise, sucking up air as it closes on me. My father does not come to comfort me. I don't know what has happened to him. My mother takes me to a Swedish doctor, who prods my stomach and prescribes some kind of medicine.

"This will help you be happy," he says in, I think, German, which my mother translates for me.

Mila and I go to a school in the middle of Stockholm. She plays with the other children. I do not. I don't want to play. I sit by myself, keeping my body very tight and perfectly still. My watch is always with me, in my pants pocket. I can't stop flipping its engraved lid open and closed. In our apartment, the clicking sound annoys my mother and I like that.

"What are you doing?" she keeps asking. "Let me see what is in your pocket."

"No," I say, defiance as natural to me now as smiling had once been.

Weeks later, I begin remembering strange things like my governess Fela, the one before Inka, who told me that Jews stole from the dead, that gold was all Jews wanted.

"Oh please," I say to myself, "not gold, not Jews."

But I know I am a Jew because my gold prize dazzles me. My heart, a Jew's heart, is beating so hard I think I will stop breathing.

One day, as we drink tea in the small dining room that is full of sunlight but cold, my mother says,

"We're going to America. We have been in Sweden for four months. It is time to leave."

A few days later, we board a train to Bergen, which I learn from a map on the wall of our railway car is a port city in Norway. Out the train window, I scan the sky for airplanes, but the sky is light blue and clear. I look around the train car for Helena, who always explains things, but she and Mila are not with us.

"Where are Emilia and Helena? Where are Aunt Eva and Uncle Lolek?" I ask.

We were eight in the Citronka and now we are four.

"Are they meeting us at the boat?"

My mother doesn't answer. My father stares at his shoes, which is where he has been looking since we picked him up in Lithuania. Oh, please look at me, I want to say, but say nothing.

As we walk from the train station, Uncle Bolek is in the lead, my mother alongside him, and my father trailing us, like a family. I flip the lid of my watch open and closed. The port opens up before us. It is full of people and ships. Boxes and suitcases all over the pier make it hard to walk. Everyone is in a hurry. I hear someone say in Polish that the Germans are on the Norwegian border.

"Where is everyone else?" I ask again. "Where are Mila and Helena?"

"They will come later," my father says.

Uncle Bolek and my mother look at the high cliffs. I don't like what is happening. I am angry, angry and weepy.

"Don't cry," my mother says, her face an angry scowl.

"Let him cry," my father says, angry himself and speaking up for the first time in a long time.

As we walk up the gangplank, the huge cliffs tower over the boat. I have never seen cliffs like these nor have I ever been on a big boat like this one. Everything is new and frightening. The air smells like coal and steam. I share a tiny cabin with my mother, who sits on her bunk, finds her little mirror in her purse, and powders her nose.

We leave shore at dusk. After a supper of mostly herring, I sneak away to the deck and stand on the rail, watching the land shrink and then disappear.

"Where are you, Mishka?" I cry quietly.

I have never felt so alone. My hands numb up to my elbow. Terrified, I turn away from the sea. No one is in sight. My knees give way and I fall asleep on the deck.

2.

Aren't we all haunted by some early events in our lives? I have begun this account of mine at a moment which seems still not only to have been central but all-consuming. You and I, Milushka, were touched by fire, born to violence. The bombs that dropped in the fields of Wieliszew were the touch and kiss of the real world. Some of us can numb-out after such a storm, others are forever linked to it. What happened to you? But even if numbing is our means of self-preservation, the painful events have a way of sneaking in and setting the stage for future actions. In that beautiful Warsaw, the parks, one light and spacious, the other dark and somber, gave themselves to me, according to my mercurial moods until my heart was blackened by three German men in three airplanes. The world ended and the dominos fell, losses gained momentum, gave birth to new losses, to hope, to unexpected curves and U-turns, collisions, to skies turning red then black, to rage. And you my little Mila, my Mishka, where are you? Where did you go?

In 1945, five years after our entrance to America through Ellis Island, I enter the third form of the Alexander Hamilton School for Boys, on the northern tip of Manhattan, recommended to my mother by one of her rich American customers. This year is to be my first living with my parents after five years in little boarding schools, the first across the East River in Brooklyn, then upstate New York, eastern Connecticut and central Massachusetts, where my strangeness was identified by head-masters as shell-shock, emotional disturbance. I was a boy apart, whose unstoppable nightmares were tolerated and pacified, usually in the lap of a kind headmistress. At the Crestview School, tucked into some New England hillside, a boarding school I'd been sent to after one ter-ror-stricken night at Brooklyn Ethical Culture, I bit a kid named Felix, a Rumanian refugee who, unlike me, had not lost his accent. I bit the kid so hard that Felix needed stitches. Sleepy Crestview did not want more to do with a damaged Michael who bit and kicked, so I was shuffled off to Mountaintop where I found a way to harness my anger and loneliness through drawing, which came to me like the English language, whole and perfect.

It began with circles, one inside the other. Having peered obsessively at the circles of my gold pocket watch, my brain overflowed with numbers and circles. "Look at Michael draw the perfect circle," was a constant refrain. Some evenings, as the kids sat in front of a fire in the fireplace and our teachers talked about the sky, the earth, the birth of cities, the sessions often ended with requests for circles, loved by the little girls and teachers, even the headmaster, Mr. Williams, my surrogate father and protector. My circles metamorphosed into drawings of animals and people. "I'll trade you for a panther," one of my girlfriends said and let me stick my hand inside her shirt. Another let me watch her pee for a picture of an apple tree in bloom. The crowning glory was displaying my little erect cock to Eunice who, in turn, exposed her not yet blooming pudenda. "No touching," she warned and we stared for a long time. A tidal wave of art swept over me. I felt its power in my head, my heart and between my legs. The emptiness inside me was being populated by a budding Michael Mendelssohn, a boy who could persuade, could forge a way forward.

Uncle Bolek and my mother, Rena, had risen in their new world from Ellis Island to 89th Street between Amsterdam and Columbus, to way West 71st Street, creeping their way towards Fifth Avenue on 55th Street, two blocks from the former Mandelbaum's, now Mandeleau Furs, within easy walking distance. My father, Zyga, had as little to do with it as possible, usually staying home by himself.

"My mother has a nose for good addresses," I tell Henry Karp, one of my new friends at Alexander Hamilton. "The war provided the opportunity for a shrewd business move, from Marszalkowska 125 to 20 West 57th Street."

Karp and I are on our way home from way uptown at the end of the IRT subway line.

Karp, small and fragile, yells at me, his facial tics fully engaged, "Don't talk like that," he says. "They lost everything!"

"Karp," I say, "I'm not saying they wanted a war to bring them to New York. I'm saying that my mother and my uncle know how to kiss asses, how to get ahead. Something my father knows nothing about. For better or for worse," I add.

"What about your father?" Karp asks.

"He's a basket case."

"He must miss his family," Karp says.

"Of course, Karp, we all miss our family, but it's more than that with him. He doesn't talk. He has no friends. He's become poisonous and I don't want to come near him."

As the train nears 86th Street where Karp gets off, he says, "I don't believe it."

"I'm not dumb, Karp. I know what's happening," I shout as Henry Karp flees onto the platform.

I walk home from Columbus Circle to 55th Street. In the kitchenette, an ugly German woman named Hedwig, with a disgusting growth near her mouth which gives her a permanent scowl, is preparing our meal. I close the door of my room behind me and on my bed I open my book, *The Chinese Room*, to a dog-eared page. *The Chinese Room* is a room of heady smells and plucked string sounds, a room crammed with jade, kimonos, dirty oriental pictures, and Chinese vases with silk flowers inside them, in which a big red-headed bear of a man messes around with his beautiful girlfriend. He is kneading her nipple, and before I unzip my fly, I have the presence of mind to grab the dictionary. "1. to work (dough, clay, etc.) into a uniform mixture by pressing, folding, and stretching." That's what he does to her nipple? "2. to manipulate by similar movements, as the body in a massage." If only I knew a girl who yearns to have her nipples kneaded. I run to my desk and grab a magazine with pictures of girls in bathing suits doing yoga stretches, just barely enough for satisfaction. My main activities in my room consist of *The Chinese Room* or magazines found in dirty little bookstores around Times Square and, mostly, filling sketchbook after sketchbook with drawings, imagined copulations, copies from books of the Old Masters, and attempts at dark abstractions.

My mother and father come home late. Zyga takes off his jacket and backs into his chair, the newspaper on his lap. He slumps into the hard cushion of the couch, emits a low moan, and turns on the radio to listen to some German named Kaltenborn read the end-of-war news. Rena hangs her mink coat in the hall closet and goes into their room. I stand at their bedroom door and watch as she unhooks all the stays of her corset which leaves bright red marks, like a zipper, all the way down her back. In her bathrobe, she lies down on her bed, closes her eyes and sighs an end of the workday sigh. After a few minutes of rest, she reaches over to her address book and looks for the number of her florist. She turns the pages, each one full of crossed out names and phone numbers. It's an indecipherable mess. Still, she stumbles onto the number and calls.

"I am Madame Mendelssohn," she says. "Yes, yes, for Madame Harrington." She listens. "Madame Franklin Harrington of Park Avenue," she says and somehow the sale is consummated.

She then looks at me, standing at the door and, in Polish, she says that Madame Harrington has just been fitted for a floor-length chinchilla. Chinchilla, Alaska-seal, ranch-mink, Persian-lamb, are the first words I learned in English.

"Bolek is teaching all America what is beautiful," Rena says.

Wrapping the robe tight around her, she moves to a chair by the window and adjusts her strawberry-blonde wig, her wigs made in Paris as they were before the war.

"Why does no one tell me what happened to Emilia? Emilia and Helena. I ask and ask. You never answer."

We communicate only in Polish. English is my language, not hers. I'm an American. She is not.

"I tell you that I don't know," Rena says. "They choose to stay in Sweden."

"Why?"

"Probably Helena finds a man she likes."

"She was a friend to Bolek."

"I know, Mishek, but some women are like that. Especially beautiful women."

"Are you like that?"

"I never knew how to be a mother, Mishek," she confesses, changing the subject as always, as if I didn't know about the quality of her mothering. "Some women know what to do. I never did."

Rena removes a necklace made of many strands of little pearls. When alone in the apartment, I fish the pearls out of their container and run my fingers through them, like tiny pebbles at the ocean edge in Long Beach where I have been deposited every summer. As Rena unclips her earrings, Hedwig coughs in the kitchen, her call to dinner.

My father is already seated at the small dinette table, slurping his soup to annoy us. No one speaks. Rena picks on the overcooked chicken and doesn't touch the potatoes. I smack the table top with a fist, my attempt to make something happen. The little bell on the table trembles. Hedwig's kitchen chair, which opens into a step ladder, scrapes along the linoleum floor. She eats her meal from a counter to the left of the sink. Rena tinkles the little bell and Hedwig serves baked apples. After spooning a few bites, Rena goes back to their bedroom. Zyga goes to his chair to listen to the large Philco radio again, his head resting on the kitchen towel provided by his wife to protect the upholstery from Zyga's head oils. After the news, Zyga gets up, goes to the door of their bedroom where Rena is talking on the telephone with one of her friends from Warsaw days. Zyga cannot bear it, especially not knowing if it is his wife or Stefa on the other end who is paying for the call. Spending money for non-essential things has become one of his major annoyances, one of many. Talking with a friend is decidedly not essential. He curses. "Blood of a dog," he hisses in Polish, "*psia krew*, cholera."

He walks into the kitchen where he picks up the extension phone. He stands there listening for minutes and then slams the receiver down into both ladies' ears. My body tenses with rage. Everything Zyga does and probably has done while I was at those boarding schools is hateful.

He has changed from the little I remember when I was a child. Some time ago, I overheard Bolek hissing to my mother that Zyga had betrayed all of us at the border. I'm not convinced that this is true though I will never forget his ashen face when we picked him up in Lithuania. Even if it is true, I don't know why he is lashing out unless he has come to hate himself as much as he hates them. I want to stay away from him, from all of them.

Karp, who knows a lot of things, tells me a week later after school as we sit on my bed at 40 West 55th Street, *The Chinese Room* on my lap, that I must try not to hate my father. Karp has an opinion about everything, a lot of it direct quotes from the books he is reading. The other day, on the subway up to school, he broke the news about the second law of thermodynamics. Every action has an equal and opposite reaction. I don't want to question him out loud, for what if he is right, but I don't believe a word of it. Now, Karp reddens and his tics go haywire as he reads the part about kneading nipples. I make him read a few other hot passages, one where the red-headed man caresses her thighs until they begin to part, another where she sticks her hand into his pocket and makes him "engorged," another word I have to look up. Henry Karp's nose and eyelids twitch uncontrollably. His face in motion distracts me as usual. Stuttering, Karp manages to ask about the kneading problem, and I rub my thumb and forefinger together to demonstrate. Karp doesn't seem to get it so, to inflict damage, I tell him about my watch.

"I stole it from a dead man," I tell him.

Karp looks aghast.

"Want to see it?" I ask, reaching into my pocket for the gold watch.

I hand it to Karp, who draws his hand back before gathering the courage to touch it.

"You didn't steal it from a dead man," Karp insists.

"Asshole," I hiss. "You'll never know who I really am unless you accept what I tell you. I stole it from a dead man as German planes were bombing me. I wanted the gold watch."

I am perspiring and breathing fast.

"And you know what else? I had a brother who threw himself under a German tank."

I used the brother lie, a little fib really, when I felt alone in the world and desperately needed attention at the Brooklyn boarding school they had left me at, the week after we arrived in America. Boy, did I ever need all the care and love I could get! Karp's eyes widen.

"With a hand grenade tucked into his belly," I add.

Karp's eyelids blink furiously.

"Okay. Enough. Just remember, Karp, you're dealing with a person the likes of whom you've never known before." I stand up. "And now, let's get out of here."

My father sits by the radio on one end of the couch and we can't avoid walking past him. Zyga's rheumy eyes turn toward us and he tries to smile.

"Keep walking," I command Karp, pushing him.

Zyga's body stirs and Karp turns toward him, extending his hand, smiling.

"Stop it," I snarl and yank him away with one hand, the other hand pushing my father back down. In the overheated apartment, Zyga's shirt is wet and I recoil.

"Leave us alone," I bark at my father in Polish.

My disgust overwhelmed me. Shamelessly, not hiding my disdain, I look down at Zyga's large nose, the bags under his eyes, the balding head full of little growths, scabs, ugly blemishes.

"I said we're leaving," I say to Karp. "I mean it. Now."

"But… but…" Karp stammers.

As I forcibly guide Karp to the front door, I am overwhelmed by guilt. I grab Karp's arm for support. With my free hand, I reach the door handle and, trying to follow, Karp nearly trips over his own shoes.

We wait for the elevator. My heart pounds in my chest.

"Are you all right?" Karp asks.

"No."

We stand silent and apart.

"Where you boys going?" asks Rabbit, the elderly black elevator man. "You best keep out of trouble."

Trouble? We are going uptown to Karp's house where Karp's mother, on many after-school occasions, hammers music into our heads. Bertha Karp is tall and boney, her brown hair knotted into a bun at the back of her head. She has a German accent which always makes me uneasy. I am happy I lost my accent during the first couple of months in America. Maybe it is just Germans—even German Jews—who are not allowed ever to lose their accents. It makes a certain sense to me, a warning to all who come into contact with them. Before she lets us in the door on West End Avenue, Bertha Karp challenges us.

"Also," she says, "this is for Michael."

She hums a theme from one of the Bach Cello Suites, which I know by heart.

"Good boy," Bertha Karp says. "And now for Henry."

Inside, Bertha hovers over the two of us. I whisper to my pal, "I much prefer your mother to mine."

Mrs. Karp puts one 78 after another on the gramophone turntable and cranks it up. Thus we listen to Schumann and Beethoven, Mendelssohn and Brahms. She watches us carefully and clears her throat when our attention flags.

"Three part fugue," she warns.

Their apartment is stuffed with books and records. I want to live here, even with Karp's tics and his mother's accent.

Want to or not, I stay in the loveless, laugh-less, music-less, dark apartment with Zyga and Rena, plus the ugly Hedwig whose sneer reminds me that I am a Jewish gold-snatching thief.

At times, I stare out the window onto the dark shaft between my room and the windows of the adjacent building. I have no family. My grandparents are dead. Everyone in school has grandparents. I do not. It's true that I am an American now, an American without grandparents and, like all my friends, I know about the war—my war, for God's sake—from newspapers. Battles in the Atlantic and the Pacific have an equal curiosity. What is it with me? I cheer for the Allies, the Americans, barely aware that Leyte and Guadalcanal are not my war, that my war is in Europe.

Two years later, Rena and Zyga upgrade from their small apartment on 55th Street to a light roomy place way east on 57th. With the money—I steal a little at a time from Rena's purse—I buy a cello. Its sound enthralled me from the first time I hear Piatagorsky on the radio. Its range descends into dark regions and transports me to a place I know well. I find a teacher, Bedric Kovic, a stooped old man with a harelip who knew Dvorak and is now reduced to sitting through lessons in his mid-town studio apartment with beginners like me.

"Cello? Cello?" Uncle Bolek cries when I tell him about it, making the word sound lewd. "You must be Mischa or Jascha to play such an instrument, not Michael, a nice name. She gives you this name your mother so you can travel and play tennis, not cello."

But I would blow into bagpipes if bagpipes could help get me laid. On the one hand there is my thirst for music and higher things. On the other, my passion screams below the waist. While my high school buddies shag pop flies in Central Park, I lurk about at the Professional Children's School, the cello in its case beside me. I try to look melancholy yet tender, contort my face into contempt and sorrow, having learned that girls lavish their favors upon select boys who know how to mock and sneer, drink liquor, punch hard. I try to coax a lock of my hair to my forehead, but my hair is too bristly and curly.

One afternoon, as I loiter at the Professional Children's School, the cello in its case at my side, a beautiful budding actress named Joy Larkin asks me to accompany her home. My heart races as she unlocks her parents' roomy apartment on West 72nd Street. Joy has dark eyes and dark hair cut in bangs. She is a knockout. Leaving me standing in the middle of the living room, she disappears into a hallway, then returns wearing a taffeta skirt and tight blouse. If I were a dog, I'd be drooling, but being a tough but well-behaved boy, I spread my legs a little and watch. She sets a chair up in the middle of the living room, takes my hand and leads me to it. I shiver with excitement, open to whatever comes next. She puts a record of Ravel's *Bolero* on the turntable and begins to dance. As she twirls, her skirt rises above her thighs, displaying her pink underpants which do not cover her belly button. As she dances around me, she hovers for seconds at a time above my knees, passing left to right, right to left. Happily, the *Bolero* goes on and on. Please don't let it ever end, though every time I reach for her, she slips deftly away. My ears begin to ring, my neck to ache, while inside my pants, the pain becomes unbearable. When the *Bolero* comes to an end, she takes my hand and pulls me to a couch, pushes me down into it, and leaps away, laughing.

"Joy, please," I beg, spreading my arms.

"Please what?" she says in a coy, whiny voice and runs out of the room.

So this is what is meant by cock-teasing. My ears feel hot and I'm sure they are red. Joy returns in a plaid wool skirt and a cardigan over another sweater. She pulls me up and out the front door. In the hall, the cello at my side, we wait for the elevator. Though forlorn, I want to smack her. I double over with aching balls. I have read reports that Ravel had tired of his Bolero, but I know I will never stop getting a hard-on every time I hear it. On the street, I rush for the subway, hoping that Joy is sorry.

Later that week, while studying for a chemistry exam at Karp's and listening to WQXR in the background, I happen to hear the announcer introduce the next piece of music, "a tone poem by Richard Strauss: *Ein Heldenleben (A Hero's Life)*." A hero's life? I reach across the table and turn the volume up.

"Come on, Mendelssohn," Karp whines. "I'm trying to study."

"You slug, Karp," I say.

Even before the music starts, I feel capable of squashing him, this puny little Karp, a worm, a piddling thing.

"Jesus," Karp says and slams his book shut.

"You know nothing about the rage of art or sex," I snap.

My whole being aches to be a hero. From its first pounding notes, the music speaks directly to me. As it storms on, I think I will explode. I am ready to assert myself, to shine, to cause a stir, to be recognized. The music is bold yet contained. It slips into loneliness, a dream. It is the beginning of the search which separates me from Karp, from everyone. I grab my books, run down the back stairs and walk into the spring afternoon. On the sidewalk, I feel like a giant, accepting the second law of thermodynamics, feeling my pounding shoes getting an equal pounding back from the pavement. At times like this, I think of you, little Mila. What wouldn't I give to share these moments with you? My arms swing confidently, defining my space. I am presiding at the birth of a lover, an innovator, a man apart.

Now the hero, I get off the subway at 72nd Street for more exquisite torture with Joy Larkin. She called me shortly after our *Bolero* afternoon and the subsequent progress of our making-out surges relentlessly forward. Week by week, my fingers push into a kind of girdle mechanism so tight that, at the end of their journey, my fingers turn blue and numb. Millimeter by millimeter, their Olympian stretch sets new records in this event. The damage to my hand is severe enough so that hours later, I still cannot hold the bow of my cello. Some such days I go home with a painful case of blue balls, others I come to a sublime satisfaction, albeit in my pants, sometimes with Joy's help. Less and less dependent on Joy's calling the shots, I begin to assert myself and we both learn the give and take of the mighty adolescent pleasures of love-making.

NOT HAVING SEEN EACH OTHER since the middle of winter, now nearly at the end of the school year, Karp finds me in the first subway car going back downtown. He takes a seat next to me. "Where have you been, Mendelssohn?" he asks.

"Getting laid, Karp, getting laid."

"Sure," Karp says, then reaches into his book-bag to pull out a book called *Airplanes of World War Two*. He opens it to a bookmarked page. "This it?" he asks. "The Junkers Ju87 Stuka," Karp reads, "with a maximum speed of 255 mph at 12,600 Feet and a maximum range of 954 miles." He looks up. "Single engine," he continues, "armed with 31-caliber MG 17 machine guns in wings and two similar caliber MG 81Z guns in rear cockpit, plus up to 3,968 lbs. of bombs beneath the fuselage."

Karp is excited. I do remember the screaming, trumpeting wail as the planes dove at me. So many pounds of bombs? Somehow, I don't know why, it is as if the airplane book has nothing to do with me, except that now I know that someone manufactured it, someone made the bombs and all of it has names and numbers. We get off the train at 86th Street.

Feeling faint, I lean against the window of a corner cigar store, then sit on the stoop and close my eyes. I am back there for a moment, then feel Karp's hand on my shoulder.

"You okay?" Karp asks and Broadway comes into focus again.

From a couch in the Karps' dark living room, I hear the noisy arrival of Henry's father. Martin Karp's forceful footsteps shake the floor, crash into the umbrella stand. A tall man, imposing in his three-piece suit, his hair closely cropped, pens, pencils, and a slide rule crammed into the breast pocket of his suit jacket, he shocks me by saying, "So, I finally meet our own Modigliani, the perfect hand with a light touch."

"Me?"

Martin Karp laughs. "Henry described what he saw in your sketchbooks."

I am blushing.

"Yes, yes," Martin Karp says, "we need more Jewish artists, you and Modigliani."

He takes off his jacket. I am a little taller than Martin Karp. I've often wondered why I am so tall—both Zyga and Rena are short, a full head shorter than me. If Bolek were tall, that would explain a lot, but Bolek is as short as my parents.

"It must be the American milk," Henry once said.

But he knows nothing about Polish milk which also comes from cows.

"Your friend looks like John Garfield," Martin Karp says to Henry.

No one stirs.

"The actor," Mr. Karp explains. "Garfinkle, Jacob Julius Garfinkle."

I'd give anything to look like John Garfield, the deep, tender tough guy, and to draw like Modigliani.

"Modigliani, an Italian Jew; Chaim Soutine, a Lithuanian Jew; and John Garfield, a Jew from the neighborhood," Mr. Karp says, looking straight into my eyes.

I am totally beguiled, seduced, by this man. I plop down in an armchair. Until another one comes along, he becomes the father of my dreams.

MID-JUNE, THE CLASS OF 1949 is graduated from the Alexander Hamilton School for Jewish Boys from the Upper West Side. In the school auditorium, we all have to sit through speeches by Dr. Bessel vander Brinckerhoff, the Dutch Reform principal whose family once owned half of Manhattan Island, plus the guest speaker, Air Force General Lisle Enders, who rallies the crowd into an anti-Soviet frenzy because "they despise Christianity." Apparently, Air Force General Enders was not told that he would be addressing mostly pushy Jewish boys from the Upper West Side.

Outside, on the edge of the baseball field, boys stand around with their parents, talking business or sports, laughing, smoking, taking photographs. They all belonged to the same club, Americans without accents. Zyga, Rena, and I stand in uncomfortable silence. In the school lunchroom, we run into my classmate Paul Metzger and his father, Arnie. Paul is on his way to West Point, just about as far as it's humanly possible to distance himself from his father, a major gangster. Since the Third Form, my entire class has been trying to pry information from Paul about his father's activities. We know that Arnie is allied with Meyer Lansky, which allows us to imagine endless scenarios; Arnie the killer, extorter, owner of whorehouses, gaming parlors, a man out of George Raft movies. Father and son live at the Mayflower Hotel on Columbus Circle. In an oversized overcoat and hat with a wide brim, Arnie Metzger greets Zyga, of all people, with an enthusiasm that suggests familiarity. Arnie is ugly with a fat nose and protruding ears. Suddenly, I feel a frisson of pleasant confusion. Might Zyga have been living a different life entirely? Could that be why he has separated so harshly from everyone?

That night, in my dream, I see Zyga as a Jean Gabin talking to fellow outlaws in an urban garage. Resolute and sly, Zyga takes a cab downtown, carrying a valise full of cash, not only cash but stocks and bonds, all belonging to Mandeleau Furs. He gets out of the cab on the corner of Ninth Avenue and 44th Street and walks west, stops in front of a store displaying car parts, fan belts, carburetors, and spark plugs. He looks left and right, then slips in through the front door. He knows his way around. He hangs his coat and hat on a hat tree, then proceeds up the stairs.

Down a dark hall, he is met by a good-looking kid, a mobster in training, his shirt sleeves rolled up, his shirt open half-way down his chest, a small Star of David at the end of a gold chain. His name is Bernie. He calls Zyga by name and escorts him to Arnie Metzger's office. Zyga deposits the stolen goods on his friend's desk—Zyga's share in the Havana nightclub they are buying together. Arnie Metzger orders coffee as the two of them talk of their sons and the wonders of American enterprise. Arnie shows Zyga pictures of Paul in his Alexander Hamilton basketball uniform, another with Arnie's ex-wife on the boardwalk at Atlantic City. Zyga then takes out the photograph he always carries of his son, a smiling little boy, beautifully dressed in short pants, jacket, and beret to match, standing in the Lazienki Park in Warsaw. Zyga and Arnie then climb into a taxi bound for the steam baths, still used primarily by old Russian men with big bellies who get off swatting each other with willow branches. The two of them enjoy each other's company, Arnie getting an Old World hit he likes, Zyga happily admitting a conspirator into his scheme of bankrupting Mandeleau Furs. After a thorough cleansing of skin and pores, after a shower, they take a cab to one of Arnie Metzger's whorehouses where they both take their pleasure with lovely young whores and, refreshed by the afternoon's excursion, Zyga hails a cab and arrives at Mandeleau's in time to lock up.

But in the morning, Zyga does not look like the Jean Gabin of my dreams. Shuffling in his slippers, in his smelly bathrobe, he settles himself on one end of the couch, pulls the newspaper to his lap, and puts his head back with eyes closed.

IN THE FALL, THREE JEWISH BOYS from the Upper West Side and me from the East Fifties, are assigned a room together. We are admitted by Yale on "the Jewish quota," a percentage whose total number none of us know. But we do know that we are special, watched carefully for communist, anarchist, or atheist tendencies.

Stevie Pepperm majors in economics, launching his "life of avarice, pilfering, and cupidity." Henry Karp and Bernie Jacobs devote their academic life to pre-med requirements. I dream of being in art school rather than here with my pals who know nothing about Goya or Caravaggio or Beethoven's Grosse Fugue.

Across from our rooms live a quartet of boys the likes of whom none of us have known before. The loudest and most amusing is Noel Perrin, a flamboyant son of a Foreign Service diplomat for whom being here is a seamless journey decided long ago by God. When I, who look the least Jewish of the four of us, am invited to join Noel and his roomies for cocktails, they are poured from a splendid leather traveling ensemble of crystal and silver bottles and glasses. Listening to their free and easy talk, mostly of the Smith and Vassar girls they have fucked, I take my serious John Garfield pose and am rewarded by ever more specific tales of conquest.

"We're sitting with a highball on her deck when she throws one leg over the arm of her chair and exposes her pussy," says John Perry from Long Island. "'Lick this, John,' she says and I get down between her legs and do as I'm told."

"Where's this? Amagansett?" asks Philip Dodge.

"Oyster Bay," says John.

"What was she wearing?" Peter Kenney asks.

"A summer dress with little roses all over it," John says and the timbre of breathing in the room changes noticeably. We are all getting a fuller picture, each of us with a particular flowered dress in mind. "She hoisted it up, exposing everything."

"And she said?" Philip prompts hoarsely.

"Who knows what she said? She put her hand on the top of my head and made sure I stayed a while."

As mesmerized by the story as everyone in the room, I am still the outsider looking in. A Roman among the barbarians or the other way around, I want to be part of this pussy-licking crowd.

"Uncircumsized hordes," is Bernie Jacobs's only comment when I report on my time with the Philistines.

IN 1951, AT THE END OF MY SECOND YEAR, I've had enough of college and embark on a life of sex and art with several Smith and Wellesley girls, lovely and eager to please, and I, eager to satisfy, hell-bent on proving my brooding, rebellious posture, totally antithetical to my father's. Every time I make my joyous entry into a hot woman, for one brief moment, I think of Zyga and thrust deeper, with more vigor and resolve. In pursuit of sex and art, Helen Ormsby, a Smith College beauty, and I decide to go to Paris together. She is a Gene Tierney look-alike, with high cheek-bones and a slight slant to her dark eyes. Like me, Helen is a budding artist, her artistic gifts, unlike mine, fall into the realm of still-lifes, as tasty as French pastries.

Having no money to speak of, the only person to hit-up is Uncle Bolek, even though I know that the payback demanded would be my life as furrier-in-chief of the growing empire of Mandeleau Furs. In the showroom again, I look up at the ceiling. Bolek says,

"So darling, I will give you introduction to the best houses, Dior and Balmain and Balenciaga. I will send telegrams."

We are sitting in a far corner of the small, exclusive showroom, the one with an ugly Raoul Dufy of sea-born tri-colors on the wall. Here, gold and ochre are the colors of choice, not the silver of the large salon which faces 57th Street.

"Of course, of course," I say in Polish. "And while in Paris, I will have a good look at the Louvre. You know the Louvre?"

"If I give you money, you must learn the fur trade."

He pulls me up from the Louis-who-knows-which chair and takes me to where the furs hang on movable chrome racks.

"Feel this," Bolek says, guiding my hand along an Alaska seal coat.

It does feel luscious, but I refrain from drawing on it with a finger as I have done in the past. Bolek is merciless. He brings a broadtail coat to the window and, as always, I am mesmerized by the gorgeous moiré patterns, the subtle changes of texture and shade. As much as I hate to do it, I must admit that beauty does exist here, piddling though it is compared with Jackson Pollock or Willem de Kooning's in-your-face paintings. I sit down, grab a Parliament out of the leather box, and light up. As I inhale, a momentary dejection hits me. I suspect that the same people buy Pollocks and de Koonings as chinchilla coats.

Charlie Steiglitz is lawyer and accountant to both Uncle Bolek and Rena.

"If you were my son," he says in his spacious office, having no children of his own, "I would insist you stay in college."

But he is writing a check.

"I think you'll be sorry you didn't finish school, and such a fine school, Yale, where people like us are not readily accepted," he says, then sits back in his swivel chair and for the next half hour tells me cautionary tales of collegial devotion, his to the NYU Law School.

From what I hear of prices in Europe, Bolek's check is big enough for a year in Paris and then some. Having begun life stealing from the dead, larceny of any kind—and this I consider petty larceny—feels like a birthright. Like Bolek, my mother gives me a sheet of paper with some names of customers and old friends from Warsaw who got out and settled in France.

Tourist class on the *Mauretania* is hot and noisy. The five days at sea, however, are an erotic Garden of Eden. After lunch each day, in a gently swaying bunk-bed, Helen performs aerobic sex-play while I, exercising my innate European sophistication, take her through what I imagine to be a graduate program of a full orchestral score of love-making.

A full orchestral score? Hardly. Diminuendos and crescendos, ritardandos, seamless modulations, emphatic codas, and da capos? Upon further examination of the past, I don't think so. A couple of years later, it was lovely Helen Ormsby who took me on as her sexual student and kindly taught me to delay, eventually for as long as a half hour until the woman under or above or to the side of me was given time for total, sometimes multiple, expressions of her pleasure. But, until then, Mendelssohn, an orchestrator of erotic symphonies you were not. You were not much more than an ardent but mediocre lover, often subject to your cock's fatigue and uncontrollable shrinkage, subject to unstoppable daydreams, descents into familiar blackness.

MAURICE TRIANCHON, A NEO-IMPRESSIONIST who teaches at the Beaux-Arts, accepts us both, his eyes glued to the spicy Helen. I cannot bear Trianchon's cheery art, replicated to some degree by each of his students, every canvas replete with finely crafted parades and sailboats with wind-blown flags, beach scenes with colorful umbrellas, some seen through hotel room windows, some from harbor-side. The nudes are bright and bouncy, all of them vibrant, luminous, twinkling, based on the frivolous and insubstantial, an art Rena and her friends would like. I can't stop thinking of the pictures I have seen on television of French collaborators and French anti-Semites. The room full of Jean-Pauls scoffs at my dark abstract images.

"You could make a bowl of apples look gloomy," Helen says.

She herself out-colors and out-draws them all while I, thinking Goya at his most rebellious, remain the precocious oozing wound, black and gray with a minimum of color, the target of many a jeer, the unbridled American.

Juicy Helen begins leaving the Beaux-Arts without me, always in the company of one of the Jean-Pauls. Every Jean-Paul in the class performs for her, pulling her suavely and relentlessly toward his little French hard-on. Trianchon plainly lusts for her, leering shamelessly at that gorgeous sloe-eyed temptress, spittle forming in the corners of his mouth.

One of the Jean-Pauls is having a cigarette with her by the tall windows that look out onto the courtyard. They banter and poke at each other's bodies with predetermined familiarity. I know that their chat must have been preceded by little enticements, merry, jolly sex play. I put down my brushes, wipe my hands on a paint rag, and walk toward them. I had recently seen *The Postman Always Rings Twice* with John Garfield for maybe the third time, and am ready to smash the lanky French punk in the kisser. And so, I walk between them and take Helen into my arms as she exhales a cloud of smoke. We both cough. The kiss is raunchy, sadistic. It is John Garfield brutalizing Lana Turner. Then I belt Jean-Paul in the belly, doubling him over. The guy falls backward, knocking down someone's easel. Then the rest of them descend upon me, pushing, jabbing, slapping, and cursing the cowboy American. One of my front teeth loosens and my left eye begins to swell. By the time I am sweating on the rue Bonaparte, I chide myself for my fractious behavior.

"Why do I do this kind of shit?" I ask myself.

Back at college, I punched Noel Perrin hard enough for Perrin's martini to fly high up in the air, only because Perrin began talking of ecclesiastic robes and surplices, an ecumenical fashion show.

"Will I ever get over being violent on behalf of Zyga," I ask myself as I take a cab to the Gare d'Austerlitz.

"When do I stop slaying the oppressors?"

Thinking black, I, twenty-one years old, leave for Madrid, beckoned by Goya's black paintings. That country—with its cult of death, its blackness made visible through Franco, through bulls and Catholicism—lures me away from the city of light.

As soon as the train arrives, I go directly to visit Goya's house on the outskirts of the city. On these walls, Goya painted the somber and private expressions of darkness and horror. Though they have been taken off the walls and moved to the Prado, I am thunder-struck by the fact that this great painter chose not to share these private images with anyone. They were his and his only. They were too close to the heart to share.

At the museum, I stand before the bearded man with bulging eyes devouring a small human form, already reduced to red meat, Saturn or Cronos eating his children. I don't know why but it doesn't sicken me. Rather, the grotesque images make my heart beat faster, make my skin tingle. The image brings me back to what, deep inside, feels like the world I was once touched by, the world of "Jericho trumpets" mounted on the wings of diving airplanes. Goya translated his darkest thoughts into an ancient crone preparing to devour a bowl of food, a witch's coven, a forlorn dog. Blackness expresses and defines the world as I, too, have come to know it. Black is the color of my heart. It absorbs the terror, the hatred, injustice, the religious urge, the love of money and furs. And to be able to express it with the passion of one's body and mind, to engage in the brutal struggle of hand and eye, this, I know, is my monumental task. From childhood, my being was laden with huge immovable masses appropriating all of space. It had enormous weight. It was threatening, sucking up all the air. In front of these hideous forms, I feel the clarity of a deeper knowledge, that of my nightmares, the vice closing in on me.

And painting has become my way, dear one, my way to honor the past, to immerse myself in it, at times to obliterate it. Shouldn't it be done with words? Especially in English, a beautiful language, a language we didn't know, not a word. We looked at the words "United States" and said, "Oo-nee-ted Stah-tess." We could not stop laughing. But, years later, I grabbed a paint brush because my right hand moved deftly and I stabbed the paint into canvas, like firing a gun or a fist or shrapnel from the black heart that has made a home in my body. My painting, Mila, chooses to scream rather than tell a tale. Perhaps it is derelict, perhaps lazy, taking an easy way out. But I don't know how else to express what happened to us when we were children. Surely, a scribbler could tell it better—and perhaps this lame attempt, written for you, will at least lay down the course of the events that define my life, but vomiting up the black blobs, symbols of horror, can express, especially for those of us whose bellies are full of bile, rage and hatred, our deepest unrestrained feelings about the dark side of humanity.

3.

My watch, my amulet and life-long companion, measures physical time but not the eccentricities, the caprices or vacillations, the speed of time passing. It gallops when life is good, and slows insanely when angsting, when waiting for depression to pass. My golden talisman has been spruced-up once every few years by stooped, Old World, mostly Jewish, watchmakers and has kept me sane whenever I disappeared dangerously into abstract thought or a vodka haze or anger. With each hour, each day, each year, I travel further into my created New World self, but the idea of time has always brought me back to the ditch at the side of the road, the beginning of my time—and undoubtedly yours—which, from then on, has passed by fits and starts, but always tied to mud and bombs, betrayal and death. When I tell my story, it is difficult to be certain about what is in fact essential, what better left out.

BOLEK AND I WALK ARM IN ARM toward Fifth Avenue, our jackets flying open in the spring breeze. The day is perfect, though bits of paper and soot swirl in little twisters. The midget doorman in front of Bendel's salutes Bolek as if he were royalty. We cross Fifth Avenue and Bolek casts a quick glance into the windows of Tiffany's, then looks up toward the drifting clouds, inhales the New York air and smiles with pleasure, a papal benediction, an expression of his gratitude for being here, twenty years by now, for being rich, for feeling free to claim 57th Street, the upper east side, perhaps also the eastern edge of Long Island as his. Half Bolek's age, I do not understand how my uncle could possibly think himself favored by fate, chosen to survive, to be rich. No one could be that stupid, especially after all we've been through, all we have lost and are probably to lose again, given the way of the world. I know that optimism is stupid, that the worst always has a way of presiding over fortunes and that one's goodness or badness plays no part in the outcome.

But Bolek cannot stop grinning. His bald head held high, his chest thrust forward pigeon-like, he bows toward a couple walking from the St. Regis. An elegant woman sends a kiss back toward him.

"That's Mr. Boleslaw, the great furrier," I imagine she is telling her husband.

"Mr. who?"

"Boleslaw Mandeleau. From one of those noble European families."

The elderly man with a finely made Irish hat on his head and camel's hair coat on his back, looks Bolek up and down.

"Polish nobility?" he sneers.

His wife tries to hush him.

"That's a Jew who took someone else's name."

No matter what Bolek does, no matter how he costumes himself—the silver ties, the hand-made shoes and perfectly tailored suits—they know, they always know. At the corner of 54th, waiting for the light to change, Bolek steps back a few paces from the street, pulling on my arm, yanking me out of harm's way as well as protecting his thin-skinned Italian shoes from being splattered as they undoubtedly were by the wheels of Warsaw's dorozhkas. Here in New York he believes in the order and civility of traffic, but even after the light turns green, Bolek waits an extra moment before crossing, the inclination to mistrust the drivers, all Cossacks, deep in his psyche. Annoyed with my uncle's Old World fears, I try to pull him into the street. At each corner for the next few blocks before we turn east again, we engage in our little tug of war.

Chez Henri is small and dark. Here, Uncle Bolek relaxes, the morning's furry theater forgotten, a splendid little meal ahead. Monsieur Boleslaw and Monsieur Michel walk in like royalty, smiling kindly as we sidle between the few tables to Bolek's usual place. Bolek orders a bottle of Merlot. His English is barely capable of communicating his home address to a taxi driver. In America, Bolek, Rena, and my father are as linguistically throttled as bottled propane. "Ach, beautifool," is among Bolek's few English phrases, usually spoken when he fits a customer.

"Bone of a dog," Bolek now says in Polish, raising his glass to clink with mine. "Let us drink to our twenty years in beautiful America." Then, "Darling," he says, after we order, "today you must think very hard about the bigger picture."

He leans back, his fingers joined behind his bald head. "Today we must talk about what is important, what is not."

"Bolek, don't spoil our lunch. Stop right here."

"Let us be honest," Bolek continues, "Picasso you are not."

Bolek heard of Picasso, though the only artist he admires is Dali who makes it regularly into the pages of Vogue and Harper's Bazaar.

"Mishek, Mishek," he says, using my baby name, saved for special circumstances, "if you do not make furs, you must learn to draw furs."

I empty a glass of wine.

"Furs, they are in your blood. It is in all our blood."

All our blood, I remember, except my father's blood, for, as I have often been reminded by Rena and Bolek, the gene for high fashion is not activated by marriage.

"I will teach you everything," Bolek says. "You are handsome and tall."

I want to get up to leave, but I can't. Bolek has bribed me all my life—the English bike early on, box seats at the opera, behind first base at Yankee Stadium, a gift certificate to Sam Goody's. So far, I have resisted, and yet I fear I have inherited a bit of the slimy materialism I suspect is embedded in this family's genes. I have made my own life, followed my own passions, as far from theirs as I could manage, but perhaps not far enough.

"You are not only nice-looking," Bolek says, unable to stop himself, "but your manners are not bad. Come to Mandeleau Furs and all America will be yours."

His fucking map of America doesn't even include the upper west side, no less Greenwich Village, where I have my little walk-up on Jane Street and a smallish studio on Grand Street, above the bridal shops. My artistic talents have earned me a teaching job at the Art Students League as well as modest successes with my dark paintings, along with, I must admit, nagging questions of true worth, while Bolek, presiding over his little furry empire, pure uselessness and hype, never questions its significance in the large scheme of things.

After a modest meal of Cervelles au Buerre Noir, I open the menu to study desserts. Tartine aux poires à la bourdaloue, clafouti aux mûres, baba au rhum, perhaps a touch of Courvoisier.

"So," Bolek says, "you are teaching your art and you are making pictures."

"It pays the rent."

"Rent? You will not rent. You will own."

"Can you not stop?" I ask, sipping my cognac.

Bolek is smiling. "I do not stop," he says.

"There is an interest in my pictures," I blurt out, sorry the moment this comes out of my mouth.

"An interest?" Bolek says, making a wry face, his lower lip over his upper, his head raised a little. When he signs the check, I realize that I have been sufficiently buttered-up and presumed ready for the big one. Still in a good mood, he nudges me to the right as we come out of Chez Henri instead of the usual route back to Mandeleau's. We walk up Park Avenue and, a few blocks uptown, mid-block, Bolek stops in front of a large store window.

"This Mr. Ritz buys furs from me," Bolek says. "Just this year, he orders ranch mink for his wife, Alaska seal for his mistress."

I look up at the store name. It is Rootes, not Ritz. My uncle, the little Napoleon-like maestro extends his arms so that his gold cufflinks travel inches beyond the sleeves of his jacket and points to a small silver-gray car parked just inside the window. A salesman is demonstrating the car to a customer, flicking orange directional arrows darting first left, then right, between the front and back car doors. I am mesmerized by the beauty of the little car, seduced immediately by the arrows. Bolek is in thrall to the west's inventiveness while I, preferring smoke signals to telephones, delight in arrows.

"This is beautiful, no?"

"It is perfect for you," I say disingenuously.

Inside, Bolek finds his salesman.

"So this is the next emperor of the fur business himself," the salesman says. "You belong in this car," he says, pulling me by my sleeve. And thus Bolek buys me the Hillman Minx, the worst car the English ever made. Bolek looks happy and proud.

"It's a beautiful gift," I tell him, "but in English we say no strings attached."

"What this is the string?"

I tell him what this is a string.

"The car, it is a gift," Bolek says, pouting. "I ask only that you think very much about the life of fur, all that it gives you."

As we get off the elevator on the third floor of 20 West, my theater of the absurd, my palace of unanswered questions, a photograph of Bolek fitting an ermine stole onto the shoulders of Pope Pius XII, no friend to the Jews, confronts me. In the showroom itself, Bolek goes to stand by the tall windows facing 57th Street, inhaling a bundle of pelts. He is now in a sensual reverie, the raw pelts for him like musk, like a woman. Having examined them carefully, he sits on the silver couch, motions me over to sit next to him. We say nothing for a long while. I have never liked being here even though, from a very early age, here or back in Warsaw at Mandelbaum's, I am showered by fawning employees, the presumed heir to this loathsome place.

We light up Parliaments and then Bolek stands up and, for a moment, looks like a double for the debonair Max Beckmann in one of Beckmann's ravishing self-portraits. He glances back at me, the wrist at his side bent away from his body in a charmingly feminine fashion, his cigarette stuck gingerly between two fingers. Bolek's charms, a gestural eloquence, a chivalry that alternates with his manly rage and bluster, turn out to be useful not only in the world of fashion but in the conquest of women who open themselves to him as they sit on the small silver chairs, crossing their stockinged legs and smoking Parliaments.

Beset with guilt and confusion concerning my identity, I walk up the back stairs to the fourth floor to see my father. The workshop hums with sewing machines, singing to the beat of little hammers tacking stretched pelts onto plywood sheets. Mr. Walter, Mr. Arthur, Mrs. Resnick, and quite a few other workers on the factory floor, came to New York before or just after the war. Mostly good, old socialists, they are loyal to their Union, here a corrupt, Mafia-connected Fur and Leather Workers Union, despised by Bolek and my mother. The workers on the fourth floor, just as the ones in the Warsaw factory, welcome me warmly. They and they alone consider Zygmunt Mendelssohn one of them and consider me royalty from the Third floor.

My father sits alone in the foreman's dark and gloomy back room, his newspaper spread before him on a corner of a table. He is a man without joy in his life. His old suit is shabby. He stopped a daily shaving routine and has a couple of days' of stubble on his face. I sit down next to him.

"Bolek bought me a car," I tell my father and, as the words come out of my mouth, I swallow hard, knowing that this must pierce his heart.

I watch Zyga lower his head and close his eyes. Years ago, in my mind's eye, I constructed a diptych, on one side a delirium of silver and gold, the family power, Rena and Bolek who make things happen. The other side is gray and black, a colorless misery, my father, and my fear that his misanthropy and weakness, perhaps betrayal, is contagious.

Zyga raises his head. "You need a car?" he asks.

"Bolek wants me to work here. That's why he bought it."

"You here? Never," Zyga says in Polish, looking straight into my eyes. "You have important things to do."

I look at him closely, at the bags that have formed under his eyes, the fingers that are always busy picking on his cuticles, hurting himself. Zyga looks so unhealthy and forlorn that I cannot escape my usual reaction, somewhere between revulsion and pity. I don't quite understand what his words mean. He must know something about me, must have been thinking about me. If so, I wonder if I don't recognize it because of propaganda fed me by Bolek and Rena or because he really has been totally absent.

"Yes," I tell him in Polish, "you are quite right. Working here is the last thing I would consider."

"Never, never," he says.

"You're the only one in this family who thinks so."

Back on the third floor, the model Yvette, in bra and a towel thrown over her shoulders, is curling her eyelashes with a weird little tool. Deep in concentration, she stares into the mirror inside her cubicle, carved out of an area of coats waiting for cold storage.

"Getting ready for a heavy date?" I ask.

"Michael darling, you scare me," she says with her delectable French accent. "I don't theenk heavy," she says.

I sidle past stacked boxes, then walk between two racks of furs, my body caressed by seal and mink, into Rena's little office. She sits, her lips pursed, a Mr. John felt hat on her head, a Balenciaga suit perfectly tailored on her small body. She has discreetly kicked off her shoes as her feet always hurt.

"My sunshine," she says in Polish and I put a hand on her corseted back, then kiss her on both cheeks.

She looks up at me adoringly, then returns to her appointment book which, like her address book at home, is full of cross-references, arrows pointing this way and that, a Sanskrit of fittings that only she can decipher. Equally mysterious is finding parts of coats in this backstage jungle, the paper cut-outs, canvasses marked with blue or red lines, a sleeve, a pocket, a collar.

"Bolek bought me a little English car," I tell her.

"He loves you so."

We sit in silence while she fiddles with her notes, putting customer orders together. I riffle through an old Vogue, looking for bra ads.

As the end of their work day approaches, Zyga locks the factory upstairs and walks down to the third floor showrooms where he appears only after the last customers have gone. He sits down on the little French couch, examining the books, a part of his job. He looks incongruous among the Empire décor, the tips of his black shoes scuffed and dusty, his necktie stained—a message to his oppressors. Bolek, who was peeing in the bathroom, comes out and notices his brother-in-law in the smaller of the showrooms, the one saved for princes and kings, the Duke and Duchess of Windsor, Gregory Peck and his wife. Furious, Bolek storms into Rena's office and pounds on her desk.

"That cretin," he screams, pointing to the showroom where my father sits. "May cholera take him!"

Zyga is now picking hard on his already bloody cuticles. My eyes tear-up. Bolek continues to rage. "He steals from us, that swine. We keep nothing."

"Borze, Borze!" Rena wails in Polish, the call to God more fitting for the dying Boris Goudonov, the Tsar of all the Russias.

Her hands cover her ears. As completely as she adores her brother, she still has to work hard at enduring Bolek's atrocious rages, many of them aimed at her.

As I stare at my dejected father, I remember those occasions, while still in high school, when I dragged Henry Karp to hear Otello at the Met. There, my heart pounded noisily in my chest as Iago and the Moor schemed to punish Desdemona. I tried to picture Zyga as Iago to Bolek's Otello.

"Be Iago, you miserable nothing."

I wished it with all my heart.

"I fazzoletto! I fazzoletto! Sangue, sangue, sangue!"

In my mind's eye, I pictured Zyga roaring and strangling them both. On our way home from the opera, I said, "I can't imagine that it was Zyga's sperm that fertilized an egg laid by Rena."

"What are you talking about?" Karp asked as we walked uptown past Times Square.

"I sometimes hope that Bolek impregnated my mother."

"What?"

Karp couldn't believe what he was hearing and stopped to lean against a lamp post.

"Don't you get it, Karp? I would at least have a model for manhood. We need models. You've got an okay one. Mine sucks."

Now, I am not at all sure if having Bolek, the glamorous, boisterous, rager, the pillager of rich men's money, the lover of their wives, would be that much better as a father figure than depressed Zyga.

"Leave him alone," I scream at Bolek, who is cursing Rena for bringing the miserable Zyga into the family.

My head is exploding. I cannot bear it any longer. I leave without a word and walk to Rootes Motors to have another look at the impudent Minx which, with its little orange arrows tucked in, stands daringly in the window, the lights of Park Avenue reflected in the silver body. Forgetting that it might cost me my soul, I revel in seeing myself at the helm of this sly vixen. Then, dizzy with the day's paradoxes, I make my way to the East River. With the insanity of family at my back, the river lets me breathe. The river air, the birds flying free above it, the slowness and sound of river traffic suggests a less tangled life.

Once, looking down to the Vistula from a beautiful iron bridge, you and I, Mila, counted the boats that carried we knew not what to we knew not where. None of the boats were big, not like the giant ones in Gdynia that your mother drove us to see or the Bergensfjord from Norway on which you were absent or the huge ones entering New York's harbor where, as far as I know, you have never been. But then, we ran the length of the bridge, played tag as our two governesses talked. I loved the river where I dreamed of what might be at its magical end. I knew that other worlds existed and I longed to taste those worlds. Who knew that the passage to new worlds would be as terrifying as it was, but then I could almost hear the songs that were being sung way beyond what I could see. I didn't know then that the river flows within us, the sea surrounds us, that rivers calm and soothe and are the source of dreams and art.

4.

DRIVEN ANYWHERE, the Hillman is trouble verging on catastrophe. And drive it I do, whipping it like a horse, daring and coddling it, learning from it by slowly transforming rage into patience, then understanding, almost forgiveness. The car plunges into New York traffic, sputtering up Sixth Avenue to 57th Street. I take on bridges and tunnels, baby the Hillman through rush hour, battling with taxis. But that little silver fox of a car, infuriating and invigorating, one day a cheetah, the next a mule, gives unexpected direction to life's opportunities and dilemmas, as if the little orange arrows which shoot out left and right between the front and back doors are a Ouija board or the I Ching.

The Hillman and I become regulars inside the Holland Tunnel where the cop pacing the catwalk above the toxic traffic calls out on his loudspeaker more times than I care to remember: "Hillman Minx, Hillman Minx, move along." Ashamed and enraged, my English pile of junk and I lurch out of the tunnel, the fuel pump once again clogged with dirt. For a year now, I've had the fuel line blown out from one end to the other. I change gas stations, but nothing helps. I am stuck with a lemon.

The trips to New Jersey begin at the Art Students League where, during the two years of my teaching, I rarely court the models who pose for my life drawing class. Mostly, they are old men or women, sometimes dressed in weird costumes, sometimes nude or partly nude, but occasionally young women with smooth, shapely bodies show up, which is the way I meet Cristine Madden. A true classical beauty, everything about her is cold as ice. Her steel-blue eyes penetrate surfaces like a welding torch. Her look is haughty, warning me to keep my distance.

"I take it that you have nothing against posing in the nude," I say when she shows up looking for a job, her frigid demeanor suggesting otherwise.

"I know how to sit perfectly still," she says.

"Good, good. Some of the work will be quick sketches, some longer poses."

"I've done this before and I'm good at it," she assures me. "When I change positions though," she says, "I will not be looked at."

"No?" The arrangement we agree on is that with each position change, I will cover her with a sheet, eliminating the possibility of lewd gazes at her body in motion. When she disrobes for the first time, I see little sensuality in her perfect body, more like a marble statue than a woman whose flesh swells and contracts, releases hormones and fluids. I find her coolness especially strange in this grungy Art Students League whose atmosphere is licentious. As in art school, I love the pony-tailed young women with paint rags sticking out of their back pockets, the camaraderie of striving artists living the wantonness of *la vie bohème.*

On her days at the League, she arrives fifteen minutes before the class starts, dressed in loose-fitting, shabby shirts and baggy pants, sits herself down on a stool, pulls a book out of her canvas sack and reads her Victorian novels. There are more Wilkie Collins, Elizabeth Gaskell, unknown tomes of the Bronte sisters and George Eliots than I ever suspected.

Crissie's poses are elegant, classical. There are no imperfections on her smooth skin. As a result, every student becomes an Ingres.

"By contrast, you make the League seem even filthier than it is," I tell her and she smiles.

She makes the floor grittier, all our clothes shabbier, the sketches not precise or clean enough.

"You are very beautiful," I tell her.

She looks up at me. More precisely, she looks through me, not acknowledging the compliment. As Princess Crissie cuts a swathe down the stairs and to the front door, her sack of books slung over her shoulders, both men and women turn to look.

When my students and model leave at the end of class, I walk down the corridor to have a peek at Petros Protopapas's class. Even though Protopapas is more than ten years my senior, we engage in a mild competition. This swarthy Greek, sporting an overgrown, dangling mustache, is a good drinking buddy, but I find his painting irksome. The year before, Protopapas won some international competition in Sao Paulo. The painting he is especially known for is an eight foot long, white canvas with a fiery sun on the left and a black asterisk on the right.

"Excuse me," I said to Protopapas at the beginning of the school year, "but I don't quite get the significance."

"Ah, Mendelssohn," Protopapas said, "it is whatever you take it to mean," which is pretty much what I feel when some asshole asks me as they're staring at my black abstractions.

I now crack my friend's door. Protopapas is projecting primitive symbols on a screen.

"Hey, Mendelssohn," Protopapas shouts, "come in, come in."

I close the door behind me.

"Ladies and gentlemen, may I present the up-and-coming Michael

Mendelssohn, distinguished teacher of the nude body, but a serious painter of raging black canvasses," Protopapas says as if talking into a microphone.

A few people titter.

"In spite of the blackness, the enemy of color," Protopapas continues, "he has a sublime touch."

One or two people clap and I bow and take a seat at the back of the room. Protopapas is an immigrant like me, but his people came over earlier, before the war. I think Protopapas's art a phony primitivism, Jungian crap. My own paintings speak from the gut, natural as an animal's growl. Before I leave the class, I whisper to a woman sitting near me, "Jung was a Nazi."

One Wednesday, I ask Crissie out to lunch. We drive down to the Village where we both feel more comfortable than mid-town. She chooses a little Spanish restaurant and selects a plate gleaming with tiny eels fried in olive oil. They look like little spaghettis and taste great when she offers me a forkful.

"I ate these almost every day on the Barcelona harbor," she says. "I spent a year following the bullfights."

When she notices my eyebrows lift, she says, "The first few times, I threw-up, but I made myself go again and again, until the day I fell for the whole magnificent spectacle."

"Sacrificing animals?" I am stupefied and sit back, remembering the dead horses and cows in the Polish countryside.

She looks up at me.

"It's not a sport," she says. "And what's the matter with sacrifice?"

I notice, staring into her mouth as she eats, her only visible imperfection, her yellowing and chipped teeth.

"It's serious stuff, Michael. It's a play about death."

She polishes off a glass of white wine and asks for another.

"You know about Eros and Thanatos," she says, "probably a lot more about Eros. Me, I'm much more interested in Thanatos."

I drive her home to Hoboken, intrigued by my ice queen whose pleasures include the goring of horses and the slaughtering of bulls. To further confuse and allure me, I receive in the mail that week an envelope with photographs taken for her NYU graduation. From the proofs emerges a magnificent, haughty Crissie, each proof with a hand-written inscription in Greek. It is a challenge. I call to thank her.

"All from the Stoics, eh?" I guess.

"I was just showing off," she says.

"I'll treasure them."

"Oh, do go on," she says. "They are just a bit of self-indulgence."

I take the lot of them to a Greek restaurant on Eighth Avenue I especially like, but no one there can read the ancient Greek. After a lunch of moussaka, I try a Greek graduate student the waiter recommends. Under a waspy Crissie, looking slightly to the left, the man translates, "The proper goal is to practice how to remove from one's life sorrows and laments, and cries of alas and poor me, and misfortune and disappointment. Epictetus," he says. Under a head-on shot, her eyes imperious, there is a quote from Marcus Aurelius: "What is good for the swarm is not good for the bee." Another snob like me, I interpret with some delight. And then, as if she were talking directly to my suspicions: "There is no great genius without some touch of madness."

To save money, Crissie lives in New Jersey, sharing a floor of a shabby rooming-house with two girls, all of them NYU students.

"My parents call it N.Y. Jew," she tells me when I drive to New Jersey to visit. "That's why I'm here, not Wellesley or Smith. Originally, they named me Christine with an H, but I've taken the H out."

Though the narrow street she lives on has a few trees planted along the sidewalk and, from the living room, a view of a tiny piece of lower Manhattan, the house itself is creaky and dark. This particular evening, I arrive with a bottle of good Scotch. Crissie, Cynthia, and Margot are from deep within the continent, Margot from a rose farm in Indiana; Cynthia the daughter of a small-time contractor in Kentucky; Crissie in flight from yeeow! aye-yip-aye-yo-ee-ay Oklahoma. They stretch out prettily on the floor and a couch while I sit at the folding card table placed between two windows, the view from which is the neighboring house, a driveway away. They talk about French symbolist poets, Masaccio frescoes, and the beginnings of polyphony, whatever they are studying fresh in their minds.

"Not so fresh in mine anymore," I say. "Except for Masaccio, Homer, some of the Greek plays," I say as I down a half glass of Johnny Walker, "the stuff I learned in college is fading away."

"Oh come on, Michael," Crissie says. "It hasn't been that long."

"Seven years. Or is it eight?"

"You're a brilliant artist," Crissie says.

I am astonished at this, her first commentary regarding my work.

"I saw a few of your paintings downtown," she adds, seeing the surprise on my face.

Cynthia and Margot are pretty enough, both with straight, sharp noses, one with small brown eyes, the other with larger ones, both with carefully tweezed eyebrows. In the sensual flush of young womanhood, their skin is clear, their bodies nimble. But next to Crissie's regal stillness, their movements are awkward, without grace.

At about ten o'clock, the three of them, in turn, go into the bathroom to brush their teeth, then change into their flannel nightgowns. All clean, they take up positions on the couch again and, as they talk, they play with one another's hair. Cynthia braids Margot's, then brushes Crissie's, who remains aloof. At midnight, Cynthia and Margot disappear.

"I've got to go to bed too," Crissie says.

"Stay here with me," I beg, putting my hands on Crissie's waist. "Or can I come with you?"

Crissie smiles a warm, charming smile.

"Stay on the couch," she says. "It's better that way."

Then, she gives me a goodnight peck on the lips and darts off, closing the door of her room behind her.

On the verge of a headache, I ponder this world of hair brushing, primping, and little-girl playfulness. I tip the Scotch bottle to get the thimble-full left at the bottom. There is something about Crissie that appeals to me, though I'm not quite sure, except for her beauty, what it is. Perhaps it's her middle of this continent's provenance, far from my depressed, angry family.

My career is beginning to sizzle. I feel dizzy with expectations. The paintings Crissie must have seen were shown in a group show of second and third generation abstractionists in a Tenth Street gallery where I sold three of the four paintings exhibited. An article recently appeared in *Art News*, written by Mel Golub, an artist and teacher I admire, about three young painters to watch. I am among them.

When I wake up early in the morning, my head and back aching, the room stinks of cigarettes. The girls come in, one by one, looking chipper while my head throbs.

"Okay if I make pancakes for everyone?" asks Crissie.

"Oh, yummy!" cries Cynthia.

I not only feel like shit, but out of place. I have some coffee and, after splashing my face with cold water, I cross back into the city in a huge pile of traffic.

A week after my Hoboken overnight, Crissie calls. She wants to pose for me in my studio.

"Don't misinterpret, Michael," she says. "I need the money."

I am intrigued and not about to refuse. When she first knocks on the door of my Grand Street studio, she is fanning herself with a copy of Daniel Deronda.

"I have to re-read it at least once a year," she says and flops down on the couch.

"It's quite a walk in this heat from NYU."

I sit on my little wooden folding chair opposite her and examine the goods. Sweating and a little red-faced, she looks more human, more womanly, more desirable. After cooling off, she meanders into the adjoining room and returns naked, the open copy of Daniel Deronda shielding her breasts. She sits down and crosses her legs.

A student of literature with a minor in art history, Crissie likes taking on nude poses she knows and loves, from Titian Venuses to Manet's Olympia. I spend the afternoon sketching Crissie stretched out like a Modigliani, with her hands behind her head like Goya's *Maja Desnuda*, standing like a Botticelli Venus. A couple of hours later, I show her some of my serious black work. She studies each painting with interest but says nothing. I lock up and we walk west to where I parked the Hillman, then drive her back to Hoboken. Before she gets out of the car, she leans over and plants a long kiss on my cheek.

For the next few months, she poses once a week, each of the afternoons more painful than the last, my body engorged, my mouth all but salivating, and yet I exercise a Zen master's restraint, never before a part of my bag of tricks, while dreaming most nights of the well-earned satisfaction that might come one day, waking every morning needing to tame the demands of my swelling, insistent dick.

One afternoon in October, Crissie poses with her back to me as the Velazquez Rokeby Venus, looking into a hand mirror originally held by a cherub. Not having a cherub in Hoboken or the Village, she holds the mirror she brought from home. Crissie Madden's hips swoop up from her slender waist. Never before have her eyes softened like this, becoming a deeper blue, looking wanton and daring. In that mirror, her soft gaze seems like an invitation.

"Are you alright?" I ask in a husky voice more basso than usual.

"I'm fine like this," she says and a half smile appears in the mirror.

"Fine doesn't describe you right now."

"No? What does?"

What does? Hot! Oh my.

"Tumid, moist, ripe, glowing…" I say, probably panting like a ghoul.

"Listen to you," she says. "I thought I was the writer."

"Crissie, you're driving me crazy."

"Yes?"

I put my hands around her hips and pull her to me. She does not resist. As I put her down on her belly, then lift her to her knees, she says hoarsely, "Not like this."

I turn her around so she is lying on her back, her thighs parting. Slowly she gets into a rhythm and her body begins to writhe with pleasure. When we finish, she tells me that she made love only once before.

"Practice isn't required," I tell her, stroking her hair.

"With a bull fighter in Spain. I didn't much like it."

"You didn't like it?"

"I had to do it because I was writing a love story about a young, beautiful torero."

"Research."

I reach for the cigarettes on the painting table and we both light up. She leans over me to flick the ashes, then, lying back down, she crosses her arms to cover her breasts, breasts I now judge as perfect as a Phidias sculpture.

"More," I beg and try to gently pull her arms apart.

"Enough," she says, climbs over me and swings her legs off the couch, straightens her hair, ties it into a bun, then takes her clothes into the other room.

When she returns, she is perfectly put together, untouchable again. Her eyes don't retain their softness, her body is back in its armor.

Though she poses for me often, in class and in my studio, love-making is rationed, irrationally rationed. At times, I make a gentle move to show my desire only to be rebuffed, as if I am the night elevator man putting the make on the lady living alone in the penthouse. At other times—and I never know when to expect it—she lightly, casually swipes her hand across my crotch, a papal nod signifying that St. Peter's gates are now open. Not only her sexuality but her moods change unpredictably, keeping me on the edge of my seat. For reasons I don't quite understand, I am happy never knowing what to expect, preferring this painful, exciting unpredictability to a tiresome routine.

Because of my persistent need to indelibly define my differentness from them, I want to flaunt my yippee-ay-yay cowgirl, as alien to my family as a geisha.

"I do want to meet them," Crissie says after a couple of drinks and a light supper she cooks for us in my J

"Let's consider, Crissie dear. My m

measure you silently as a model among

Are your breasts small enough, your leg

Crissie looks at me with a quizzical

"On the other hand, Rena might reco

to Bolek"s immaculate costuming, she jumps out like a cactus in a poppy field. In Polish, Bolek pays homage to her beauty, but expresses little comprehension of her proclivity for sartorial self-abasement. As a matter of fact, he finds her fashion statements unforgivable.

"Tell Miss Crissie I will send her to Pauline who will dress her."

Blood rushes to my head and I jump up. "She is not yours to dress," I snarl in Polish.

"Michael," Crissie reprimands.

"He thinks he can buy you off."

"Whatever do you mean?"

"Like he buys me off."

Bolek strides off toward the kitchen to order a bottle of champagne. Hasegawa-san pops the cork and even though it is the middle of Sunday afternoon, we drink together as one happy family, the undercurrents of incomprehensibility from each one of us fading into a pleasant champagne fog. And thus, slowly and not without mishap, Crissie Madden of Tulsa, Oklahoma, begins her introduction to the Mendelssohn-Mandelbaum clan.

In spite of my family, life with Crissie and painting is deeply engrossing and satisfying. In my Grand Street studio, I attack an empty canvas with gusto. I sing along with John Coltrane's "A love supreme, a love supreme." Then with the Mozart Requiem, *Lux aeterna, lux aeterna.* I am at the top of my game, whistling every morning as I walk east to the Bowery and down to Grand Street. I stop seeing hot Helen Ormsby, stop our weekly research into better sex. As far as I know, she is still exhibiting in a Lower East Side gallery. I no longer visit with Debbie, the curator of decorative arts at the Brooklyn Museum, or Marjorie, bored wife of a Professor of Geology at Fordham. I am entirely focused on my neo-classical Crissie, Crissie the unpredictable, Crissie of debilitating migraines and excruciating periods, immersed in the saga of her Seville toreador. And I feel in my gut that I am on the brink of being discovered big time, a trajectory as uncertain and promising as the road out of Poland. From a Chock Full of Nuts coffee can, I choose a brush and, with a passionate flourish, I write on the wall of my studio, in dripping black letters, words from a Mayakovsky poem.

"Mamma?

Mamma!

Your son is gloriously ill!

Mamma!

His heart is on fire.

Tell his sisters, Lyuda and Olya,

He has no nook to hide in."

5.

As I sit at a small table inside Minetta's, drinking a cappuccino and reading the paper, I look up and spot Henry Karp. I have not seen him since college. A doctor now, Karp tells me how excited he is about the state of neurology, its technology on the point of breakthrough, its possibilities enormous.

"As you know, Michael, I thought about psychiatry for a long time," he says. "In the final analysis, it seemed stupid compared with real hard science." He orders a coffee. "Do you know what I mean?"

While he talks, his cheek and eye twitch as they did when he was younger. I still can't help being distracted by it.

"Can you imagine what it's like to explore the brain, the actual brain? All those neurons have a purpose, just waiting to be discovered."

"That's great. You will save lives."

Karp smiles.

"On the other hand," I say, tapping my friend's shoulder playfully, "don't altogether disregard the arts. They are as essential as chemistry. They transport us to a level of consciousness that we don't even recognize without it."

But Karp is still Karp. He says, "Neurology is not playing around," he insists, his face pink and twitchy.

"Karp, Karp, you haven't changed a bit."

I lean back in my chair, finish my croissant.

As we walk east to the Bowery, Karp is deep in thought.

"How's your father?" Karp asks, another dangerous subject, bringing my father muddle to the forefront. "I'll never forget how badly you treated him. I hope you have come to your senses."

I never realized how important this was to Karp. Now I wonder why, there being so many other memories from our student days, my father problems remain fresh in his mind.

"Well no," I report, "nothing is really resolved."

"We're grown men," Karp cannot stop. "They did the best they could, all of them, yours and mine."

We turn onto Grand Street. I feel quite bothered that my father thing is more than a private affair. I'd sort of like to push Karp into traffic.

"I've been wanting to come see you in your studio," Karp says, "ever since Morty Steinmetz gave me Mel Golub's article in Art News."

Scrubbed and clean in jacket and tie, our required daily costume at the Alexander Hamilton School for Jewish Boys from the Upper West Side, Karp looks seriously out of place in my grubby studio. The walls are spattered with paint, smelling of turps and resins, oils and varnishes, putting Karp's allergic nose into a mild spasm. He sits down gingerly on a chair I wipe clean for him. He wrinkles his brow as he reads the Mayakovsky poem on one of the walls. I show him the canvasses stacked within racks I built for them, black shapes troweled on with a palette knife, eating up the available space, as well as a sketchbook of nudes. Each black abstraction makes Karp flinch.

"I can understand good craftsmanship," he finally says.

"The black paintings don't speak to you?"

They are hot, these black paintings, hot and angry.

"I don't know how to look at them. They're just a lot of black and white paint to me."

I am still in explication mode, a gentle teacher.

"There's a new freedom here, a new way to look inside and find deep and honest ways to express what lurks there, dying to be set free."

Karp has a quizzical look on his face.

"You must use your imagination to picture these paintings a lot bigger than they are. One day they will be monumental."

"Aha," Karp says, his expression unchanged from its usual grimness.

"Oh come on, Karp, try a little harder."

Old feelings about Karp, the smartest kid in the class as well as the puniest, return in full force and I want to hit him, to smack him around the room, to smear his seersucker suit with black paint. I get a hold of myself, soothing the demons inside which are scratching to get free.

"We all need to explore new ways of seeing and understanding," I tell him in as even a tone as I can muster. "We should recognize the precedents in the art conversation that led to these new, risky adventures."

Karp's right eyelid is going wild. "Don't you think it's… what? Facile?" Karp runs his hand over the short bristles of his brown hair. "I can't help feeling," he says, "that your painting lacks discipline and therefore promotes an 'anything goes' mentality, not just in painting but in society."

Though now I really want to throttle Karp, I cannot avoid my own familiar struggle between the bad boy and the pretty Polish Prince, the bad boy who cannot pass up an easy petty larceny or unpleasant fight, the one who bit a kid in boarding school as they wrestled, the one shunned by the Yalie preppies after he beat the shit out of Noel Perrin.

Yes, that is one Mendelssohn story, but not the only one. There is also the dapper man of the world, the hand-kissing charmer who, in spite of his best intentions, smiles and changes his underpants daily. There is the certainty of Bolek and Rena, Alaska seal and chinchilla. There is also my scream of anguish and rebellion, risk-taking and irony in my painting. It is suddenly all up for grabs. I fear that my life and work don't exist for their own delicious sake but represent, along with everything else, my insane way of vindicating my miserable father. I am pacing now. Karp sits and looks straight ahead.

"Look, Mendelssohn," he says, "I could be wrong…"

"You wrong? How can that be? You're never wrong."

Karp hunches his shoulders as if to avoid a blow. He is half my size, a little punching bag. I want to pull Karp up by his little red ears, but the good knight of fashion chivalry prevails. The deep suspicion that my work may indeed lack depth, that it might suffer from manners, comes into focus and makes my knees weak. I suspect I might be holding back from the outrageous, just like the whole lot of them at the Alexander Hamilton School. Karp is about to stick his grubby paws into the gray matter, a gesture bolder by far than the angst expressed by black and white pigment. I take a deep breath.

"All you twits from school did everything right. Mama said be a doctor and the lot of you became doctors, off to fucking neurology school. Get out of here, Karp."

Karp runs for the door and speeds down the stairs.

I light a joint and spend the rest of the afternoon looking at my work. Surely that arrogant German Jew does not have the power to undermine the art house I have so carefully constructed. It's probably not uncommon for anyone's art edifice to be, at times, threatened by disintegration. It is such a precarious, sometimes pretentious world one creates. But rejection is my devil, one of my devils, and even a sniveling little Karp, a termite, has the power to make me question everything. Some hero. Not all that long ago, I stumbled, chest forward, head held high, into that Strauss Nazi superman shit. Only Karp could bring it back to me, that bunch of squabbling, cackling flutes and oboes, philistine imbeciles, little Karps who meddle.

I walk down the stairs and out into the street for a breath of fresh air. At the corner of Grand and Bowery, a cop is beating the shit out of a drunk and a small cluster of people look on. No one will ever know how much I want to clobber the fucking cop. Unleashing wisdom I can't always rely on, I walk past, feeling like an old Jew wandering the Warsaw streets outside the ghetto. Just a couple of days before, I began to grow a beard whose stubble is at its most ungainly. I find a phone booth on the east end of Grand and dial Henry but get Bertha instead.

"Ach, my favorite, Michael Mendelssohn," she says.

"Do you know where Henry is?" I ask.

"Henry lives in Ithaca. He is here briefly in New York."

"Would you tell him that it's okay what he said?"

"Vot did he say?"

"He'll understand."

She says nothing for a moment.

"Henry is a doctor," she then tells me. "He is a neurologist. He vas first in his class." Henry's mother taught him that analytical thinking is important in the world. Mine still assures me that as long as I don't smell badly and smile a lot, I could own a fleet of ships "like that nice Mr. Onassis." I hate the fact that the same fucked-up chromosome produces both art and fashion, art and leisure, the one probably as unnecessary as the other.

A couple of days later, I go up to the Met to look at the Goyas, mostly courtly portraits which have become friends. They turn out to be dispensable and redundant. As most courtly portraits, they now appear shallow, flamboyant, and banal. If Goya, who I love, is under suspicion, then Velazquez, Caravaggio and Titian cannot be far behind. At home, I pull reproductions of Goya's Black Paintings from the bookshelf and begin to doubt even their sincerity. Provoked by a twit of a neurologist, I push my way into an aesthetic, ontological crisis.

That evening, at the White Horse, I down several Scotches. A woman I recognize from the few years between Art School and the Art Students League when I would occasionally prowl the New York parks for luscious young mothers sits at a table near the window. Mendelssohn, Mendelssohn, I warn myself, you don't need this. You drink too much and you don't know how to pass up any opportunity to get laid. No control? No control. So I keep checking her out to make sure she is the Annette of yore. We did have some good times, addicted to the danger of making love even in her marriage bed, when her husband Lou went off to work. Annette notices me, turns to her friend, then looks again and smiles.

"Michael Mendelssohn," she says and introduces me to her girlfriend who soon leaves.

Annette loses no time to tell me that Lou is away on business and she is horny. Oh, Jesus. Oh, shit, shit, shit. I follow her into a taxi and we drive to her fancy high-rise next to NYU. Upstairs, she sends the baby-sitter home. Annette massages me into shape and sets herself down on me. She gets into a lovely rhythm and suddenly I hear the double lock on the front door click and Annette slips off and runs to her bedroom. Lou Fisher walks into the living room to find a stranger with a hard-on, hiccupping. Suddenly sober, I spring up and grope for my clothes.

"I've seen you before," Lou says.

Annette runs in, fully robed, her hair wrapped in a towel as if she has just stepped out of the bath and acts as surprised as Lou regarding my presence. As I pull up my pants, Lou, a big burly guy, grabs me by the arm and begins beating the shit out of me. I crumple but Lou doesn't stop, making my ears ring. I hear my nose break and blood gushes all over the fuzzy wall-to-wall carpet.

"You fucker," he says and starts slapping Annette.

Instead of trying to get back at him or to protect Annette, I grab my remaining clothes and slip out the front door, sliding down several flights and stumble into Washington Square Park. I have never been beaten before. My face hurts terribly. In this park where bad shit happens all day, the scion of Mandeleau Furs and wonder boy refugee artist, might very well die. As my brain begins to fog up and stars appear behind my eyelids, the little bit of focus that remains assumes that it is my idiocy to make up for Zyga's weakness, my yearning to be my father's savior, that rules my womanizing self. Once a Polish prince, now a broken bum, I lose consciousness.

Some time after midnight, a cop finds me and shines a flashlight into my eyes. He asks if I want to file a complaint.

"I never saw the guy who mugged me," I murmur.

"You look like shit," the cop says. "I'll give you a ride to St. Vincent's."

There they set my nose, stitch me up, bandage my face, and send me home in the middle of the next day.

I call Crissie.

"I broke my nose," I tell her. "I got into a stupid fight at the White Horse."

A moment's silence.

"You? I don't know this part of you. You're acting like one of my uncles."

I emit a little moan.

"Jews don't do this sort of thing, do they?"

"Crissie…"

"If you ask me," Crissie says, "the whole agenda was set when you stole that watch."

A long pause.

"I must admit I love that part of you."

"Crissie," I begin again, then pause.

I can't tell her the truth. Betrayal lurks large in my life and it scares me.

"What was the fight about?" she asks. "Are you sure you're not from Oklahoma?"

"What I'm sure about is that I'm an asshole."

My face throbbing with pain, I drown in vodka, straight out of the bottle, sip by sip. The next day, with one pain on top of another threatening to bust my temples wide open, I want a mommy or a daddy, a mamusia or a tatush. In the early afternoon, I leave my cramped quarters on Jane Street to stare at the ocean-bound ships from a bench in Battery Park at the tip of Manhattan. It's an unusually warm, sunny day in October and I lose myself in the river traffic and, past that, the ocean. The sound of large ships carrying cargo, the bells, the whistles, the honk of ferry boats and sea gulls give me respite. I close my eyes and listen. What do I really have? What is entirely and exclusively mine? My painting. At this time in my life, color still seems extravagant, picturesque, frivolous. Life is heavy, a prison. Its borders, like Poland's, are surrounded by barbarians, by lies and avarice. On its way to the canvas, my brush flies, pokes, makes indelible structures, empties me. In my studio, I am delirious, feverish, about to explode. These large blocks of black are a dare, my dare. They are protection against disappearance, against all that threatens the world. I spend the night in my studio, these rooms having once been—who knows?—the interim hovel for a Jewish émigré family from my part of the world in an age preceding mine.

A few days later, I get a call from Suzi Schwab, a slick middle-aged European gallery owner who visited my studio a few months before. She wants to give me a show, to talk contracts. Madame Schwab, related by a former marriage to the international financiers, offers me an exhibit nine months from now, between a Bruce McCallum exhibit and "drawings of modern masters." I like McCallum's work, which looks as if the pigment were spread with the guy's thumb, fresh and urgent.

Madame Schwab wants to talk about the show over dinner. Before our meeting, with the hand-held spritzer, I shower and, just in case, cut my toenails. We dine in her neighborhood, somewhere in the East Seventies.

"What happened to your nose?" she asks.

"I got into a bit of a brawl at the White Horse."

She seems to like the idea of a brawling male. Smiling, she reaches across the table to take my hand.

"Come," she says when we finish dinner, "we'll have a drink up at my place.

Her place is a showplace, her walls crammed with important drawings and paintings, a small de Kooning, a Max Ernst frottage and a wine bottle labeled and decorated by Magritte, as well as a host of carefully chosen photographs and manifestos. I am thrilled to be surrounded by all these objects in a private collection. After a couple of drinks, Suzi pulls me into her bedroom where we spend a noisy hour in her bed, with its tall four Renaissance bedposts turned in Barcelona and crowned with small carved birds.

After a few minutes of post-coital sweet talk, she slides to the floor and assumes yoga stretches. Her feet are now behind her head.

"What I am doing is called The Plow," she explains.

We then explore the erotic possibilities of this Plow which offers many pleasures. She shows me Downward Facing Dog, Pelvic rocking and the Mountain, the latter with her wrists gently tied to the top of a door.

The next day, exhilarated by last evening's activity, by the promise of a major exhibit, I try to put my guilt aside and call Crissie.

"I must teach you the Plow and the Shoulder Stand," I tell her.

"What are you talking about?"

"Yoga positions."

"Where did you learn yoga positions?"

"I signed up for a yoga class."

I drag Crissie to Bloomingdale's. She looks stunning in a couple of beautiful dresses. Her compulsion from early on has been to downplay, even deny her beauty or any effort to enhance it with clothes or ornament, but she now stands before a triptych of mirrors, looking pleased. Her half-smile brims with satisfaction. As I sit there, a pasha nursing a hard-on, strangers stop to look at Crissie in a low-cut black dress, in summery prints of tiny wildflowers, in a warm light-ochre suit which makes her hair blacker, her eyes bluer.

A couple of months later, to my astonishment, my mother calls on the phone. "Bolek says your lady is very beautiful," she says in Polish.

"Yes, she is."

"I must meet her," Rena says.

"Why don't you come to see her here? You've never been in my apartment."

Of course she will not, so a week later, not very happily, I bring Crissie to East 57th Street. Zyga looks clean-shaven, still smelling from the barber shop; my mother, as always, in some Balenciaga suit or its facsimile. Crissie is resplendent in one of her new Bloomingdale's dresses, cool as Grace Kelly.

Zyga, who does not stop smiling at Crissie, takes her arm and walks her into the living room. My mother pulls me into their bedroom where she sits down in her emerald green chair, takes a magnifying mirror in one hand, and begins to tweeze little hairs from her chin.

"You are happy?" she asks me. Her lower lip is pulled over the upper.

"You have always been a moody boy," she says while pulling out the unwanted chin hairs without showing pain.

"I am okay."

"We come with nothing," she says in Polish. "We work hard and America gives us all we need." She stops tweezing and looks out the window. "Your girl is beautiful, but you can have any girl you want. No one can resist you. You are tall and handsome. Everybody tells me how intelligent you are and how talented." She puts the mirror down on her dresser. "Do you know that I fit a sable on Madame Jacqueline Kennedy when I am at the White House? She runs around to get me tea. It is very good to have friends like that."

As I listen to stuff I don't really want to hear, I imagine Karl Marx coming to visit at 400 East. Marx is nearly unrecognizable. Knowing he had to be presentable, Marx got a haircut and shaved his beard. My mother continues her cautionary tales.

"He is an ideal husband, Mr. John Kennedy," she says. "Baron de Gunzburg tells me that Mr. President has many amours which, of course, is the way of men, but he surrounds his wife with flowers and furs."

I'm beginning to tire of this. I'm also curious about the hushed talk I barely hear coming from the living room.

"Remember, Mishek," my mother says, "that to be with many women is natural for men."

This wakes me up.

"What about your husband?" I ask her, probing brand new territory.

"Zyga?"

"He is your husband, isn't he?"

"Zyga is not a man like Mr. President. He does not act like a man."

"You would like it if he had girlfriends?"

"He can do what he pleases."

Two photographs in leather frames look out from her dresser; one of a smiling Bolek, the other one of a sullen me.

"And do you know," she says, "that Bolek has a new lady friend, an elegant, beautiful woman, Ursula?" She begins tweezing again, then, very quietly, she says, "Your girl must have a new coat." She points to the dresser. "Give me my handbag," she says. "I will give you money. Go to Bergdorf."

I cannot bear any more. I leave her and walk into the living room where the scene stops me short. On the couch, facing each other and holding each other's hands, sit Zyga and Crissie, quietly engaged in conversation. They are sitting on the most uncomfortable of sofas, an Empire satin thing made for the likes of Rena and Madame Pompadour, over which hangs a second-rate neo-Impressionist painting of a lady in royal blue chiffon looking down from a balcony. I lean against the Victorian armoire, stocked with liquors and wines in case anyone important comes by. Crissie and Zyga are a picture of contentment. Crissie looks at me and her smile broadens. Not meaning to, I bare my teeth like a rabid dog. Zyga looks down and Crissie bites her lip. I pour myself a half glass of Polish vodka and turn away.

"One for me too," Crissie yells across the room. "And what about you, Zyga?"

I pour her one and bring it over.

"Your father is telling me about the time between the wars."

I stand there transfixed, my mouth open. They look like a father and daughter reunited. It never occurred to me that my father wanted a daughter and she a different daddy. I study my father's face, the thin, dry lips now turned up at the corners into a smile.

"Fuck this," I say to myself and, in the guest room down a short hall, turn on the television where a studio full of happy faces cheer as the camera zooms to a shiny white refrigerator.

"What is it, Michael?" Crissie asks, looking alarmed.

"I'm fine," I tell them and sit down for a minute to cool off.

Crissie comes to me and lifts my chin.

"You don't look fine," she says.

I kiss her hand. "I'm really okay," I tell her.

My father stands at the door, looking warmly at us.

In the elevator, Crissie looks up, her smile generous and tender. Eddie the doorman doffs his cap to us, the happy couple, and, walking west on 57th Street, Crissie clutches my hand and swings our arms back and forth. We're like little kids claiming the territory.

"I love your father's Polish accent," she says.

"Crissie, your being with him startles me."

She squeezes my hand and says nothing.

"He and I don't have much to do with each other."

We walk a long block in silence.

"Listen, I was a child of eight, but some of those memories are embedded forever and, as you know, Rena and Bolek never let up."

"Do you really trust your eight-year-old memories?"

"No."

"Why don't you ask Zyga directly?"

"I'm afraid."

"What a lot of old baggage you carry around with you."

We take a taxi downtown to Jane Street and run up three creaky flights to my rooms. On my bed, as we hold each other close, Crissie says, "Every once in a while, I try to examine my feelings about my own parents. There's very little there to love. Still, I keep telling myself that I must simply love them for no other reason than that they're my parents."

"Chrissie," I say, overcome with emotion, "I love you very much."

She is crying now and says that they are tears of happiness.

"And then there's the fact that you're a witch," I say.

"I am not," Crissie says and tickles my ribs.

"You can't fool me. I saw what you did. You transformed that miserable apartment of theirs. When you sat at that Empire dining table, it didn't tip over as it usually does."

She runs her fingers down my back, scratching me gently.

"And those ugly green Limoges tea cups, they actually looked good in your hands." She sighs.

"Until you entered that apartment, every object in that living room was an expression of disdain—paintings hung as dares, tchachkis waiting to have their little necks broken."

She puts her head on my chest and caresses my belly from hip to hip. It takes great self-control to keep talking, but I do, saving the best part of the pie for last.

"It's true that knives are never thrown."

Her lovely fingers roam on my belly.

"Skillets are never used to crack skulls open, but every object in that apartment is suffused with reprimand and rage."

"Both their doing? I thought you said that Zyga was a weakling, never defending himself."

"It's both of them."

Then, her face radiant, her body in slow deliberate motion, she makes love to me, her exclamation point—and what a juicy exclamation it is—I surmise that it's partly in honor of my admitting Zyga's power as equal to Rena's. After a few moments of inactivity—what the yogis, I have read since my initial yoga experience, call "receiving the posture"—she extends her arms toward me, pulling me back to her. We turn each other over and over like tumbleweed. When we stop, wet and exhausted, she says, "There are a few things you don't know about me."

"Impossible."

"I am partly American Indian."

"American Indian?"

I'm stunned into silence for a moment, then an electric current runs through my body. I want to jump, to give a whoop.

"Oh my god!" I cry.

"Michael, Michael, what does this mean to you? In my family, it was hardly mentioned. In Oklahoma, native people are seen as rattlesnakes."

"Who is the Indian?"

"My mother's mother was a Cherokee. All of them on my mother's side, but they never spoke about it."

She smiles and puts both her hands on my cheeks.

"You're not the Junior League or a Daughter of the American Revolution."

She is laughing now and I want to get up and dance around a bonfire, to revere falcons and jaguars. My beauty turns onto her belly and up on her elbows. She looks deeply into my eyes.

"Don't ever leave me," she says.

Flooded with a sense of renewal and optimism, with a love I never experienced before, I tell her,

"Never, Crissie, never."

IN THE MORNING, while Crissie is still sleeping, I leave quietly, take the subway uptown and, from the lobby of a building across the street from

Mandeleau's, I wait for my father to re-emerge after opening the place, as he does every morning. I've had fantasies of my father conducting a life somewhere outside the hell of family, but this is the first time I act on that dream, hoping to discover a mistress, a labor hall, friends. I have no great expectations, but now feel an unfamiliar sympathy for this poor, poor creature, so full of anger and sadness.

Zyga steps out of the entrance of 20 West, stops to look left and right, pulls his shoulders back, rotates his neck and takes a deep breath, then walks to the corner for a newspaper. He crosses 57th Street and heads for the park. His steps are mincing, his head thrust forward, he looks uncomfortable. At 58th, a quiet block, he turns east. I follow him from the other side of the street. Walking down Fifth Avenue, my father stops in front of DePinna's and my body clenches as I will him to go inside to buy a suit. He looks at the window display for a while, then resumes walking. After passing a big, blind guy with a guide dog inching his way down the avenue, jingling his tin cup, Zyga stops and returns to drop some coins into the cup. Zyga's steps become longer, his body more upright. For moments, I witness a man given a full pardon, free from his prison. Though I now see only his back, I wouldn't be surprised if he is smiling. Like everyone else, Zyga is navigating the streets of this city, the heels of his exile shoes making a mark on an alien sidewalk. This is his city, as much his as anyone else's. I wonder if in Warsaw, also not strictly his, he felt like an owner of those Polish sidewalks or if he knew that he was given guarded permission to temporarily use what belonged to them. I am becoming aware of my father's isolation, his alienation, the events that forced him into someone else's streets. About to walk past the Rockefeller Center skating rink, now set with tables and umbrellas, Zyga looks at his wristwatch, opens his newspaper and lays it on the parapet wall overlooking the rink. Leaning on his elbows, he begins to read. After a while, he looks up at the sky, takes a deep breath and spreads his arms wide to stretch his shoulders, an eagle—a Polish eagle?—spreading its wings. He is fully a man with a claim to the air around him. Slowly, he folds up his paper and sticks it back in his jacket pocket. Exuberant and generous, he steps aside to give others the right of way, bowing politely, a gentlemanly courtesy.

Zyga crosses Sixth Avenue and I follow. On 57th Street, Zyga ducks into the automat. I post myself across the street at the Buckingham Hotel, giving Zyga time to settle down. Now I can imagine that he is about to meet a mistress and take her next door to the Great Northern Hotel. I cross the street and see my father sitting at a table in back, close to the counters where they serve hot meals, away from the sandwiches and wedges of pie inside turntable slots on the side walls. The tables begin to empty, people hurrying off to work. A few walk in, one of whom, a tall, bald, thin man, brings his coffee to Zyga's table. They smile and shake hands. The tall man gets up again, then comes back with two plates of pie. They eat and drink, talking the whole time. Zyga's eyes look clear, even sparkling. He reaches into his pocket and hands an envelope to his friend who then stands up to kiss Zyga's cheeks. They know each other well. At home and at work, I hear only grunts and moans and fragments of complaints, mockery or rage. Inside the automat, I have a glimpse of a social man.

When the two men finish what is in front of them, Zyga refills their coffee cups. The thin, bald man has big lips and a sallow complexion. He opens one of the several books he brought with him, finds the place he is looking for, and reads something aloud. Zyga puts two fingers to his temples, listens intently, then comments. His friend smacks his lips and nods, puts the book back in his briefcase and opens another. It is possible that Zyga's headaches and depressions disappear when he is out of the family orbit. Good one, I think, way to go, tatush. This family, my family, is toxic. I have found my way out. Perhaps my father has as well. The men sit for a long time, each of them talking in turn. When they get up to go, I dart across 57th Street and watch them walk west, both with their hands clasped behind their backs, heads down, like two philosophers. Clothes obviously mean nothing to either of them—Zyga's wrinkled suit a bit too small for him, the other man's too large. They make a comical pair. And what am I to do with this hoped for discovery? I walk down to the Carnegie Deli and order a pastrami on rye with a half sour pickle. Munching away and eager to get back to my Crissie, I wish that my father were here with me.

6.

Crissie and I are products of gross marital misalignments, especially the Rena-Zyga one, not to discount the utter boredom and stupidity she tells me about regarding her own parents. When we talk of marriage, we assure each other that a history of bad marriages is not hereditary. Still, we know, deep down, that a careful study of family histories, psychological propensities, a thorough investigation of preferred songs, plays, and books ought to precede any leaps into commitments destined to last even a little while.

"Each of us should make a list of things we love," I say.

"Sounds like a good idea," Crissie says, kneeling by the Goya books stacked on the floor of the Jane Street rooms that we are about to share.

"Okay, here's a start."

She sits down next to me on the couch I brought up years ago from a throwaway pile on Mulberry Street.

"The Charlies—Parker and Mingus."

"Check," she says, clapping and badly imitating a Charlie Parker riff.

"The Bach Violin Partitas."

"I'm with you there as well."

I name three painters—de Kooning, Motherwell, and Franz Kline.

"No problem," Crissie says, slapping my knee happily and then taking my hand. "My turn."

She puts her head on my shoulder.

"*Middlemarch*," she says.

"Read it and loved it."

"*Bouvard et Pécuchet*, my favorite Flaubert."

"I'll give it a try," I promise.

Before we stop, she adds the essays of Montaigne.

"Perfect," I say, satisfied that we are meant for each other.

We are married by a civil servant on Centre Street, telling no one and without fanfare or ceremony but with great elation, each of us convinced that we are doing the right thing. We do in fact read the Montaigne essays aloud to each other, a welcome change from my old, lonely German philosophers who are never a great remedy for sleeplessness.

"Even in sleep," I confide to Crissie, "they appear in my dreams wagging their bony arthritic fingers, reminding me that we should regard our lives as a useless episode in the blissful repose of nothingness."

Crissie cuddles up closer, says nothing.

"Before you came into my life, those ugly bastards used to remind me that no matter how bad it is today, tomorrow it will get worse."

"You know what?" she says. "I think that books by depressives are reassuring. They're company. At least they make us feel that we're not alone."

If she had told me that a few months ago, I would have married her at that very moment.

"I hate people who won't read stuff because they find it depressing. Not reading it, they miss what most of the world is doing. For me, pessimism is my birthright, probably inserted during circumcision."

We are perfect together, I tell myself. How lucky is that?

"Whenever happiness enters my bloodstream," I go on, "the regulator eventually brings me back to reality, to worries about body parts, worthlessness, and death."

"Michael, I love you," she says into my chest. "We're so much alike. Not angsting is shallow and uninteresting," she says a millimeter from my lips, and I realize that I have never been happier.

"And now we've got Montaigne who thinks that happiness comes from living the life of animals, paragons of health and virtue," I say, unbuttoning her blouse. "The two Michels, Montaigne and Mendelssohn, agree that natural pleasures, whether of body or mind, should be gratefully accepted."

And thus, in Montaigne's name, we continue to tear each other's clothes off, certain we have never experienced this kind of fierce hunger, not ever.

Much of the time, Crissie is tough as nails, full of energy and curiosity. Her obsessions are captivating. In our crowded Jane Street apartment, in the middle of the night, she taps me lightly on my shoulder.

"What? What do you want?"

"I was just thinking about Richard III."

She is sitting up, books spread on the bed before her.

"Michael," she says, "he was so maligned."

"Can't you turn out the light? What time is it? I was in the middle of a dream." Now awake and pissed off, I stammer, "Jesus, Crissie, what are you doing? Why does this Richard matter? Anyway, wasn't your Richard a hunchback?"

"There, you see," she says angrily. "That's all anyone thinks about when Richard is mentioned. It's all a lie."

"Aha," I say, wanting to introduce no more controversy or commentary this night. "It's two o'clock in the morning."

But she cannot be stopped. It turns out that Richard Plantagenet, the youngest son of Richard Duke of York, became Duke of Gloucester and was made king in 1483 and killed in 1485 at the Battle of Bosworth by the invading Henry Tudor who became Henry VII, a descendant of King Edward III. Civil strife was never quelled among these irritable, argumentative people, Richard having hardly left the north of England except to invade France and Scotland.

"My God," I say after a drink of water and a pee, "all those Richards, Edwards, and Henrys. Exiled, deposed, reinstated, murdered, their lives like a paranoid's worst nightmare."

"I've begun my Richard III book," she says. "The Bosworth Chronicles."

From then on, it is Plantaganets this, Lancastrians that. We begin to receive a newsletter in our mailbox which she reads as avidly as I read the Nation, except that her news is from 1485. As a couple, we do not believe that Richard was evil or a hunchback with withered arms or a killer of his little nephews.

"Shakespeare's sources were the hostile Tudor chronicles. Could he have really thought that an evil mind must dwell in a twisted body? Contemporary portraits show no sign of a hunchback. Come on, Michael, sit up and look at these portraits. He had delicate arms and legs as well as a great heart."

"Isn't there a statute of limitations? Why don't you turn your anger toward McNamara and Rusk? With them it's not a matter of libel. It's fucking war crimes."

She was quiet for a moment.

"Once your Richard injustice is cleaned up, we'll still have a few million villains to go after."

"We have to start somewhere," Crissie says.

So, what to tell you, my sweet doppelganger, about Ruth? We are careful about eating well, better than well. We swallow anti-oxidants, fish oil, and flax seed, all in moderation. She tells me which cheeses are nourishing, which life-shortening. She tells me about rennet, food coloring, and nitrates. She launches into the correctness of this, the correctness of that. She pronounces—superbly gurgles—the word Nicaragua with all the gutturals, and then some. She never defines anyone by skin color or sexual preference while I need that, plus job descriptions and approximate net worth, to compare and connect. I like goading her with stories of feasts gathered in rain forests, bald eagle soup or the delicacy of bovine growth hormones. That's us at our sweetest.

TWO YEARS AFTER WE MARRY, Blanche Madden, Crissie's mother, calls to tell her that her father Marvin is recovering from his second heart attack. On the phone, Crissie lapses into Oklahomese, a saccharine drawly sweetness.

"Fuck," she says the moment she hangs up, a word she rarely uses.

The Jane Street apartment now houses her Indian chotchkes, as well as piles of books and records stacked against every wall. For weeks, she has been immersed in her matador book and now she pushes the typewriter to one side of the card table and stares down at the street below. Pensive, she grinds her teeth and bites her lip. Even though I have been curious enough to want to meet the Cherokee mother, Crissie has avoided visiting home. As a matter of fact, she works hard to dismiss her past in Oklahoma, impressing on me her love for the city.

"Is this very upsetting?" I ask.

"I should be more upset than I am."

"Maybe you should go. Maybe we should both go."

When I get home late in the afternoon, the typewriter is clacking away.

Crissie's concentration is complete, even though she is humming some off-key tune, then turns to me, smiling, her hair a bit mussed, falling over one eye. I pull a chair up to her writing table.

"You don't have to come with me, Mishek," she says, using my Polish baby name, "but should you decide to come, bring a lot to read and draw on, for you'll be bored out of your mind."

She pours each of us a glass of vodka. As we lay back on the springy couch, half full of papers and books, we get more sloshed on our second drink, and Crissie says, "Zyga makes me want to be Jewish."

I nearly spill my drink.

"He's hardly Jewish himself," I tell her.

"He told me that first he was a human being, then a Social democrat, and then a Jew."

She runs her fingers through my hair.

"My father said that?"

"Yes, Mishek, he did. I love all of those three aspects of him. Jewish is a third of it. And if you think your family is awful, come meet mine."

Even though I am not that eager to meet folks who despise the New Deal as well as the UN, I am curious about witnessing another fucked-up family. And so, the next day, we pile into the Hillman and head west. Wrenching that flawed silver Minx away from New York City is like separating the heart patient from his cardiologist. The farther west we venture, the weirder that little car seems to all who see her. Mechanics run out of their garages to have a look. They smack her, kick the tires, ask for demonstrations with the directional arrows, gawk at her and think her hilarious. Both Crissie and I have learned to take the fuel pump apart with our eyes closed. Driving into the interior, I begin to feel jittery, a deep craving to drop bread crumbs behind us.

"What do you folks do to Jews out here?" I ask my philo-semitic wife as we pass through Wheeling, West Virginia.

"We keep them out of our country clubs and swimming pools."

"Are there many of us in Oklahoma?"

"There was a little Jewish boy in my third grade class. Smart and pushy."

She puts her head on my shoulder as we drive through Zanesville and Terre Haute.

"Do you want to know one reason I love you so much? I love the little boy who figured out how to survive. And the man who makes big statements."

Some 50 miles from St. Louis, she becomes agitated. We are approaching her private hell. A hot wind is blowing in our faces through the open windows. Crissie fans herself with an illistrated history of the Jews. After a while, she tells me that Hasidism had once taken place in the smaller Polish towns, not in the cities.

"Lots of singing and dancing, lots of joy and ecstasy transformed religious worship into an escape from the horrors of everyday life."

"Aha."

This damn country is huge. On Route 66, where a nation is moving east and west at will, I feel the vague threat of barely concealed violence. The newspapers we buy along the way glow with kidnappings, near-lynchings, torched houses, embezzlements, and widespread corruption.

"In the midst of your rugged individuality," I complain to my Virgil, "we have, in front of our very eyes, a lot of bad shit."

She puts her hand on the top of my head.

"Satan," she says, "get your grimy fangers off'n God's property."

As we pass the welcome to Oklahoma sign, Crissie grinds her teeth uncontrollably, then confesses that when she was younger she was cutting.

"Cutting?"

I have no idea what she is talking about.

"In high school, I cut my arm with a razor blade."

"You what? You wanted to kill yourself?" I'm astonished.

"Not really," she says, biting her lip hard. "This was high school, Michael. I was a drama queen."

I pick up her left arm and barely see the faint shadows of scars. I lay her arm gently on the steering wheel and kiss the tell-tale remnants of scars, then lick them. It is confession time.

"In boarding school, I bit a kid so hard he needed stitches."

"We're both a little crazy," Crissie says and massages the back of my neck.

"I liked biting him. I like hurting people who piss me off. You know why? I lash out in Zyga's name."

"What does that mean?"

"To make up for his wimpy behavior."

Crissie takes the wheel as we approach Tulsa. We pull up at the curb in front of the Madden"s house, more than ready to get out of the car. A pre-war suburban house, simple and ugly, stands on the corner of 27th Street. It is already late in the afternoon and Blanche Madden, not too steady on her feet, comes out to greet us. She is small and very thin. Her black hair is cut in bangs. The skin on her face is heavily lined, shriveled, like a preserved head from the Museum of Natural History.

"Mama," Crissie says and kisses her mother very gently, as if she were afraid of shattering her to pieces.

In a flowery dress that hangs loose on her frail, shaky body, Blanche holds steady on her daughter's arm.

"And this is the famous Michael Mendelssohn," Blanche Madden says, more a judgment than a statement of fact.

Her voice is high in register and gravelly, an unpleasant combination.

"May I call you Mike?" she asks. "After all, I'm your mother-in-law."

"I prefer Michael."

and shouted in Russian for the prisoners to wake up. *"Proznut'sya! Proznut'sya!"*

Next, they blasted the Russian national anthem just in case the screaming and banging didn't do the job. That was followed by a song from Putin's favorite pop star. Shaman. *Ya Russky!* 8 p.m. was lights out, and for the next nine hours she would lie in the dark, listening to the scuffling of cockroaches and the occasional rat that climbed out from the hole in the floor.

The 5 a.m. lights at least scared the roaches and rats back into the stinking hole. She could hear the prisoners in the other cells. One man constantly ranted and raved in Russian. Sometimes he'd scream day and night. Another prisoner had a horrible hacking cough. It sounded like he was dying, and maybe he was. They never let her out to exercise. Perhaps because she was female. Or a foreigner. They told her they'd be transferring her to a women's penal colony soon. The dreaded IK-14 prison for women in Mordovia. But since then, she hadn't heard another word about it.

Two weeks into her captivity, guards dragged a new prisoner inside and tossed them into the cell next to hers.

"Bloody hell! You're breaking my bloody arm! Get off me, you wanker!" The cell door clanged shut. He shouted at the guards through the food slot. "You can't do this! I need to talk to my embassy! You hear me? Hey!"

Bettina knelt next to the food slot and called out into the hall. "Are you a Brit?"

"Who are you?"

"I'm a reporter for *Rolling Stone*. Bettina O'Toole-Applebaum."

"American?"

"Yep."

"What are they accusing you of?"

"Spying. What about you?"

"They haven't told me a damn thing. They just grabbed me up off the street and pumped me up with some kind of sedative. The next thing I know, I'm in Russia."

"Where'd they snatch you up?"

"Solvang, California."

"Jesus."

"Right? I'm guessing we're somewhere in Siberia."

"Polar Owl Prison."

"*Polar Owl?*"

"I came here to interview Oleg Ivanov."

"Did you get the interview?"

"I did. And now I'm being charged under Article 276 of the Russian Criminal Code for espionage."

"Bastards."

"So, what's your name?"

"Duncan Dankworth."

■ ■ ■

Even with his heavy woolen peacoat, lambswool scarf, stocking cap, and fur-lined gloves, Kalishnik continued to freeze his balls off. He hated the cold. Especially damp cold. All his joints ached. Even his bones hurt. Standing in line to enter Polar Owl was torture. The frigid wind made his eyes water and his teeth hurt. He stamped his feet to stay warm, but that didn't do dick.

Luckily, he was here to see Ivanov and, once past the front gate, a young guard led him directly to Ivanov's cell block. The smell of piss and shit and sweat and fear began to fade, overtaken by the sweet aroma of some kind of delicious stew and freshly baked bread. Upon seeing Kalishnik, the massive prisoner guarding the large steel door at the end of the hall knocked three times. Instantly, the door opened.

Kalishnik entered to find Oleg Ivanov sitting at a butcher-block table, wearing a Fila tracksuit, and enjoying his midday

One afternoon in October, Crissie poses with her back to me as the Velazquez Rokeby Venus, looking into a hand mirror originally held by a cherub. Not having a cherub in Hoboken or the Village, she holds the mirror she brought from home. Crissie Madden's hips swoop up from her slender waist. Never before have her eyes softened like this, becoming a deeper blue, looking wanton and daring. In that mirror, her soft gaze seems like an invitation.

"Are you alright?" I ask in a husky voice more basso than usual.

"I'm fine like this," she says and a half smile appears in the mirror.

"Fine doesn't describe you right now."

"No? What does?"

What does? Hot! Oh my.

"Tumid, moist, ripe, glowing…" I say, probably panting like a ghoul.

"Listen to you," she says. "I thought I was the writer."

"Crissie, you're driving me crazy."

"Yes?"

I put my hands around her hips and pull her to me. She does not resist. As I put her down on her belly, then lift her to her knees, she says hoarsely, "Not like this."

I turn her around so she is lying on her back, her thighs parting. Slowly she gets into a rhythm and her body begins to writhe with pleasure. When we finish, she tells me that she made love only once before.

"Practice isn't required," I tell her, stroking her hair.

"With a bull fighter in Spain. I didn't much like it."

"You didn't like it?"

"I had to do it because I was writing a love story about a young, beautiful torero."

"Research."

I reach for the cigarettes on the painting table and we both light up. She leans over me to flick the ashes, then, lying back down, she crosses her arms to cover her breasts, breasts I now judge as perfect as a Phidias sculpture.

"More," I beg and try to gently pull her arms apart.

"Enough," she says, climbs over me and swings her legs off the couch, straightens her hair, ties it into a bun, then takes her clothes into the other room.

When she returns, she is perfectly put together, untouchable again. Her eyes don't retain their softness, her body is back in its armor.

Though she poses for me often, in class and in my studio, love-making is rationed, irrationally rationed. At times, I make a gentle move to show my desire only to be rebuffed, as if I am the night elevator man putting the make on the lady living alone in the penthouse. At other times—and I never know when to expect it—she lightly, casually swipes her hand across my crotch, a papal nod signifying that St. Peter's gates are now open. Not only her sexuality but her moods change unpredictably, keeping me on the edge of my seat. For reasons I don't quite understand, I am happy never knowing what to expect, preferring this painful, exciting unpredictability to a tiresome routine.

Because of my persistent need to indelibly define my differentness from them, I want to flaunt my yippee-ay-yay cowgirl, as alien to my family as a geisha.

"I do want to meet them," Crissie says after a couple of drinks and a light supper she cooks for us in my Jane Street apartment.

"Let's consider, Crissie dear. My mother would look you up and down, measure you silently as a model among the walking dead of her profession. Are your breasts small enough, your legs long enough?"

Crissie looks at me with a quizzical expression on her face.

"On the other hand, Rena might recognize that you are perfectly capable of the haughty coolness required for the fashion show runway."

"You think I'm haughty?"

"Not really. Only when you want to be."

She does not look pleased.

"And then there is my father Zyga. I'm afraid that one look at him and you might fear that I will follow in his footsteps."

"What's wrong with your father?"

"It's a long story," I begin, not really wanting to continue.

"Tell me," she says, stretched out on my bumpy couch, her head on my lap.

"It's hard to talk about."

"Try."

"He has given up all hope since we left Warsaw."

I stop for a moment, not knowing what to say. "That's not it, not only that. Something devastating happened at the Lithuanian border on our way out of Poland. I'm not sure about any of it, but my mother and uncle keep harping on that time." I swallow hard. "They say he betrayed us."

Crissie sits up.

"How?" she asks.

"I'm not sure but, even though the memory is murky, I do believe it."

"How awful," Crissie says.

"With his melancholy, his misanthropy, his weakness, he is not a father to me and I'm not a son to him."

So we begin with Bolek, Bolek the Bold, Bolek the Conqueror, Bolek the Clown. As we walk up on the park side of Fifth Avenue, Crissie points out that neither of us have great marriage models in our families.

"At least yours talk to each other."

She laughs. "You should hear what they have to say. There's a lot of Jesus talk. They get down on their knees and pray for no socialized medicine."

My turn to laugh. "That would be intimacy in my family."

"I thought Jewish families yell and scream and cry," Crissie says.

"I grew up in silence. If you want a history of yelling and loving and stuffing your face with matzoh balls, you're with the wrong Jew."

When we arrive at 1016 Fifth Avenue, Uncle Bolek is his usual charming self. He takes Crissie's hand in his, bows down to kiss it. In Polish—for there is no English equivalent to these chivalrous gestures and words—he says, more or less, "I kiss your dainty little hand, esteemed Madam." When I translate Bolek's words, Crissie nearly swoons. It is chivalry, among other anachronisms, that she requires and, after that, she can be won over whenever I kiss her hand, bowing.

"Say those words in Polish," she would beg, already breathing hard.

Bolek's apartment is beautifully appointed by Pierre Delvaux, "the interior decorator used by the whole family Paley," he says, "and the Shah of all Persia." The leather couches are long and plush, the dining table primitive chic, with an ancient wooden Egyptian funerary expedition its center piece. The entrance hall is tiled with a large black and white checkered design, all kept in immaculate shape by a male Japanese housekeeper, Hasegawa-san.

"What sublime taste," Crissie drawls.

Although she had long ago shed her incomprehensible Oklahoma drawl—she can't bear anyone, especially her parents, to "talk Oklahoma"—her Tulsa accent now returns, making her English even more incomprehensible to stupefied Uncle Bolek. Then there is the matter of her dress, a sign of her sensitivity toward the poor and oppressed, both conditions central to her caring identity. She wears a hand-me-down blue, rayon dress, too tight and nearly threadbare. I do not pay much attention to her taste for ill-fitting, stained clothes, her beautiful face commanding most of my attention. But here, in contrast to the apartment's perfection and

"And how is my only child, my baby?"

"Fine, mama, just fine."

Marvin Madden comes out of the house, leaning on an aluminum cane. He is a tall Oklahoma replica of LBJ and a bit stooped. Under his cowboy hat, his hair is thinning.

"Hello there, Miss Crissie," he says. "How's my Yankee girl?"

His hand is large and rough as he grips mine.

"Michael Mendelssohn," he says, trying it out for size, then leads the way inside.

Marvin Madden is the first of his family to go to college, then an undreamed of leap into medical school. A successful eye and ear specialist, he is also a shrewd businessman. He bought the building which houses his office, then the one next door. The Maddens moved into their present house on a quiet, tree-lined street in the Forties. Their furniture is plush, all corners rounded and covered with plastic.

"The plastic covers never come off," Crissie tells me, "summer or winter."

Crissie fits the house and its activities more snugly than I would have guessed. Like a trained sous-chef, she cooks with her mother and, after dinner, the clean-up proceeds like a well-oiled machine while Marvin and I stay at the table, drinking coffee. Madden offers me a cigar and we both puff away.

"American cigars," he says. "So young man, you paint pictures, do you?"

I own up to it.

"My daughter likes everything that's out of the ordinary," he says. "She lives in a world of her own."

"Quite a gal," I agree, American man to American man.

"Here, she could have everything any girl would want."

"Crissie needs a large canvas," I tell Madden as we toke on our cigars.

"Her people aren't good enough for my girl," he says.

"Crissie is a loving and generous person," I say, a little pissed off.

She comes in and stands behind me, rests her arms on my shoulders and nuzzles the back of my neck.

"We're both pretty tired, Daddy," she says and moves toward him to kiss her father's cheek. The phone rings and though Crissie hasn't lived in this house since going away to college, she runs to answer.

"Zyga!" she cries. "How good to hear your voice."

I can't believe what I'm hearing.

"My father? It can't be."

She puts her hand over the receiver and says,

"Isn't that wonderful?"

She then talks quietly while Marvin drones on about his daughter's high school career.

"She'd go to nigra revivals," he says as he pulls his chair away from the table so he can cross his long legs. "They carry on like cannibals," he says.

I should be expecting this, but it's the first time I hear this kind of raw hatred in America.

"Cannibals?"

"Come speak to Zyga, Michael," Crissie says. "He just wants to know if we arrived safely."

I furrow my brow as Crissie hands me the phone. Zyga says in Polish, "Are you alright? And that car? Did that car take you to Oklahoma?"

"Just barely," I report. "We had to fix it at least five times."

"Do they want you in Oklahoma?" he asks. "They are nice people?"

"Very nice."

When I get off the phone, Crissie, beaming, sits down with her father who picks up his newspaper.

"What's your new book about?" he asks as he scans the real estate section.

"About Michael," she says.

"What?"

This is the first time I hear of it.

"About a Jewish artist trekking through the southwest. You want to know the title?"

Marvin appears not to hear.

"*Chaim on the Range*," she says, the mistress of words.

Marvin turns his body away from both of us.

"What a great title," I say. "Don't you think so, Marvin?"

He says nothing and I'd like to smack him.

Crissie's ancestral bedroom has twin beds, the other one across the little night table I assume served sleep-overs of little girlfriends also being bred for the Junior League and country club. The pinkness of beds and walls is hard on the eyes, the teddy bears not conducive to fellatio. Still, I climb into her bed with her and, from some deeply ingrained biological imperative induced, I suppose, by the color pink and the presence of fuzzy old bears and rabbits, Crissie broaches the subject of children. We talked about it abstractly in the past but never in bed as I hover over her. She wants to be impregnated here and now.

"Wouldn't it be fitting if we conceived a baby on the bed I was practically born on?"

I move off her and sit on the side of the bed, thinking that a terminally self-absorbed papa and the mama who would rather have been a courtesan locked in the Tower of London than a mom dispensing cough syrup to a row of bawling brats, is not a promising scenario.

"Look Crissie, we are two artists, not parents. You can't be both."

"You can't?"

She pulls me back and stretches out under me, puts both her hands on my chest.

"Why not?"

"Would you really want to bring children into a world of nuclear bombs, wars everywhere, rock and roll?"

Crissie pushes me off her.

"And not only that," I say, holding on to her hand, "but consider the fact that no one taught me to be a father and it's pretty clear that you haven't been smothered with love either."

With my elbows on my knees, my face in my hands, I tell her that my genes are suspect.

"Betrayal runs deep in my family," I explain.

"Oh come on, Michael. What betrayal? We're all capable of little betrayals."

"Probably true, but I think I have the dominant gene."

"What are you talking about?"

"It's in the family."

"You're crazy," Crissie says, sitting up.

"That too," I say.

"If you don't want children by the time I'm thirty, I'm off to get pregnant elsewhere."

"Children will change our lives. We'll grow apart."

"My whole body, everything in me wants to give birth."

"It's exceptional people who resist that biological urge."

"Who told you that?"

"Tell you what. We"ll talk about it when you're thirty. Five more years. Is it a deal?" She nods and the love-making takes a rest for that night, but I assure myself as I fall asleep I will supervise the insertion of her diaphragm, measure the amount of spermicide she squeezes around its perimeter, and hope for the best.

Relatives arrive for dinner the next afternoon. The sing-song of their chatter is not unpleasant though often incomprehensible. In the conversation pit, a dangerous two steps down from the non-conversational level, Crissie and I face the jury of aunts, uncles, and cousins, who believe that God put oil under Oklahoma. Marvin elaborates, proclaiming that God had a reason.

"And what might that reason be, daddy?"

I sit up, look intensely into Madden's eyes, and wait for an answer. My eyes dare him to answer.

"Something you don't appreciate about our oil?" Madden asks, glaring at me. "You got something against that, boy?"

"Why don't we just let it go for now?" Crissie suggests while getting sloshed on the Bourbon she is sharing with her mother. "Let's just have a good time."

"Tell us, Michael, how are your fur coats made?" asks Aunt Belle.

For a moment, I'm taken aback. Why is she asking me? I cough and sputter.

"I have no idea," I tell her. "I am not a part of their business."

"What a pity," Aunt Belle says. "They make such beautiful things."

"Isn't it lovely to have some Hebrew influence in our part of the world?" Crissie asks.

This upsets everyone. Everyone looks at everyone else, eyes rolling back in their heads. There goes Crissie again. Crissie gets up, pours herself another shot of bourbon, and goes down the rows of armchairs kissing her relatives. Blanche hiccups.

"Mama, mama," Crissie says and Blanche hiccups again.

Everyone is shifting positions, followed by many throat clearings. They have all been through countless Crissie eruptions and exuberances. They undoubtedly hoped that the end of adolescence, then marriage, even to a Jew, would put an end to her rebelliousness, but it doesn't.

Crissie's Aunt Janet turns to me. "We have a very nice new delicatessen right here in town," she says.

Now I want to inflict damage. Who are these morons anyway? I want to ask if their ancestors are Polish.

"And that man's cousin is—what do you think, Michael? A furrier."

Jews are slowly moving in. Furs and pastrami are one thing, but everyone knows that the banks are next. I get up from the hard corduroy couch, its plastic cover removed for the occasion.

"Madam," I address Aunt Janet, "My father is not in the fur business or the delicatessen business. He is a political man, a thinking man, a Social Democrat, and I am his son."

Crissie looks stunned. Aunt Janet nods agreeably.

The conversation pit is silent. Crissie breaks out into a lovely smile which buries all my rage and makes me love her even more. A few aunts and cousins also smile in my direction while the men begin to talk of guns and oil. When I sit back down from my podium and Crissie comes over to sit by me, I feel a strong kinship with my father, the human being and Jew and Social Democrat.

Just before we intend to head back east, Crissie announces to her mother, father, and me, to our horror and shock, that she intends to become Jewish. I can see in her eyes the perverse satisfaction of pounding a stake through both her parents' hearts. To me, too, it seems like a tactic to assure Marvin Madden's next and probably final heart attack.

"I'm sure your father will set you up with a delicatessen," I tell her as Blanche and Marvin start walking up the stairs, holding on to each other as if they are walking into hell itself.

She and I step out the back door into a pretty little garden with statuettes of black people smiling happily. We sit down on two uncomfortable Adirondack chairs.

"Don't be funny with your delicatessen shit, Michael. I mean it," she says, swatting a bug flying around her head.

"You've chosen a path that will satisfy no one."

Actually, it throws me into a head-splitting confusion; Blanche Madden, probably, at best, to her hidden bottle of bourbon; and Marvin into a drooling spiritual coma.

"You will become the only observant Jew in my family," I say to my wife, trying to put this into a more rational context.

"Worse things could happen and, as for you, Michael, it won't hurt to learn something about your own religion."

"Listen to me, Crissie. Being Jewish is important to me because it's my fuck-you to all the Jew haters of the world. On the record, though, I declare all religions dangerous and vile."

"I'm not going to argue with you," Crissie says. "And stop playing with your watch. The clicking is driving me crazy."

"What more do you want? You've already trapped your Jewish refugee artist, so why this rage for a Star of David on your own lapel?"

So here we are, each of us having married—in part, to spite our tribes—and now Crissie's spiritual enthusiasm is leading her into becoming the object of her tribe's obloquy. With mosquitos raging and hungry now, in the late afternoon, we run back into the house. From a liquor cabinet, I grab my first drink of the day and swill it down as if it were orange juice.

Upstairs, with me at her side, she knocks on her father's door. He is lying on top of his bed and points to a couple of chairs by the window.

"Daddy," she says, "I want to tell you why I will convert."

Madden closes his eyes and I close mine.

"Daddy, you know how I love words, how I love to discuss everything."

Sotto voce, I say, "You Christians don't know how to discuss?"

"Shut up, Michael," she says.

Sotto voce again, I say, "Let's talk resurrection and transubstantiation. And, by the way, you can be a New York Jewish intellectual without converting."

"Fuck you," she answers.

Marvin Madden's breath becomes heavy. He cannot stop the gurgling that accompanies his breathing.

"Well, Daddy," Crissie says, "the more I read about the history of the Jews, the more I love how they examine every word. Everything is open to question, to discussion and argument."

Sotto voce, I say, "You're about to join company with the God who commands that we should smite the infidels, including women, children, and animals and burn the whole fucking place down. No questions asked."

"Michael," she warns. "Daddy, it's a life of seeking and inquiry, rational skepticism, living life ethically. They have suffered so much."

"You love the niggras too," Marvin says quietly.

His eyes are now open but unfocused.

"Paint your pretty little face and you can be a niggra too."

Now I want to strangle this cowboy motherfucker.

"They are beautiful," Crissie continues, as if she doesn't hear her father, "and they have beautiful names, names like Mendelssohn and Blumenthal."

This makes my head turn. Who ever thought of that? I whisper in her ear: "What's wrong with Yellow Bird, Spotted Horse, Iron Hawk?"

She gives me a look that could kill.

"How about Woman Who Reads Torah?"

Unabashed, she says,

"My name is Mendelssohn now and I'd like to change my first name too. I was thinking of Ruth."

This is the first I hear of the Ruth plan.

"And listen, Daddy, the Jews have always been scapegoats and I think it's because they're good, just, moral people, unlike the rest of us."

If another heart attack were to visit Marvin Madden, it would be a lot more than merely his bad genes or diet. It would be the stresses of an evangelical disposition, his Jewish son-in-law, his nearly-Jewish daughter, the end of America as he knows it. Marvin Madden closes his eyes. Perhaps he is dead, but at this point, Cherokee Blanche bursts into the room. Her face is swollen, her eyes bloodshot, the puffiness under them grotesquely enlarged.

"Crissie is my only child. How can anyone not love her only child?"

I await the answer and watch Crissie cover her face with her hands.

"Michael," Blanche says, "about that Jew business. I'm trying to understand. After all," Blanche says, "our Lord was a Jew."

"What?" I turn to Crissie. "What the fuck is she jabbering about?"

"Mama," Crissie says, "your Lord has nothing to do with any of this."

"He's your Lord too," Blanche says, blanching.

"No, Mama, he is not. He hasn't been since 6th grade."

Blanche drops to her knees. Marvin, who is not dead, sits up, finds his Stetson, the bottle of bourbon, and pours one for himself and one for his wife. Carefully, they walk down the stairs, recently fitted for a lift. Crissie and I pack up the few things we brought, including a stack of books on Jewish history she studies daily. Crissie sits down in the kitchen and cries.

"My sweet baby," I say, on my knees beside her, "in spite of my rants and bigotries, you impress me with your strength. I totally respect each of the paths you try."

Crissie, the Ruth-to-be and I, leave Tulsa a lot messier than it was before our invasion. The Jews came and, as Jews will, changed the house on the corner of 27th Street forever.

"Some would say we sullied the place," I say to Crissie in the car, "not simply changed it."

I drive fast as we zig and zag toward the Atlantic Ocean, propelled by my need for a coast, the edge of the continent. From Oklahoma, it is an endless strip of gas stations, roadside taverns, and tourist shacks with mementos of Broken Arrow and Muskogee, Last Suppers and crucifixions. A huge Buick pulls onto the road in front of me. I almost hit the damned thing and fly into a rage.

"I'm going to get that son of a bitch," I cry and step on the Minx's puny little accelerator.

"No!" Crissie cries.

I manage to pass the old bitch driving that tank, reach across Crissie and scream. I try to nudge the Buick off the road.

"Stop it!" Crissie yells and pushes me back.

I slow up, pull over, and breathe hard.

"I've never seen you like this," she says and lays her hand on my beating heart. "Did Oklahoma do this to you?"

With my eyes closed, I, too, wonder what did this to me. Here I am, a Polish Jew, transcending the boundaries of Jewishness, becoming all Pole. On the other hand, Jews were merciless as they pilfered Arab land, while Poles, defending honor and gallantry, had no problems slaughtering the Jews. I am sweating and breathing hard, the tangle of nature and nurture unable to solve the genesis of my behavior.

I sit up and head east again. Curled up in the front seat next to me, Crissie reads from books on Judaism she took out of the New York Public Library. She reads silently until St. Louis. New highways continued to be built across America, but my wife insists on Route 66, this, she assures me, being her last trip home.

"Have you ever heard of Shabbatai Zevi?" she asks when we turn north.

"Can't say that I have."

"He proclaimed himself the Messiah in 1655."

As we hurtle toward Columbus, she is on the last quarter of the 18th century and, as she shares this material with me, I begin to see it not only as interesting but I feel closer to my long gone ancestors, some of whom must have been practicing Jews.

"So," she says, "we're on to the Baal Shem Tov. No wonder people flocked to him and his Hassidic teaching. Hasidism became a major force among the Jews," she reports, then tells me about more scholars and moral guides, Elijah Ben Solomon Zalman, the Gaon of Vilna, and how eventually a truce was negotiated between Hasidic ecstasy and rabbinical learning.

"I love these Jews," Crissie says as wee zoom into New Jersey.

Anger is not a great choice and yet anger has infiltrated my bones from the age of eight, maybe even before. Did you experience my anger in the Citronka van? Did I scare you? Now, it's Crissie's insane cowboy father who has triggered my fury. Another father, Milusha, another terrible disappointment. And you, do you even know—I certainly don't—who your father is? If you do, if he has been in your life, I hope it has been better for you than for Crissie or me. My own hands have always felt best when tightened into fists. I know that no one loves a guy with road rage. And yet rage sits here in this body. I think that it must also stimulate the creative channels to open and throb. Cowboy America, land of oil and guns, soil fertile for Crusades, has deepened my rage and further blackened my painting and my heart, my sinews and arteries, my cells.

7.

As I settle back into my work, I stretch canvasses that barely make the turn up the stairs and into the door of my woefully small Grand Street studio. The only music that accompanies my explorations is the third movement of Beethoven's A-minor Quartet and a Shostakovich Trio. At the end of each day, though, a joint plus a swinging of my ass to the Benny Goodman band or sextet, bring me back to the life I must lead by walking home, aware of my surroundings, my petty hatreds and uplifting loves.

With a ferocious resolve, Crissie finds a rabbi in Brooklyn who agrees to instruct her while she, with manic energy, takes a job as a copy editor for Dell, who are considering publication of her bull-fighter book, *'Olé!* With Rabbi Teitelbaum, she studies and prays. Once, during this initiation period, she drags me on the subway to deepest Brooklyn for a talk with the man. Talk? Not a talk but a harangue. A sanctimonious patriarch with eight children of his own, the rabbi tries to convince us that we, the beautiful couple, have a unique opportunity, not to speak of moral duty, to have little ones, God's will. Crissie wants to believe it, but I can't square it with what I have experienced so far on this planet.

"You can change all that," Rabbi Teitelbaum says. "Just look at you, two Jews, such perfect specimens, two beautiful creations of God."

He says a lot more, but I hear little of it, my ears ringing with scorn. Sitting on the other side of the Rabbi's desk, I hold my face in my hands and hope I do not commit a felony. Larcenies, especially petty larcenies, suit me best.

According not only to Rabbi Teitelbaum but to Crissie's old friends, she and I are meant to propagate, to combine her straight black hair and my black curls, both of our blue eyes, non-Jewish noses, and shapely bodies.

"You both have good bones, stamina, and a sensitivity to higher callings," says her ex-roommate, Margot, who herself escaped from her family's rose farm in Indiana.

But no one knows the vastness of the shadows that lurk in our psyches, the potential damage we might bring to our union—hers from generations of drunks, including the Indians, as well as from reactionary mediocrity, mine from an equally ignorant merchant class whose consanguineous preferences sometimes led to the occasional betrayal, frontal lobotomy, or suicide. Though the picture of the indigenous, middle-class, mid-American beauty queen and rebel, the writer, who is my wife, steadily deepens, becoming ever newer and more attractive, her depressions and headaches are no longer rare.

Crissie, almost Ruth, spends a lot of time with a group of young men and women who are converting to please their spouse or spouse-to-be. She alone is doing it in spite of her spouse. She lights candles every Friday evening and finds a Yeshiva student to teach her Hebrew. When the time comes, she asks me and Zyga to be present for her conversion ceremony. I stand with her, holding her hand. Zyga holds her other hand. Ritually bathed clean and smiling, as tears run down her face, the rabbinical court of three men pronounce her a Jew. Christine Margaret

Madden, now Ruth Mendelssohn, becomes the most Jewish person in my family, including a slew of Jewish atheists and agnostics slaughtered by the Germans.

"Now all three of us are Jews," she tells me and my father as we eat Chinese food on Mott Street.

"My dear Ruth," Zyga says, "I am a Jew because I must be true to my family in Poland. They all die because they are Jews. I am also a Jew because everyone in the world hates Jews and it is not honorable to deny it."

Ruth's new Jewishness is, for a long time, a solemn affair. Lovemaking becomes a semi-spiritual practice. For a good couple of months, our attempts at sex are like Errol Flynn trying to seduce Simone Weil. Happily and slowly everything begins to change as Ruth relaxes into her chosen identity, abandoning her occasional thoughts of martyrdom, abstention, Puritanism.

"What is happening?" I ask her one evening as we begin to engage in delicious foreplay in bed. Once preferring Thanatos, she now begins serious research into Eros.

"Isn't this what Jewish girls are known for?" she asks.

Straddling my chest, she tells me that she spent all day Saturday with Zyga.

"Ruth, this may not be the best time to talk about my father." She wiggles closer, indulging in a teasing of the most audacious, inflaming kind. There is little question about her awareness that her moist lusciousness is approaching my lips.

"There, baby," I say, pulling her even closer.

She does not pull away.

"Conversion must be responsible for this," I manage to murmur.

I wish I could recite some Hebrew prayer so that her teasing would never stop.

"Tell me, darling, is this like the Jewish girls?" she asks, moving daringly back and forth, beginning to breathe hard.

"I don't know," I mumble coyly.

"You liar, yes you do."

"I'm going to chant now," I cry and wail in a Middle-Eastern sort of way.

Our laughter blends joyously with our moans and squeals.

"Oh Ruth, Ruth, Ruth," I manage to say, "my tasty, delicious Ruth."

"Now, where were we?" she asks when we finish the first act, two to go, both of us still panting.

"We're not done."

"Later," Ruth says, slides down my body and gets up to bring us a second cup of coffee.

"And now I'll tell you about yesterday. I've got a notebook filled with Zyga's stories and his thoughts."

In fact, our little apartment is filling with books on Poland and the Jews.

"At the Central Park Zoo," she begins, "Zyga and I stop to look at the polar bears."

"The bears?"

I lean back against the pillows and cannot imagine an animal resembling my father more.

"Transplanted," I say, "lonely, unclean, pissed-off, like him."

She thinks for a moment and looks sad.

"I never thought of that," she says, "because he has changed so much. He's not like the polar bears anymore."

Another few moments of silence.

"You know how he walks with his hands clasped behind him, looking at the ground? As we walk on, he's looking down and I'm yacking away, my arms going in every direction."

"He's looking for coins."

"Well, he found a dime in the grass and his face lit up with pleasure."

"He and I are both seekers of metals. Nickel, copper, and silver for my father. For me, only gold."

"As we walked inside a tunnel under the roadway," Ruth says, "I told him that I've always been attracted to communism, and he wagged his finger at me saying that ideology leads to slaughter."

Ruth climbs back on top of me and kisses me. I roll off the bed to cut a grapefruit in half, pare around it, and cut it into bite-size morsels in two bowls.

"I am always surprised at how good his English is," Ruth says when I come back to bed. "He and I sat down on a bench and I asked for more between-the-wars history. Coming from Oklahoma, I told him, I saw a very different kind of oppression. I'm a student of oppression, I told him, and the richness of Jewish experience doesn't come with conversion. He laughed and leaned over to kiss my cheek, then put his head back to catch some sun on his face. He said that he was a very young man after the war when Poland got its independence at Versailles. He said that at home you all spoke Polish and they also spoke German and Russian, no Yiddish, not even one word. He was having a hard time explaining your family's assimilation."

"None of them," I tell her, "not the Mendelssohns or the Mandelbaums, in spite of the misfortune of their names, wanted to be associated with those Jews who they considered primitive, noisy, and smelly."

"Well, yes. Your family thought itself enlightened, part of the western Jewish community who value education and intellect."

"He said that? Or are you making it up? I've never heard him speak like that."

"His words," Ruth says.

"They were furriers," I tell her, "a very Jewish profession at the time."

"Not your father," Ruth corrects me. "Zyga always hated the fur business. His brothers and sisters were professionals who lived on that land almost from its historical beginnings. They were more Polish than Jewish."

"Jesus, Ruth, you're becoming a biographer of the Mendelssohn clan."

"I'm totally engrossed," she says. "The Mendelssohns accepted the Polish values of romantic patriotism," she continues, "love of land, ancient hospitality, the courtly values of honor and bravery and gallantry. "

"As for Rena and Bolek," I add to the family history, "the riches were handled in a Polish way, a Christian way. Then, as now, the Mandelbaums were valets to the rich. In Warsaw, it was exclusively the Polish Christian rich. In New York, it's anyone who enters the hall of furs and mirrors, no matter how Jewish."

Ruth takes my face in both her hands and kisses me.

"As for me, I used to stand at attention and salute the tomb of the Unknown Soldier. How do you like that?"

"A little Polish patriot," she says.

She stretches out again.

"You probably won't believe that in the park Zyga wore an aftershave, some English lavender cologne, which I liked a lot. I'm going to buy you some."

She lifts one leg, then the other, stretching her toes. As her feet climb the wall at the foot of the bed, she tells me about the various parties that Jews in Poland joined, the Socialist Bund one among them.

"For Zyga, it was a statement of his solidarity with the Jews and with socialism. I think it was also a reaction to your uncle and mother not hiring Jews to work the salon at Mandelbaum's. Their best Polish customers preferred it that way."

She lowers her legs from the wall and snuggles again.

"Zyga joined the Bund," she goes on, "after he was beaten up at his university by a bunch of students."

"What?" I sit up straight. "He was beaten up?"

"Yes, Michael. And yet he didn't lose faith in Poland's essential goodness."

"You're not making this up?"

"The students and their professor jeered as Zyga fell to his knees, blood in his mouth and nose."

I turn toward the window, close my eyes, and imagine my father coughing blood. My father is taking on new shapes, a new depth coming into light. As Ruth holds me tight, I begin to understand—oh what a fool I have been!—that there is so much history back there that I know nothing about, that, as a matter of fact, they probably wish they could forget there ever was a history in a place they'd like to forget.

Ruth resumes with their Central Park idyll. They are on the west side now, at a dairy restaurant called Steinberg's.

"So," she says, "Zyga orders something he calls 'shadwe mleko,' pardon my Polish. It is potatoes in curdled milk. I try a bit and love it. 'You like that, lady?' the waiter asked waspy me, looking bemused. I confessed that I love it."

"Me too," I tell my wife, who is not only Jewish but, specifically, becoming a Polish Jew.

"From Steinberg's, I suggest a taxi home," Ruth says, "but Zyga is not tired and wants to walk. We've got to buy him some better shoes and socks," she says. "All the walking made huge holes in his socks. His heels were rubbed raw."

I turn toward my sweet Ruth, put my head between her breasts. We lie like this for a long time, then I doze off for a while. In the early after-noon, we get dressed and go out for a breath of fresh air. Walking uptown on Sixth Avenue, trucks rumble and taxis weave in and out of lanes, their horns blasting. A few women are yelling up to the Women's House of Detention across the street, "Hi, angel baby!" and "Hey, peaches, it's me!" We walk west to the river, Ruth's arm around my waist. Her beauty startles me every time I look at her. She is my Vermeer, her face flushed pink, her hair a bit messy, a few strands arching across her forehead. Her light blue eyes have softened, though her teeth are still a bit imperfect, a bit yellow. My Ruth is fragile, unstable, dark, traits that add to her beauty. She is perishable, mutable, evanescent. Near a pier where huge ocean-going ships dock, I stop in the middle of the block to take her in my arms.

"Do you know how much I love you?" I ask.

She says she does.

Back home, while she soaks in the bathtub, I bring two glasses of wine and sit on the toilet with its lid down. She is immersed in sweet-smelling oils and asks me to scrub her back. I soap and scrub. I watch her dry herself, wrap a towel around her hair, and slip into her little-girl-pink terrycloth robe. Her body, once immutable as porcelain, has become as luscious and alive as creamy rose petals. In bed again, she rests her head on my chest. I play with her hair, twisting it into ringlets. She reaches over to the pile of books and picks up her notebook.

"I wrote a poem for you."

She reads:

> *"Why can't I paint like Caravaggio, you said, his brushes*
> *innocent of indecision, mine thought clogged.*
> *Rage is quest not art, you said Monday afternoon.*
> *I want to make elegant spaces of perilous precision*
> *like a bull dying in Madrid*
> *like a poem's silhouette."*

I cover her body with mine until she falls asleep under me. Quietly, I get up and close the door, step into the unkempt living room. My mind and my body feel complete. Before I pick up the cello, which stands leaning against the couch, I insert a tape of a Brahms cello sonata minus the cello. It doesn't take long to lose myself in the E-minor Brahms which suits my usual nocturnal mood, mucking about in the lowest registers. Even with my frequent flatness and squeaky overtones, even when the piano runs ahead of my playing and I have to lay the cello down and rewind the tape, my imperfect sound can still make me smile, even though I'm pretty sure that my cello playing will never improve. I must say that I am persistent, accepting my fingers' fumbling. I seem to have little talent for any of this glorious instrument's demands. The cello is the chink in my creative output.

In the course of that year, the images I create are more pregnant with meaning, spewing energy, anxiety, the richness and absurdity of life. In November, my exhibit at Suzi Schwab's gallery is successful beyond my measured expectations. She sells most of the fifteen canvasses she and I have chosen. The Museum of Modern Art buys a middle-sized painting named *Border Crossing* in which a thin jagged white-and-ochre line separates two massive, black rectangles.

Henry Karp, whom I haven't seen since the torment of his visit to my studio on Grand Street, shows up with his German wife, Gabrielle. He finds me and gives me a hug.

"I have learned to appreciate your kind of painting," he tells me.

"Oh yes?"

"Mostly though, I favor artists who can draw."

I wonder if this man, once the bane of my existence, now a successful neurosurgeon who performs miracles with pituitary gland tumors, will ever leave me alone.

Zyga, Rena and Bolek attend the opening. My mother and uncle thank Suzi as if she had done me a life-saving favor. My father stands at the door between two gallery rooms, beaming.

8.

ON THE BED TABLE NEXT TO ME is a small stack of poetry books: Rilke; François Villon, who haunts me with his *"ou sont les neiges d"an-tan?"*(where indeed?); and Lucretius' *On the Nature of Things.* Deep within my bedside drawer rests my gold pocket watch—my Buddha's belly, my lifelong obsession. On Ruth's side, next to her water, lay stacks of Polish history. Though she can delight me with her hyperbolic passions, she can also exhaust me. She spent the evening before with long recitations of Polish history and this morning, as she pours grits into boiling water, her brain is still stuffed with unfinished Polish business. We sit down at the foldup card table. I am slowly learning to tolerate grits, Ruth having assured me that they are an American Indian porridge. She herself is learning to appreciate Nova Scotia salmon and white fish.

"Picture this scene, Michael," she says. "It's the inter-war parliament of Dmowski, Pilsudski, and the socialist Gabriel Narutowicz—president of Poland for three days before he was killed by a Nationalist fanatic, the painter Eligiusz Niewiadomski."

"Whoa, Ruth, dear Ruth, did my father teach you to pronounce those names? Eligiusz? Niewiadomski? Did I say them correctly?"

She disregards my astonishment.

"Just think, Michael," she continues, "this Niewadomski asks permission from the Church, consults with the fascists, then stalks the President of the Republic and stabs him in the courtyard of the presidential palace."

She is pacing and I am amused.

"As for this Polish Catholic horror, I hardly need more reasons to convert. Reading about the Polish church makes me want to puke."

"You are an obsessed woman," I tell her.

Richard III is hardly Ruth's only obsession. It has long been accompanied by the Spanish Theater of Sacrifice; Art among the Philistines; Zyga and the Polish question; the Mendelssohns; and the Jewish question.

"Yes," she says, "if something interests me, I immerse myself in it."

Nevertheless, her moods swing up and down. There are times when she sinks very low and takes to the bottle.

"Just like my mama," she says, "my mama and a few mamas before her."

Although I sometimes think that we both drink too much, her down times affect me deeply. As she lies on the couch for hours at a time, as she slurs her words and can't stand up without leaning on me, I begin looking through real estate brochures for a house in the country, to serve mainly as Ruth's Marienbad, her sanitarium and refuge, something I have never considered before. Now that I do, the idea seems promising. Perhaps, I think, a temporary change of scenery will do us both good.

To cheer her up, I invite my father to our Jane Street apartment, unseen by anyone in my family. Zyga climbs the three creaky flights, out of breath when he arrives. He hands a bouquet of six red roses to Ruth and a pound of good coffee to me. I am beginning to be surprised by most everything Zyga does these days. He is especially happy to be here, more comfortable in dinginess than on 57th Street.

"I am very concerned about you, Ruth," he says. "You look very pale, not your usual healthy self. Maybe you should go for vacation," he suggests, "away from New York."

He and I seem to be thinking alike. I look at Ruth.

"Listen to him," I say.

"Soon," she says. "I have work to do."

"Now that you are a famous artist," Zyga says to me, "you can buy a little house not in New York."

We have not been conspiring so his suggestion surprises and pleases me.

Early Saturday morning, I bring Ruth breakfast in bed which she pretends to enjoy and, when she stops picking at her scrambled eggs, I tell her, as lovingly as I can, that we're driving upstate to look at a couple of old houses.

"We are? Michael, I don't want to go anywhere right now."

"Last weekend I drove up there and saw a nice little cottage. But don't worry, we'll just look," I assure her.

At noon, we arrive at the Hillsdale general store across from the Methodist Church.

"Look, honey, that's Fred's barber shop and, next to it, Muriel's Laundromat."

She nods. Beyond the one paved road through the village the road winds into farmland, in the middle of which stands a rundown farmhouse, its clapboards rotting, its roof line concave, the bricks of its chimney mostly gone.

"Don't you love it for its distance from Mandeleau's, from the whole fucking Upper East Side, a safe distance from the fancy ladies, their overbred dogs, children and husbands?" I ask.

"I'm surprised that this appeals to you," Ruth says.

"Don't you think that my father would love it?"

"I think he might," Ruth says.

An old codger named Harland Morse, who represents the deceased owner of the place, drives over to walk us through the house and the little bit of land, points out the hand-blown window panes, their bull's eyes refracting a spectrum of light, and the gaslight fixtures. The place smells old and rancid.

"Yes sir," says Harland, "these walls are filled with corn cobs."

There isn't a right angle in the place—not the unpainted clapboards, not the old roof, not a window or a door. Ruth drags along after us. We walk out the kitchen door into a yard run amok with wild grasses and a couple of unkempt apple trees which probably have not produced an apple for decades.

"I guess it's no surprise," I tell Ruth, "that I yearn to own a piece of America." Harland Morse tells us to poke around and leaves us alone. I drag Ruth into the little backyard, touch a tree or two, pick a wild flower whose name I don't know, get splinters from running my hand over the gray boards of the little horse barn. My classical beauty's black hair is pulled back into a bun and I stick the wild flower into it. Ruth sits down on a smooth rock and I kneel in front of her.

"Does it excite you even a little bit?" I ask her.

She runs her fingers through my hair.

"Maybe one day," she says.

She is quiet for several minutes, then says, "I understand your wanting to own a piece of this country, but there's a lot to be said about not owning. In the city we are part of a huge transient population. Everyone is in motion. Owning in New York doesn't matter. No one even knows who owns, who rents, who is leaving, who is coming back."

She is reminding me of truths I have learned in my life and seem to be forgetting. I like the way we feed each other, each of us at times the teacher, at times the student.

"We really are city people," I agree. "It felt different to be bombed in Warsaw than to be personally bombed in a country house in the middle of nowhere."

I think that one day we will buy this dumpy little house or one like it, but we leave with the understanding that we will give the whole matter more thought.

Toward the end of September, the High Holy days Rosh Hashanah and Yom Kippur arrive and Ruth's observance kicks into high gear.

"Come with me to *schul*" she says. "At least as an observer."

"Maybe another time," I tell her, dreading the thought.

"What other time? This is the only time."

At a temple just off Fifth Avenue, walking distance from Jane Street, I listen dutifully to the chosen reciting and praying, some, like Ruth, pounding their chests with deep devotion. After the service, she prepares a meal for the first night of Rosh Hashanah which, she informs me, requires a lot of yellow foods, "a sign of joy and happiness." In Gristede's I find saffron. I cannot believe the price and pull a couple of packets into my pocket, then feeling fairly invincible, pull a bag of cashews off its hook and wander through the aisles eating the nuts for lunch, thinking that I should abandon petty larceny and focus on big ticket items.

Zyga is the only family member who agrees to come, "only to please Ruth," he whispers in my ear. Rena is in Paris; Bolek and his new woman aren't interested. A couple of Ruth's friends arrive, all crowding into our tiny apartment. Ruth announces that this is to be a happy time, requiring apples dipped in honey; challah with raisins; herring and chicken soup; honey cake; and teiglach, a pastry of figs, dates, nuts and raisins.

"How do you know all this?" Zyga asks her.

I also turn to her, awaiting the answer.

"Study," she says, "like a good Jew."

After her friends and Zyga leave, Ruth and I sit together on the couch, each of us with a glass of vodka, with all the dishes and leftovers piled high in our tiny kitchen. Ruth glows like one of those early Siennese paintings of saints radiating haloes, sparks, and rays of light.

"You want to hear some Mendelssohn history?" I ask her when we cuddle in bed. She says she does.

"I'll start with tales from before I was born."

"Okay," Ruth says, her head on my chest.

"My mother sent Zyga on a mission to negotiate with the rabbi of Warsaw regarding the naming of the baby in her belly."

"That's you," she says and tickles me gently.

"Should the child be a girl, Rena liked Anita, easy to pronounce even if a trifle Spanish. If a boy, she did not want to give him a Jewish name, not even a Polish one. She wanted a name like Michael, no Mieczyslaws or Boleslaws, no Solomons or Chaims. In their wisdom, Zyga and Rena had chosen names which needed no translation, international names, easy to pronounce beyond the borders of Poland."

"Smart lady," Ruth says.

"Rena Mendelssohn, nee Mandelbaum, did not like being pregnant, hated the ugly proof that she allowed this man, Zygmunt, entrance to her body. A year had passed since their arranged wedding of the two well-to-do Jewish families and within that short period of time, they both came to the conclusion that they did not like each other."

"So why did they stay together?"

"A sad and stupid story," I tell her. "Rena's mother, a dowager lady who I did not know—though in a photograph, I once saw, looked stupid, like Queen Victoria—made Rena promise, from her death bed, that she would never, not ever, divorce Zyga."

"What a horror," Ruth says, "and she is keeping that stupid promise."

"So listen. I'm putting this together from bits of conversations here and there."

"You're making some of it up, aren't you?"

"I am. With my mother."

"So tell me more," Ruth murmurs.

"Zygmunt Mendelssohn climbs into the first *dorozhka* in line on the corner of Moniuszki and Marszalkowska and gives the driver the address of the great synagogue of Warsaw, on Tlomackie Street. He had never been inside it before and does not look forward to doing so. The horse clops through the city, past baroque palaces and mansions, handsome apartment houses and churches. Zyga always said that this city was as beautiful as Paris. He called it 'the Paris of the north.'"

"I want to see it," Ruth says, as involved in my little history as she is in the several partitions of Poland.

"So, Zyga does not look forward to his private meeting with the spiritual leader and chief negotiator of Jewish law. Stepping down from the carriage, Zyga is surprised by the imposing synagogue, looks up at the cloudless sky and takes a deep breath of Polish air, protecting himself, I am sure, from the Jewish air he was about to inhale inside."

"I love this story," Ruth says.

"I'm embroidering it a bit," I tell her, "but it's mostly as it happened."

"Don't stop now," she says.

"A Star of David is perched on the dome of the synagogue. 'Why advertise it?' Zyga asks himself. He walks in through a side door and is struck by the beauty of the place, its spaciousness and subtle decoration, careful stonework and colorful marble. He has to admit that it is breathtaking. It is a giddy moment as he struggles with his identity."

"Yes," says Ruth, "that's one of the things I love about him."

"What things?"

"He seems always to be open to change. He is what he is but he's open. You know what I mean?"

"In return for rabbinical permission to give me a most un-Jewish name, he is willing to pledge a large donation to help poor Jews find their way to Palestine. After a brief lecture from the educator-in-chief, permission is granted to name the child Michael or Anita or Andrew."

"I love Michael," Ruth says.

"So, after a long labor, Rena gives birth to a perfect little boy who they name Michael and call Mishek, a soft diminutive that would do until my launching into the world. As I grow past infancy, Rena loves having the governess display her son to the workers of Mandelbaum Furs, where women bend from their sewing machines to touch me, as the pinners and the pelt stretchers stand back to admire cute little Mishek, their hands clasped before them, their smiles wide. And little Mishek loves being loved."

"He still does," Ruth says, "and the workers still behave like that when you go up to the fourth floor, don't they?"

We take a minute off to kiss, then try to keep our hands off each other.

"When they took me to visit my Mendelssohn grandparents' mansion in a small manufacturing town in western Poland, my governess—Inka or Ola or Fela—would come on her hands and knees to chase me out from under the dining room table where I love to play. I could see my mother sitting alone by the window, looking out. This is Mendelssohn territory, all professionals of one sort or another, and they are not enamored of the merchant class Mandelbaums. And vice versa."

The next day, looking happy and gorgeous, she says that she loves the intrigues of both Mendelssohns and Mandelbaums.

"Let's visit Bolek again. Your mother said that his new woman was transforming him into a happier man."

"You're sure? It wasn't so pleasant last time."

"If you promise to be nice to him," she warns, wagging a finger at me.

A few days later, we trudge up to 83rd Street, just off Fifth Avenue. I greet the elevator man as if we lived in the building. Somewhat uneasy about meeting a new Bolek, I put my arm around Ruth and ring the bell. We are greeted in the hallway by a tall, handsome woman who welcomes us to 1016 Fifth Avenue as if it were hers. She is obviously from a different world than Bolek's bimbos with zebra blouses and feathers in their hair. This one is a rigid, stern, correct young woman in a perfectly tailored beige suit, smelling of a subtle perfume. Her ashen blond hair is severely swept back, her short fingernails colored a light rose madder. Ursula takes both our hands and leads us to the couch. She deftly twists the wire around the cork of a bottle of champagne and hands it to Bolek who, with a cloth napkin on his arm and, head held high, pops the cork.

"I shall be the mother," Ursula says with a slight German accent.

She takes the bottle from his hand to fill our fluted glasses. I am uneasy, expecting a military toast, an oath to blood and soil, but Bolek suggests we drink to his Ursula, adding almost in a whisper that this drink shall mark the first celebration of their imminent marriage. *"Blitzkrieg! Anschluss. Drang Nach Osten,* from the Hudson River, across the park to Fifth Avenue," I think, my heart sinking. I inflict on Bolek my indigenous American in her dowdy attire while he reciprocates with a perfect square-jawed German straight from the pages of August Sanders' specimen photographs. Clever and opinionated, she assures me that she is a citizen of Switzerland, which I don't believe for a moment. But given my devotion to Brahms, Schopenhauer, and Richard Strauss, my German bigotry does seem irrational. Bolek's woman is the very definition of Aryan; mine, the Homecoming Queen from Oklahoma—both decidedly from a different tribe than his and mine.

I follow Bolek into the kitchen where he orders caviar from a middle-aged Germanic woman named Erna, who has replaced Hasegawa-san. Ruth and I sit primly on one couch, Ursula and Bolek on the one opposite. We spend the late afternoon sipping champagne and listening to irritating talk about a fashion industry which Ursula plans to join in some unspecified way. When Ruth and I leave, we run downtown through the park like escaped caged birds.

As mysterious as Tahiti must have been to Gauguin, terrifying as the wilderness might have been to Lewis and Clark, my uncle and I plunge into our chosen unknowns; into Oklahoma where the waving wheat sure smelled sweet, to an Aryan woman who will protect Bolek's Jewish hide. In my case, I am also hell-bent on exogamy. To totally preclude any unsavory chromosomal soup, I choose a gene pool that is an ocean and half of two continents from the European land mass. Bolek's attempt at distancing himself from his Jewish roots in Poland, whether via his ice blue showroom walls or his very proper woman, is, I suppose, no more outrageous than my choosing an indigenous Indian. So, here we are, each with a woman who the other of us suspect will make us wish we were dead.

A month later, Bolek and Ursula marry in an intimate ceremony performed by a pastor friend of Ursula's in their large living room overlooking the Metropolitan Museum of Art and attended by a few luminaries from the fashion world: a magazine editor or two, Ursula's brother Peter, and my parents. I pull my Ruth down a hall to the master bedroom, close the door behind us and, still dressed in our best clothes, make love to her on the newlywed's king-sized marriage bed.

In the dining room, Rena is preoccupied with the catering staff, making sure that everything is clean and polished, that the canapés are arranged as perfectly as an Escher design. Zyga is in a corner speaking

German to the pastor. I have never heard my father speak German before; the fluency of that language coming easily from his lips shocks me. Rena has told me that she wants her brother well cared for, putting her money on the Teutonic race to bring order to his volcanic nature, while Zyga undoubtedly wishes for mayhem and misery, a German victory.

The dining table is resplendent with bulging silver platters, the Egyptian funerary expedition still its centerpiece. The door to the kitchen swings open and shut as servers dressed like, I think, Romanian country dancers, mix among the guests, serving champagne and canapés. Ruth and I are now sitting on one of the living room couches with Ursula's brother, Peter, a taciturn civil engineer from Hamburg. Ruth who, like me, has already had too much champagne, suddenly shoots up from our couch.

"I should be helping," she says.

"No," I cry and try to hold her back, but she plunges into the middle of the room, knocking a tray full of champagne from the hands of one of the dancers. Though wobbly myself, I rush toward the wreckage. Rena is already there, her eyes full of venom directed at a sobbing Ruth who is on her knees trying to assemble the shards. Silence reigns all around. A secret believer in omens, my mother undoubtedly suspects that the incident promises the beginning of an ill-fated marriage. In Polish, she curses Ruth.

"Don't talk like that to my wife," I scold my mother, who covers her ears and rushes to one of the bedrooms while Ruth runs off into one of the bathrooms.

Trying to help, Ursula follows Rena and closes the door behind them. When I arrive in the bathroom to deal with Ruth, Zyga is already there, holding her and stroking her hair.

"Why do I always have to interfere?" Ruth sobs. "Why can't I mind my own business?"

Zyga assures her that trying to help is never bad. "You have a beautiful heart," he tells her.

"I can't stand watching servants, especially dressed up like clowns," she says.

"There, there," Zyga says.

I push my father aside and stroke Ruth's wet cheeks.

"Michael, I'm so sorry," she says.

"I never know what to expect from you," I say, holding her close. "I love that about you."

My father and I slip away with Ruth and sit in the park behind the Museum for an hour or so. When we get back home, I tell her that I've been thinking of taking Zyga for a drive in the Hillman.

"It was once as improbable as your crashing into a poor Romanian folk dancer."

"That's not funny," Ruth says, giggling. "I love you, too, when you do unexpected things: steal a gold watch or saffron, when you suddenly want to buy a house in the country, that kind of thing."

"The truth is that you are introducing me to a father I don't know. You are bringing him back to me."

"Oh, Michael, I'm so proud of you."

A few days later, I pick my father up at their East 57th Street apartment. As we make our way across town to the West Side highway, Zyga fidgets in the front seat.

"It's very small, this car," he reports, then gingerly touches everything within reach. "I am not often inside a car," he says. "Where do you learn to drive? I never have a car, never."

A taxi tries to pass us and I cut him off. The honking behind us brings a smile to my face, while Zyga turns white and picks hard at his fingernails. Sick of Rena's droning "don't pick, Zyga," I stop myself from echoing her words, though the sound of the picking and the damage it's inflicting is so irritating that it is hard to concentrate. Wounding his fingers might be Zyga's penance—I don't even know for what—and I am not about to deny him that.

"Try to relax," I say and put my hand on top of his damaged one.

We cross from highway to highway until the Merritt Parkway. We say very little. I cough. Zyga blows his nose.

"It's good to be in the country," I say.

Zyga agrees. We get off at some Connecticut exit and drive along pleasant country roads with fully leafed trees arching above us.

"This is not like Long Beach," Zyga says. "I like Long Beach. Do you remember?" He then sits up and says, "I must make pee. Where to do this?"

We stop on the side of a nearly deserted road and Zyga rushes out to pee. I walk around the car and pee a few feet from him. We look at each other and smile. Father and son are simply peeing together but it feels like a great shared intimacy. Zyga's is a slow pee, stopping and starting. I do not put my penis back into my pants before my father does his. Solidarity. When Zyga is done, he slides back into the front seat of the car and I walk around to my side. Behind the steering wheel again, I sit motionless for a minute, looking out the window. This familiarity between me and my father feels a little like the beginning of a love affair, its future unknown but full of possibilities. I am thinking of the many times I have seen Bolek pee. In one motion, he zips up his fly and, manly man that he is, he lifts one Italian shoe to press down the plunger. I especially like toilets with that kind of flushing mechanism so I, too, can pee like a man. Debonair, that's what it is. Turning toward Zyga now, I notice a black swath of hair at the back of his head, surrounded by gray. I do not remember seeing it before.

The damned Hillman doesn't start. I have long known how to take the fuel pump apart, clean the copper filter, and put it all back together again. Zyga comes out with me, looks into a car engine maybe for the first time. It is still fairly pristine and my father observes, his eyebrows raised, astonished.

"Where do you learn to repair cars?" he asks.

"So far, just this filter. Gasoline passes through and, for some reason, dirt gets into it."

Zyga looks at me with admiration.

"You are amazing," he says. "I think the first Mendelssohn to know so much about cars."

"Am I the first artist? I'd prefer being that."

I wipe my hands on a dishtowel I carry around in the back of the Hillman and put my arm around my father's shoulder.

"A Jewish artist?" he quips. "Absolutely. Never before."

"I like being with you," I tell my father as we find a coffee house not far from the Merritt.

I mention that I saw him with a friend at the Automat.

"Ah, perhaps Rytek," Zyga says.

"There are others?"

"Not too many."

"Who is this Rytek?"

"A very sad man; one of those lifetime scholars who does not know how to take care of himself. He lives on air, only air."

"You've known him a long time?"

I note that my father likes his coffee black while I take a little cream and a little sugar.

"Very long," Zyga says.

"What do you and Rytek talk about?"

"What do people our age talk about? The past. We talk of the time we hear Lenin lecture in Switzerland. Also Leon Trotsky, and so far and so far."

"You heard Lenin and Trotsky?"

"We are still very young men. Lenin and Trotsky are the most interesting men in Europe," Zyga says. "Maybe also we listen to Leon Blum, but that is later. You know Leon Blum?" he asks. "A Socialist and a Jew."

I look at my father with admiration. He did have a whole life in Europe. I could weep thinking about his losses; not just a childhood but a whole life.

On the way back to the city, I glance in my father's direction. He is sitting quietly, his hands at rest. We get off the parkway at the 72nd Street exit and drive through Central Park. Before he gets out of the car in front of 400 East, he leans toward me and gives me a sloppy, wet kiss on my mouth. When Zyga disappears inside the lobby, I lick my wet lips to taste him.

9.

I have always had difficulty thinking of Germans as human. It took a long time to understand that human is exactly what they are, Germans and everyone else. What a terrible mistake to think of what they did— and certainly not only they—as "inhuman." Hating, killing, lying, betraying, torturing, all too human. I still have a problem imagining Mozart or Schubert—for some reason, not so much J. S. Bach—speaking that language as they write their very human, stretching to celestial, music. Still, the older I get, dearest Mila, the more I accept everything: from Bach"s Chaconne in the D-Minor Violin Partita to their stacking Jews like sardines in mass graves and shooting them in the back of the head, one by one; all of it as human. We are all both good and bad, don't you think so? The fur business cannot be all bad. The insurance, pharmaceutical, advertising, arms business? I have to swallow hard. All my life I have been trying to transform my natural "may they die" into "may everyone be happy." Everyone? Everyone. Not just me. Kissinger? Everyone. Nixon? Everyone. It hasn't been easy.

In late Spring of 1970, Zyga, quite unexpectedly, flies off to a spa in Bad Gastein, a German resort. I don't know what to make of this. A

German spa? I wonder if he has friends there, perhaps a girlfriend, but still, had he asked me, I would not have approved. At nearly the same time, five years after we marry, Ruth flies off to England. I am preparing for a show so it's a perfect time for her long desired introduction to English battlefields. She calls from Leicestershire where she is scouring the historical countryside.

"I spent the day walking the hills and found the site of the battle of Bosworth," she reports on the telephone. "It only lasted a couple of hours, but it's where King Richard was betrayed and lost his life."

"Michael," she says, "this land is soaked in blood."

"Your kind of place," I shout into the bad international connection.

"Everything is still here, just as it was in 1485, Even the farmhouse where the Earl of Stanley took a position on Richard's right flank, from which he betrayed his king. Even the swamp at the top of the hill where Richard's horses got stuck is still a swamp."

When she returns, she weeps for poor King Richard, for things totally out of her control, for the seconds that separate Desdemona's murder and the discovery of Iago's perfidy. Surely it is not only world-weary cosmopolitan Jews who are capable of taking it all in with a shrug of the shoulders and a knowing nod. But just as surely only Ruth believes in the goodness of the U. S. Postal Service as proof that humanity is capable of altruism. She is a free spirit, mischievous, unconventional, and untrammeled, most gloriously alive. In the English countryside as during weekends we spend in Maine or Vermont, she is the beautiful, flower-loving wood nymph, always hungry for more sun, more rain, more life. She is the reckless girl whom I adore.

I have become an ever hotter property. My paintings are selling briskly, the price of each monumental. The work itself, once black and white exclusively, is beginning to contain more than hints of Naples

Yellow, sometimes ochre, sometimes alizarin, which appear subtly along the edges but are still mostly obscured by the heavily applied black. In the studio, a quiet joy accompanies the addition of color. When I scoop up a blob of yellow with my palette knife and spread it into a thin wall of happy color, my heart skips a beat with anticipation and guilt. I am entering forbidden territory. My suggestions of color receive some mention in the art magazines, news flashes about Mendelssohn reversing the expected and admired images. I chuckle, thinking of the recent outrage when Bob Dylan substitutes an accompanying band to replace his folksy guitar and harmonica. When he comes to visit, my father seems delighted to see the change in my painting from what Ruth calls "total gloom."

With the substantial increase in revenue, we buy a cottage in Hillsdale and a loft on Lafayette Street, the loft big enough for working and living and then some. Floor to ceiling windows face north and west, the ceiling high enough for canvasses more than ten feet high, brought on the huge freight elevator previously used to haul machinery. The street noise, the hubbub of the tumultuous Lower East Side, provides the nervous energy that feeds both our work.

Ruth is immersed in a big novel of Poland between the two world wars, Zyga Mendelssohn, renamed Mieczyslaw Kagan or just plain Mietek, in the role of Marshal Pilsudsi's cavalry adjutant. For days at a time, she inhabits that world, making it hard for us to talk about anything else. Only one or two martinis at the end of the day can pull her out of the campaigns of 1920 and beyond.

Our new building is rich with artists. Two floors down lives a pop artist, his psychologist wife and two children. Noah Radetzky paints enormous blow-ups of scenic post cards, banners of names like Ausable Chasm or Carlsbad Caverns or Petrified Forest above folksy landscapes.

Surprisingly, they sell to collectors and museums all over the western world. In spite of their rather comical popness, Radetzky is a Luddite and a Buddhist.

At lunch in the Radetzky loft, served on a huge spool once used by the telephone company to store cable and now their dining table, they serve a Nicoise salad. Noah's wife Sonia (a psychologist recently returned from a Carl Rogers symposium and smitten with process, gentle love and understanding) is obsessed with her children's anger.

"Now, Nate darling," she says to her bratty ten year old son who is throwing peas into the hole in the center of the spool, "let's find a safe way to get your mads out."

Sonia is tall with a high ass, the only body type that attracts Radetzky in wife and student girlfriends. He teaches at Cooper Union where there are plenty of gifted high-assed young women. The Radetzky's ill-mannered children make me grateful for having none.

After lunch, Ruth and I, not prone to this kind of excursion, get into the ancient Radetzky station wagon and drive out of the city to browse through garage sales in pursuit of the old and worn, the toasters that still have a couple of years of life left in them, the forlorn lamps needing minor repairs. Making do with the used and worn, finding uses for useless objects, afflicts the Luddite rich.

Among Radetzky's many activities, he plays the double bass and we attend not only gallery openings but many a concert in the city and as far afield as Philadelphia in one direction and New Haven in the other. He and I drink together and, at times, whore together, the latter bringing great guilt upon me. Once, from a massage parlor known for its blow jobs, I almost call Ruth to tell her where I am and what I'm doing. If she's anything like my mother—which she is not—she would take it as a function of men's need to follow the demands of their unruly dicks. Some of my illicit behavior is still intended to counter Zyga's perceived weaknesses. Less now than before, I am inclined to fuck women in his name or get into stupid brawls or swipe an occasional tube of paint. Radetzky's rebelliousness includes painting itself, his father an ultra-orthodox rabbi.

At one of the Radetzky's musical soirees, he introduces Ruth and me to a musician he has known from student days, a rising star of the violin world, one Isaac Getlin, the winner of the Queen Elizabeth of Belgium competition three months before. A large man, no taller but much broader than me, he invites Ruth and me to hear him play in his Riverside Drive apartment. His arms, his entire torso is round and hairy. He plays nearly in the nude, exposing much of his abundant flesh. He is ugly, with a frog face, wears heavy horn-rimmed glasses and sweats a lot, and yet he loves being looked at and adored, to be listened to, especially by Ruth. He smiles at every difficult turn, every flight into heavenly musical territories.

"No problem for a genius," he seems to be saying—not saying, but shouting.

Nevertheless, he plays the Brahms Violin Concerto so beautifully that it brings tears to my eyes.

"O the virtuosity," I think, "that sexy virtuosity. How can a painter"s slog through a canvas compare with this?"

Ruth ogles Getlin lewdly as, violin under his chin, he paces the length and breadth of his living room.

"Ah, another Jewish refugee artist," I conjecture.

"He is shameless," Ruth whispers, almost salivating, "and the way he looks at me makes me shiver."

The cost we are required to pay for the pleasure of listening to Getlin's music is abject adoration, and somehow I pay the price, not wanting to be encouraging Ruth"s flirtation but accepting that that is precisely what I'm doing. I cater to all of Getlin's needs, becoming the sycophant extraordinaire. For a while, it costs me nothing. What I get in return is the respect due to a friend of Orpheus at Tanglewood concerts, Carnegie Hall recitals, and the private chamber music evenings in Park Avenue apartments. After his unexpected competition victory, Getlin owns the musical world, his energy and virtuosity captivating. I would like to talk music with him, to get to the essence of compositions I love, but Getlin resists the topic. Dabblers are allowed to watch and adore, but not to question.

"The narcissism of painters doesn't come close to that of performers," I tell Ruth, who is looking out the window, in a world of her own.

We visit violin shops where store managers and owners welcome him, bowing.

"Maestro," they address him, "do try our prize Guarneri."

And Getlin obliges them with mercurial scales and fragments of Bach Partitas. Flunkies bring chairs for Ruth and me. We lunch at the Russian Tea Room, where fawning waiters serve Isaac a cup of hot water into which he dunks a special tea bag he carries in his violin case. Though I fear the wounding of my male ego if this continues, I also realize that my past sexual disloyalties become tacitly condoned or at least shared.

One evening, Ruth goes alone to hear Getlin play an all Brahms program at the Frick while I meet with my dealer, Suzi Schwab. Late in the evening, I return to the loft, but Ruth is not there. I sit up reading. Just before dawn, the elevator clangs to a stop on our floor. Eventually, Ruth lets herself in. When she sees me sitting quietly on one of the long leather couches, she approaches and plants a kiss on my forehead. Out of a pocket of her skirt hangs the bra she'd been wearing. I cannot stop staring at it.

"So," I begin, fingering her bra.

"We took a drive to White Plains. He wanted to show me his Thunderbird."

"Aha! What else did he show you?"

"Whatever do you mean?" Ruth drawls. "I'm parched, Michael," she says and disappears into the kitchen.

Plainly, and not for the first time, not really wanting to, I open the door to what these days is called "an open marriage," in which sensuality trumps loyalty.

"Honey," she says from the kitchen sink, "do you want some soda?"

"You pretty little cunt, get your ass out of here," I yell.

She doesn't answer.

"Such an innocent, this Tulsa homecoming queen. She even forgets to put her fucking bra back on. How natural, how organic, what naïve outdoor frivolity. It's like a Goya happy peasant tapestry. She doesn't bother to think of trivia like this."

Still, no sound from the kitchen.

"Couldn't that ugly fiddler help you put it back on?"

She sits as far from me as she can and sips her soda. "That's as far as we went," she finally says.

"Ha!"

"And anyway, you haven't exactly kept your hands out of your students' pants. I know that for a fact."

"Perhaps it was Brahms who made you want to get laid?"

"I didn't get laid."

"No? She gets her tits sucked and, pulling her panties back up, she demands that he stop, that this is as far as she goes."

"You don't know what you're talking about," she says, squirming a little. "Not only that, but I don't want to talk about it anymore."

Over the next couple of years, I spend a lot of time at the Radetzkys', mostly without Ruth, but not always. Interesting guests show up. A Japanese oboist, a Hungarian conductor of a mid-western symphony orchestra, a German theater director, and a Polish movie maker named Kostek Krajewski. Krajewski brings copies of his and his pals' films. When I tell her about it, Ruth jumps with excitement and begs to see the Polish films.

"It will be essential research into my Zyga book," she says.

"You don't understand a word of Polish."

"Will you help me?" she asks.

We sit through not only Krajewskis', but Kwiatowski's, Piwowski's, and Pulaski's. It takes days. Talk, talk, talk. Those Poles never tire of it. What we see on Radetzky's screen are not movies, they are manifestos, sporadically interrupted by little visual wake-up calls, images of long-maned, white horses galloping through cities; slow, painful deaths on garbage heaps; the fancy carriage wheel stuck in the mud. Ruth is ecstatic while I doze as the procession of images lumbers on, accompanied by a Polish language much too complex for my understanding. Layer upon layer of history is painfully uncovered. It takes lovers of oppression like Ruth, scholars of allegory and allusion, experts in partitions, insurrections, and consolidations, to appreciate them.

"I should tell my father about this," I tell her later that night.

"Oh, yes," she says, pours us two cognacs and sits down beside me.

The films must have made a deep impression for, all night, I ache for the urgency of art, yearn to be free of the vulgar oppression of the marketplace, and to enter the oppression of political ideology and the small, furtive, cultural guerilla actions that inflict casualties. These Poles remind me that the possibility for battle, for anguish and struggle, is endless, no matter the genre. It can be film or marriage, art or the slippery self. "It is the human condition," one of those German philosophers—Nietzsche? Schopenhauer?—said, something like, "All our lives are a misery. We nurse our wounds trying to find worthiness.

Then we get laid and we're in heaven. Moments later, we're back to our old wounds again."

Krajewski has obviously taken a shine to my wife and spends a good deal of time upstairs in our loft. Ruth makes more exquisite meals than she has ever cooked up in the past. She and Kostek Krajewski steal glances at each other and I think I see Ruth swipe her hand across the back of his shoulders when she walks past him. I watch their little show and, for reasons I must examine one day, it turns me on. I like seeing her desired by other men and, at the end of the day, I want to fuck her even more than before.

My father comes over to meet Krajewski who shows him a recent film about a fire fighters' convention whose clandestine metaphors poke and jab at the communist regime.

"It is very Polish," Zyga tells us afterwards. "It reminds me that there are many things to admire in the Polish character. I am speaking about being clever and rebellious and independent."

Ruth is smiling and takes his hand in hers.

"Probably they are not all anti-Semites," my father says.

I'm a pretty damn clever Polish Jew and yet, during the past few years, I have come to believe, stupidly so, that Ruth's and my marriage is inviolable even as she takes more interest in her looks and begins buying blouses with lower necklines, exposing, at first, a tiny bit of cleavage, but now enough of it to attract pubescent boys. Little by little, she begins to pile pillows between us in our bed, pillows or books or magazines.

"I want to read," she says from the other side.

A few nights later, the bed light turned off, she announces that in order to make love, she requires "sweet nothings."

"What the fuck do you mean 'sweet nothings'?"

"You're incapable of finding words? What about in Polish? What about that chivalrous Polish crap of Bolek's?"

"You can't be serious."

"Not you. With you it's all wordless. Painterly silence? Well I need more."

"Yes, we all know you need more, but apparently not from me. By the way, am I still on your list?"

"Oh, listen to him," she says. "The innocent artist speaks."

Partly to annoy her, I buy a dog, a small Golden with silky fur. Ruth names her Cherokee and she does serve as an outlet for our clogged marital emotions. My desire to knead Ruth's hardened nipples is severely rationed, so I get down on the floor with Cherokee who willingly turns on her back.

"Upside-down dog," I murmur, as my hand runs up and down her chest, while Ruth whispers sweet nothings, her face an inch from Cherokee's.

"I love your sweet body," she says, "but it's not only these sweet paws and eyes, it's your being, your innocence I adore."

Later, as we sip our late afternoon vodkas, a thought pops into my head which had never been there before. I am a little astounded.

"I want to go to Poland," I tell Ruth.

"You do? I thought you hated the place."

"I do, but I need to explore."

"Explore?" she asks.

"Explore my origins, look for the places where I was happy, where I was terrorized, where they died, where they were gassed, where they are buried. Maybe there is someone left who knew us."

"Michael, I'm glad you want to go."

"I'd like you to come with me."

Ruth puts her head on my shoulder and caresses my chest.

"You can shove yourself in their face," she says. "Finally, you can vent your rage on people who deserve it."

Aside from my studio and our more than ample living space, Ruth occupies a pleasant room facing north. Some years before, she published her bullfighter novel named *olé!* Although the book was remaindered quickly, she was thrilled to have it out there. She did get some decent reviews which, at the time, seemed to satisfy her. More recently, the same publisher brought out a small printing of the *Chaim on the Range* book, renamed *The Painted Desert*, which was optioned by an eager Hollywood producer, then imprisoned in the limbo of unmade movies. So far, no one wants her Richard III book as written, but she isn't quite ready to abandon it, though her main professional concern these days is her Zyga book, for which she has been gathering material for a few years and which she stores inside a large armoire in her office. There are days when she hardly leaves her desk, others when she rummages through libraries and goes for long walks in the city.

We work on opposite ends of the loft, some days coming together for a meal, some evenings apart, she with her friends, I with mine. When we're out in our separate worlds, we come home smelling of booze, cigarettes, cigars and alien odors. One evening after we eat some Chinese takeout, she says, "I want to see the bridges where Zyga and Pilsudski repelled the Soviets."

"What are you talking about, Ruth. Zyga and Pilsudski? You're a fabricator of weird stories."

"Michael, the two of us, I mean this marriage, sure can use a little shake-up. Also, there's a lot you still don't know about your father."

She plans a dinner for Zyga, Rena, and, for the first time in ages, Bolek and Ursula. Neither of us is surprised when Zyga refuses to come.

"He probably never in his life sat down for a meal with Bolek," Ruth says. Nevertheless, she makes an impressive effort to be gracious and welcoming. Earlier in the day than usual, Ruth downs a couple of Bourbons.

"It's a matter of will," she says, "that's all it is."

She makes chopped chicken liver to be spread on matzos and washed down with the Dom Perignon provided by Bolek.

My mother, Bolek, and Ursula arrive together, undoubtedly feeling strange in this neighborhood. The streets below are alive with people, mostly young, running, singing, selling watches and hot dogs from carts or blankets spread in doorways. My mother, uncle, and Ursula walk around the loft dutifully, remarking on our furniture, on our kitchen, designed by Ruth, its appliances on display, even the little German coffee maker which sits not far from the sink in spite of all my principles. But, like Wagner, this piece of Teutonic equipment is a great product which I do not want to do without. Its brand name is no longer I.G. Farben but Farbineau or Farbinetti or some damn thing. Rena admires everything, as if she were at her friend Helena Rubinstein's triplex on Park Avenue.

"Ach, how beautiful," she says over and over again.

I put my arm around my mother and show her my studio. She is quieter here, wanting, I am sure, to say something, the right thing, but unable to do better than a charmed and charming sigh. She looks even smaller than she is as she stands next to a very large black canvas leaning against a wall.

Without provocation, Ursula, who has been married to Bolek for ten years, philosophizes about life.

"I love everything that isn't easy to accomplish," she says, skipping the chopped liver. "I love mountains, marriage, physical perfection, order and beauty," giving a disapproving nod, I notice, to a black and white painting of mine, not intended to satisfy one's aesthetic longings.

"I cannot understand why anyone would want to underscore flaws in nature or in the human body. No one wants to make art in praise of mediocrity or deformity or weakness."

Her own face is now lined and rugged, like the old Leni Riefenstahl and, like that Nazi bitch, Ursula has become hard and impenetrable.

For the main course, following a cook book she bought for the occasion, Ruth makes a Jewish meal. Who knows where Jews ate such shit unless it was another of those plagues, grasshoppers or locusts. Everyone's nose is twitching and noses are being blown after inhaling the smells wafting in from the stove.

"What's this, dear?" Ursula asks.

"Boiled tongue with a sweet and sour raisin sauce," Ruth says demurely.

"And this?" I ask as I stab a slug of hard dough with my fork.

"Michael," she says solemnly, "you know very well what it is. It's a knish."

Rena, who always eats the minimum of food required for life, doesn't even make a stab at any of it. Bolek picks on it for a little while, then gives up. Ursula is the bravest.

"It's very interesting, dear," she says.

Ruth clears the table and brings dessert. "This is a pudding made with rice flour, milk, sugar, and cardamom," she says, "but it didn't thicken properly." She sits down and takes a bite. "Oh dear, I did try to serve it warm."

Bolek grimaces. The dessert has finally done it. He whispers something in Ursula's ear and they both run to the bathroom.

"What's wrong with him?" I ask my mother.

"I told you that Bolek is not well," Rena says, "but they visit the best doctors in New York and Berlin."

Rena always has access, through her customers, to someone somewhere who performs miracles, cures or replaces a sick body part with a healthy one.

"I am praying," Rena says.

Bolek returns from the bathroom looking pale and haggard while Ursula steadies his uncertain gait. The knishes cannot possibly be at fault, but Bolek has a hard time staying upright. Ursula announces that it is nap time for Herr Bolek now. Bolek looks like he is about to faint. He simply nods, says nothing and, as the door closes behind him and Ursula, Rena breaks into tears. In Polish, she wails,

"He is so sick. How will I survive without him?"

Ruth puts her arms around my mother who sobs as her body heaves.

"Except for Zyga, you can't look to any of the rest of them for any depth at all," Ruth says as we do the dishes. "One might label Bolek a pre-conscious man. The idea that deep currents might be stirring beneath, seems impossible."

"That's pretty harsh stuff," I tell my wife, who undoubtedly believes that she has done her job for humanity and now she can say whatever she feels. "It's a European thing," I say inside the bedroom door. "They don't believe in the psyche. Life is what happens day by day."

"There's something to be said about an unexamined life," Ruth says. "Until now, I thought, like what's-his-name that an unexamined life is not worth living. Well, I think that's bullshit. Look at me, look where an examined life gets you: into a whole lot of trouble, into depression, and nearly into the loony bin."

A few days after the Jewish dinner and while Ruth is out shopping, Zyga comes over to discuss our plans for the Polish trip. I make tea. He and I sit on the leather couch.

"So, you are going to Poland," Zyga says.

"I have second thoughts about the whole trip."

"I am not very happy that you go," Zyga says.

He sips his tea in a jaunty, sprightly way, one elbow on his knee, the other hand balancing himself on a cushion. He puts his cup back on the saucer, leans back and puts both hands behind his head and looks up at the tin ceiling.

"Poland does not want you or me there. It always treats us like a stranger. When I am there long ago, they say to me that I am an internationalist, that I worry about all humanity, but not my own nation's misfortunes. You must be careful, Mishek, for any Pole can attack you because he is a defender of Polish culture and you are a Jew and therefore not human."

"Why did you go to Germany for your vacation?" I ask.

"I know," he says, "but I go only for the baths. Also, I have a few friends there. Jewish people," he adds defensively.

When Ruth sticks her key in the door, Zyga's face breaks into a broad smile.

"My Ruth," he sings and, standing up, he spreads his arms to welcome her.

She settles down between the two of us.

"I look forward to being a Jew where they are famous for hating Jews," she says.

"I too am a Jew, but also an agnostic," Zyga says, a twinkle in his eye.

"An agnostic?" I am surprised. "That is hedging your bets, covering all the bases," I assert.

"I am covering bases? What this is? I am like Pascal," Zyga says, an unexpected reference.

"Headmaster Michael means that he wants you to be totally negative, like him," Ruth says. "But he's wrong. No one can be certain about things like this." Then, as she pours tea from the pot in the middle of the coffee table, she peers at me. "And listen to who is preaching to his father," she says.

Zyga is still smiling. "You are looking beautiful, as always," he says to Ruth.

"I'm not feeling too beautiful these days," she says. She lifts my father's hand and kisses it. "And Poland can't be as bad as the two of you say."

He takes both her hands in his.

"Not so long ago," he says, "they go after all the Jews that remain. They call them a Fifth Column. They have to make a story they like for the murderous war years. So, what do they do? They re-write history. Everything we know about Poles who send Jews to the death camps or stand by to watch, is now censored."

I continue to be surprised by my father's thoughtful understanding of the world he comes from and the one he now inhabits. I mourn for the years he was absent from my life. And I from his.

"No one of us is left in Poland," Zyga says. "There is Lolek and Eva in Brazil, a cousin I meet once or twice in Warsaw, Mietek Mendelssohn who is now in Australia, and that is all."

He takes out his handkerchief and blows his nose.

"I am sorry you will have no help from a Mendelssohn or even a Mandelbaum," he says, "but if you want to hear stories, call Herman Tauber in Berlin."

"He's the one who delivered the reparations money?" I ask. "That was Tauber?"

"What reparation money? Ruth asks.

"Years ago," my father tells her, "Tauber helps them get a lot of money from the Germans who take their furs to Berlin. He was a witness. Tauber is not the nicest of men, but he is there for the whole war."

Zyga is pensive for a moment, then adds, "And while you are there, go to see if that wonderful chocolate shop remains on Marszalkowska."

10.

In mid-November of 1976, we fly to Frankfurt, then change planes for Warsaw. I would not have guessed that they could fill a plane whose destination is Warsaw, but packed and sweaty it is, as are, without doubt, daily flights from Dar-el-Salam to Jaipur, from Oslo to Bergen, Kwala Lampur to Singapore, all of them packed.

We wait forever to deplane and then the cold November winds blow grit into our eyes as we run Inside Okencie airport, a pre-fabricated Scandinavian cow barn, where two old women are sweeping cigarette butts from the cement floor. It is dark and smells of mold. There is no Kostek Krajewski to meet us.

"He promised," Ruth says, despondent. "I don't understand."

As our taxi approaches the city, I recognize nothing. These must be the streets I walked or drove through, but they hold no memories.

"I expected an 'Aha' moment, a shortness of breath, an astonished gulp," I tell Ruth, "but nothing of the sort is happening."

"I bet this part of the city was flattened and newly rebuilt," Ruth says. "One ugly building after another."

At the Hotel Europejski, in whose lobby Rena and Bolek once displayed their furs, I ask the clerk in Polish if they have any messages and she gives me a look which says: "You're not in New York, asshole." She shouts for the bellhop who—young, pale and smelling of alcohol—picks up our bags and leads the way upstairs. He tries to open the door to a third floor room with different keys and when that doesn't work he kicks at it with his big black shoes.

Suddenly filled with the accumulated rage from the time the Mendelssohns and Mandelbaums crossed that border into Lithuania, I push the bellhop aside and, even though Ruth tries to stop me, I lunge for the door, knocking it off its hinges. We burst into the dark room like a swat team. As the bellhop puts the hinges back together, Ruth unstraps the wardrobe bag and hangs it on the back of the bathroom door. The wire hangers provided inside the musty armoire are useless, drooping with the memory of heavy gabardine.

Through the rain-splattered window, the city huddles under the darkening sky. Ruth runs a tepid bath. I call Kostek Krajewski.

"For me too, this has been a terrible day," Krajewski says over the crackly phone line. "Believe me," he says, "everything here could not be worse. Otherwise I would have picked you up at the airport."

The bellhop opens the drapes and stands by the tall windows looking down at the street. Krajewski says, "Do you know what it is like to live in this country?"

Pause.

"How can you?"

Pause.

"They spit on us. I am well known here, but I wait on line like every-one else."

With the phone wedged between my ear and shoulder, I slip out of my coat and tip the bellhop. The room is overheated, yet a cold wind whistles outside, rattling the window panes, blowing the curtains.

"These are bad times," Krajewski is saying. "Here we have empty stores, resistance, prison, war."

Next, I expect to hear about the misfortune of being stuck between Russia and Germany. I grip the edge of the bedside table.

"No sign of war coming in from the airport," I grumble, "no tanks, no artillery."

Ruth comes in from the bathroom to chide me.

"If you're talking to Kostek, be nice," she whispers.

Still on the phone, Krajewski laughs.

"Even in war, we never know if we are winning or losing. Even when we win, we lose," he says.

We agree to meet in a bar off the Europejski lobby. While Ruth dresses, I go downstairs and find the place. A tall, young woman in a black hat and coat, straight out of Toulouse-Lautrec, sits on a barstool, exposing a tantalizing white thigh above her black stockings. She strikes a Moulin Rouge pose, her elbows on the bar, hands holding up chin, legs splayed apart. On my napkin, I doodle a sketch of Josef Pilsudski, Marshal of the armies, madman, dictator, protector of the Jews. Zyga taught me when I was a little boy to sketch this grim face and, like then, I now scratch in the thick black stand-up hair, the bristling eyebrows, the ferocious mustache.

"Pilsudski!" the bartender exclaims as he brings me a coffee.

The woman at the bar comes over to look.

"Everyone loves Pilsudski," she says, taking a seat next to me and rubbing her knees against mine. "You are Polish?" she asks.

"Born here," I tell her in Polish.

"You stay at the Europejski?"

I nod and add that I am waiting for a friend. She leans over.

"I do everything," she whispers in English.

She turns her body away from the bartender, who is already facing the mirror in back of the bar where, on a ledge, he read his newspaper. She blows a lock of loose hair off her forehead and opens her tight-fitting black jacket, giving me a peek of her lovely white chest, a chest that can belong only to the owner of those white thighs. She gives me her calling card and just then, the bar door flies open and, looking over her shoulder, she squeals, "Kostek!"

Kostek Krajewski puts his arms out and smiles.

"How beautiful," he says, "you have already found Pani Maryla."

Maryla gets up and they hug.

"Pani Maryla is my best whore," Krajewski says in English as she primps, dabbing powder on her nose. He sits down facing the door to the bar.

"Whore parts don't come every day," he explains as he empties his first hundred grams of vodka. "She makes more money here at the hotel than in a film."

Krajewski's features, like a fox's, are a little too close together, a little scrunched. His eyes dart everywhere. He takes Maryla's chin in his hand.

"She is beautiful, no?" he announces and the two of them begin talking in rapid-fire Polish, way too fast for me.

They sound like neighbors remarking on the shortage of light bulbs, on the recent shipment of herring.

"Maryla was just telling me about your Pilsudski. He is well known in America?"

"Only to me, I think."

Ruth then makes her appearance. Maryla gets up, brushes some imaginary debris from her heavy black suit, and kisses Kostek goodbye. Though Ruth puts her hand on my knee, her overheated pink face is turned toward Kostek. Ruth is, I am sure, precisely where she wants to be, back in the presence of the man she cooked for so lovingly in our loft. And I am responsible for the heat that is being generated in this little bar.

Krajewski invites us both to a viewing of more of his confiscated films. Ruth tells him that she is honored, while I would rather have toothpicks stuck under my fingernails. Still, I go, unable to keep away from the torrid high-wire act of my manic wife. We walk at a brisk clip to the church where the films are to be shown. In a white sweater and an open leather coat, Krajewski looks like a diminutive long-distance skater, his body leaning forward as his legs stretch into long strides. Unlike us, he doesn't seem to mind the cold. Ruth and I peer into the nearly empty shop windows, some with a few random objects defying description, gathering dust. Price tags lay in the vicinity of shapeless brown and gray suits and cheap shoes. But, surprisingly, the streets are full of window-shoppers, as if prize turkeys and hams are being displayed. Couples parade up and down the avenue as if this repellent frozen avenue, street cars screeching, had morphed into a sunny, Sunday morning on some Mediterranean waterfront. We catch up with Krajewski to ask why the streets are so crowded with leisurely strollers. He tells us that most days at this hour, people go into the streets to protest the lies of the evening television news aired at 7:30. As Krajewski takes the lead again, Ruth says that she is precisely where she wants to be, a place where life is on the edge, where people can be heroes.

"We're finally in a place where window-shopping is a protest, a political act, where allegorical movies attract standing-room-only crowds, where art and poetry are dangerous," she says.

I don't want to admit that I feel pretty much the same. Thoughts similar to hers are coursing through my blood and my heart beats faster.

As we turn the corner, the narrow street is packed with people. Police cars block the street to traffic. Plainclothes police with crackling walkie-talkies stop everyone who tries to go into the church where the screening is about to take place.

"They won't dare go inside the church," Krajewski says.

The young policemen are businesslike and friendly.

"They are just doing their job," Krajewski says.

At one point, two uniformed cops try to ask Ruth and me a few questions. When they realize we are Americans, their tough demeanor becomes welcoming. One of them bows toward Ruth, the other slaps me playfully on the back.

Aside from a dim light hanging in the entrance of the church, the street is illuminated only by the cops' headlights. Krajewski treats the festivities as if they were his own private party. Everyone wants a piece of him. Like a good host, he leads Ruth and me around, introducing us to men and women wrapped in overcoats, shawls, and ear muffs, their faces clouded by the vapor of their breath.

"They are all actors and writers," he whispers, "and that is why the cops love this assignment. They know them all from television."

People begin jumping up and down to keep warm, swinging their arms against their bodies. As they jump, they coalesce, become a unity, a troupe. Ruth starts jumping with them as I watch. Jokes and poems and bits of theater are shouted back and forth in a kind of choral antiphony. Krajewski is in heaven. The street events become so operatic that I would not be surprised to see the window shutters fling open as the Queen of the Night or the Bartered Bride or the Cunning Little Vixen appear on the rooftops. The cops shuffle uneasily, talking self-consciously among themselves and, little by little, they start their cars and slip away. No one else leaves. A two hour postponement means nothing.

"I've never felt so at home in my life," Ruth says.

Inside the basement of the church, the film session is like those concerts in Beethoven's day when the maestro conducted two or three of his symphonies, played a couple of piano concertos and, to round it off, performed a few early sonatas. After an hors d'oevre of documentaries on a convention of masseurs and one on the inefficiency of a local fire department, comes the main course, *Voyage on a Train*, a talk piece, visually arid. The audience is riveted from the moment the program starts, and once started, it does roll on. And on. In spite of the cold, hard benches in this frozen church basement where hundreds of them are squeezed together, everyone wants more. As the lights are turned on, Krajewski gets up to field questions. I might be the only one there who is shaking with cold.

Even though Ruth does not understand a single word, she cannot be pried away. I walk out into the church's cobblestoned courtyard to breathe. The weather has improved a bit, a slice of the moon now visible through thinning clouds. I am lost in thought. What do these people do when they are not here getting their rocks off on solving the story beneath the story? They figure out the day's riddle, then they go back to their gray room, nibble on the vodka ,and look at the dying fly buzzing in the sooty rain-splattered window. Then they sleep and dream of ice-spitting refrigerators. They don't look for the keys to the universe but the little joke, the allegory that makes it possible to survive one more night. For a moment, I think of my art as irrelevant, chest-thumping bullshit, yet another heretofore Karp-inspired ontological crisis. I envy Krajewski, all the poets who sneak their Fifth Column ideas past the censors, talking of real things, life and death.

Across the street, I notice a lonely figure, standing very still, looking directly at me. He has a long beard and a yarmulke on top of his head.

I am shocked to see a Jew advertising himself in the streets of Warsaw. The man steps off the sidewalk and walks toward me.

"I know who you are," he says. "I come here to introduce myself."

I turn away as the church begins to empty and lose myself in the crowd. The specter of that impudent Jew makes me uneasy. That night, Ruth is wild with passion.

"I love your Poland," she says, sitting on top of me.

The next morning, in the hotel lobby, the clerk hands me a note which he says was written on the premises by a Jew.

"He was wearing one of those Jewish hats," the clerk says, cupping his hands over his skull.

"I am a fellow Jew," the note reads, "almost family. Poland is a book, but who can read it? I know many things about your homeland and about you, and I offer you my services. Szymon Bolynski."

He printed his address and phone number. Having no desire to meet him, I tear the note into little pieces. I am sure that he sells his services to every Jew who comes back to the motherland and I want no part of it.

Outside the hotel, we are mobbed by money-changers. Though the city had been reduced to rubble by Germans and Russians, the area near the hotel escaped most of the damage and, in any case, is somewhat rebuilt, fragments of it stirring memories, though not with the force of the avalanche I crave. Ruth and I walk to the edge of the dark, somber park of my childhood. She takes my hand.

"When I was little," I tell Ruth, "my governess had to choose between two parks, one light and cheery on the other side of the city, or this one which she knew suited my many dark moods."

Ruth squeezes my hand.

"On this very path, I once picked chestnuts from the ground and, splitting the prickly green bur to expose the shiny, smooth, umber, irregularly shaped nut, I had my first aesthetic experience, not just aesthetic but erotic."

"There are no chestnuts on the ground now," Ruth says.

"They probably stopped falling during the war, a big fuck you to the population."

A little boy is sailing a toy boat on the tiny pond.

"He could be me," I say.

Well-dressed men and elegant ladies with fur muffs on their laps used to sit, watching the children play, pointing out the chestnuts on the ground. Now I want to axe that barren chestnut tree into pulp. This fucking little park got through the war and the kid playing with his boat probably never heard of Jews.

"Do you suppose that there are any Jews left here?" Ruth asks.

"Between zero and a couple of thousand I heard somewhere."

As we walk some of the barren paths of this park, she says nothing for a while. Then, "even though most of the European Jews were killed here," she philosophizes, "it was the Germans who gassed the Jews, not the Poles."

I try to calm myself. This defense of Poland being just another victim enrages me. It always has and now I have to control my instincts so as not to smack my wife. "These fucking Poles should have lined up ten deep to welcome me back, to say how sorry they were for their part in what happened."

Ruth assures me, with numbers she has found somewhere, that as many Poles as Polish Jews died in the war.

"It's not about numbers," is all I can come up with.

As we walk past the tomb of the unknown soldier where, as a kid, I stood at attention saluting, I spit as I pass the damn thing.

"I wish I could extinguish that fucking flame, all flames, all fallen heroes, all flags, crosses, stars of David, all patriots," I growl, enraged.

"Michael," she says, out of breath from running to keep up with me, "these people aren't all bad. They're writing poems and music, even great movies."

Now, for sure, nothing will stop me from knocking her to the ground and kicking her. In this most violent part of the world, it doesn't seem far-fetched. I remember from a Dostoevsky novel that here or somewhere in the neighborhood, they kick old horses to death, horses and Jews.

"You're imagining better times? There were no better times. Even the trees are ugly."

"Don't go totally crazy on me," Ruth begs.

I wheel around. She stops. I close my eyes and get ahold of myself.

"Michael," she says, "you saw some of these buildings crumble. It wasn't the Poles who bombed you at Bolek's."

A bit calmer but still breathing hard, we walk into the old town. The market square has been reconstructed, modeled on paintings from the 18th century. We find a bench in the middle of the square and sit down. It takes a while to start breathing normally. I cannot fathom how poetry comes from this place, or music from the "Brutality must breed art."

I try to be rational. It's not easy.

"Especially in Europe, brutality and barbarism have no boundary between them."

She leans toward me and takes my hand.

"You needed to come back. And for very good reasons. If you can just look around and take it all in, you might find what you are looking for."

We sit in silence for a while, watching crowds mill around, going in and out of stores, standing in groups talking and even laughing. Pigeons are pecking at bits of garbage.

"We know why I came," I say, my head down between my knees, "but what about you? Why did you want to come?"

"To be with you," she says.

"Me or your movie maker?"

Stop it, Mendelssohn, I tell myself. Ruth freezes, the old ice queen again and now, yards away from each other, we walk down toward the Vistula whose waters had once pointed to a whole world I knew nothing about. Now it stinks of war and rebellion, corpses and shit. We sit on the scrubby dead grass, beyond reach of each other.

"That's where in 1920 your father fought the Russians. Zyga and Pilsudski," she says. "The miracle of the Vistula."

"What are you talking about?"

"Your father was barely twenty when he joined Pilsudski's army," Ruth reports, "believing that the Field Marshal would save the country and the Jews."

"This cannot be true," I tell her. "It could not have happened without my knowing something about it. You made this up."

"Believe it or not, I'm telling you what happened."

From history books we both read before coming, I know that during the last two centuries, Polish soldiers had to their credit only one unaided victory. Once and only once, the Poles won in hand-to-hand combat with their neighbor to the east. Apparently, how it happened was due more to chance and stupidity than superior military power or strategy.

"My father had nothing to do with it," I try telling my hallucinating wife.

"They were maniacs," Ruth says, her eyes looking inward, her voice pitched evenly. "They were full of stamina and fortitude, able to improvise. In defense of the mother country, they were careless about their own safety."

She stops and lies down on the grass. "I love that about them," she says.

I heard Ruth tell tales before, but seldom with this intense concentration, with this flailing of hands and arms. The words are coming so fluidly that it sounds like she is reading.

"Warsaw was about to be stormed," she says, sitting up again. "The scene was strangely calm, as if the Bolsheviks were a thousand miles away and the country in no danger. Your father was on horseback, a messenger to Pilsudski's adjutants. He felt out of place in his ill-fitting uniform, his boots and spurs."

"Ruth, stop. Is this a Babel short story or a Ruth Mendelssohn novel?" She gets up and walks toward the river. I close my eyes and can almost see the page in one of the history books we read. The Pilsudski miracle happened at the end of summer. Warsaw had been occupied so many times in its history that it hardly caused a stir, even though a huge Soviet army was ready to pounce. To the surprise of Tukhachevsky, the Soviet General, Warsaw's fragile defenses held firm. The attack on the Vistula bridgehead was repulsed and the Polish assault force sliced through Tukhachevsky's rear, encircling his entire army. It was a miracle, the miracle on the Vistula.

Ruth is satisfying her need for legend, enlivening the armies inside her skull. She loves the idea of the fighter, a man who stands alone to face oppression, face history. Perhaps she no longer needs me, who once served that purpose. She needs the solo violinist, the trickster film maker surrounded by the malevolent state, and Zyga Mendelssohn. I love the spinner of tales, but worry about her sanity and her need to supersede me with other heroes. We buy a bottle of good vodka and, in our hotel room, we make desultory love. When she falls asleep, I sip vodka and watch apparatchiks on the television screen.

In the morning, I get out of bed, stumble into the bathroom to pee and gape at my bloodshot eyes. The phone rings.

"Mendelssohn," says the voice, "I am Bolynski in the lobby."

I knew this was coming.

"No Mendelssohn here," I say and hang up.

The phone rings again. "What no?" he says. "This is not the Jewish artist Mendelssohn?"

"Who are you and what do you want?"

"I have plenty to tell you," he says.

His English, though accented, is very good. A familiar guilt sweeps over me.

"How do you know I'm a Jew?"

"It doesn't take a genius," he says.

I let it go and say nothing for a couple of seconds.

"You eat breakfast," he then says, "I eat breakfast. So why not eat together?"

"My wife is asleep," I tell him.

"I am not a big eater," he says and moments later knocks on the door.

He has a yarmulke on the top of his balding head. His eyes are rheumy. He might be my age, but looks older. The suit he wears has no color, threadbare, stained and shiny from overuse. I look down at his feet, expecting sandals, straight from the bible, but no, he is wearing canvas shoes. Bolynski looks up at me, still in my pajamas.

"You are a big man, Mendelssohn," he clucks disapprovingly, "a real Goliath."

I make way for the man and close the door behind him. I put on my bathrobe.

"What were you doing in the street the other night? Why are you hounding me?"

Bolynski carries a package which he unwraps carefully, then puts his scarf down on the bed. Ruth stirs. He smiles as he uncovers three shiny herrings.

"For you," he says, as he releases the sharp, pickled smell into the room.

Ruth is wide awake now, the covers drawn up to her chin, watching intently.

"Hold on to them yourself," I say and crack the window open, then call room service. "You take coffee?"

"Tea," Bolynski says. "Milk and sugar. Boiled eggs, two minutes, bread, butter, nothing more."

"Two eggs?"

"Three," he says, as he brings the open package of fish to his nose and inhales deeply. "What a smell," he says, pushing the herrings toward Ruth who takes a whiff and smiles. "Don't you think so, madame?"

He scratches one of the herrings with his fingernail and sucks it, smacking his lips. Like an enraptured wine taster, he raises his eyebrows.

"Pickled in heaven," he decides, and I suspect that every sound the man makes, every movement, is intended to annoy me.

"I am a serious man," Bolynski says. "I am here to instruct you. I will take you to the important sites."

A waiter wheels in breakfast and shoots my visitor an impertinent glare as Bolynski loses no time pulling a chair up to the breakfast table.

"I don't need a guide," I tell him. My head is splitting. "Also, I don't need a lecture."

"I will go with you to the death camps," Bolynski says as he stuffs a napkin under his collar. "You, too, lost everyone."

"If I need help, I'll let you know," I say and just then the phone rings.

It's Krajewski on the line saying he will be right over.

"I have many friends in Warsaw," I tell Bolynski after I hang up.

"Did I hear the voice of Konstanty Krajewski? What does he know about death camps?" he asks, dismissing the idea with a sweep of his hand.

He knits his brows. "On the other hand, who knows?" he says. "Even

Krajewski could be a Jew."

Every Jew knows this kind of claim. The strangest people—Columbus's first mate, one of the Avignon Popes, Marlene Dietrich, Darwin—all Jews, a Jew behind every theory, every big philosophy, every thought.

"Yes," he reassures me, slicing the top off his egg with a knife. "Either a Jew or an anti-Semite."

He scoops the top part out of the shell, then the bottom, mixing them in a bowl. As he chews, the bone that hinges his jaw to his skull clicks loudly, more loudly than the hum of traffic in the streets below, more loudly than the flushing toilet in the room next to ours. The more deafening Bolynski's mandible becomes, the more refined my table behavior. Bolynski stops his clicking to observe me.

"Why do you move your fork from one hand to the other hand?" Bolynski asks. I blush, not having made such ridiculous transfer of utensils since boarding school.

Ruth asks Bolynski to turn his head while she gets into her bathrobe and sidles past us to use the bathroom. When she comes back, she sits on the edge of her bed, as entranced by this clown as she is by everything in Warsaw. Bolynski slathers butter on the soft white bread.

"Tell me, Bolynski, what do you really want with us?"

"My parents knew your parents. We were only a few cars behind you at the border."

I am astonished. "You were?" My skin breaks out in goose pimples. "You got out as well?"

"We spent the war in a Soviet labor camp," Bolynski says. "My father died in the camp."

I look into Bolynski's eyes for the first time.

"After the war, my mother, sister, and I came back to Poland. My mother, too, is now dead."

My hands are shaking.

"Are you all right?" Ruth asks me.

"So what else do you do, Bolynski?" I ask, pushing the border crossing out of my mind. "Surely you don't survive just standing in the streets."

"What do I do now?" he says, exposing a mouthful of egg. "I am in the streets to give reason to my existence," he says, slurping his tea. "I want to rub their noses in it. Also, I am a coach. I coach the Yiddish theater," Bolynski says, getting up to brush crumbs off himself.

He spots some egg on the cuff of his suit jacket and rushes into the bathroom to wash it off. "I teach the goyim," he says from the bathroom. "I teach them Yiddish, I teach them history."

He comes back in. "You too should be concerned with these things, Mendelssohn," he says.

Ruth's expression says, "See? That's what I think too."

"Listen," I say as I put down my cup of coffee, "I don't need this."

"My opinion, you need this," he says.

Ruth smiles.

"You don't know you are a Jew. You are lucky to meet me. I am a teacher. This is my job."

He tears a corner off the newspaper in which the herrings are wrapped and writes his address and telephone number. The moment he puts it on top of the dresser, Ruth gets up and buries it in her bathrobe pocket. Just as I know that she has the hots for Krajewski, I know that she will show up on Bolynski's doorstep for more oppression news. But I, too, am trying to evaluate Bolynski's usefulness in my search for clarity about the border crossing.

The Europejski front desk calls to announce Krajewski. Within moments, the film maker arrived carrying a bunch of carnations.

"It is easy to find flowers these days," he says, handing them to Ruth.

"These were on a doorstep, a memorial for a dead party hack."

He and Bolynski shake hands and quietly exchange a few words in Polish.

"How do you think I know the esteemed artist Mendelssohn and his wife are coming to Warsaw?" Bolynski asks. "The eminent director Konstanty Krajewski told me, of course."

Krajewski lights a cigarette, offers one to Ruth, Bolynski and me. When I refuse, Krajewski says,

"In life it is not always good to be so safe."

He takes a deep drag. The room is filling with smoke.

"Here, time passes slowly," Krajewski says. "Cigarettes and vodka, it is our little adventure."

Bolynski sits quietly. Ruth hangs on Kostek's every word.

"I'll have a cigarette," she says. "Light one for me please, Kostek."

I disappear into the bathroom to get dressed and soon Ruth follows and—usually a non-smoker—brushes her teeth.

We all walk down the stairs, for the elevators aren't working. We find a table at the Europejski café which is bustling with party hacks, according to Krajewski, and American Jews like me, needing a hit of mother Poland; a good cry in the killing fields. Ruth asks Bolynski if he feels threatened by the Poles, always at the ready to take mental notes on the Polish and Jewish questions.

"Here it is different than in your country, madam," Bolynski says. "In America you are too sensitive. You smell Jew hatred everywhere. Someone says he doesn't like you and immediately he is an anti-Semite. Here it is very subtle. If you are seen as a Jew in public, you are seen as someone different, not one of them. This explains why I dress always like their nightmare Jew."

He takes a big sip of his tea, sighs deeply.

"But I am not sure that there is any more anti-Semitism in Poland than, for example, in France. The difference is that in Poland it isn't disreputable. In fact, here what you call anti-Semitism is irrelevant, shrugged off as if it doesn't matter. It is here in everyday thinking, in everyday language."

"The Poles did a lot of killing of Jews for the Germans," I say. "They didn't seem to mind."

Krajewski objects. "Those were not official acts, but the work of a few bad people," he says. "You must understand that holocausts make people crazy."

Holocausts make people crazy? I want to smack the son of a bitch, have done with him once and for all. Holocausts make people crazy. I reach into my pocket for a valium. Before it begins its good work, I stand up abruptly, knocking my chair backwards and, ready to slug him, tell Krajewski to go fuck himself. In the blink of an eye, Ruth jumps in. "Let's go for a walk," she proposes and tries to drag us all out into the street.

"Fuck the lot of you," I yell and turn back to the hotel lobby.

In my address book, I look up the Berlin phone number of Herman Tauber, the eyewitness to wartime Warsaw events, the man who gave important testimony for the reparations money recovered by Bolek and Rena. I wait a couple of hours for the Europejski to put through the telephone call.

"You remember the Mendelssohns and Mandelbaums?" I shout into the phone.

"How could I forget?" Tauber says, his accent more German than Polish. "Mendelssohns and Mandelbaums have been a part of my life for a long, long time. We have benefitted handsomely from our shared business relations."

"I want very much to talk with you. Could I entice you to come to Warsaw?"

"Oh no, my dear. I may not come. You see, my wife is not well."

"Then, may I come to Berlin to talk further with you about those times," I ask.

"Of course, my dear, of course."

Late that night, Ruth fiddles with the lock on our door and finally manages to let herself in, dead drunk. My whole body tenses. It screams with rage and jealousy. I want to take the next plane back to New York but fly to Berlin instead—as distasteful a trip as the one to Warsaw. On the plane, my body is tight as a drum, my hands clenched into fists. I'm going to kill that bitch, I snarl to myself. And her motherfucking moviemaker, as well.

When I get off the plane, having this language all around me is like being in the middle of a bad war movie. Everyone speaks it, unashamedly so. Valium helps transform the language into comic strip characters growling, then into the background, like listening to *Die Walküre* on the radio while vacuuming.

Tauber and I meet in the lobby of the Schweitzer Hof Hotel where I'm staying. A rotund, rosy cheeked man, he wears an expensive suit and a tweed coat with a belt that would have gone around me two or three times. He has pulled a matching tweed sporting cap down to his thick eyebrows. He enters the lobby jovially, his arms spread in warm welcome. I put my hand out, but Tauber pushes it aside, slipping in for an embrace. With mugs of beer, we settle in two Biedermeier armchairs in a quiet corner of the hotel bar, which is dark and elegant.

"Ach," Tauber says, "this divided Germany is a nuisance. Who can get from place to place?"

I want to say "May it ever stay divided," but say instead, "So Herman, you were in Warsaw for the entire occupation? You saw everything?"

"I had little choice," he says defensively.

"Of course, of course."

"It was terrible what I saw, unbearable to witness to all that suffering."

"I forgot what you did during those terrible years," I prod.

"I continued to work for Mandelbaum's. It was always my profession to cut skins. Now, of course, I am retired."

He orders two more beers and insists on paying for them.

"As soon as Warsaw was taken over by the Germans, SS Hauptsturm-führer Fassbender marched into Marszalkowska 125 and aryanized it."

"Strange verb, to aryanize."

"Yes, but we must call things as they are," Tauber says, then proceeds to tell me that this SS man began an affair with one of Mandelbaum's models, a beautiful woman named Slava.

Tauber pauses to empty his large mug.

"You know, of course, that the SS man and Slava moved into your apartment. Where was it? Moniuszki?"

Bolek and Rena must have heard this from Tauber when he came to New York, but, of course, they said nothing.

"Slava was half Russian," Tauber continues, "and married to a Polish officer. She became Fassbender's accomplice and lover. He made her pregnant and arranged for her husband to be arrested and shot by the Gestapo."

"In my blue bedroom?" I can't help murmuring.

They fucked in my bed? They planned her husband's death in the dining room where I played under the table?

"Soon, there were constant orgies in the Mandelbaum showrooms," Tauber says. "The place became a bordello. The appetite of the German authorities for elegant fur was insatiable. With fur, one manages to have good political relations and good friends. Hermann Goering and Generalgouverneur Hans Frank also took many coats from the premises back to the Reich."

Goering at Mandelbaum's? Goering, the commander of the Luftwaffe and second only to Hitler? And an SS man in my bed? I wonder if this kind of information remains only a story, a piece of my history that hardly relates to me, but a story I will never forget. Or is it only an interesting footnote that elicits surprise, like a little known fact about the Napoleonic invasion of Russia?

"I am really interested," I say over our third beer, "in hearing what you remember of my family, especially my father."

Tauber blows his nose into a red and white checkered handkerchief, as big as a dishtowel, then rests his head on the back of the armchair. He closes his eyes.

"Excuse me for saying so, Mr. Michael, but your uncle was not very nice to your mother. The story is not pretty. He humiliated her, yelled at her in front of the workers and in front of customers as well. It was not pleasant to see her, such a small woman, treated like this. Everybody talked about it."

He sits up and puts his meaty hand on mine.

"As for your father, no one in the business knew him well. Mr. Zygmunt and I, however, shared a love of boxing and wrestling, so we were together from time to time." He loosens his necktie. "Mr. Zygmunt had another life altogether. He did not appreciate the fur business. A very nice man, an intelligent man, a political man."

Tauber is sweating through his shirt. "How they heat these hotels," he says, fanning himself with his handkerchief. "If we do not leave this place, I will have a heart attack."

We leave the smoke-filled bar to get some fresh air. Tauber, who looks like the photos I have seen of the fat, sweaty Goering himself, takes my elbow and leads me to the Tiergarten. He has a hard time carrying his weight, so, in spite of the cold and darkening sky, we sit on a bench from which I try not to think of the horrors that once took place in this neighborhood. I can almost hear the shattered glass of *Kristallnacht* when most any German could enjoy the spectacle of Jews being humiliated. I think not only of a bearded rabbi on his knees, but Zyga, beaten by Polish students.

"We were talking about your father," Tauber reminds me. "He was a quiet man, a melancholic." He takes a deep breath. "Your uncle and mother, with reason or not, thought that he looked down on their enterprise. Perhaps, they thought he knew nothing of life, nothing about making money, his head in the clouds. Who knows? I am guessing."

The sky is gray and threatening.

"But I can tell you this. He was a man of the left, and did not favor the merchant class. You will tell me please if I am saying too much."

I assure him that he isn't.

"My wife and I never understood why your mother and father remained together."

"It is one of those things that doesn't happen much anymore. My mother swore to her dying mother that she would never leave my father, even though they didn't like each other from the start."

"Is this right?" Tauber asks. "Of course, he did have other women."

He turns to look carefully at me.

"You are smiling," he says. "This makes you happy? Very good, very good."

In fact, betrayals do not make me happy, but I am smiling thinking of my father as a man who has not always been squelched, a man with a purpose, a will of his own. Tauber loosens the belt of his great coat.

"There was Jadwiga Krapinska and Stefa Karczmar. But we do not need to name names."

He studies my face to assure himself he is not overstepping the limits of civility.

"To tell you the truth," he says, "I think he was driven to it. Your uncle and your mother were not very kind to him. My wife always thought that he had mistresses not only for enjoyment, but to make a scandal."

A wind blows across the Tiergarten. A cold drizzle gets us to our feet. As we hurry back toward the hotel, Tauber says,

"Of course, your father had wealth of his own. What was it? Cooking oil?"

"And margarine," I add just for the record.

Inside a booth of a coffee shop, we sit across from each other. The smell of cakes baking makes me hungry and we order Linzertorts.

"Your father was not a happy man," Tauber says. "By this, Mr. Michael, I mean he was often depressed. I am different and—knock wood—I do not suffer from the curse of depression. This curse," and here Tauber tapped his temples in that universal sign of disturbances in the brain, "makes a man appear a little crazy. He was driven to it; I am sure, not only by his melancholic condition but by Madame Mendelsohn, your mother, and Mr. Boleslaw."

We are drinking good coffee served by a young blond Aryan woman.

"You say that they drove him crazy?"

"I am guessing only. How can one really be sure of these things? But it was said that Madame Rena and Mr. Boleslaw spread the word among all their friends, even some customers, that Mr. Zygmunt is a communist."

"I don't think that was true. Do you?"

"This I do not know, my dear. But, whether he put himself there or he was forced by others, he spent a few months in a beautiful sanitarium in Zopot."

"This was well known?"

"Warsaw was a city full of gossip. Everybody knew about everybody else. Personally, I think your mother and father stayed together not just for the sake of their only son but to punish each other."

He straightens up and adjusts his cap. "And one more thing, something you are likely to know already. My wife and I have heard that your uncle, Mr. Boleslaw, fathered a child."

"What?"

"Now, if you please, Mr. Michael, this, of course cannot be proved and, as I told you before, Warsaw was populated by busybodies."

"What happened to his child?"

"I don't know," Tauber says.

For now, I have little choice but to accept this collaborationist's information, at least provisionally; to mull it over, enter it into the growing unproven testimony of lives lived, witnesses and whole cultures disappeared. My father's deep depressions and his vitality fill some of the unknowns of pre-war Zyga, as do the intrigues of Bolek and Rena, the Claudius and Gertrude of my life. But I wonder if I can ever find the truth, not sure even what "the truth" means.

Tauber's body begins to slump, his energy depleted.

"If you will be so good, Herman," I say to him, "permit me to come another time or perhaps to correspond with you by mail."

"Of course, of course," he says amiably as his eyes close half-way.

I stuff him into a taxi. He waves and puts his head back and, I'm sure, immediately falls asleep.

The Berlin rain turns to snow. I try a walk in the city, but don't last long, still unable to stomach the language, the language which, I remind myself, Beethoven spoke: and Bach, Mozart, Schubert, Brahms and Mahler. It was Schopenhauer's native tongue. But Mozart? I never thought of Mozart, in spite of *The Magic Flute*, speaking German before.

In Warsaw, Ruth is not only sober, but welcomes me back with an ardor I have not seen for a while. I recount the many stories Tauber told me and she not only listens with rapt attention, but questions me particularly about Zyga's depressions and the sanitarium about which I can't say more than that he spent time there.

"And everything that Tauber said must be taken with at least one grain of salt," I tell her. "For instance, he said that Bolek is the father of a child."

"That doesn't surprise me," she says. "Knowing him, he's probably fathered more than one. And this might be a good time to tell you something very important I've been saving."

"Saving for what?"

"It's about Zyga," she says, taking both my hands in hers. "First, remember his friend Rytek who he met from time to time? Well, Zyga has been supporting Rytek all these years. Rytek had no money and your father paid all his bills."

"I like that," I tell her and remember the envelope that was passed between them at the Automat, in return for which Rytek kissed Zyga's cheeks. "My, my," say I.

"That's just a little preface," she says. "Now, something a lot more important."

"How come you know all these things? Or do you really?"

"Your father likes talking to me."

"And the news is?"

"They're liars, Rena and Bolek. They planted the whole story in your head."

"What story?"

"The border crossing," Ruth says triumphantly. "He betrayed no one."

I stare at her and make a wry, quizzical face.

"I remember what happened. I remember him white as a ghost as he stood alone, waiting for us at the side of the road in Lithuania."

"Do you remember your father's beautiful gold pocket watch?"

"His watch? He wears a cheap wristwatch."

"I'm talking about a watch he had in Poland."

"What?" I pry my hands from hers and move to another chair, a bit further from her.

"Zyga gave his beautiful gold watch to the border guard to bribe your way out of Poland."

I'm getting angry and gnash my teeth together, hurting my jaw. "He couldn't have told you this. It's not possible. Why didn't he ever tell me?"

"Michael," she says, getting up to come close to me again. "After he offered the guy the watch, something awful happened to him. I don't know what it was. He wouldn't elaborate. Something awful happened, then the guard pushed him into the car that was about to drive across."

"So, this is the story you're selling. I steal a gold watch from the dead man in the ditch and my father gives his own away to buy our freedom?" I grasp Ruth's hand hard as my own hands shake. "What a nice story, but I'm having a hard time trusting you, you who have good stories to tell about everything. What about Pilsudski?"

"Up to you," she says. "Take it or leave it."

What I know in my heart is that Rena and Bolek are capable of any duplicity to demolish Zyga, but how could the real story, whatever it is, not come out somehow, as little overheard secrets or mere suggestions or confessions?

"Why didn't he simply come out with whatever the truth is?"

"That's the beauty of Zyga," she says. "It's one reason I love him so."

"You love him for keeping silent?"

"He wants to do no harm, not even to them," she says. "He's a hero, a quiet hero."

I cover my face with my hands. Ruth's fingers are massaging my scalp, then my neck. Is it possible that Zyga has not only become a father to me, a human being with his particular frailties, his nostalgia and melancholy, strength and dignity, a man of substance, a political man, a lover, a hero? I want to leave this miserable Poland. I want to hold him. I want to throttle my mother and Bolek.

We hire a taxi and Bolynski accompanies us to the major death camps. Ruth insists on doing this even though, aside from an interest in actually seeing the murder factories, I have no illusions about my ability to place individuals from my family in one atrocity location or another. Among Auschwitz, Treblinka, and Majdanek, the number of Mendelssohns and Mandelbaums, gassed and thrown into pits to rot, is huge. There is my grandmother Paulina who stood with me in her field, covered with wild flowers, as we watched the sky turn scarlet a few weeks before the war began.

"This is a sign of war coming," she said.

They murdered my aunts Zosia and Ola, together with cousin Henio and his beautiful wife, Flora. They slaughtered Bolek and Rena's parents, Grandmother Bronka and Grandfather Maximilian; Uncle Julek who taught me to ski in Zakopane. And many more, unremembered and unmourned. Inside the taxi, Bolynski talks numbers, names of villages, techniques of killing. Ruth weeps as she holds Bolynski's hand while I stew in the front seat fending off the good humor of our insufferable driver.

"Let bygones be bygones, Mr. Michael," Ostrowski says, "that was then, this is now."

The taxi speeds north, swerving to avoid the nastier breaks in the asphalt. We are heading toward Wilno, now Vilnius.

"Wilno was once Poland," Ostrowski says.

I turn to Ruth. "In this miserable country, no one knows if they will wake up in Poland or the Ukraine, Lithuania, Belorussia, or Germany."

Ostrowski says, "I was not born until after the war, Mr. Michael, but I know Polish history."

He looks at me.

"Yes, I am a student of history."

He is talking so fast that I have a hard time keeping up. "And so," he says, "not long after the war began, the Litvaks and Huns sneaked over the border, destroyed the Polish army, and stole half of Poland."

"Yes," I agree and put my hand on his shoulder, "it must have happened right after we crossed."

We stop in a town named Lomza. Studying his map, Ostrowski tells us that this is the last place with a restaurant before the border. The day is damp and cloudy. Inside the local hotel dining room, the four of us order soup and chicken from a bored, pale waiter in a greasy tuxedo. Ostrowski and I ask for a couple of hundred grams of vodka.

"Ah, Mr. Michael," our cheery driver says, "this is the way to forget the unpleasantness."

I don't know if he means the unpleasantness of this decrepit hotel, all of Poland under Soviet rule, or the war. Sporadic sunlight enters through the dirty windows, highlighting the dust motes floating all around us. The wallpaper is peeling. We can't be mistaken for anyone other than who we are: Ruth in a fancy plaid skirt and cashmere sweater, me in turtle neck and jeans, Bolynski, as always, in his Biblical outfit. Ostrowski, who speaks no English, is reading the paper. The chicken arrives and is inedible. We're all hungry and suck on the stringy bird. I have a recollection of sucking on a chicken, probably not too far from here. Bolynski chews loudly as he talks about those terrible September days long ago. He, too, was a little boy, a couple of years older than I. He, too, screamed all the way from Warsaw, but by the time he and his family arrived within sight of the border, the border was closed, hundreds of cars stranded, soldiers with rifles pointed at them, guarding the invisible line that separated the two countries. Bolynski dabbed at his eyes while Ruth held his free hand. I try to bring back the war sounds, the revving planes, the thud of bombs and rattle of gunfire, the wails and cries, the orders shouted, the terrible shrieks of the wounded. Neither the red and white border barrier nor the guard house appears. Perhaps they are merely a story, the whole war a story. How much comes from a René Clément movie, from Napoleon's retreat from Moscow, from the Iliad? And where was Zyga? Inside the van or out? Bolynski puts three spoonfuls of sugar into his tea. I get up from the table, leave them struggling with their chickens, and find my way outside. The day is still, with only an occasional sound of a truck, of a horse neighing in the distance. The fields are fallow, the trees barren, the houses unpainted. It is ugly now and was most likely ugly then. Nothing opens the floodgates of memory, no Freudian eureka moment. I remember thinking, a long time after the fact, that somewhere in the endless line of cars, a tire must have blown out, then another. Engines must have died. The spark plugs had to stay clean; the planes had to stay busy elsewhere. I was in a ditch somewhere, clutching my ill-gotten gold pocket watch. Gazing at this forlorn landscape—flat, colorless, scrubby, where crops have grown and died forty times since then, trees sprung up to give shade where no shade existed before. I stand here for a long time, then walk around to the entrance of the hotel.

Back inside, I pull my chair close to Ruth. "Nothing here but an ugly landscape," I report.

"No memories?"

"Nothing."

The taxi driver is drinking too much and I wag my finger at him.

Bolynski is having a post-chicken nap, his head back, his yarmulke on the floor behind him.

WHY AM I TELLING MY STORY? When we suspect that our fate is sealed, what to do? Struggle? Accept? Suicide? Do we laugh through it? Some say that there is always hope. I don't think so. Are we here to have fun? I don't think so. So, why write it all down? Even though I am a painter, in the final analysis, painting does not do the job. Not music either. So these are all memories and we all know about memories. They lie or, at the very least, they skirt the truth. And truth? As slippery as memory. On top of all that, this is the only story I have. If I can figure it out, then my life might get some meaning. How else to do it? Probably not via black shapes screaming from my canvases. no details in sheer blackness, trumpeting murder and betrayal and depressive misery. It's so much easier to lay down the black pigment and let it conceal the story. Can the telling bring understanding or peace to you, Mila, or to me? It is a comedy of struggle and survival. You and I, Mila, had no such concerns. We played and sang and held hands, amused each other, all because it felt good, only because our possibilities were limited in that closed van, vulnerable to the power beyond our understanding, beyond our capacity to know. Was it better to be the children we were, enclosed and powerless, than to live with the illusion of freedom, free of the sound of war, able to roam, to examine, to open one's throat, one's eyes without blinking, without stuffing fingers into ears, breathing deeply and fully, taking small pleasures, able to exercise what we are fooled into thinking as freedom?

IN WARSAW, KRAJEWSKI INVITES US to a grand party at one of his actor friend's' dacha somewhere on the other side of the Vistula. Ruth, of course, is going whether I do or not, so Krajewski drives us both in his little Polonaise, a tinny Fiat manufactured for the Polish market, darting insanely in and out of traffic. We speed out of the city, on the way, it seems, to nowhere. There are no signs, no lights, no shoulders at the edges. We are in no man's land, a closely guarded secret, unmapped and unmarked.

"Lupek owns several restaurants in and out of Warsaw," Krajewski says, "a gift from the government for winning a couple of Olympic gold medals in boxing. If there is no duck to be had in all Poland," Kostek says, "you can always find duck at Lupek's Metropole."

At a seemingly arbitrary point, Krajewski swerves off the main road, bouncing from the asphalt into dirt.

"Lupek is also a good actor," Kostek says, all our teeth now rattling. "He played the prison guard in *Waves on the Water.*"

Without transition, we are in the country. The car lists from side to side. A few random poplars mark the sides of the road. We turn into a clearing and stop abruptly. Dozens of other cars have stopped before us, looking as if they have been abandoned in an air raid. Cheerfully, Krajewski leads the way through a break in a stone fence. In front of us stands a Polish version of all sleazy bungalows everywhere, this one, according to Krajewski, "in the California style."

Lupek Bikont is taking a leak from the second story deck. When he notices us, he greets us with spirals of pee like strands of beads. "Kostek, Kostek," he bellows, "and who is with you? The great artist and his beautiful wife? What a fortune."

He zips up his fly and slides down the bannister from the deck to the ground. In spite of the cold, he is in shirtsleeves and sweating. After lifting Krajewski off the ground in a bear hug, he falls towards Ruth and kisses her hands. He slaps my back.

"We love Americans," he says.

Inside, Krajewski pulls us toward the bar, threading our way past sweaty actors, cameramen, directors, and hangers-on. Melancholy drinkers stand three-deep at the kitchen counter. Glasses full of vodka are passed back over the crowd's heads. Two elderly women work feverishly to refill empties. Everyone's head turns to Ruth, her beauty shining a light before her, like Grace Kelly entering a pig sty. She disappears into the crowd. Everyone is tripping over an old decorated general who has slipped to the floor. From there, he is singing fragments of the national anthem.

"One of our Dostoevsky characters," a bearded young man explains.

Someone then claims the general as a true Pole, a historic Pole. I catch a glimpse of Ruth, a glass of vodka in one hand, dancing happily with one man, then another. I fear that here, in this drunken place where she knows no one except Krajewski, the hero of the pack, she can give herself permission to run wild. Dance music is booming from two imposing speakers. Though people are milling around me, I spot Ruth and Krajewski from time to time. Out of nowhere, Ruth appears at my side.

"I'm having such a good time," she says and vanishes again.

As I lean against a wall sipping my vodka, the scene becomes dreamlike, a time out of time, a place unlike any I know, the sound coming at me in waves, sometimes a roar, then a hum, a weird dissonant music. During the next half-hour which blurs with drink and anxiety, Ruth comes in and out of view, suddenly at my side, wrapping her arms around me, then disappearing again. Inside this nightmare bungalow in Poland full of drunken strangers, I want to grab my sexually aroused unleashed wife and throw her over the railing of the deck. Jostled this way and that by inexplicable surges of the crowd, a bald, wrinkled cameraman named Stanislaw Kaper comes over to introduce himself.

"These things," Kaper says in English, referring, I think, to the many discrete groupings inside this dacha, "provide us with very good material."

He pours more vodka down his throat.

"We are at our best with ultimate things," he says.

I have no idea what he's talking about, but the weirdness of his intrusion doesn't strike me as especially strange. His dull, gray eyes telegraph that he has seen it all and is past caring about rationality.

"Here it is always simple and clear," a young man in jeans says, "always terrible." They all seem to speak a fairly comprehensible English.

"What is clear?" Kaper asks. "We start as Catholic moralists, change to Communist moralists, then dissident moralists. God willing, we will one day be free market moralists, all in one lifetime. This is clear?"

I am beginning to reel. Everyone is yelling back and forth just to be heard. All of our drinks are spilling, as if we were plowing through stormy seas. In fact, the bungalow is swaying. Stilts are involved in holding up the second floor and surely they are bending and buckling. But I am among survivors, drunk out of their minds, but strong and resolute, endowed with Polish fortitude.

"Enough heroism, let someone else do it for a while," a portly gentleman in a suit and tie says.

He adds that his needs are well satisfied with good vodka, a little pig, and herring.

"I need to fuck my wife every day, and once in a while," he says, poking the man next to him in the ribs, "to fuck yours, Lolek."

"You are a Jew?" Kaper asks me.

Why would I not be expecting this?

"Of course he is. Is Mendelssohn not a Jew's name?"

"But the composer Mendelssohn converted," someone says.

The matter is becoming ever more complicated.

"They say you speak Polish," Kaper says, hiccuping.

"I am a Jew and I speak Polish badly," I say with an appropriate smile.

Mock yourself a little, Mendelssohn, and the situation will lighten up.

"You speak very well, very well. You are born here?" Kaper asks.

"Before the war," I tell him. "I have not been back since we left."

"Only the richest Jews left. The rest were looked after here."

"Looked after?" I ask.

"Like Lupek, like Krajewski, I have Poland in my blood," Kaper says.

"Yes?"

We are entering dangerous territory. My body stiffens. I want to tell him that, unfortunately, I am stuck with a drop or two of Polish blood and that I would gladly rid myself of it completely. All eyes are focused on me. I am now the entire show.

"Inside me is a soup of Polish and Jewish blood. It is good to have a blend."

I try to smile, but no one is smiling.

"You have a real Pole in your ancestors? Mixed blood? And so you are a real Pole too?" Kaper asks and closes his eyes, looking as if he is silently fighting a bad dream. "You have Poland in your blood?"

"Stash," someone says, taking Kaper's arm, "let us go out on the balcony."

Kaper shakes the man off.

"I am going out for some air, Stash," the man says, pulling gently at Kaper's sleeve.

"Why do Jews hate the Poles?" someone asks. "The war was not our fault. We didn't do it, the Germans did it."

A sweaty, bald man in a checkered sport jacket says:

"Tell your friends, please; we are not guilty."

"All right," I say, knowing that we haven't hit rock bottom yet.

In a sweet, didactic voice someone says, "The house it is ours. But we lived in it together with Jews. When the Germans came, they killed Poles and they killed Jews. We are guilty only because we mourn more for our own kind than your kind."

I now try to push my way out of there, but Kaper, zombie-like, blocks my way.

"I think Poland is not in your blood," he says. "Poland is not in the blood of Jews. Poland is only in the blood of Poles."

I am sweating profusely. I look carefully at my tormentor: a thin, rather frail-looking man whose collar is loose around his scrawny neck. My Jewish blood is beginning to boil and I know I cannot contain myself much longer.

"You don't like Jews, Kaper? You think we brought it all on ourselves? You think we deserved to be slaughtered?"

I grab him by the collar.

"Tell me what you think, Kaper."

I am choking the son of a bitch and Kaper rasps. For the briefest moment, I think of my father being beaten by fellow students at the Jagiellonian University.

"Tell me, Kaper. Can't you talk?"

Arms grab me from all sides. I hit Kaper so hard that blood spurts from his face. His knees buckle and he falls at my feet. I kick him, roll him over, then sit on him, smacking his face to the left, then the right.

"I am a Jew knocking the shit out of you, Kaper."

The feeling is delicious. I have never been opposed to a little violence, but none has provided the equal of this rush, as if my lifelong anger and predisposition to unseemly battles led to this moment, the grand relief, the orgasm for all time. I would kill Kaper if many arms didn't pull me off him. I stand over him to remind him and everyone standing there that I am a Jew beating the shit out of a Pole. I am breathing hard.

Poland is making me more Jewish than I have ever been.

"You're a fighter," Lupek says as, in a boxer's crouch with fists rotating about his face, he shuffles over to see the last of the fray. Someone drags Kaper by his feet to get him out of the room. The place becomes eerily quiet. Lupek, the boxer, could throw me over the railing of his deck if he wanted to, but, instead, he puts his hands on my shoulders and says,

"We haven't seen a good beating for a while."

"Kaper is from the old school," someone says. "He is a famous drunk."

All my life, I felt entitled to act out on behalf of my father who probably never put his body on the line, to hit for him, to fuck women in his name. My hands and wrists hurting, my knuckles bleeding, I want this to be the last time I act on his behalf. This immense satisfaction cleans the slate. Each of us is now on our own. I sit down on a couch in a room where people are dancing. My knuckles and wrists are on fire. A very pretty lady who had taken her blouse off asks me to dance. On the dance floor, the woman, Dora, is not the only one who has partially stripped. Probably this too is another aspect of Polish rebelliousness. My knuckles are bleeding. I am wet from sweat and vodka. I unbutton my shirt so I can feel Dora's breasts on my skin. She pulls my hand into her mouth and sucks the bloody fingers, one by one.

Lupek's dacha empties a little since "the beating." The music, too, is softer, lilting, a gentle Artie Shaw tune. Suddenly, as in a circus, a couple of whores storm into the house.

"Ordered by Lupek," Dora whispers, "like pizza."

Loud and brash and not very attractive, the whores throw their coats off, exposing large breasts and cleavage, and are surrounded by men. They negotiate briefly, then one of them pairs off with a director in his sixties and the second whore with some other movie world dignitary. Up the stairs they rush where, I fear, my wife is probably fucking

Krajewski. Even though I am despondent about what I imagine is the upstairs scene, Dora is pawing me pleasantly. I extricate myself to face the bedroom events and, half-way up, I pound the wall, hurting my hands again. I keep pounding.

"Fuck you, Ruth," I yell, but instead of knocking the doors down, I walk down the stairs.

I either kill them both or work at letting it go so I can get on with my life. I go out onto the deck where the air is fresh and cold. It feels like snow.

Early in the morning, when the house is quiet, worn out, and every one of the upstairs revelers hardly able to stand up, I drive Krajewski's Polonaise back towards Warsaw. Ruth, up front with me, is seriously hung over, as is Krajewski in the back seat. I am not in great shape either.

"So what did you and your boyfriend do all night?"

"Not all night," she says, half asleep.

"You fucked all night," I say and urge Krajewski's little Polish car forward through accumulating snow.

We skid but move on. Nobody stirs.

"Poor Kostek has a terrible headache," she slurs.

"I'm so sorry to hear that. You nursed him back to health?"

"I helped with the suppository."

"Suppository? Up his ass? You pushed it up his ass?"

"He needed help."

"Are you telling me that he couldn't find his own asshole?" She squirms in the seat and I swing my forearm into her face. I never imagined that I could hit her. She is sobbing and her nose is bleeding.

"Both of us had terrible headaches," she says through her tears.

"Aha! So, each of you shoved suppositories up each other's ass."

Krajewski is snoring in the back seat and I am ready to stop the car and beat the shit out of the drunk lover of my drunk wife. I pull over, still a mile or two before the Vistula bridge, pull the son of a bitch out of the back seat, and whack him so hard that he crumbles like a dying animal onto the accumulating snow at the side of the road. I gun the stupid little Polish Fiat and the tires sing their plaintive get-me-out-of-here song. The snow stops, but a couple of inches have already fallen. I cross the river and drive slowly through the city. There is a surprising number of cars, probably going to work, most of them skidding.

"Why don't you stay here? I've had enough of you."

She is in tears, wailing for her Kostek and now looks shocked.

"Stay here?"

"See if there's a place for Miss Oklahoma in Warsaw."

She says nothing.

"Get out."

She doesn't, sobs for a while, then calms down and dries her tears. Her face, which had been burning from the evening's activity, is drained of color.

"I am so ashamed," she says. "It's not like me. "

"Not like you? It is you."

Ruth manages to defend herself.

"What about all the women you've been with? Infidelity keeps us alive."

I park Krajewski's Polonaise a few blocks from the Europejski and leave the motor running. Ruth tries to get back to turn it off and I pull her away from the door handle. If this Communism shit works, someone will get back to Krajewski about the location of his car, provided he is still alive. I drag Ruth away and she straggles behind me back to the hotel.

11.

THE FACT THAT THE MAN SITTING across from me in the Oak Room of the Plaza Hotel is not Krajewski or Bolynski or Kaper is reason enough for celebration. I want a rest from the Polish question, the Jewish question, the dilemma of marriage, the problems of art and reality. But now, sitting with my Scotch, I am scarfing up the peanuts as if I had been in Poland for years, not weeks.

Petros Protopapas, once my Art Students' League nemesis, now in his late fifties, has, over the years, become a friend and drinking buddy. We meet at art openings as well as jazz clubs. In the Oak Room, surrounded by serious men in three-piece suits and silk-clad women, Petros and I are talking about doing our private art while continuing our known and lucrative signature work, my large monuments of angst and Protopapas's inscrutable symbols. Petros has already spent several years working at the simpler world of etching and engraving, created with patience in stages, its methodology glorified by old tools, acids, resins, metal plates, rollers, and presses.

"The process," Protopapas says over our second Johnny Walker Black, "is quiet and private."

"I love the idea," I say. "I, too, feel a need for smallness."

"What's with us, Mendelssohn?" Protopapas asks, slapping a handful of peanuts into his mouth. "Are we getting wise in our old age or jumpy and bored and dissatisfied with everything?"

"As for me," I say, "I no longer need to shriek for attention or interpretation." Protopapas, whose belly has grown quite large over the years, orders a plate of hors d'oeuvres.

"I'm ready to take up the inks and charcoal," I tell him, "cook up a private art, work with small strokes, carefully, not wantonly. I want to put a loupe in one eye like a watchmaker."

I finger my precious watch, always in my pocket.

"For a long time, I've been thinking of illustrating Odysseus' journey from Troy to Ithaca. I love the tale of a man who, through many trials, was hell-bent on going home. My homes have been anything but ancestral," I say. "What to call them? Manufactured, rented, occupied. Maybe the journey home is an illusion, an unfulfillable obsession. It's back to the womb, Mom's warm and caring lap, the kitchen with bread baking, the story books read aloud, the attic trunks filled with photographs, none of it a part of my life. And think of Odysseus's women, Petros, women like Athena who made sure he was safe, then Circe, the Sirens, Nausicaa and, best of all, Calypso who, for seven years, knew how to satisfy this long-suffering Greek with food and drink and sex, lots of sex. "

"Maybe only wandering Jews know that the boundaries of home, not just the self, is one's skin," Protopapas says.

"It's like Ruth said. Perhaps shlepping one's ass from place to place, not owning any of it, not yearning to own any of it, being a refugee, defines freedom."

At home, sitting at a drafting table rather than in front of my easel, I fill sketchbooks with Odysseus's temptresses, in their comely little huts and caves, by the river gamboling about with playmates, as well as Odysseus's shipwrecks, misfortune after misfortune. In place of the Laestrygonians, instead of Scylla, monster of the ocean caves, and Charybdis, the whirlpool, I also begin to substitute leveled Warsaw, the ditches along the road to Lithuania, the hideous face of the dead man in a brown three-piece suit, the faces of the German pilots, the hatred on the faces of Jew-hating Polish soldiers, even poor Zyga, face contorted by grief, moaning by the radio.

Since our arrival back in New York, Ruth's skin has become blotchy, her hands cold, her eyes dull. We hardly talk. I see little of her. She spends time with friends, often comes home drunk and collapses into bed. Drinking, once just a way to get blotto, a way of forgetting or soothing herself, has become a political act, endorsing her native American roots—shabby as they have turned out to be.

"You look like you're getting sick, Ruth," I tell her.

"I'll be alright," she says.

"Where have you been?"

"At the library."

"What are you doing these days at the library?"

"I am reading about American Indians, about the shoot-outs at Wounded Knee and Pine Ridge, the transcripts of the Leonard Peltier trial."

"Why do you stink of liquor?"

"I stopped in to see Wendy."

"Who is Wendy?"

"Wendy knows all about Nicaragua."

Zyga comes as often as he can to visit. He seems altogether comfortable with each of us. When Ruth is present, I speak differently than when she's not. When she's absent, I ask him about Pilsudski.

"Pilsudski? I met Pilsudski. He is just another Pole, but, when it suits him, he is good to the Jews."

"Ruth told me a complicated story about you in Pilsudski's cavalry, at the battle on the Vistula."

Zyga smiles. "Ruth makes stories," he says quietly. "Don't worry. She is not crazy. It is charming. She wants me to be a hero."

"Not one bit of her story is true then?"

"I am not a hero," Zyga says.

"She does need heroes," I say, but stop short, offering nothing about Krajewski.

"Do you run into that film maker, what is his name?"

"Krajewski," I tell him. "We saw him from time to time. But let me tell you about Tauber."

"You fly to Berlin to see Tauber?" he asks.

"He remembers you very well, mostly gossip, gossip about you and all the others."

"Yes, Tauber and I are foolish together when we enjoy wrestling and boxing."

"He remembers how very depressed you sometimes were."

"And who is not?" Zyga wants to know.

"He also said that Bolek had a child, maybe more than one."

"Yes, I think so," my father says, "but this is his business. I never think Bolek is a very nice man."

Fixing the discord between his Mishek and his Ruth becomes Zyga's mission so, after he and I finish a couple of sandwiches I make for our lunch and Ruth comes out of the bedroom bleary-eyed, he greets her with open arms. She is wearing her pink terrycloth bathrobe given to her when she was in her teens by her uncle Albert. She takes a couple of aspirin out of her bathrobe pocket, washes them down with a glass of tonic water, then falls happily into his arms.

"So what do you think about our Poland?" my father asks her.

"Ruth loves oppression," I pipe in before she can answer.

"Stop it, Michael," she says.

"Jews, Poles, English kings, and now this. Next it will be Angola or East Timor or some other damn place."

She talks of Polish bravery, of the rebellious arts.

"Ruth's friends think that holocausts make people crazy," I blab like a vengeful kid.

"What?" asks Zyga.

"They mean that Poles can't be responsible for their actions in the middle of chaos," Ruth explains.

Zyga looks puzzled.

"They excuse the soldiers who spat on our car because Jews represent dirty money," I say.

"What soldiers spat on our car?" Ruth wants to know.

"Before your time," I tell her.

"The soldiers are walking past us toward the border crossing," Zyga explains, then produces his analysis. "Why are they not angry with all the rich people who get out? There are many more rich Poles than rich Jews. Why not class hatred rather than Jew hatred?"

Since our unhappy departure from Poland, apart from our bruised egos and entitlements, Ruth and I have nearly come to blows not only about our infidelities but about art's formation. Depending on our moods, art is cooked in a mind that is quiescent or turbulent. It thrives either in a society whose fridge is empty or full. There are moments when, like Ruth, I am smitten with the grandness of art as necessity, art with a function other than commodity or a self-referential game or, like French art, exhausted.

She then tells Zyga that she has been reading about her roots.

"Mine, not his," she says. "I never paid much attention to North American colonialism," Ruth explains to Zyga. "The stories and myths were appealing, but I never thought of them as mine. Now I know that they are."

"This gives you a lot of energy," Zyga says.

"It will," Ruth tells him, "when the depression loosens its grip."

"She won't take her depression medication," I say, snitching on the bad girl.

"Oh shut up, Michael."

"Unless it's a suppository delivered up the ass," I murmur, sotto voce.

"Why not to take medication?" Zyga asks.

"I'm strong enough to get through this without drugs," she says. "Depression takes its place with all of our vulnerabilities and weaknesses."

I wonder if Zyga was medicated in the Zopot sanitarium. I have no idea what medications existed then.

"Depression is a part of human complexity," Ruth says. "Knowing yourself is always revealing. 'Take notes,' wrote Virginia Woolf, 'and the pain goes away.'"

I used to beg her to be more concerned about the vile actions of McNamara and Rusk, then Kissinger and Nixon, rather than the events of 1485, and now she begins to concentrate entirely on the injustices of the day, reading the alternative press, corresponding with people engaged in similar thinking. As she gains strength, she becomes passionately critical of the Reagan presidency.

"The Guatemalan oligarchy has begun their genocidal project against the Mayan population," Ruth tells me. "And who stirred it all up? Reagan."

She hears of a sect of Christian evangelists who are sending people to Nicaragua to help in the struggle.

"People down there are being murdered and the Christians are trying to help save them."

"Ruth, they're missionaries. Missionaries are dangerous."

Having made contact with the Moravian sect in the mid-west, Ruth is getting ready to join them to save Central America, and in early spring of 1981, she flies with the missionaries to the Miskitu territories in northeastern Nicaragua.

Ruth is somewhere in Central America in December, when martial law is declared in Poland.

"Really?" my pal Radetzky says when I report the startling news.

He is not overly concerned about Poland, even though his own roots go back to some stetl near the Ukrainian border.

"I heard it on the radio this morning," I tell him.

"What does that mean exactly?"

"In an attempt to crush political opposition, thousands of activists are being imprisoned without charge and more than a hundred people killed. The bits of permissiveness Ruth and I witnessed is over. Krajewski is probably in jail, Bolynski incarcerated in some parish priest's dungeon, Kaper appointed to the secret police. A whole new cadre of martyrs are now leaving their dingy rooms to man the barricades, an ideal time for a visit from Ruth, Miss Liberty leading the people, a musket in one hand, the tri-color in the other."

Usually, when alone these days, I begin to enjoy my solitude, liking the image of myself as the middle-aged proprietor, the caretaker, the host, the cook, the captain of my ship. I equip the loft with an etching press, the supposed facsimile of Goya's, and I take to etching as avidly as a child to finger painting, concocting like a cook lines and shades of varying qualities, playing with the resins and acids, with aquatints, the burins and burnishers, the important images of my and Odysseus's journeys making pastiches of his delights and my horrors. I continue drawing with charcoal, inks and graphite. My large canvases are changing as well, their aim no longer tragic, not even entirely serious. A broad swath of a color, say the rough, imperfect ochre in "Bacchus," splotched with small drippings of umber, takes up almost half of a large canvas in which the ponderous blacks move to one side, no longer the cry of anguish but a reminder that the tragic has not altogether disappeared.

Occasionally, I drive up to our Hillsdale cottage to walk in the nearby woods or lie quietly in a hammock I have recently set up behind the house. Next to the cottage is a small horse barn where I store my 1960 Hillman Minx. The interior of our little bungalow is largely unfurnished and I sleep on a futon, eat meals at a little metal table on the grass in back. When Ruth returns exhausted from wherever in Central America or the North American southwest she has been, she drives to our shabby country estate, sometimes for weeks at a time.

This early fall, six years after our return from Poland, she comes back looking like shit. She has lost too much weight, bites her lip and grinds her teeth. She and I avoid each other, I concentrating on my drawing and etching, she sleeping. On a crisp September morning, I get up very early and walk to the horse barn. Over the past couple of years, I taught myself a bit about the Hillman's entrails. The little car is now more than twenty years old. Never having been one of those boys who loved soldering the insides of amplifiers or rebuilding car engines, not even knowing what makes televisions or telephones tick, I often hoped that, one day, I will wake up to discover that all the new technologies are a bad dream, that life will untangle itself and become comprehensible again. In the meantime, my city fingers inside fuel lines, carburetors, and transmissions are meddling with my state of ignorance and grace. Thus I learn to replace or clean or file pieces of the Hillman and rebuild others. Keeping it up to snuff, learning to build new parts, to substitute filed down facsimiles, to re-wire, to re-tool, has become a welcome pleasure. Sitting on an old hay bale, I study catalogues and manuals. I communicate with a few Hillman lovers in different parts of the country and, though we never meet for fear of breakdowns, we exchange plans and diagrams and methods of using parts of Yugoslav or Korean cars, imports of Anglia or Sunbeam-Talbot fuel systems, Vauxhall carburetors or Lucas ignitions.

After a couple of hours of car play, with the fuel line well tightened and operative, the no longer fleet little Minx is ready to roll. I dawdle in front of the house, stare at a flock of birds picking orange berries from a mountain ash, then walk into the house, the badly patched screen door slamming behind me. I take a Genoa salami out of the ancient fridge and make myself a sandwich.

"You want a sandwich?" I yell to her.

"No."

Resentment, like a virus, infects us both. When she is here or in New York, we talk a little between our first drink and the one that knocks us out. We rarely have sex and if we do, it's desultory and unsatisfying.

"You've got to eat something," I say, but she doesn't answer.

I go out back and sit at the white metal table where I munch my salami with a slice of cheddar on a baguette brought up from the city. I suspect that Ruth has a better chance of changing the world than I—anger and angst a poor substitute for distributing food and drugs to those who have neither. Still, success in altering perception from moral turpitude and ethical blindness is not exactly nothing, I tell myself. In fact, I respect both our paths even though the differences between us are beginning to destroy us. It used to be otherwise. Those differences once filled us with wonder and admiration, but no more. Impermanence rears its ugly head.

Ruth has made friends with a widow named Olga Cleary, a woman who teaches environmental studies in a community college nearby. Olga is tall and grim, with long gray hair. She and Ruth met at a farmers' market and now, whenever Ruth comes to Hillsdale, they go on excursions to catalogue the flora and fauna, explore the wetlands, brooks and streams, bogs and swamps.

"In the forest," Ruth mentions today, a relatively pleasant day because we are talking, "we catalogue the wanderings of white-tailed deer, beavers, black bear, gray foxes, and red squirrel."

I picture Cherokee Ruth walking through the tangle of green things as silently as in the movies, leaving no scent or sound or footprint behind.

"How are you at killing meat?" I ask peevishly. "I need protein," I say, earning both of their enmity.

When Olga leaves, I walk across the dirt road into a field which, during the few years of our ownership of this little plot of land, has reminded me of the field in Wieliszew: the bombs, the bicycle. I walk tentatively into the rough terrain of the unplanted acreage, sit on a patch of grass. What could have passed through my eight-year-old mind? At moments such as those, there is no room in one's body or brain for anything but terror, a glimpse of the end of the world. This field, that field, scrubby, dreary, uncared for. Here the sky is quiet except for the drone of a harmless airplane approaching the city. Then, too, it was quiet except for distant thunder and my laughter, until the three planes appeared and droned over the treetops. Until that moment, I knew only safety, the uncaring certainty of changelessness, predictability. Within seconds, all certainty collapsed. Anointed by fire, by unknown forces, forces that ruled then and, I now know, will rule it always, I inhabit the world of uncertainty and change. Now, I put my hands on my thighs, the same thighs as the eight-year-old's, though the skin is new, the muscles and bones as well. And yet, every cell in this body retains the memory of forty-some years ago. I hear the voice of the German pilot inside the Junker talking to the German man sitting next to him. "Let's kill that little boy, Dietrich, eh?" "Waste the only bomb we have?" He looks down. "Ach, he looks so happy, so vy not?" says Heinz and they both laugh and I am anointed, touched by fire. In that field, I was as alone as I would ever be, my world shaken to the core. And now, I am about to be alone again.

Later that day, in our forlorn living room, half of its floorboards rotted out, Ruth says, "You never did understand that I have a life of my own. None of this is about you. It's about me."

I shoot up from my rickety chair and it falls behind me. I punch the wall which threatens to break apart. "Take a deep breath, Mendelssohn," I chide, exhaling. "Yes, it's about you. Your shit is about you, mine about me. There used to be stuff that concerned us both, but those days are over, Ruth."

I follow her into the bathroom and watch her wash her face, never bothering to look in the mirror. She brushes her teeth, abraded by constant grinding and denuded of enamel, no longer capable of eating an apple without pain. She winces from the cold water rinse.

"I'm going back to the city," I tell her.

"I'll have no car," she says.

"You'll have the Saab."

I grab a pair of khakis and a black turtleneck from a shelf.

"You're taking the Hillman?" She laughs.

The Hillman starts after some coaxing from a neighbor's starter cables. I back out of the barn, scraping the little car's bottom. In a nearby village, I stop at a general store to pick up a paper and a cup of coffee to go. I drive the back roads, pass under scraggly pines, houses with their paint peeling, broken-down farm machinery, ugly dogs barking and pulling on their chains. Carpenters pound away, finishing jobs before the big freeze sets in.

Neither of us really cares that much about the Hillsdale cottage, though I am beginning to love the country sights and sounds, the hammers and chain saws, the wind in the trees, a whiff of lilacs, of apple trees in spring, the pine resins. I sip my coffee, then fish around in the glove compartment for a mint. The sky is a deep blue, the fields all shades of ochres and siennas. As I drive through this peaceful country-side, the fate of my city studio, the whole loft, suddenly feels vulnerable to our imminent separation. I will never give up the studio. I guess I will if it's absolutely necessary. I console myself by suspecting that Ruth is not and has never been the vengeful woman who would try to pry stuff from me. I pull the car over to the side and think of the studio's finely crafted racks and shelves, drawers that slide open with a finger's pull, heavy easels. Ruth had arranged for our beautiful loft's blankets to be made by skillful weavers, rugs hooked and quilts sewn by hippie women, cabinets cut from cherry trees and expertly crafted, their hinges and knobs pounded on an anvil by the young son of a friend, the kitchen counters tiled in creamy white by an accomplished potter. If it comes to that, I have no idea how we divide the goods. It's a scary thought. On one wall of the loft, hangs a large, nearly all black canvas, *Ithaca*. I love this painting. Its three heavy oval impasto shapes are surrounded by a hint of white, the painting itself one of the very first of this great size and meaning. I never put it up for sale.

The sun is buried in the trees and a breeze cools me off. Fleeing the traps of family, I am thinking, running from marriage, a fixed place, becoming untethered from carpets and woodwork, must have its own rewards. I take a leak beside a bush turned red. A buck and doe run across the road not far from where I'm standing. I note it, but my country pleasures center on its peace and quiet, not its flora and fauna. Whether here or in the city, I am in favor of the outside staying outside, not encroaching on interiors. Interiors belong inside walls, paintings belong inside frames. I jump back across the ditch and into the Hillman. Of the two orange arrows, only one works. I light a cigarette, which I rarely do any more.

What was it like for Zyga, Rena, and Bolek? My loft and cottage have been mine for a matter of years, theirs for generations. What a brave decision they made when so many others stayed behind. Zyga said that they tried to convince the whole family to leave, but they didn't want to give up their houses, their friends, their possessions. And so, Zyga said goodbye to his parents, beloved brothers and sisters, cousins galore, not to speak of Bolek's giving up his commodious modern apartment, his house in Wieliszew. Surely, he was in love with the damask drapes and large windows that looked down to the Vistula. What about the Wedgewood dinnerware, the Scandinavian furniture, the rows of immaculately tailored suits from Saville Row in his walk-in closet? Each of them must have dreamed of a favorite chair or headboard or carpet left behind; my portrait, age six; the ancient grandfather clock in the dining room. In their middle age, with no language or knowledge of their new home, they performed the improbable, creating a new life. In my own mid-life, I will try to find a comparable ingenuity and courage. Maybe that, too, is hereditary.

12.

Still a few miles from the city, I fill the Hillman's gas tank. And now the old junk heap won't start. I hear Hillman parts hitting the pavement under me. Water gurgles and steams from under the hood. Dejected, I sit behind the steering wheel, ready to cry or beat the shit out of this tin box.

"What a history we've had, you fuckhead car," I tell it, my eyes closed. "Breath by breath, Mendelssohn. Loss by loss—self-inflicted or not."

The garage mechanic is at the window.

"You okay?" he asks.

I open my eyes and look straight ahead.

"Want to buy a car?"

"You better get out before the damn thing explodes," he says and after the Hillman entrails stop peppering the ground, stop growling and sputtering, the guy tells me that it's not worth fixing.

"Dead as a door nail," he says, holding back a smile—the same smile that has greeted this car since its first trip across the country.

He then pulls his wallet from his back pocket and waves a bill in front of my face.

"I'll give you twenty bucks for it," he says.

I consider for the briefest of moments.

"It's a deal," I tell him and grab the twenty from his hand.

"It's called unburdening, releasing the chains that bind you," I tell myself on the train to the city.

From Grand Central, I call my father. We meet in a coffee shop on Lexington Avenue.

"Ruth and I have been heading toward this for a long time," I tell him. "It is the right thing to do, but it hurts nevertheless. I don't even think that it's either of our faults, just the end of something which has become all wrong."

My hand shakes as I lift the coffee cup to my lips. Zyga reaches across the small table to put his hands on mine.

"This is the most terrible news," he says. "But there is time, no?"

"I don't think so. And yet you never know."

Zyga takes out his handkerchief and wipes his eyes. He says nothing for a while, then,

"Here is an idea, Mishek. Let us go away together for a few days."

"You and me? That sounds wonderful. Where would you like to go?"

"Long Beach," my father says and, a couple of days later, we take a train to Long Island.

When I was thirteen and the war was coming to its end, Rena hired one of the fast growing Mandeleau Furs fourth floor workers to drive me, and sometimes them, to a couple of rooms they rented for a respite from the city's summer heat. The house was owned by Leo Stillman, a local banker and his Polish wife Jadwiga, who had worked for them at Mandelbaum's in Warsaw. Rena and Zyga showed up some weekends, Rena entirely out of place in an enclave of old socialists and union activists. My first year there, I learned to smoke cigarettes from a cross-eyed girlfriend named Lenore and gravitated toward a group of bad boys. We vandalized cars, stole from mom and pop stores, and drank cheap whiskey while listening to Frank Sinatra records, sometimes copping a feel of the edge of a bra strap, even the fabulous, unexpected edge of a breast. The one thing Rena and Zyga agreed upon at the time was the importance of fresh air, mountain air or blowing in from a sea. But Long Beach sea smells were not that pleasant, not the salty freshness that might have been expected from the vastness of the ocean, but rather smelling of rotting fish, sea weed, and the garbage which collected in heaps under the boardwalk.

"If the Hotel Lieber is still there, that's where we will stay," Zyga now says in the taxi.

The hotel is there, a block from the beach, probably not as run down as it was at war's end, but it remains shabby enough to suit my father's taste. A few elderly people sit on the front porch facing east, though the beach itself is partially hidden by the houses on the other side of Willow Street. Zyga bows politely toward each pair of eyes that turn to inspect the newcomers.

"I come here so long ago," he says, "to play checkers on this porch."

An old woman checks us in.

"Madame Lieber?" Zyga asks. "I am Mendelssohn from a long time ago."

She looks at him. "Time is not our friend," she says.

"And Mr. Lieber? He is here?" She picks up the phone and dials. "Come to the front," she says. "Nothing goes wrong but an old customer is here." In a few minutes Lieber, clutching a walker, pokes his way through a door behind the desk. He is a little shaky, but his face looks fleshy and pink.

Zyga says, "Mr. Lieber, I am Mendelssohn. You cannot remember. It is long ago."

The old man's face lights up and tears come to his eyes. "Remember? Who can forget?"

He leaves the walker behind the desk and shuffles toward Zyga, who opens his arms. Tears now pour down both men's cheeks. Zyga holds Lieber up and I move behind them in case they tilt backwards.

"Dear Mendelssohn," Lieber says, "do you remember the hurricane? What was the year? During the war still. You stayed a week and we boarded up the windows. You and me, no?"

I am amazed that even then, when I was a pre-teen then a teenager, and wanted nothing to do with my depressed and disdained father, he had a life. He had friends. He played checkers; he boarded up windows in a hurricane. What adventures! Zyga is now stroking Lieber's back.

"What a wind it was," Zyga says.

They stand clutching each other for a long time without speaking.

"And this is my son," Zyga says.

Lieber looks me up and down. "He is so big, so strong," Lieber says. "Why this should be that our children are so big? My Munia we never see. She lives in Hawaii. How far can she go? If America owned as far as China, she would live in China. And big? She is big like a Hawaiian queen."

Old, tired Mrs. Lieber comes out from behind the desk.

"Go take a little rest in your room," she says, "and I will make coffee. The help they are away in the afternoon."

I mistrust the ancient elevator, so Zyga joins me on the staircase. I walk ahead with our suitcases and on the second landing, out of breath, Zyga stops to rest. I put the suitcases down.

"Are you all right?"

He nods.

"Let me buzz for the elevator."

He does not want help and we walk up one more flight to our room. Inside the door, still a little out of breath, Zyga puts his hands on my shoulders, then pulls my face down to kiss it. I put my arms around him and we stand holding each other.

From the open windows the scent of sea weed blows in. Sea gulls squawk a block away. I sit down on the bed and watch as my father lies down and inhales deeply, his hands on his belly. I am thinking that my mother feels at home wrapped in blankets on the terrace of the Palace Hotel in Montreux; Bolek and Ursula sit under a colorful umbrella lakeside at Villa d'Este. Zyga is at his best at the Lieber Hotel in Long Beach.

"I am not like the others," my father says to me after a short nap. "I don't know why, but I am comfortable in places like this." He wrinkles his nose. "Fancy places are not for me."

As for me, I vacillate between the two, think that I belong in both. In the bathroom, Zyga wipes the sink clean with a wet end of a towel, then closes the bathroom door. The bedroom floorboards show signs of many weather changes, some edges turned up as if by frost heaves, all the floor varnish scuffed and peeling with years of sand and shuffling. The curtains are musty, even though blown by decades of sea breezes. One has to have a broad-minded view of neglect not to be offended by spider webs, discolored porcelain sink and bathtub, acrid smells.

We meet the Liebers in the hotel's small dining room. Mrs. Lieber brings hard rolls, butter, marmalade, and coffee. The plates and cups are thick, chipped restaurant ware. The coffee is instant, and though I can't, Zyga drinks it as if it were an Automat brew.

"Business is good?" Zyga asks.

"The only thing good is we sell the hotel."

"And where will you go?" I ask, smitten with premature nostalgia.

I wonder where indeed they will go, where will the old Unionists go, and the unrepentant socialist refugees, even the Social Democrats like Zyga?

"They buy the whole block," Mr. Lieber says. "They take down everything and make very big apartment houses. Soon there will be nothing left of long ago."

"If Munia likes it or not," Mrs. Lieber says, "we go to Hawaii for the rest of our days."

"I am happy we are here before you go away," Zyga says.

Zyga and I finish our snack and walk toward the beach, then up to the boardwalk, busy now with cyclists and strollers, the sleaziness of thirty years before replaced by condos and smart apartment houses with balconies. We sit down on a bench facing the water.

"Do you see that boat?" Zyga asks.

We both look at the slow moving freighter almost at the horizon line.

"Do you remember the big ships in Gdynia? You always liked the sea. You liked to play alone and talk to yourself. You were your own best friend."

"Wasn"t I lonely?"

"Always smiling," he says, "always nice to everyone, always well-behaved." He turns away from the boat to look at me. "I think you were very happy alone."

"Now I am learning to be peaceful alone all over again."

Zyga takes my hand and I put my other hand on top of his. Feeling the torn cuticles, the hanging, prickly skin, I want to protect these wounds from further damage. I stroke them gently. "There is so much I want to ask you. All my life, I have wanted to learn what really happened inside our Citronka."

My father's face turns toward the horizon again.

"I want to know about Emilia and her mother, Uncle Lolek and Aunt Eva."

"Lolek and Eva live in Brazil."

"You are hiding things from me," I tell him and watch his lips and brows pucker into a worried expression.

"Emilia and Helena disappeared," he says. "I write to Sweden during the war, but the government knows nothing."

"You don't even know if they are alive?"

"No," he says with a finality that makes me shiver.

"Did you cross into Lithuania ahead of us?"

I stop, take a big gulp of air.

"It is a terrible time," my father says, his gaze still elsewhere. "Something very bad happens at the border."

"Yes?"

I wait for more, fearing what is to come.

"Mishek, I cannot talk about it, it is too painful. I try to be sure they permit us to go and then there is only trouble, very bad trouble."

I want to yell at him. "Answer me!" I want to cry. "Clear it up, damn you." But the words won't materialize. They are in my throat, my mouth, but won't come out. I get up, sit back down.

"I don't even know Emilia's last name."

"Pinoszewski," is all he says.

"I will find her," I tell him.

We sit in an uncomfortable silence for a long time, both of us staring off into space. Then I come back to the present, to the sea breeze, the clatter of roller skates, the putrid smell of cheap candy. Somewhere below this boardwalk, I used to make out with Joyce Diamond. For a moment, I wonder if a son who shares baseball games and dinners at Broadway steak houses with his father could share memories of adolescent lust, the days of incomparable early making out. Would Henry Karp share such things with Martin? But I can't imagine Henry Karp making out at all. I get up and lean over the railing, focusing on a spot which might very well have been where Joyce and I used to lie on one blanket and cover ourselves with another, both brought by overheated Joyce, a couple of years older than me. We adhered to the rules of the time, its Presbyterian prohibitions testing our dissolute lechery, our sanity, as her long scarlet fingernails explored, with the slowness of the tides, just under the elastic band of my bathing suit, while my fingers began their journey downward in hers, praying that she wouldn't come to her senses.

Sea gulls now poke through the remnants of sandwiches left on the beach. A wind blows up from the sea and we walk back into the streets of the neighborhood. A corner drug store, now part of a chain, was once one of my hangouts. Here, I shared with some of the Long Beach bad boys what I knew about being rebellious, macho, oppositional, daring, insolent and brash, qualities not readily found or shared at the *Alexander Hamilton School for Pushy Jewish Boys from the Upper West Side.* Inside the drug store, Zyga buys a newspaper. The malted milk mixers, the Drake's Cakes once on display are gone. The whole damn counter is replaced by rows of non-prescription tonics, salves and capsules, drops and ointments, cleaners for bodies inside and out. Hand in hand, we walk back to the Lieber Hotel where, after a dinner of pot roast and over-cooked vegetables, we go out to sit on the porch. The sky is almost black. Noise and smells reach us from the boardwalk. This is Zyga's porch, not what he knew in Marienbad or Carlsbad, but his post-war porch, its unpretentiousness most suitable for post-calamity depressives. I look at my father's calm face and tell him that I would like a drink.

"Unless Lieber's policy changes," Zyga says, "drinking alcohol is not allowed here."

Allowed or not, I run up the stairs for the traveling bottle of vodka and ask an elderly waiter for two glasses. I pour myself a fairly stiff one. Zyga lifts his glass for 'just a taste'.

"No drinking here," an old man on the other side of the porch yells at us.

Zyga lifts his glass.

"A little schnapps is good for health," he says amiably.

"You are Jewish?" the man asks.

"What else?" Zyga says, emptying his finger's worth of vodka.

With some difficulty, the man on the other side of the porch gets up from his lounge chair and disappears inside, slamming the front door behind him.

"Tell me, please, about your painting," my father says from nowhere, surprising me. "Why do you paint?"

He puts out his glass for another finger's worth.

The question, the topic itself, has never been broached, not by any of them. It feels strange and yet delicious. What a gift if I could share my deepest feelings with him. If the question came from Bolek, it would have been followed by "instead of make furs?" From Rena, by "instead of be ambassador to France?" I take another swallow of vodka and feel its comforting warmth.

"I would like to say that I am driven by demons or by angels, or that inside me is stored something so unique and valuable that the world cries out for my painting."

"Why not say this?" Zyga asks.

"I paint because I like the way it makes me feel. Also, I paint because I can."

"I think very good reasons," Zyga says.

"I have to admit that I also want to be admired because of it, to be recognized as special."

"You are special, Mishek," my father says and leans across a little side table to pat my cheek. "I love your art, but you are my son. Otherwise, I must confess that I have no patience for art. My eye is not trained for it. I look sometimes but it does not talk back."

"In a way, it's easier to say what art is not. To be moved by it doesn't make you a better person. You know what I mean? Art is not the truth. It's another level of knowing."

"I think your Ruth believes that truth can be found and it can save the world."

"Yes, I think she does."

"I wish this is true," Zyga says. "Where is she now?"

"I think Nicaragua."

He then asks for a little more vodka, sips it and walks over to the edge of the porch. He looks up. "This is a beautiful night," he says. "I see many stars."

I GO OVER TO LOOK. We stand there, our heads bent back, our hands clasped.

"Without art, without poetry or music, I would live a more shallow life," I tell my father. "In art there is hope."

"This vodka makes me sleepy," Zyga says. "I am sorry. I don't know how to drink alcohol."

In bed, I listen to his snoring.

"You have given me a precious time," I whisper. "You give me joy. I am grateful that you are alive. What a gift you offer me. I can look into you because you have opened yourself to me. I can almost hear your thoughts, feel your itches and spasms and aches."

Back in the city, I go with Zyga to St. Nick's Arena where he loves watching big beefy slobs throw others like themselves around, smashing each other to the mat, kicking and beating and pulling hair. Ruth has gone with Zyga a number of times, asking me to go with them, but I never did. Now, even though I hate the whole idea of this farce, I am eager to share every aspect of my father's life. Zyga is and apparently always has been a passionate aficionado of this theater of grown men practicing this dangerous choreography. The place is packed. Every once in a while, Zyga shoots up from his seat in the throes of excitement and appreciation. His face is red. He is sweating and smiling, hitting his knees with a rolled up program. Among the sadistic screamers in the audience, all sweating profusely, squashed in the midst of the noise and stench of overheated bodies, I am flushed with happiness that he finds satisfaction in so many different ways. Later, a simplistic thought strikes me. Is this one of Zyga's outlets for his hatred of Bolek? Is he imagining that it is his brother-in-law being burned on the ropes or slammed to the mat? What a wonder to discover that he chooses the space he inhabits, that he regains the stature he attained before the war.

In the life he is leading outside the family insanity, he meets on a regular basis with people who, like himself, have strong views about the fate of human society.

"I don't know if you are interested, Mishek," Zyga says on our way home from St. Nick's Arena, "but I love it if you come with me this weekend to a Chinese restaurant where I will be with a few friends."

At a dim sum restaurant on lower Broadway, a few elderly gentle-men, including Rytek of Automat memory, sit in friendly communion, talking mostly politics as they eat dumplings wheeled around by little grim servers in a cavalcade of spicy carts. This band of European exiles, munching dumplings and sipping tea, veterans of old political battles, discuss the urgent need for social justice, equality, the welfare state. Ruth and I attended anti-war rallies in the Vietnam era. We were chased on the steps of the National Archive by a phalanx of paratroopers in riot gear. We were enraged and even thought of joining the Weatherman people. We wanted action, no matter how bloody, to punish the evil-doers. We thought we knew exactly how to fix the corrupt, lying world. But here, among these elderly men, I have to take a deep breath and consider, from their reformist perspective, the overall picture, consider it from a sober distance, rather than with my animal reactions to the particular upheavals of the day. The five men I sit with have long ago rejected Marxism, revolutionary socialism, and the dictatorship of the proletariat.

"It is very clear," says Rytek in clipped but decent English, "that the world abandons the poor and the needy; that our goal is always to promote a more caring state of affairs. Even in wonderful America, we live with a bigger and bigger space between rich and poor."

Zyga declares that perhaps humanity has not yet reached the stage of caring for others and the battle would not be easy. "We never again look for utopias," he says, "but a decent society."

"We lack collective purpose," a Mr. Frankenheim, a white -haired man in a natty gray suit and a German accent, says. "We live in a materialistic, selfish society and believe only in the individual, everyone for himself."

"Do your own thing' it's called," I pipe in.

"Yes, this is right," adds Mr. Levy. "It is private objectives, not public good."

"We have been talking like this for years," Zyga whispers in my ear, "and look where it gets us." Zyga smiles. "The world does not listen."

"Capitalism cannot stand," says Mr. Lavy.

This produces a mild argument as Mr. Etinger, a businessman, insists that there is such a thing as an honest capitalist.

Rytek says, "We are getting too old to do anything about unregulated markets, the impossibility of endless growth."

Dr. Finkel says, "In our time the state counts on support of the industrial unions, but now the unions are shrinking and workers are hurting."

Zyga brings up the need for freedom from all discrimination. Mr. Frankenheim includes the freedom from religion.

"Who are these wonderful people? Where did you find them?" I ask my father quietly.

"Mr. Levy is the only one of us who goes to synagogue during the high holy days," Zyga whispers back. "We love Levy, even though he prays to God. He believes that God will help end capitalism."

As each one of them points to a desired dumpling on its way by, they try to engage the Chinese person in conversation, but to no avail. The most they get in return is a perfunctory head nod. No question that all five men would like to engage these workers in talk about working conditions, satisfaction with the rest of the staff, the relationship to their boss. And now their talk gradually descends to more pedestrian topics which include the new location of Dr. Finkel's wife's dental office, east 78th Street; the rising cost of public transportation; an evaluation of Zabar's smoked whitefish.

My father and I walk the few blocks to my loft where he plainly misses Ruth's presence. "Ruth is like my daughter," he says and, to my surprise, I offer him solace.

It is plain that his loss is as real as mine. Inside her office space, I open the armoire full of her research material, much of it histories of Poland, the Jews, exile and war. Ancient maps and books are everywhere. The wall behind her desk is a portrait gallery, beautifully arranged, of several Plantagenet kings; a photograph of a schoolroom in pre-war Poland in which an old rabbi instructs a group of little boys; a stern Pilsudski covered with medals; Zyga in Central Park facing the camera and smiling; another of him reading the newspaper; seated on his favorite armchair upholstered with colorful embroidery.

"This is remarkable," he says tearfully, then begins to turn the heavy pages of a photo album, studying the many photographs of me, standing in front of a partially destroyed number four Moniuszki where I was born, in the old Warsaw market square, in front of my easel, at Suzi Schwab's gallery openings, throwing a red rubber ball with Radetzky, bowing the cello, listening to music with my eyes closed.

"I never see this before," Zyga says with difficulty. "Darling Ruth comes one day to take all her things," he says. "This is so sad, so terrible. And there is so much."

"Twenty years together," I tell him, surprising myself by the number.

When my mother returns from Paris, she is renewed as always after her stay at the Plaza-Athénée and her visits to the grand fashion houses, but plainly stunned to see me warm and smiling in the company of my father. At a safe distance, she tolerates the heretofore unsuspected bond. She is accustomed to my sharing her disdain for Zyga, she once being the unquestioned source of power in the family. Now, at a late age, she is witnessing the dissolution of those early alliances. The day after her return, I take her for tea and pastries at Rumplemayer's. We sit outside, a blue-jeaned but proper middle-aged son listening to his chic, aging mother describe the fall Paris collections.

13.

Late in the afternoon of a perfect autumn day, Protopapas, Radetzky, and I attack a pitcher of martinis in my studio. We have agreed a long time ago to skip adding vermouth to good vodka, simplifying the mixing process. It has been a busy summer and early fall during which I have worked almost exclusively on etching and engraving. When I show them some of this recent work, Protopapas says, "So, who do you think you are? Goya?"

"I'm calling them *Disasters of War*," I quip. "Has that title been used before?"

I have always loved Goya's *Disasters of War*—the depictions of horror utterly human, the artist obviously a weeping member of the human race. Though my technique still lacks the skills I expect in the future, my touch as I scratch through the resins is nevertheless within sight of my modest expectations.

"What's this?" Radetsky asks.

In his hands rests a print of an ashen white figure which looks like it is constructed with sticks and papier mache, like a complicated kite, standing in a dark landscape.

"It's an eerie shadow of a man standing at the side of the road," I tell them both. "It's like the ghost, Hamlet's father, a father figure, slain by Claudius and Gertrude, who are implied in the black aquatint."

They look puzzled—my intention.

"A wronged husband, a father," I repeat and I think they sort of understand.

My *Disasters* include images of ripped apart horses, the carts behind them partly burned; a man in a three-piece suit with his face torn apart, propped by the side of a ditch; a man raped by men in uniform; a little boy in the middle of a field, saluting three airplanes. When Goya etched his *Disasters*, he continued to paint court portraits and I, like my hero, continue to supply large canvases for sale; my *Disasters*, like Goya's, a private art, not meant for public consumption and, like Goya's, they are "memories that know no forgiveness."

I love our little fraternity of weirdo artists. Often it is just the three of us, but others join us from time to time. We shoot the shit—art shit— and yell at each other. It is one of the wonders of the universe that what most of the world would consider Jungian crap, Pop funnies, and gloomy black smears are satisfying collectors, serious or speculative, both pro- viding great material comfort to each of us; work whose existence we would defend unto death, whose serious intention and value we would proclaim with our last breath. When we are not engaged in art talk— which often includes philosophy, history or the other, lesser, arts, each according to his unmentioned limitations—I serenade our group with the cello, Radetzky with his cumbersome double bass, and Protopapas with a little flute he carries around with him or an upright piano when we're in his apartment on Wooster Street. When a bit high on weed or booze, the cacophony we create is astonishing. We love jazz from the Forties and Fifties, but our attempts at jazz riffs are cheeky and ludicrous.

"Better stick with Shostakovich," Radetzky says, madly plucking his instrument.

What could be better than this? I ask myself when they leave. Radetzky's wife left him long ago, Protopapas's hasn't slept with his for ten years, and my Ruth is gone. This is not an altogether bad way to spend my days and nights, to remain involved, occupied and sane.

The next day, however, the shit begins to hit the fan. My father calls to tell me that Bolek has cancer. "Your mother is—how you say?—a basket case."

I understand that when Rena loses Bolek, she will not recover. For a brief narcissistic moment, I also realize that no other loss, the loss of me included, would be the equal of this. In the best European tradition each of them protects the right not to know, denial and looking the other way built into their genetic code. As for me, I am torn between my long-growing hatred of the man who hates my father, the man who spent many years courting me to accept him as my real father, and the uncle who loves me, the uncle who has forever been part of my life.

As more of Bolek's daily activities are curtailed, Ursula finds ever newer treatments. She believes that no effort in that pursuit is wasted, making him swallow vile concoctions in Mexico, lie on a cot in a small town of the Philippines where a deft magician showed her the tumor he extracted from Bolek's stomach. A visiting nurse suggests prayer, another urges him to visualize his body as it once was, free of cancer.

"Listen to them, *liebchen*," Ursula urges, but no one can fix Bolek and he slowly understands.

When I go uptown to sit in his Lennox Hill hospital room and listen to his difficult breathing, surrounded by unpleasant medical smells, I am sorry that we never spoke the truth about our family, about his role in its unhappiness, its ugly divisiveness.

"Now is the time to turn to God," Rena tells me in Polish, as we share the only armchair in Bolek's hospital room.

"What? To God?"

"There is no one else who can save him," my mother says.

She is totally incapacitated by her brother's illness. She taxis up from Mandeleau's at least twice a day, sits in Bolek's hospital room, crying quietly. Just before he dies, Ursula hears him say "something like a prayer, I think in Hebrew," she says.

Rena tells us that she wants a funeral befitting the king of furs. She lobbies hard for a royal casket of shiny hardwood with brass fittings and is appalled when Ursula makes different arrangements. Ursula and I consult a friendly reform rabbi who tells us that Jews are buried in pine boxes, their bodies wrapped in simple shrouds. Rabbi Waxman delivers an ecumenical eulogy at a posh funeral home befitting the royal furrier. Most of it is written by Mandeleau's PR lady, Anna Voroshliva, a flamboyant Russian *émigré* who wears turbans and is Rena's closest associate. In a solemn rabbinical tone, Rabbi Waxman extolls the courage of a man who re-made his life and who was responsible for opening American eyes to European chic and luxury. Rabbi Waxman seems to choke as he calls Bolek "the king of ranch mink." I am so embarrassed that I scrunch down in my seat. My body shivers as I recall that, for many years, I wished that the King of Ranch Mink was my real father.

The cortege of limousines speeds up the West Side highway to Westchester where Bolek's simple casket is lowered into its grave. A few of us shovel dirt onto it.

"Bolek's cortege would have been much larger in his heyday," Ursula says.

I try to console my mother but she is inconsolable. Zyga does not want to talk about his feelings toward Bolek, who did so much to make his life a misery.

The day after the funeral, Rena takes to her bed. "I have enough of life," she says.

A couple of years before, she cut her time at Mandeleau Furs by a third and now, without her brother, she wants no further part in it. Rena's and Zyga's housekeeper Flora, who speaks only Polish, begs Rena to reconsider her decision to surrender. "Madame Rena," Flora says, "you are a healthy woman. You must remain in the world."

When Flora goes back to the kitchen, Rena says with shameless cruelty, "She is afraid America will send her back to Poland without me. She steals from me."

"What is she stealing?"

"Shoes."

"You won't need any if you don't go out," I tell her, pissed off.

"Ferragamo himself made them for me."

So she is losing it, an old woman's paranoia, but when she warns that she is ready to spend the rest of her life in bed, she means it. She begins to lie there, motionless and with her eyes closed, eating little. But because her doctor impresses upon her a deep human need for potassium, she becomes a conscientious banana eater. Why, in her renunciation of life, she cares about potassium is a mystery. On the other hand, she could never say no to a doctor.

"He speaks beautiful French," she says, referring to Dr. Richard Petlin, an Upper East Side provider. "And do you know, Mishek, he is doctor to Diana Vreeland?"

"Oh," I say, as my big toe begins sketching daisies inside my shoe, a well-proven way to distract myself from unpleasantness.

"I love America," my mother says.

In our various ways, each of us think we have become American in spite of Rena and Bolek's ignorance about this land's culture and history, its bigotries, class struggles, and predisposition to violence. But there is no reason to quibble about culture and history when, like me, they have benefitted and exalted in their differentness, momentary exoticism, their outsider status. Their European charm, bravado, and will to succeed, sells furs and—the thought is odious—paintings.

Rena turns to her side and takes my hand.

"You are still so beautiful," she says, then puts her hand on my graying beard. "So why hide your face like this?"

Her soft, warm hand strokes my face lovingly. It feels good. Her fear of touching, of motherhood, her neglect, has become comic, a farce. As the cliché goes, I tell myself she did the best she could.

"America has given you so many wonderful gifts," I tell her. "So many rich customers and beautiful jewels from Van Cleef and Arpels in the safe deposit box at Chase Manhattan."

"Yes," she says, "and all of it will be yours."

Then she smiles as she remembers an incident from her business life.

"One time," she says, holding my hands, "a woman comes up the elevator into the showroom. Mishek, you cannot believe it, but she is wearing a very dirty jacket like a person working in the fields. Can you imagine? Mr. Edgar and Mr. Frank, the salesmen, they take her by her elbows and put her back in the elevator."

Now Rena is giggling, radiant. "Well, Mishek, she is Mrs. Rockefeller and when they bring her back to me, she buys many fur coats."

Quite a few people visit the bedridden Madame Mendelssohn—bedridden and changed into a different woman. She stops wearing her wig altogether, a sure sign of her abdication from her previous life. She looks quite pretty with her gray hair cut short, like a boy's. And so, my mother, paragon of European chic and ass-kissing, no longer bothers to put on her wig or take her false teeth out of the glass on the little table beside her bed. Among her visitors, her turbaned associate and friend, Anna Vorishlava arrives with her lawyer husband Charlie. Anna, who, like most of Rena's friends in the haute couture industry, never utters a genuine word, now corners me by the bedroom windows.

"I cannot believe what I am seeing," she says. "Your mother has always been the zenith of propriety and good taste."

Anna Vorishlava's face reddens. She looks like she is about to cry.

"Look at her, Michael. She is not wearing her beautiful wig. And," she nearly chokes as she says it, "her false teeth are in the cup for everyone to see."

"What an amazing statement," I say to an astonished Anna Vorishlava. "Appearance no longer matters to her."

"Michael," Anna Vorishlava says, her hand in front of her ruby red lips, "what does this mean?"

"She is—excuse my French—saying fuck you to the world. She is exhibiting her originality and boldness. I am proud of her."

Anna Vorishlava flees toward her husband Charlie, who is exchanging niceties with Rena. She whispers in his ear. Gentle soul that he is, he kisses Rena's hands as he is vigorously pulled away, into the front hall and out the door.

As she falls asleep, I remember that this little woman, my mother, whipped the men, Bolek and Zyga, making sure they would not go back but keep driving to the Lithuanian border and beyond. If the men in the van had their way, our little band of escaping Jews would have returned to the comfort of home and sure death, no small matter to be thankful for. Rena was tough and relentless.

A few months later, my mother's heart gives out as she sleeps. Not a peep out of her, lying there on her back, her hands folded under her breasts. Surely, she puts an end to it because she wants to die, to meet Bolek among the other angels, but also it is out of her hands, normal wear and tear, the body's depletion of its rugged, prodigious heartbeats. Flora finds her in the morning and Zyga calls me. I jump into a cab and arrive as the funeral people are preparing the gurney to cart her away. Her face and hands, though cold, are as soft as baby skin. Zyga sits at the bottom of her bed, his head in his hands. I kiss her on her cold forehead before the ambulance people transfer her little body to the gurney and wheel her out the front door, proceeding toward the service elevator. I scream after them.

"Not that one! The main elevator!"

They refuse and I run after them, howling like a madman, blocking the service entrance where all the smelly garbage is. The fighter in me, the hero reappears, fierce and resolute. I would rather be crushed under the tread of a tank than allow this indignity. It is, I think, the only time in my life that I ached to fight for her sake. She would have been surprised while recognizing that blocking the service entrance was a worthy cause. Though Rena and I have never been as I think a mother and son should be, I am ready to fight unto death to preserve the stature of the person she was. The ambulance people and I push and shove until, finally defeated by this brawling lunatic, the gurney attendants wheel Rena toward the main elevator. Out of breath, I wait with them for the damned thing to arrive on the 12th floor. When the elevator door opens, a gasp, then a shriek, comes out of it. A woman, wearing a little broadtail wrap probably made by the woman on the gurney, shouts, "No corpses on the main elevator!"

I watch as the woman flees into the hall. Into her face, I yell that on this gurney rides the great Madame Mendelssohn. Then I accompany the two men and my mother into the elevator and out into the street where they transfer her into the back of a van.

Rena's life-long financial advisor, Charlie Steiglitz, mild-mannered husband of Anna Vorishliva and, in my youth, the writer of the check that paid for my trip to Paris and Madrid, now in his eighties and in excellent shape, comes to their apartment a couple of days after my mother's death. Zyga and I sit opposite Charlie as he puts on his glasses and picks documents out of his briefcase.

My father says quietly to me, "I know what she owns. I look at her statements every quarter."

Charlie clears his throat. "With 20/20 hindsight," Charlie says, "she could have been a lot richer, but, as her advisor, I chose very safe investments. No losses, no killings either."

He reads through the list. A killing? Her earnings from the business, from German reparations and I don't know what else, are as safe as a rock in a blizzard, with built-in hedges against inflation, deflation, stagnation, against a plunge in mutual funds, against a spike in the bond market, safe in case of war, global warming, safe in case of nuclear disaster. Her fortune, though plentiful, would have been much larger if she hadn't allowed Bolek to reap most of the benefits from the German reparations. Still, Zyga, together with his own savings from who knows where, now has plenty of money to continue living as he did when my mother was alive. Rena's will also specifies that she be buried next to her brother in Westchester County, the plot having been bought together with Bolek's.

A memorial service is held in the same posh funeral home as Bolek's. For her, the auditorium is packed with loyal customers, directrices from some of the main fashion houses in Paris and New York, the cream of magazine editors and workers from the fourth floor of Mandeleau Furs, which had recently been sold to a venture capitalist and dealer in Mexican government bonds named Edelman who is arranging to sell cheaper versions of the furs in department stores nationwide. I am surprised to discover that so many people loved my mother. During her lifetime, I heard from her friends and customers that she was an angel. I dismissed this as more hype from the fashion industry. I still have problems putting her into the angel category. Nevertheless, these people's love seems genuine as they gather to tell stories from her life, most of which I have never heard before. Her taste, above all, is singled out as perfection itself.

"I say to her, 'No, Madame Rena darling, I do not want a long coat,'" old Mrs. Harrington recalls, "I want a bolero.' But Madame insists and, of course, as always, she is right. I have never loved a coat as much as that floor-length chinchilla."

"I would not have believed that anyone could make a sable stole so perfectly for my old, bent body," enthuses Suzi Lazard of the Parisian banking family. "Every person I know adores it. Only Madame Rena could have made it."

Her lifelong friend from Warsaw days, Mrs. Prokocimer, weeps as she tells of the time when Rena sent money to her sick daughter in London when times were tough for the Prokocimer family.

"An angel, that is what she is," Mrs. Prokocimer says.

I am touched by these memories, but can't help thinking: What about your husband, Rena? And, narcissist that I am, what about me? A very old scene pops into my mind, that of her coming home from the store on Marszalkowska in the middle of the day to stand outside the little toilet in our Warsaw apartment, waiting for me to have a bowel movement.

"You never took off your mink coat whose bristles released the cold of the Warsaw winter. You stood there with—who was it? Fela, Inka?—and waited for me to produce. I don't remember if I was proud of my gift to you or embarrassed by your admiration of my shit. What does it matter? You cared. I accept your regret that you never knew how to be a mother. But how to accept your and your brother's torture of Zyga?"

Later in the week, my father and I walk west on 57th Street to the Russian Tea Room for dinner. We look into the windows of the Polish store which sells amber and badly made decorative overcoats. At the corner of Fifth Avenue, we wait through two red light sequences, absorbed in talk of Rena.

"Did you and Rena have any good times?" I ask him.

"Good times?" Zyga says, looking as if he's unable to put the idea of good times into the same part of his brain as the one occupied by memories of his wife.

"I mean did you ever enjoy anything together, say like a concert or a movie?"

"We never go together," he says glumly.

"Did you ever want to?"

He doesn't seem able to comprehend wanting to be together.

"Probably she wants a man different from me," Zyga says, "Maybe a man who treats her badly."

"You didn't treat her badly?" I ask, a bit astonished.

"It is hard to understand, but I think she likes me more when I am not very nice. She likes a man to yell, threaten, take charge, take a mistress."

"Like Bolek?"

"Yes," Zyga says.

Just before opening the door to one of our favorite restaurants, I ask him if he ever took a mistress.

"Not in America," he says inside the door, "but the only time she looks at me is when I am misbehaving."

"Misbehaving?"

"When I am angry, make noise, break things."

"You were good at that?" I ask even though I know that he was.

Zyga smiles as we are shown to our table. Both of us seem to feel totally comfortable in this rich pre-revolutionary atmosphere.

"Why on earth did you stay with her? Wouldn't you have been happier elsewhere?"

"My time is so different from yours. We are not used to leaving. We forget our pain and find a way to endure."

He is wearing a decent enough suit; his necktie a little stained, but not enough to matter.

"We are the only ones left," Zyga says. "Rena is gone and so is Ruth gone. We are alone."

"We have each other," I say, each of our fingers now around a stem of a martini glass.

"Their business is finished," Zyga says and lifts his martini.

"Unless some unknown member of the Mandelbaum tribe is trading leopard pelts in Sri Lanka or alligator hides in Ecuador," I say.

"I never like that business, never," Zyga says, "but she builds it from nothing. She is an artist with furs."

We both order a Chicken Kiev.

"Was she beautiful when young?"

"Not beautiful, but not ugly either. You know that her mother and father always tell her that she is ugly and must find something important to do for herself because her looks will not help her."

"What a terrible thing to say."

"Now Ruth," Zyga says, slathering butter onto his Russian black bread, "that is beautiful. You must be strong, Mishek. Maybe you do not lose Ruth forever."

"She found something of her own, something that doesn't involve me. She is gone. I was selfish. Now I must find my own way. I need to do what you did."

Zyga's face is relaxed and every once in a while, he smiles a beautiful smile. Each time I see my father, he seems more handsome.

"Do you want to stay alone in that apartment?" I ask him. "You should move in with me."

Zyga is plainly moved. "I will stay on 57th Street," he says. "You must be alone so you can see your ladies when you need them."

While cleaning out some of Rena's clothes from their bedroom closet, we come across several Mandeleau silver boxes, stamped with Bolek's familiar scrawled signature logo.

"I never look inside her closets," Zyga says.

I imagine an old passport, letters, the railroad tickets from Warsaw to Marienbad. And so, I pull them out and drag them into the living room. As I open the first of three, the putrid smell of furs makes me cough.

"She probably does not open them for years," Zyga says.

One box is full of newspaper clippings, reviews of Mandeleau's many shows, articles from *Women's Wear Daily*, torn out pages of ads from the fashion magazines and editorial commentary on the king of furs and his worker bee of a sister. We riffle through a bunch of fashion designs on stationery marked Christian Dior, some from Balmain, 44 rue Francois I, vendeuse Solange. We skip ahead to drawings of suits and coats from Balenciaga, 10 Avenue George V, vendeuse Florette, notes in Rena's handwriting naming places to buy wholesale scarves at 4 rue Volney, embroidery for linings at 277 rue St. Honore.

In another box, among ermine tails and small patches of mink and sable, lay packets of letters, mostly from satisfied customers, but some whose return addresses make my heart skip a beat. Some are from Poland, some from Brazil, some from the Swedish consulate in

Stockholm. Of the Stockholm letters, the first is dated February 21, 1946.

"Dear Madame Mendelssohn,

We have made inquiries about Helena and Emilia Pinoszewski, mother and daughter, and thus far have not been able to locate them. If you can gather any further information about them, we will try to look further, but many records from the years 1939 and 1940 have been destroyed or misplaced."

"What?" I cry and look at my father whose face shows no emotion. "You know about this?"

"I know we look for Pani Helena and Emilia," Zyga says. "We never find them."

Now, I'm digging through the piles frantically and find a couple of letters from the American Consulate that speak of further unsuccessful efforts to locate the pair. Then a cache of treasures from Brazil, all of them in Polish, from my aunt and uncle who, together with Helena and Emilia, were in the Citronka with us after we abandoned the Packard.

"My dearest Rena," Zyga translates. "'Lolek and I are well settled in a nice neighborhood in Rio, a beautiful and interesting city," Zyga reads slowly. "'Lolek has learned Portuguese much faster than I, and has found work as a salesman for a kitchen appliance company while he studies to get back his lawyer's license. We are hopeful that he will return to the law. I was truly shocked to hear the news, dearest Rena, that Bolek would not allow Helena and little Emilia to travel with the rest of you to America." And then the bolt of lightning. "After all, Emilia is his child.'"

"That pig! That prick of misery! He left them in Sweden. He didn't want to be bothered by them anymore. It's unbelievable. Did you know all this?"

"Yes," Zyga says. "Boleslaw Mandelbaum was a cruel man."

"Why did you never tell me about this?"

"It is very painful. I cannot speak about anything that happens then. I am a coward. All my life I try to forget."

Old feelings of wishing my father were a thundering Iago, an associate of the killer Arnie Metzger, convulse my stomach. I don't know what to say and say nothing. He walks over to the window, then comes back and riffles through more letters. Another letter from Rio describes their unexpected South American existence and the good friends they have found in the community of European Jews.

"Lolek is finally practicing law in Rio. We hope to visit you in New York soon and, by the way, quite by accident, a little bit late in my life, I am pregnant."

"Did they come? Do you know their child? He's a grown person by now."

My father stumbles, looking for words.

"They never come. Eva does not come for Bolek's funeral. When Rena dies, she has an airplane ticket, but becomes very ill with pneumonia."

"Why does no one tell me about any of this? Do you think I'm not involved, not interested? Those people—Emilia and Helena, Eva and Lolek—were present at the turning point of all our lives and you don't mention them to me, not ever? How could you do this to me?"

My hands turn into fists. I gnash my teeth. Breathing hard, I go into the spare room. I sit on the couch and pound my forehead. If Bolek and my mother were alive, I would want to strangle them, but what to do about my father?

"Poor bastard," I think, "he has suffered as much as anyone. Let it go, Mendelssohn, just let it go."

Back in the living room, we sit at some distance from each other. Zyga begins to pick on his fingers, an act he had almost abandoned. I pace, make myself a drink. My father too begins to pace.

"I'm going to Sweden," I say quietly and Zyga stops and palms his eyes. "If Mila is alive, I'm going to find her."

Zyga says nothing in response, sits down again and continues to read.

"'I hope you can find a way to be nice to Zyga,' Eva writes.

My father is agitated by this sentence and swallows hard.

"'He is a good man. To be depressed is a terrible thing, Rena darling. It is a disease. Bolek is the one who deserves your anger, not your husband.'"

He puts the letter down and closes his eyes.

"So much shit in our past," I say and walk over to the armoire to replenish my glass of vodka.

"Betrayals seem to be a mark of this family," I murmur.

My mind fills with recollections of Mila's braids and the ribbons which held them together, of her crying and singing little tunes as we held hands lying on top of the diminishing pile of fur coats. And Helena feeding us both, kissing us both, running with us to the ditches. I walk past the wobbly Empire dining table and look out the window. Nothing is in focus. I pull a chair over and feel my father's hands on my shoulders. A deep love for this man sweeps through my body.

"I don't understand any of it," I say quietly. "Why the hatreds and the angers? Would it have been very different without a war? Of course it would. Would you have stayed with Rena? Would nostalgia and depression not been a part of your life?"

I don't understand the ease or the irrelevance of betrayal, the need for secrecy, the lies. I'd like to slam shut every door to the past.

"Have you been in touch with Lolek and Eva?" I ask my father.

"Very little."

"Did they have a son or daughter?"

"A son," Zyga tells me.

"One day soon, let's go to Brazil to see them."

My father thinks for a moment.

"Yes, Mishek," he says. "We will go."

14.

Dear one, you cannot imagine what this country is like. When I visited my friend Radetzky in one of his Vermont retreats, the town displayed signs posted by practitioners announcing their cockamamie specialties: forgiveness-based therapy, psychic makeovers, respectful therapy, drumming therapy, people barely out of adolescence offering life coaching, massage people who dig deep into your flesh and guts, others whose hands hover above you, never touching but generating heat and redistributing energy. Energy was being redistributed all over the place. Everyone was doling out hope for a better life, for a better death, a closer relationship to God, the Dalai Lama, the universe. People were being born again to yet another Messiah. If you took a central position at the corner of Elm and Maple at lunchtime, you would witness dozens of people, colorful yoga mats strapped to their backs, walking in different directions to the yoga class of their choice—Bikram, Ashtanga, Iyengar, Kundalini and God only knows what else—looking for perfect health and a long life. The whole damn place—and who knows how many other places just like it—was magic bullet central.

ON A HOT SEPTEMBER DAY, Noah Radetzky urges me to observe the

High Holy Days with him. My father reluctantly comes with us. We assemble at Temple Sholem Aleichem, or whatever its name, where Ruth used to chant and pray, for the sundown ritual of Kol Nidre, a part of the Yom Kippur services.

Before we go, I consult Radetzky about what I am getting myself into. He is my connection to things religious from Buddhism to Judaism. As a matter of fact, he calls himself a "Ju-Bu-Lu." I've never seen this written, but I suppose this is as good a way as any. A Jewish Buddhist Luddite.

"Isn't it all about God, shit like doubting or blaspheming or not paying attention?" I ask him.

"Somewhere along the line," he says, "in Poland or Lithuania or maybe in the desert, twirling a live chicken around your head until the bird died was supposed to help wash away your sins and cleanse your mind of filthy thoughts."

"Do they still do that? Will they hand out chickens at the door? One chicken per Jew?"

"No more chickens, pal," Noah says, poking me in the ribs. "I made it up."

Inside the synagogue, it is crowded. Some people I know, most I don't. I do know that, without question, each Jew has a different political agenda, a different conception of human beauty, taste in food, diets and places to vacation; that the issue of faith runs along a spectrum substantially different from other religions. Among any crowd of non-fanatical Jews, most are atheists or agnostics, attending the synagogue only because grandpa did so in the old country. In my case, it was great-grandpa.

Surprisingly, I am received warmly, hugged and kissed.

"Good *yontiff*," everyone says to everyone else.

"Where's Ruth?" asks Judy Hoffman, the weaver.

"Nicaragua," I tell her.

Judy Hoffman looks puzzled. She wants to know more. I walk on with Zyga and Radetzky to find a place where we can sit together.

"You look great in a suit," Sophie Glass, a painter in Suzi Schwab's stable, says, straightening my pink tie.

When we find a seat at the back of the synagogue, Radetzky, aware that I know nothing, tries to fill me in.

"This is a complicated negotiation with God about vows and oaths, either for the past year or the one to come. It's a dialogue with God," he says, and pulls a book out of his pocket and quietly reads. "'All vows, and prohibitions, and oaths, and consecrations, and any synonymous terms, that we may vow, or swear, or consecrate, or prohibit upon ourselves, from the previous Day of Atonement until this Day of Atonement and from this Day of Atonement until the Day of Atonement that will come, we repudiate them. All of them are undone, abandoned, cancelled, null and void, not in force, and not in effect. Our vows are no longer vows, and our prohibitions are no longer prohibitions, and our oaths are no longer oaths.'"

"What the fuck?" I whisper into Radetzky's ear. "Holy shit."

He tweaks my cheek like my aunt Zosia used to do. I slap his hand away. A couple sitting in front of us turn toward us, scowling. My father is snoring blissfully.

My chin on my chest, sitting among these singing Jews who know all the tunes, who belt them out like an Oklahoma revival while the cantor sings back, I slump down in my back-destroying bench and dive into myself. I know I could have gotten off my self-absorbed ass long enough to pay more attention to Ruth, my yipee-ay-yay cowgirl. I might have worked harder at the marriage. After all, I love her passions for the Jews, the Poles, Richard III, Zyga, even Isaac and Kostek, and now indigenous people everywhere. I recall daily moments of our existence together, playing chess, getting off on each other's highs, the booze highs and the intellectual ones, the precious moments of playfulness in bed, changing our sheets together, loving the Greek plays and histories, reading aloud to each other, her introducing me to hominy grits, her learning to love gefilte fish straight from a Manischewitz jar. No one can say that it was all bad. It was just enough. We loved each other's snobbishness, our mutual disdain for pop music, pop movies, and pop psychology. Plunged into the familiar despair of loss—a painful nostalgia—I surface to the sound of two hundred Jews singing their hearts out, wailing and chanting. I sit up and Zyga whispers, "My grandfather makes me hear all this in Poland. If you promise God that you will pray every day if he sends Ruth back, and she comes back, but you lie about praying every day, you can say here that you are sorry."

As in a bad dream, the congregation now really lets go, raising the roof. Radetzky shouts into my ear.

"Atonement has nothing to do with vows made between two people. You are just asking for protection from divine punishment."

Zyga shouts into my ear, "Anti-Semites say that you cannot trust Jews because, in the secrecy of the synagogue where no one hears except other Jews, Jews can cheat you without guilt for a whole year or even lie about the Holocaust."

I can't take any more. I grab my father's arm and we rush out of there into a drizzly September afternoon. I hail a cab for Zyga and head downtown. My need to have drinks with Ruth, so salutary at times like this, chokes me up. I pour enough vodka for both Ruth and me into a pitcher and, an hour later, fall asleep on the couch. The next day, I sit in front of an empty canvas and just stare. In the early evening, I make a noodle soup from a package, then walk down the back stairs to Radetzky's, who is packing a small bag.

"I'm off for a month, Mendelssohn," he says. "Going to northern Vermont to an ashram."

Radetzky's son Nate is working as an assistant sound man for a rock group in California, while Rosie waits tables in an upscale bistro in Westwood Village, hoping for an audition. His wife Sonya, long gone, works in an adult day care center in south Los Angeles, not far from her children.

"It's not the way it was supposed to turn out," Radetzky says. He lights a joint and inhales deeply, holds his breath and coughs. "Come with me," he says. "It can't hurt."

"What do you do in ashrams? And why should I go? I don't believe any of that shit." I take the joint out of his hand and inhale deeply. "I've been trying to integrate all my new family stuff—the loss of Ruth, the love for my father, being alone. Why mess with what I've got?"

"You'd find ways to integrate even better," Radetzky assures me, "And enlightenment is not shit. Look, Mendelssohn, we are both artists, damn good ones. I have come to believe that there is more that needs to be done and I don't mean looking for god," he says. "Do you know what I'm talking about when I talk enlightenment?" He pours himself a Scotch and leans back on the couch. "Enlightenment is seeing into one's true nature, It is understanding how to liberate oneself from the prison of craving and suffering. For me," Radetzky says, "I need to control my lust and learn humility."

He sits up and gives me a poke in the ribs.

"You could do with some humility yourself, Mendelssohn."

"I tried atonement. It sucks. And as for humility, Noah, I don't need or want it."

"How can anyone not want to be enlightened?"

"Look, Noah," I say after another toke of his weed, "you have sold me on impermanence, even though it doesn't take a genius or a Buddhist to be pretty damn certain of this. Not too enlightening to know that nothing is predictable about who we are going to be tomorrow or whether or not a bomb will go off or conditions will be such that our brains will fry. Only fools can believe in permanence or absolute truth or certainty."

Radetzky stands up, arches his back, then leans hard against a door jamb to stretch his calf muscles. "I'm talking process, Mendelssohn, not absolute anything."

"Take another of your truths," I say, as he flinches with back pain. "Take the illusion bit, the everything is illusion, all reality is illusion. My question is: who gives a shit? Reality is whatever you sense it is, no matter what that is—a dream, a fantasy to jerk off with, this coffee table, everything. It's just atoms you say? Fine. It's mahogany? Okay with me."

He lies down on the floor, tries to stretch torso and limbs. "I advise you to look deeper," he moans. "You're too damn smart not to."

"One more thing, at least for the moment," I tell him. "As much as I'd love to look forward to reincarnation, it is as hokey as heaven and hell."

He says nothing.

"Karma?" I ask. "Collecting points to be a prince next time or a pet dog rather than a cockroach?"

Nevertheless, not quite able to suppress my curiosity, a week later we drive to Siddhartha, or whatever its damn name. Radetzky's Luddite beat-up station wagon is the only one of its kind in the ashramic parking lot, full of shiny new cars. In the lobby of the mansion, a movie is being shown on a big screen, accompanied by music from, I think, *Chariots of Fire.*

"That's the man," Noah says, "the guru giving a dharma talk." Quiet words in a high register drone on and on. The staff greets one and all, the weekend's spiritual warriors. I sign up for "Inner Quest Intensive." There is little choice. "Deepening Your Love" is available only to couples. We meet in groups of a dozen or so and, as oceanic massage music plays, we sit cross-legged on mats around a central candle. A young man with a shaved head and a wireless mike is leading the proceedings and, as the votive candle is passed, each of us is to have our moment to say why we are here. People are "in recovery." Everyone is in recovery. Recovery is *de rigeur*, abuse a painful badge of honor. I can't focus. In the room, there are addictions to food, drink, unhealthy behaviors, sex. How can you not be an addict to sex? We are all addicts to sex. It's an evolutionary imperative for Christ's sake. Everything people are recovering from I personally require just to survive. The staff—acolytes of the spirit world—run around providing boxes of Kleenex. Where does this dipshit kvetching fit on a spectrum that includes torture, slaughter, rape, war? Give it up, Mendelssohn, I tell myself, as someone pokes me in the ribs.

"It's your turn," the guy next to me says.

"'Life is bad today and every day it will get worse.' Schopenhauer," I say.

This place brings the wonders of despair back.

"Sickness, old age, pain, and death is coming to all of us," I continue.

I want to play a late Shostakovich quartet or Mahler's Kinder-totenlieder. I mumble that, "Without malice, Nietzsche wished his closest friends suffering, desolation, sickness, ill-treatment, indignities."

Then, loud enough for all to hear, "Difficulties should be sought in order to reach fulfillment," I quote from some damn book of Radetzky's.

Now I am ranting in spite of the tinkling bells and my fellow weekend warriors seeking solace. At lunch, no one sits next to me.

Very early the next morning, we are asked to be mindful of our breath. As I breathe and try to concentrate on my belly rising and falling,

I can't let go of my mind's exigencies, the loss of childhood and country, the loss of family, of mother and wife. I am breathing, but I have plenty of space left for feeling bad. We begin to transfer our awareness from breathing into the belly to breathing into the left toe. How can a big toe matter in face of the maldistribution of wealth? There are some forty left feet in this room, each left foot the center of some wounded psyche in dire need of consolation.

"Bring the attention to the left heel," the leader says, "without judgment."

I have a repulsive little bunion on the sole of my left foot. It scratches people in bed with me and grows back after I pare it down with a single-edged blade. I judge it to be fairly disgusting.

"When you feel ready," the leader says, "let the left foot be and bring your attention to the left knee."

We send our breath to one body part after another and I suppose I could be as relaxed as I have ever been if only I was someone else.

We shift from big to little groups. An acolyte of the guru calls our attention to mindfulness. A little bell rings. I like the sound and the quiet that it so gently demands, the change in tempo and mood whose possibility it announces. I like the idea of mindfulness, which seems so slippery in the company of others.

"Mindfulness is the considered attention we give to the activity we are engaged in," a man with a sweet tenor voice tells us.

I fall in love with the peaceful little bell. I need this bell to mark the transition from one thought, one flourish of paint brush to another. I want a little tinkling bell of my own.

That night, on my cot, I think of my mother who, all her life, craved messiahs. On each of her business trips to Paris, she frequented smelly apartments on the right bank where little shawled women read cards or tea leaves, broke the code of her smooth palms or head bumps. Madame

Rosa apparently told her that she and Bolek should offer the world a line of perfumes. I laugh out loud as I remember this, although it probably would have made them much richer than they were. And in August 1939, Madame Coco told Rena that war was coming, the only fortune teller in Europe who considered this a revelation.

Breakfast the next day is gruel and after it we sit facing a fellow weekender who first listens then repeats what the other says, without comment, without judgment. A sad, lonely woman is telling me her history. Hers, mine, all of ours seem like supper the previous night, a lot of indistinguishable vegetables in a bed of unsalted rice. My personal misery banquet, probably like most of us here, consists of existential angst, aesthetic crisis, cosmological nausea and dread of death.

"We're not all that different," the woman across from me says.

The grandness and triviality of all our lives are clear. My woes are as puny and as immense as hers. Depression and panic visits us all. As Ruth knows, they are a function of life, woven into life's fabric. Ah Ruth, what would you think of this place? You'd probably love it.

Unlike most of us, Radetzky is among the cadre of penitents who engage in menial work directly related to the guru. He says that he considers it a privilege. He was here at ashram Siddhartha a few times before and, like penitents everywhere, he sweeps from the moment we arrived, sweeping being an important part of developing spiritual disciplines.

"By the way, you're nothing but free labor," I tell him when we share a moment in the lobby. "Why are you doing this?"

"To learn humility," he says. He straightens his body and recoils in pain. "Fucking backache," he says.

I am feeling humiliated on Radetzky's behalf. Noah is a large man, impressive, important. And who is this little dinky guru? A nothing, a puny smartass who knows how to make money and get laid. Just then, the guru materializes. We stop talking. While cleaning the floors, Noah moved all the shoes and boots from one side of the entry hall to the other. In his reedy voice, swami asks the pile to be moved back to where it was.

"From there to there," he points.

Then, with my eyes closed tight in disgust, I hear bones hit the hardwood floor and fear that Noah either decked the guru or fainted. In fact, Noah is prostrate, in total submission, arms wrapped around the guru's legs. My heart pounds so hard in my chest that I fear I will explode. I pounce to disentangle them. The guru steps back and I hear the patter of little feet leaving the room.

"My God, what horrors did you inflict on the world to justify this humiliation? This asshole is no guru," I cry. "He's a putz."

"I'm looking for the limits of my ego," Radetzky says as he gets up, vertebra by vertebra, leaning hard against a wall to realign his back.

"There's no way either you or I should give up angst or judgment," I say as I pick up one of the boots in the entranceway and heave it across the room. "If you think you're going to get something in return for your humiliation, forget it. The universe is not about to make gifts to some poor schmuck like you or me who might be thirsting for gifts. Jesus, Noah, it was Beethoven, not God, who wrote the Cavatina. You know what I'm saying? It was Jason Giambi who hit that long-distance home run in the 14th inning. God had twelve games to watch that night, close to five hundred players asking him for a base hit."

Sunday morning, we are instructed to lie head to foot with a partner, our toes north and south. For reasons known only to that putz of a guru—and who knows, maybe this is the moment everyone is waiting for—we are to concentrate on each other's bodies, from the toes up, to talk body parts. My partner, Catherine, is lovely in a lime green yoga suit and my heart beats fast as we begin with a narrative about our toes. Catherine says she loves her feet, wants them to live outside her shoes and socks, barefoot, on sand, in water. I confess that mine are always cold and resemble flounder fillets. We feel equally estranged from our knees, knobby and asexual. When we arrive at our crotches, she, almost inaudibly, speaks of miscarriages and pain. I tell her that mine is stirring, always asking for attention. I wait for more, but she proceeds with her upward journey and I admit that my belly button and nipples are oversensitive, too tender to play with and, after a moment's silence, she claims she can change all that. I sigh.

"Mine are a source of endless pleasure," she confesses.

Her arms reflect an empty nest; mine feel debilitated by panic, yet spastic with the desire to wield brush and palette knife. In some detail now, we discuss our appetites concerning mouths and ears, then revisit the lower erogenous zones, this time with meticulous precision, whispering the nature of each of our sensations. I begin to breathe hard. Clasping hands, we wait for the session to end and, without a further word, we take off in her Volvo to a nearby hotel. It's women, always women who provide the answers.

Still, in spite of a hefty push from the Far East and the New Age, I remain true to myself, a snob, an elitist, secure in my renunciation of things trite or touching on faith, perhaps a little more attuned to compassion. Compassion?

"We"re all such schmucks," I tell Radetzky when we are both back in our lofts, "schmucks looking for a respite from meaninglessness, insignificance, from rage and evil."

"It"s not outside the realm of possibility that, along with compassion," he tells me, "a touch of enlightenment has broken through your self-satisfied carapace."

"Though the prison of lust remains a delightful given."

"We are all seekers," he assures me. "We all yearn for renewal."

Little by little, some of my friends peel away. I'm not surprised to learn that this often happens when couples split up, but I am surprised by some of the virulence of the occasional animosity, such as occurs one day at noon over coffee at Ferrara's. Sitting with my longtime sparring partner, Henry Karp, and his wife Gabrielle, the little man gets himself into a nervous attack mode.

"Frankly, I think you could have taken better care of Ruth," he says. "You've always been engrossed in yourself. No?"

"How would you know this, Karp? You hardly knew her."

Karp is a big time neuro-surgeon at Mt. Sinai Hospital, well known for his exploits in removing pituitary tumors, his instruments piercing either nose or throat to reach the base of the brain where the gland resides.

"Being with dozens of other women didn't help," he dares to spit out at me.

I am not about to make a case for lower numbers. Karp, as always, is the evangelist of good behavior and high morals. Every time I run into this man, he brings out the worst in me. I have been relatively well behaved for years, but I want to smack Karp. Struggling to remain civil, I change the subject.

"Remember the book you showed me a long time ago, the one about airplanes of World War II?"

"Sure I remember," Karp says. "The Junker dive bombers, the ones you said bombed you."

"Well," I tell him, "I've been reading a lot about that war, my war."

"Your war," he repeats with a hint of contempt.

"It turns out that you were quite wrong."

Karp looks up at me with his "I'm never wrong" mask on his face.

"Those dive bombers did not carry the thousands of pounds of bombs you thought they did. The plane you showed me was not introduced until 1941. The only version of the Stuka dive bomber in service in 1939 had a crew of two, with two machine guns in each wing and carried a single 500 pound bomb between the wheels."

He is silent.

"One bomb from each of the three airplanes," I tell him.

He leans over and, nose to nose, says, "I've been wanting to tell you this for a long time. You've been trading in on your escape from Poland long enough. Well, let me tell you right now that I see through all that. I know many people who have survived the Holocaust or who are children of survivors. You are neither. Sure, you had a few bombs explode in your ears. You got out because your family had money, but you've seduced women all your life with your little war stories. You were not involved in the Holocaust. Go read Elie Weisel and Primo Levi." He slams his paper down and runs out into the street.

I am aghast. I cannot believe that this puny asshole talks to me like this. I must have turned white.

"Don't take it too hard," Gabrielle Karp says before she runs after him. "He's been in a lot of pain with kidney stones."

"May he never be out of pain," I grumble and leave.

Except for the very few people who remain loyal friends throughout life, the rest are no more than acquaintances bound by circumstance. In my dreams, friendships are formed by a primal blending, a coming together of inexorable forces. In reality, most of the species is disappointing to one another, especially at moments of need. Who among any of my friends, anybody's friends, sees the other's true portrait? We mistake one another for who we assume they are or who we want the other to be: a father, a son, the life changing teacher, the Great Forgiver.

The whole exercise is profoundly depressing. "What need is there to weep over parts of life?" Seneca asked. "The whole of it calls for tears."

Radetzky now tells me that to really get a handle on who I am and how circumstances have shaped me, I should look for a psychoanalyst.

"Good ones do amazing work," he says. "I just finished three years with a shrink who changed my life."

"How did he do that? What did he do?"

"It's very subtle," Radetzky says.

"So subtle you can't describe it?"

"It's a long, introspective process," he tells me.

"Aha."

Pause. "I can do that all alone. Or with music," I tell him.

"But this is like telling a friend who has no other agenda than you. You know what I mean?"

So, fool that I am in pursuit of—what?—a better me, a me I might still know nothing about, I begin psychotherapy with a Philadelphia-trained psychoanalyst named Samuel Zeitfinger. What I know about Philadelphia is the Museum, the Barnes collection nearby and the orchestra when it was led by Eugene Ormandy. What I should have paid better attention to was the Walter Arensberg collection of Dada objects, principally the anti-retinal jokes of Marcel Duchamp. For a couple of sessions, Samuel Zeitfinger pays about as much attention to me as Duchamp did when he painted a mustache on the Mona Lisa.

"I never dealt with the damage done when I was eight years old," I whine, thinking, from the little I have just read of analytical practice, that this might be a perfect way to start. Radetzky had assured me that it"s all about the mother.

"I don"t know," I tell Zeitfinger, "but I sometimes think that I need a woman so desperately because my mother never gave me much except words, half of which I was busy translating from the Polish."

I wait for a response. Nothing. We are in the middle of a silence, "a pregnant silence," Zeitfinger is undoubtedly thinking, but pregnant only with unease, an annoying discomfort, with the hope that a bolt of lightning will rattle this office, light up the sky, break the goddam window behind Zeitfinger's chair.

Nevertheless, I continue jabbering into our second month together. I tell him about the border crossing, the suspected betrayal, the discord and near-violence between all of us, the only survivors in the family. I tell him about the vanished Mila who has been the powerful silent witness of my life, the only one in the theater watching this movie.

Toward the end of the month, I unload even more. "My whole body is tight with revenge fantasies."

"I'm beginning to hate you, Zeitfinger," I want to say.

"I hate everyone," I do actually say. "I love to hate." Now it is spilling out of me. "I like hitting people. I drink too much. I can't forgive. I think only of myself." Once begun, there is no end to self-flagellation. Zeitfinger finds a new position in his listening chair. I am quiet for a while, then I swing my feet down from the couch and sit up.

"You know what?" I say, "I can't stand being here. Let's end this farce. Let's call it a day."

Like a pop-up toy, he shoots up from his chair.

"A day?" he asks, his voice gruff like that of someone who speaks his first word after a night's sleep.

"I've had it," I tell him.

"Okay then, Mr. Mendelssohn, let me tell you this."

Zeitfinger comes over and sits on the other end of the couch.

"In your case, I suggest that you stop looking outside of yourself for answers. Here, our aim is to look deeply inside. After all, you have a rich history, plenty of reasons to be angry and fearful. You have reason as well to be proud of all you've accomplished, including, may I say, the stirring rapprochement with your father. It seems to me that you have very important work to do. Just as your—what to call it?—spiritual quests seem not to have touched you, thus far you have not immersed yourself in the psychoanalytic experience. That's fine. It is your choice, Mr. Mendelssohn. Do understand, though, that your life, like mine, is one damned thing after another. You cannot change the past. Life is a continuum, the bad and the good following upon each other. Perhaps this is not the right time for you to pursue analysis. Perhaps you will find ways to probe more deeply into yourself in the future. I certainly hope so."

O Mila, I do get depressed, although I don't want to admit it or talk about it very much. Maybe you were able to sense it when you were little. Is that possible? Probably not. But all these people in my life now want to save me from depression. They say I am a caterpillar ready to become a butterfly and I say that a crow will eat this caterpillar before change happens. And yet, I've been searching for a shape to my life, a parabola, a circle, a sonata, ever since it was driven out of shape on the way to that border and then crossing it. Uncertainty, unpredictable currents and eddies, undermine clarity. My life, special as any narcissist's, must be more than a muddle of random events, each one contradicting the last. I'm not searching for my place in the universe. I'm not anguishing over the impenetrability of ultimate things. And then, I say to myself, "Give us a break, Mendelssohn. You have always wanted what everyone wants: answers, the truth.

15.

AS A PLEASANT SUPPLEMENT to my serious work, I spend an hour or so each day on the cello. One day, as I arrive at Weingarten's Violin Shop to pick up my partly refurbished instrument, I hear some very uneven playing of a Bach Partita behind a closed door. A large stooped man eventually comes out, a glum expression on his face.

"Isaac Getlin?" I say.

"Yes, yes, it's Isaac," Getlin says and gives me a bear hug. "It's been years."

He blows his nose. His hands are all over me, patting me, squeezing, hugging, sucking air to stop his nose from dripping. "How's Ruth?" he asks.

"Gone."

He takes me in his big arms again and cries.

"I can't make music anymore," he says. "Look at my hands. They're frozen into claws. It's fucking arthritis," he says.

"We've all got our tsuris," I say and we walk over to Central Park. Getlin shuffles, can't keep up, needs to take small steps, unable to move without his cane. He is a mess. We sit on a bench. He pops a pain pill and I pop a Xanax.

"Where did Ruth go?" he asks.

"You want an address?"

"No, no, Michael. Believe me." Sobbing, Getlin's body rocks forward and back. "She is a good woman," he says, then thinks better of it.

Kids are playing all around us. The sun beats down.

"She never stopped talking about you," Getlin is saying. "She was so proud of you and your work."

I don't want to hear more. Ruth's frantic manias were her illness, as well as her health. I think of her bra hanging out of her pocket when she came home from a night with Isaac. Now that body parts hardly matter, I smile thinking of her naiveté.

"I like your work," Getlin says.

"I like yours."

"Our meeting now must be determined somewhere, by someone, by a higher power," he says.

"Not you too. Are you recovering from something?"

"I'll never recover," Getlin says. "I think I might kill myself. What am I going to do if I can't play the fiddle?"

Getlin proceeds with a full medical report, bone by deteriorating bone, nerve by unplugged nerve. Pity is not my forte. If it is called for, forgiveness for Getlin's having fucked my wife is not the next step in my quest for improvement. Please, not forgiveness, screwing up my face in disgust. First forgiveness, then absolution, the end of anger, then what?

Getlin unloads all his sorrows, as if he hasn't spoken to a soul in years. His son Henry is a junk bond trader, his present wife, a young flutist, is on tour in Europe. His teaching at the Curtis Institute has come to an end. But it isn't only Getlin who kvetches about everything, far from it. With Radetzky, with most of my friends, the first order of business before a meal together or even a phone conversation is "How's the prostate, the lower back, the memory and oi, the bowel movements?"

As a matter of fact, in my early fifties, belly aches have become my default state. Stomach pains stop me in my tracks. Often, they send me to the side of a building, doubled over. The gastro-intestinal vampire Dr. Auguste Binochet believes that my gall bladder is implicated and, with my hypochondrial acquiescence, removes the organ. When, a couple of weeks later, I recover enough to take long walks, the belly aches resume.

I report all this to Radetzky as we sit in my studio. "I can't believe I fulfilled his monthly quota for gall bladders."

"We do what those vultures want," Noah says. "We've got to believe that someone out there is looking out for us, especially since, given the tininess of tissues and cells standing between us and total breakdown, having all the organs and neurons work in harmony and in a proper sequence, a relatively healthy survival past middle age is itself a matter for wonder."

"I'm going to tell you something, but you've got to promise you won't repeat it ever."

"Shoot," Radetzky says.

"I signed up for a minimum of a dozen sessions with a myo-fascia massage therapist for belly work," I confess. "As the witch pressed hard into some critical part of my psoas, she told me that I had the body of a 35 -year-old. Not 40, not 50, but 35."

"The lady knows how to get a guy your age to come back every week," Radetzky says.

"'I'm going into a theta state,' she said and, closing her eyes, one hand under my sacrum, the other on my belly, she asked the theta people whether my discomfort was medical. 'No,' they answered immediately. 'Is it musculo-skeletal?' she then asked and poised as they are to make a diagnosis, she told me that they have given her an emphatic yes."

It is well past midnight, a time we often choose to talk, sleepless nights afflicting us both.

"So listen to this," I continue. "Last night, I'm lying in bed, the ball game on the radio, and suddenly my heart starts pounding."

Noah is as aware of body parts deteriorating as I have become.

"I've been with you when I thought you'd have a heart attack in the ninth inning," Radetzky says.

"I feel that artery in my neck. My pulse was racing, then slowed down, then raced again."

"Irregular heart beat," he says. "I've got that too."

We are co-kvetchers from way back.

"Normal wear and tear," he says, having been through two mild heart attacks.

I get to the point.

"You know what happened to Seth Abrams?"

"The poet?"

"He's in great shape, swims a mile a day, plays tennis three times a week. Well, he felt a little out of breath on the 18th lap in the pool. He went to his doctor who did an EKG and found him just fine. Seth knew it wasn't just fine, went to a cardiologist who did a stress test and said he was just fine. You know what he then did? He checked himself into a hospital at his own expense and said he wanted an angiogram, that he'd pay cash out of pocket for it because his doctor wouldn't recommend it. It cost some gargantuan amount, but, naturally, they did it and you know what? They found he was over 95 percent clogged and performed a quintuple bypass the next morning. They fucking saved his life. The story proves that you never know. Even the experts don't know."

When Radetzky leaves, I begin breathing into my belly, do some pelvic rocking, spinal twists, cat and dog stretches. I breathe deeply again. Every time, I am surprised at the pleasure this gives me. I push myself up, stretch my hamstrings, then take my cello out of its case, rosin the horse hair of the graceful bow, pull the instrument between my legs and begin tuning. I don't practice enough these days, immersed as I am in my painting and etching, but when I do, I play almost exclusively for my father. Most of the time my cello lives in a corner of the 57th Street living room, ready for a little consolation music, hopefully a momentary solace to Zyga's loneliness.

One evening after work, I let myself in, hear no noise in the apartment and take the cello out of its case. I sit in the middle of the living room and plant the instrument's pin on the colorful Persian carpet. I hear stirring from the bedroom. The toilet flushes and Zyga, rosy-cheeked and smiling, appears.

"No tea first?" Zyga asks.

"I want you to hear a piece I've been practicing," I say.

Zyga sits down on his embroidered armchair, closes his eyes and listens. I begin playing the Prelude from Bach's first cello suite. Zyga and I were at Carnegie Hall together to hear all six suites played in two concerts by Rostropovich, a strapping, grunting Russian who plays from his big Russian heart. Zyga and I have the Rostropovich sound in our minds, guarding against my awkward, bumbling fingers and the irritating scratching of my bow. Ruth was right. I am to be congratulated on my sheer tenacity, my refusal to give it up.

Suddenly, Zyga's head falls forward and I hear Polish words.

"What is happening," Zyga whispers as his body slumps and one of his legs kicks forward.

I drop the cello and leap toward my father, grab his arms, put my lips on his forehead. I hold him and hear his breath slowly come back to normal again. Still, I hold on to him, my own body shaking with fear, with what turns out to be premature grief. Zyga returns from some distant place, lifts his head and sits up.

French-speaking Dr. Petlin, my mother's potassium prescriber, a carnation in his lapel, arrives the next morning and diagnoses a mild stroke. The left side of Zyga's body is somewhat weakened and his speech just a little blurred, both symptoms remediable, if Zyga agrees to physical therapy, which he refuses. My father's certainty about this matter surprises me. I wonder if it has anything to do with his experience in the so-called sanitarium in Zopot, recounted by Herman Tauber.

"I'm staying with you," I announce.

"You will keep me company from time to time, just like now," Zyga says.

"I'm moving in until you are altogether well."

And I do. Flora stays on to cook us meals and clean the apartment. Because Rena left her nothing, Zyga has written a large check, assuring her that the amount, enough to buy a house in Poland, is specified in Rena's will.

Over the course of a year, my father seems to regain strength, but one day, as we eat the overcooked chicken, baked potatoes, and canned white asparagus Flora serves us, he asks me to get in touch with Ruth.

"I want to see her one more time," he says, his eyes momentarily closed. "I want to say goodbye."

Zyga's self-prognosis frightens me, but I locate Ruth on the Navajo reservation in Arizona and hand the telephone to Zyga.

"My darling Ruth," he says. "I think I do not stay a long time and, please, can I see you soon?"

She agrees to fly east right away, making Zyga breathe a huge sigh of relief and smile with happiness.

I hold his elbow to steady him as we walk to the duck pond just off

Central Park South. In the middle of the week, this is a sanctuary, the noise of the city a distant hum. The ducks quack and birds sing, as much country as Zyga requires. And here our conversations seem more intimate than anywhere else, though it is I who need to talk, to unload, to share everything with him.

"You are the reason my heart is no longer in my huge black paintings," I tell him. Zyga looks up at me with a quizzical expression.

"Now that I feel so close to you, I've lost the need to make big, narcissistic statements."

Zyga raises his eyebrows.

"I guess I once felt that I had to make a lot of noise, to be impudent and daring , bold enough for both of us."

Zyga smiles. "You do not anymore?" he asks peevishly.

"Now I can be quiet."

What else to tell him, what to confess, what to learn? I've been avoiding the burning topic that has plagued me from the time I was eight years old. Sure, it has lost its urgency, how could it not? Guilt or innocence, who cares? It doesn't matter, but that inscrutable central event has molded me, defined my relationships, my loves and hates, my life's work. As we walk slowly around the duck pond, I don't ask, I tell.

"You know, Zyga," I say as a couple of ducks paddle quietly by, "what happened at the border more than forty years ago doesn't matter. Everyone suffered. Everyone has an opinion. But it's so over, so finished, that whole thing. We are all capable of good and evil. Everyone. So why not accept this simple fact and get on with it?"

Zyga is staring at the passing ducks who are now quacking.

"As I see it, the intriguing thing about that moment, the irony, is that I stole a gold watch and you tried to give yours away. You are a hero. I want to be, but I'm not. What is a hero anyway? We all muddle our way through life, one damned thing after another." We walk out of the park, head slowly toward 400 East.

"The important thing is that I have my father. I love him with all my heart, warts and all."

I'm not sure he heard or if "warts" is a word he understands. Zyga holds my arm tightly. His body shakes a little and he stops every few steps to take a breath.

"And he has his son whose warts abound."

A week later, Ruth arrives, looking beautiful. I meet her at the airport and we taxi back to the city. She is radiant, soft and beautiful in a white skirt and top, the neckline decorated with colorful embroidery, around her waist a metallic belt encrusted with turquoise.

"So how are you?" I ask. "You're looking great."

"I'm in pretty good shape," Ruth says, "starting a new life, one that seems to suit me very well."

"We're all getting on with it, doing what we need to do."

I don't want to think excessively of the effect her beauty and radiance makes me feel. A bit shaky, I look out the window at the ugliness of Queens.

"I'm so glad to hear you say that," she says, looking out into Queens through the other window. "What about you? How are you getting along?"

"I'm mostly with Zyga. It's your doing."

"What do you mean my doing?"

"You brought this father and son together and I will be forever grateful."

We cross the bridge into the city.

"Oh Michael, you would have found him without me. He was there waiting. You were both waiting. You were so ready for him and he for you."

As we step out of the cab at 400 East, I can't help being attracted to her every motion, her legs and arms brown from the sun, her eyes a deep blue, her dark hair tied back with a bright red kerchief. She is in her mid-forties and obviously thriving.

"Do we even know how old Zyga is?" she asks inside the elevator and I tell her that, among other pre-war mysteries, there are no documents, certainly no birth certificates.

"But he must be more than eighty. And if he fought with Pilsudski," I say, sotto voce, "he must have been at least 20 in 1920 to qualify as a cavalry officer."

Upstairs, her reunion with Zyga is emotional and moving. Now they are unashamedly father and daughter, loving without reservations. Out of her bag, she pulls out two books.

"One is for you, Zyga, the other for Michael."

Both are books of Zbygniew Herbert's poetry, one in the original Polish, one in English translation.

"You're looking good," Ruth tells Zyga. "I was so afraid that you would be in pain and depressed. But look at you, like a man in his sixties, early sixties."

Then she digs into her purse and pulls out a little stone object and hands it to my father who holds it in his palm, then looks at Ruth.

"It's a fetish," she says, "a bear and cub."

"Fetish?" Zyga asks. "This is a Jewish word?"

Ruth laughs. "No, it's a sacred object to the people I'm living with, a bear and cub, you and Michael."

Zyga looks at it carefully, then lifts it to his lips and kisses it. Tears are now rolling down his cheeks. He hands it to me and I kiss it as he did. Until this moment, I perceived only Zyga's fading strength, the relative shortness of breath, the slight shaking of the hands. Ruth's presence rejuvenates him. His cheeks look rosy, his face relaxed, his smile genuine. Even though I realize that I will lose both of them, one to death, the other to her new life, I now feel only the warmth the three of us share, though it isn't easy to stop craving Ruth all over again.

She is staying with a friend of hers in the Village, but doesn't leave us until late in the evening. She returns midmorning and, while Zyga naps, she and I have coffee together. At the Empire table, she tells me about her new life.

"I have become totally dedicated to the worldwide plight of indigenous people," she says.

"You've been heading in that direction for quite a while. Where do you work? Where do you live?"

She looks down at her hands which are darting nervously around her saucer.

"I am living with someone," she says.

"Yes?"

I am curious yet don't want her to go on. I can't stop thinking of the Ruth who once, a long time ago, was entirely mine and I entirely hers, the Ruth whose body opened up to me a little at a time until it screamed its openness, its vulnerability, in full bloom like a lush dahlia. Once, for me, all flowers were daisies, but since Ruth and Olga's cataloguing the wonders of fields and woods in upstate New York, I have made a perfunctory study of flowers, and thus I know about dahlias which, like chrysanthemums, are lush but have little scent. In any case, those pale violet petals are gone, dropped to the earth, desiccated. They are blooming again elsewhere, but not for me. I look out the window and ask myself if I am turning toward masochism, another gate to pass through on the way to enlightenment.

"His name is Miguel, a Native American man who lacked formal education, was terribly abused when a child, the son of lunatic drunks. I like the way he fought his way into wanting to help others."

I am torn between jealousy and amusement, the latter by inserting her Miguel's heroics into the same camp as oh-so-many of us at different times in her life.

"What does your Miguel do?" I ask her.

I am now playing nervously with my coffee cup. The horrible little table is wobbling.

"He and I are very involved in educating his people. We're concentrating on teaching how capitalism works, particularly the politics of the greedy coal company that is stealing the tribe's natural resources."

Zyga comes in, looking refreshed.

"I am afraid that you are a dream," he says to Ruth, "so I am full of joy that it is you and that you are really here."

They go off to the park together and spend the day there. I take the opportunity to have a few hours in my studio.

"We had a fabulous day," Ruth reports when we meet again.

Zyga nods, smiling so broadly that I can see his molars.

"Lunch at the zoo," she says.

"The food is terrible," Zyga says.

"But we were happy," Ruth says. She takes Zyga's hands in hers. "What do you think, Zyga? Enough walking for a day or two?"

After drinks late in the afternoon, Ruth agrees to have dinner out with me. Zyga is pleased.

"You are really back," he tells Ruth.

In a Japanese restaurant, we sit uncomfortably cross-legged on cushions. She tells me about teaching writing on the Navajo reservation, proud of her students' accomplishments.

"I love turning people on to your Polish poets, to Flaubert and my old Victorians."

"You're in full bloom," I tell her sullenly. "I must admit that it hurts a little to see you so well without me, but I, too, am doing well."

"What a marvel if we can keep doing this well," she says.

We touch on specific aspects of our life together, times when our agreements were joyous and heartfelt, times when, both of us lonely, we went our separate ways, either coming back to each other or widening the rift, making reunion hard or impossible.

"I was pretty awful at times," Ruth says. "I'm not proud of some of the things I did." She takes my hand in hers.

"Michael, I forgive you for your—how to say it?—indiscretions. Do you forgive me for mine?"

"You know how I feel about forgiveness."

"A forgiver you've never been."

"I'm still not. But I no longer think of it even as an option. I do not forgive, I accept. You know what I mean?"

"Yes," she says, "I do."

"When I did things to hurt you, I don't forgive myself. I accept that part of me, even though I don't particularly like it."

Ruth stays nearly a week. There are moments when I want to take her in my arms and beg her to come back, but I manage to maintain sanity and self-control. Ruth's most difficult parting is leaving Zyga.

"You must come back," he says, taking her in his arms.

"I will if you promise to keep improving."

They are both sobbing until I glance at my pocket watch, newly refurbished, and announce that it is time to leave.

On the way back to the airport, she says,

"Eventually, I know that I will work myself up to be some sort of an international advocate, perhaps a fighter [and here she laughs a self-deprecating laugh] a fighter for a very important cause. Imagine, Michael, what Marvin and Blanche would have said about my wanting to work for the United Nations."

For days after Ruth's departure, Zyga is forlorn and does not want to eat. I try to entertain him with my improving cello scales, arpeggios, and the occasional tune from Brahms, Bach, even pop melodies that elicit smiles, even laughter. I spend most of every day and all my nights with my father.

As his eyesight begins to fail, I read him the paper every day and passages from books, especially the two poetry books Ruth left for us. I read aloud from the English translations of Zbygniew Herbert while Zyga, with the help of a magnifier, tries to make out the original Polish.

"This one is about what an artist should do while tormented by the world's horrors," I tell him. "'So, why have I been writing unimportant poems on flowers?' This is what the poet is asking himself," I explain, even though Zyga needs no explanation.

I look up and see that he is fully engaged in the original Polish. Still, I continue to read aloud.

"'Thus, one can use in poetry names of Greek shepherds; One can attempt to catch the color of morning sky, a rite of love and also, once again, in dead earnest, offer to the betrayed world...a rose.'"

Zyga looks up, visibly moved.

"A rose," he says softly.

I cover his hands with mine, a gesture I have been making for years to soothe his wounded cuticles, now recovered and healthy.

"A quiet gift, the rose," I say, "and the emblem of the social Democrats, no?"

He nods.

"One of these days, I will bring you a red rose."

He is smiling.

"I love your beautiful smile," I tell him. "I wish I knew what you did to get rid of your anger. You were angry so much of the time. How did you let it go? What took its place?"

"You did," Zyga says softly. "You took its place."

He says it in Polish, then English. It feels like the most ardent declaration of love I have ever heard. This much love is almost unbearable. It fills me full and, from the pit of my stomach, it also brings regrets. Why not long ago? Why all those wasted years?

I compose myself and clear my throat.

"But there is so much to be angry about. I still don't know how to stop it. Probably your anger with Rena and Bolek was even more painful than mine."

He looks into my eyes, but says nothing.

"But what about the anger with all those hateful people who rule nations, who hate Jews or gypsies or blacks? What do you do with that?"

My father turns away from me, maybe nursing a petty hatred of his own or regretting an unjustified one, I don't know.

"When I'm angry," I say and he turns back to me, "my whole body tenses so hard I think I'm going to break, like a string on my cello. And what a waste, these revenge fantasies, this wishing for better outcomes, for harm to strike people who we know deserve harm."

Zyga nods, knits his brow, becomes thoughtful and serious.

"I am not a wise man," he says, "but it is not necessary to be wise to understand that anger brings nothing good. How do I know this and when does it come to me?"

He sits up straight and takes my hands in his.

"Many years ago, I have terrible stomach aches and terrible headaches, so much pain I think I am going to die. This happens from time to time all my life. In Poland, I go for a month to a beautiful sanitarium in Zopoet. When I come back to Warsaw, everything is the same, but I am different. I say to myself that I can live with difficult people if I do not pay too much attention. And so it is until the war."

"The war, the war, all fucking wars," I blurt out.

He looks up at me, then back down, his face now more wrinkled than before.

"The war does not make me angry," he says. "It is much worse than that. It takes my life away from me. Headaches come back and stomachaches. Depression takes the place of anger. I don't know what to do. Then, after years of what they call in Europe neurasthenia and what I call terrible sadness, I say to myself, 'Idiot, you cannot change it so if you want to live, (and I want to live because my Mishek lives), you must climb out of this ditch no matter how hard this is.'"

"My god, Zyga, how did you climb out of the ditch?"

"First, I know that I must get out of my chair, away from the radio, away from the house and away from that business."

"During all those years I was gone, you, too, were gone."

"Not far," Zyga says, "but, with Rytek, we make new friends, talk and read, and with Frankenheim, we watch wrestling." He laughs. "I take long walks, look for what is beautiful, like beautiful women who walk on Fifth Avenue. Suddenly I am smiling."

I have never heard him talk like this. I am overwhelmed by love and even hope. I swallow hard to contain my emotions. I suspected that anger was hereditary. Now, I hope that it is good sense if I allow it to penetrate. Still, I know everyone in the world is angry and depressed, some more than others. Why they're not if they're not, I don't comprehend. I know that conditions everywhere call for anger, though perhaps not the unfiltered anger that has felt like my patrimony.

"I am always so negative, so aching for a fight," I confess to my father.

"I liked hitting people. I started hitting in boarding school, then in college. Did you know that?" Zyga shakes his head.

"I once nearly killed a Jew hater in Warsaw. I have imagined a huge hole in the earth where Poland once was."

I reach for the Zbygniew Herbert book again.

"Here are a few lines from another of his poems. It speaks to those of us whose people have perished.

> *'But in these matters*
> *Accuracy is necessary*
> *One can't get it wrong*
> *Even in a single case*
> *Despite everything we are*
> *All our brothers' keepers*
> *Ignorance about those who are lost*
> *Undermines the reality of the world.'"*

Zyga takes it in, clutching the bear fetish which never leaves his sight.

"We know nothing about how they die. I think this all the time. It makes me crazy."

I watch as my father begins to sob, then lists them, one by one.

"My brother Stash," he says, "Marysia and Henio."

He swallows hard and begins to choke, remembering their names.

"Oh my god," he gasps, "your grandfather, my father Solomon, and Paulina, my mother—that angel of a woman."

I try to hold his hands, but he wrests them free, hits himself on the sides of his head as tears flow like a torrent down his cheeks.

"How did they die?" he cries in a rage. "The Germans? The Russians? The Poles? How could they push my mother into a grave of the dead? How can men shoot babies? Oh Myszek, my Myszek, I will never know who murdered who and how each of them died."

I dab at his tears and he quiets down. My tears have been flowing with his. He lies down on the couch and we both begin to cough. I kneel at his side and lay my head on the pillow next to his. We are cheek to cheek, like lovers, and I wouldn't want to be anywhere but here, a sacred moment, a lot more than a moment, perhaps a half hour of silence. But I have more to confess.

"I don't know how to forgive. I do not forgive," I tell him and he reaches for my hand. "Listen to this, Zyga. I really can be insane. Once, I lived with the idea that if anyone licked my heart, he would be poisoned. It isn't an original idea. I don't think you ever went to movies, but there was a movie called *Shoah*. I wish you had seen it. It was about Polish Jew hatred. In it, one of the two surviving Warsaw ghetto fighters said those very words. I've never seen anyone so full of hatred. He said that if anyone licked his heart, he would be poisoned."

I look closely at my father's calm, relaxed face, seeing, I think, for the first time, that he has a few black hairs in his eyebrows.

"I've always wondered if anyone in his right mind could put his arm around that brave ghetto fighter and suggest, 'Now, now, you'll feel much better if you forgive?' You know, Zyga, that's what some of my friends would advise. Of course," I assure him, "My heart has not earned that fighter's passion to hate."

He listens. My father listens and understands. What could be better than that? When he falls back asleep, I make myself a drink, then play a little on my cello.

Zyga seems to be gaining some strength, enjoys our meals together and our short walks. Suzi Schwab displays my "small work," the etchings and drawings, which get modest attention in the press, while the occasional new large painting is gobbled up by one or another of a substantial number of collectors. And so, for the next year and a half, our days pass. And then, in the course of a single week, Zyga is shaken by two more strokes, each one stealing more vitality, capacity for walking, even talking. In desperation, I read aloud, waiting for a word or two of response, and if they do not come, I wait for signs, a squeeze of the hand, a little smile, guttural sounds which I learn to interpret as an expression of agreement, the need for a bedpan, a sip of water, the beginning of a deeper sleep. Organs begin to fail, depriving Zyga of breath and move- ment. The nurse now stays every night in the spare bedroom, checks Zyga's vital signs, turns him over, washes him, cleans up after bowel movements. Dr. Petlin, a carnation in his lapel, supplies the morphine he says will keep Zyga pain-free.

"No one must know," Dr. Petlin warns us, as he undoubtedly warns all his dying Upper East Side patients. "I am offering you a very special service. It's worth a lot, I assure you."

As my father drifts into morphine hazes, I sit on the side of his bed and watch him. In spite of twenty years of my hiding from him, we did find each other. What would it have been like if we weren't interrupted by war, displacement, by having to learn a new language, live in unfa- miliar places? My father's breath changes into a gravelly rasp. I listen hard, then run off to call Ruth on the kitchen phone. I worry that she won't be able to catch a plane in time and I'm moved when, two days later, she arrives and sits by his side.

"Do you remember that monster," she asks, leaning close to my father's ear, "the fat guy in a zebra swim suit, the one who came into the ring with a tiger mask on his face?"

Zyga is trying to smile, I'm sure of it.

"What about the Gorilla George?" she asks.

He blinks an eye.

"Those were the days," Ruth says.

Zyga's breath comes in spurts now, one breath followed by seconds of silence. Ruth lays her head on his chest. Alone and in unison, Ruth and I tell him how much we love him. And then, when we leave the room for a minute, Zyga breathes his last breath. In spite of my strategies, days spent jabbering non-stop, tender touching and wiping spittle from his mouth, it is an unwinnable battle and Zyga stops breathing. Ruth collapses to her knees and I go down on mine, not to pray as Ruth might be doing but my legs won't hold me.

"What didn't I tell you, Zyga? Did you hear how much we both love you?"

Her head is on his chest. The bear and cub fetish lies beside his hand. Radetzky who sat beside his mother as she was dying, told me he felt the swoosh of her soul leave her body and head out the window. I move close to my father to test for an escaping soul. In spite of my despair, I can't help smiling.

"When Zyga's cells died," I say to Ruth, "everything that is Zyga, except for the memories, dies. Like everything in the universe, whatever lives, dies, the ultimate existential absurdity, the end."

A few days later, I drive the Saab across the Atlantic City Bridge into Long Beach. Having changed dramatically over the past few years, it no longer seems like Zyga's kind of place. The Lieber Hotel is gone, now a high-rise apartment house with balconies. The beach is clean and white. I take off my shoes, roll up my pants, and walk the two or so miles of warm sand. The beach is crowded, kids playing by the water's edge, riding the waves onto shore. Zyga would not recognize the place. I miss Ruth. She and I could be walking hand in hand on this beach, swinging our arms as we once did. I climb toward the dunes, sit down, take my shirt off and put it behind my head for a pillow. I take off my sunglasses and close my eyes.

Now that everyone is gone, Mila. It is time for me to begin my search for you. But where? Have you become a Swede or did you return to Poland? Did you emigrate to Australia or Israel, Chicago or Argentina? If you are alive, living somewhere, are you married? Do you have a different name? Children? And your beautiful mother? Are you as beautiful as she was? Did you try to numb your childhood out of existence or did you face it with all the unpredictable consequences? Do you wake up in terror in the middle of the night? Do you like Chicken Kiev or Duck a l'Orange?

None of them carried, in their bodies or minds, the religion or rituals of their past. Zyga was aware of all of it, but he suffered with nostalgia which sent him into years of aloneness and depression. Like him, I am stuck with nostalgia, now for his old Long Beach, the breeding ground for those argumentative Jews, depressed refugees and the rabble-rousing Unionists. Mila, you probably remember Zyga only as a miserable, non-functioning man, but he had become so much more. Don't think of him as a betrayer or coward. Who knows what he did or did not do at that crucial moment? He was a caring man, a thinking man, a loving father. I want you to know and believe that he was a complicated man whose life, like yours and mine, was stolen from him, a life he managed to rebuild in spite of the fact that family ties were buried with those who perished. Nearly all records, letters, photographs, documents, have been destroyed, if not by war, then willfully. There was no reckoning with the past, a past that was too painful to face.

As I lie here in the sun, Milusha, a painting is forming behind my eyelids. You might ask—and rightfully so—why, at a time like this, with the loss of a beautiful father and a wife of many years, I am making a painting behind closed eyes. All I can say is that it feels right. Half the canvas is a wash of yellow, a lemon yellow mixed with a bit of ochre. I say it's a wash, but, in fact, I will lay it on with a palette knife, maybe a trowel, the canvas being huge, and the paint a bit pockmarked, more ochre in places, more yellow in others. Somewhere on this skin of pigment, I will squeeze a blob of a light cadmium red, oily and gooey, squeezed into a lively, maybe insect-like shape, dripping and oozing with oil. On the right side of the canvas, perhaps two-thirds of the way, black shapes begin to form, but not the weighty shapes of yore. Rather a brushed web of black, in clusters, suggesting musical fugues, spindly and organic. I have never been much concerned with what is generally called beautiful, but the images forming in my mind's eye are beautiful, the colors and shapes evoking spasms of joy from heart and belly. But it's so hard to describe this new child, still in the process of being born. The moment I'm back in my studio, I will put brush and knife to canvas. I only hope that one day you will see it.

THE HAPPY SHRIEKS OF KIDS AT PLAY and the pounding of a passing boom box penetrate my daydreams. I sit up. The beach is in frantic movement, kids running, little red balls making arcs in the sky, bathing suits mere ribbons and strings, a jumble of delights: ruby red towels; turquoise blankets; electric green and orange pails and shovels; multi-colored umbrellas; the white sand, the deep blue sea; sailboats in the distance. Though a bit too French for Maître Mendelssohn, my body responds to the change of tempo, like a dog shaking off the dullness of sleep, ready for whatever comes next.

Since my midmorning arrival, a bunch of kids, their number growing by the hour, is near completion of a huge sand fortress, castles within castles. Hefty fortress walls surround towers and turrets, a labyrinth of paths and underground tunnels, all of it encircled by a moat, not yet filled with water, though already populated by toy alligators, undoubtedly absent from medieval European moats. I walk down to the construction, delighted by the enthusiasm that surrounds it.

"Is this based on an actual fortress?" I ask a tall boy who seems to be the master planner.

"Fourteenth century," the boy replies.

"It's beautiful."

"I know a lot about fortresses and fortification," the kid says.

"Can you tell me what all these structures are?" I ask and listen to a lesson I hardly expect, words I know only vaguely, if at all.

"See the flying bridge from the counterscarp to the other side of the moat? Near it," the young man goes on, "stands the keep, surrounded by the bailey. See this curtain wall? It's a fortification high enough to make ladders useless and thick enough to withstand siege engines, with portcullises and arrowslipts on all sides."

Some of the kids brought beautifully made replicas of catapults and perfect little armored soldiers and horses, either inside or outside the castle walls.

"Battlements like these," says the young man, "have crenellations, hoardings, machicolations and loopholes."

"I can't keep up with you," I tell him, laughing.

Aside from its historical correctness, which I cannot question, the sheer beauty and absolute impermanence of this work of art touches me deeply. The castle keeps growing, even though its lower walls are being threatened by the incoming tide. Parents, friends, and strangers are now snapping pictures, elbowing one another to get the best shots. No one seems to mind that there will be no evidence of the chateau's short-lived magnificence.

I walk to the shore to dip my feet in the water. My head and chest are in the hot sun, my feet in the cool waves, the tide pulling on my toes as they sink into the sand. Mila, dear Milushka, I feel fully alive. Much is missing, but there are these lines from one of the poems I read to Zyga.

"Thus one can use in poetry names of Greek shepherds, one can attempt to catch the color of morning sky, a rite of love and, also, once again, in dead earnest, offer to the betrayed world...a rose.'"

Acknowlegdements

With enormous gratitude, I want to thank Chris Lynch for her invaluable help in editing this story, as well as my wife, Loie, who managed to remain her wonderful self during the years of my writing.

Fomite

Burlington, VT

A fomite is a medium capable of transmitting infectious organisms from one individual to another.

"The activity of art is based on the capacity of people to be infected by the feelings of others." Tolstoy, *What Is Art?*

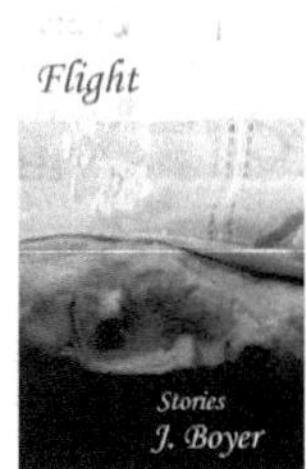

Flight and Other Stories - Jay BoyerIn *Flight and Other Stories,* we're with the fattest woman on earth as she draws her last breaths and her soul ascends toward its final reward. We meet a divorcee who can fly with no more effort than flapping her arms. We follow a middle-aged butler whose love affair with a young woman leads him first to the mysteries of bondage and then to the pleasures of malice. Story by story, we set foot into worlds so strange as to seem all but surreal, yet everything feels familiar, each moment rings true. And that's when we recognize we're in the hands of one of America's truly original talents.

Loisaida - Dan ChodorokoffCatherine, a young anarchist estranged from her parents and squatting in an abandoned building on New York's Lower East Side, is fighting with her boyfriend and conflicted about her work on an underground newspaper. After learning of a developer's plans to demolish a community garden, Catherine builds an alliance with a group of Puerto Rican community activists. Together they confront the confluence of politics, money, and real estate that rule Manhattan. All the while she learns important lessons from her great-grandmother's life in the Yiddish anarchist movement that flourished on the Lower East Side at the turn of the century. In this coming-of-age story, family saga, and tale of urban politics, Dan Chodorkoff explores the "principle of hope" and examines how memory and imagination inform social change.

Improvisational Arguments - Anna Faktorovich
Improvisational Arguments is written in free verse to capture the essence of modern problems and triumphs. The poems clearly relate short, frequently humorous, and occasionally tragic stories about travels to exotic and unusual places, fantastic realms, abnormal jobs, artistic innovations, political objections, and misadventures with love.

Carts and Other Stories - Zdravka Evtimova
Roots and wings are the key words that best describe the short story collection *Carts and Other Stories,* by Zdravka Evtimova. The book is emotionally multilayered and memorable because of its internal power, vitality and ability to touch both your heart and your mind. Within its pages, the reader discovers new perspectives and true wealth, and learns to see the world with different eyes. The collection lives on the borders of different cultures. *Carts and Other Stories* will take the reader to wild and powerful Bulgarian mountains, to silver rains in Brussels, to German quiet winter streets, and to wind-bitten crags in Afghanistan. This book lives for those seeking to discover the beauty of the world around them, and will have them appreciating what they have—and perhaps what they have lost as well.

Fomite
Burlington, VT

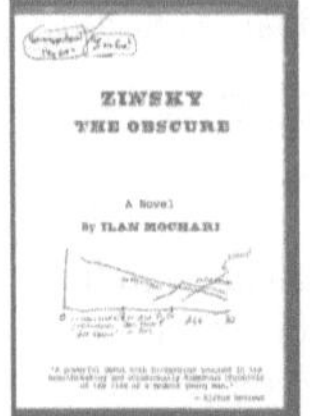

Zinsky the Obscure - Ilan Mochari

"If your childhood is brutal, your adulthood becomes a daily attempt to recover: a quest for ecstasy and stability in recompense for their early absence." So states the 30-year-old Ariel Zinsky, whose bachelor-like lifestyle belies the torturous youth he is still coming to grips with. As a boy, he struggles with the beatings themselves; as a grownup, he struggles with the world's indifference to them. *Zinsky the Obscure* is his life story, a humorous chronicle of his search for a redemptive ecstasy through sex, an entrepreneurial sports obsession, and finally, the cathartic exercise of writing it all down. Fervently recounting both the comic delights and the frightening horrors of a life in which he feels—always—that he is not like all the rest, Zinsky survives the worst and relishes the best with idiosyncratic style, as his heartbreak turns into self-awareness and his suicidal ideation into self-regard. A vivid evocation of the all-consuming nature of lust and ambition—and the forces that drive them.

Kasper Planet: Comix and Tragix - Peter Schumann

The British call him Punch; the Italians, Pulchinella; the Russians, Petruchka; the Native Americans, Coyote. These are the figures we may know. But every culture that worships authority will breed a Punch-like, anti-authoritarian resister. Yin and yang—it has to happen. The Germans call him Kasper. Truth-telling and serious pranking are dangerous professions when going up against power. Bradley Manning sits naked in solitary; Julian Assange is pursued by Interpol, Obama's Department of Justice, and Amazon.com. But—in contrast to merely human faces— masks and theater can often slip through the bars. Consider our American Kaspers: Charlie Chaplin, Woody Guthrie, Abby Hoffman, the Yes Men—theater people all, utilizing various forms to seed critique. Their profiles and tactics have evolved along with those of their enemies. Who are the bad guys that call forth the Kaspers? Over the last half century, with his Bread & Puppet Theater, Peter Schumann has been tireless in naming them, excoriating them with Kasperdom....
from Marc Estrin's Foreword to Planet Kasper

Loosestrife - Greg Delanty

This book is a chronicle of complicity in our modern lives, a witnessing of war and the destruction of our planet. It is also an attempt to adjust the more destructive blueprint myths of our society. Often our cultural memory tells us to keep quiet about the aspects that are most challenging to our ethics, to forget the violations we feel and tremors that keep us distant and numb.

The Co-Conspirator's Tale - Ron Jacobs

There's a place where love and mistrust are never at peace; where duplicity and deceit are the universal currency. *The Co-Conspirator's Tale* takes place within this nebulous firmament. There are crimes committed by the police in the name of the law. Excess in the name of revolution. The combination leaves death in its wake and the survivors struggling to find justice in a San Francisco Bay Area noir by the author of the underground classic *The Way the Wind Blew: A History of the Weather Underground* and the novel *Short Order Frame Up*.

Fomite
Burlington, VT

Short Order Frame Up - Ron Jacobs

1975. America as lost its war in Vietnam and Cambodia. Racially tinged riots are tearing the city of Boston apart. The politics and counterculture of the 1960s are disintegrating into nothing more than sex, drugs, and rock and roll. The Boston Red Sox are on one of their improbable runs toward a postseason appearance. In a suburban town in Maryland, a young couple are murdered and another young man is accused. The couple are white and the accused is black. It is up to his friends and family to prove he is innocent. This is a story of suburban ennui, race, murder, and injustice. Religion and politics, liberal lawyers and racist cops. In *Short Order Frame Up*, Ron Jacobs has written a piece of crime fiction that exposes the wound that is US racism. Two cultures existing side by side and across generations--a river very few dare to cross. His characters work and live with and next to each other, often unaware of each other's real life. When the murder occurs, however, those people that care about the man charged must cross that river and meet somewhere in between in order to free him from (what is to them) an obvious miscarriage of justice.

All the Sinners Saints - Ron Jacobs

A young draftee named Victor Willard goes AWOL in Germany after an altercation with a commanding officer. Porgy is an African-American GI involved with the international Black Panthers and German radicals. Victor and a female radical named Ana fall in love. They move into Ana's room in a squatted building near the US base in Frankfurt. The international campaign to free Black revolutionary Angela Davis is coming to Frankfurt. Porgy and Ana are key organizers and Victor spends his days and nights selling and smoking hashish, while becoming addicted to heroin. Police and narcotics agents are keeping tabs on them all. Politics, love, and drugs. Truths, lies, and rock and roll. *All the Sinners Saints* is a story of people seeking redemption in a world awash in sin.

When You Remember Deir Yassin - R. L. Green

When You Remember Deir Yassin is a collection of poems by R. L. Green, an American Jewish writer, on the subject of the occupation and destruction of Palestine. Green comments: "Outspoken Jewish critics of Israeli crimes against humanity have, strangely, been called 'anti-Semitic' as well as the hilariously illogical epithet 'self-hating Jews.' As a Jewish critic of the Israeli government, I have come to accept these accusations as a stamp of approval and a badge of honor, signifying my own fealty to a central element of Jewish identity and ethics: one must be a lover of truth and a friend to the oppressed, and stand with the victims of tyranny, not with the tyrants, despite tribal loyalty or self-advancement. These poems were written as expressions of outrage, and of grief, and to encourage my sisters and brothers of every cultural or national grouping to speak out against injustice, to try to save Palestine, and in so doing, to reclaim for myself my own place as part of the Jewish people." Poems in the original English are accompanied by Arabic translations.

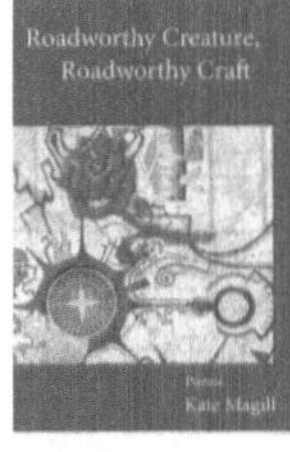

Roadworthy Creature, Roadworthy Craft - Kate Magill

Words fail but the voice struggles on. The culmination of a decade's worth of performance poetry, *Roadworthy Creature, Roadworthy Craft* is Kate Magill's first full-length publication. In lines that are sinewy yet delicate, Magill's poems explore the terrain where idea and action meet, where bodies and words commingle to form a strange new flesh, a breathing text, an "I" that spirals outward from itself.

Fomite
Burlington, VT

The Listener Aspires to the Condition of Music - Barry Goldensohn
"I know of no other selected poems that selects on one theme, but this one does, charting Goldensohn's career-long attraction to music's performance, consolations and its august, thrilling, scary and clownish charms. Does all art aspire to the condition of music as Pater claimed, exhaling in a swoon toward that one class act? Goldensohn is more aware than the late 19th century of the overtones of such breathing: his poems thoroughly round out those overtones in a poet's lifetime of listening." John Peck, poet, editor, Fellow of the American Academy of Rome

The Derivation of Cowboys & Indians - Joseph D. Reich
The Derivation of Cowboys & Indians represents a profound journey, a breakdown of the American Dream from a social, cultural, historical, and spiritual point of view. Reich examines in concise detail the loss of the collective unconscious, commenting on our contemporary postmodern culture with its self-interested excesses, on where and how things all go wrong, and how social/political practice rarely meets its original proclamations and promises. Reich's surreal and self-effacing satire brings this troubling message home. *The Derivation of Cowboys & Indians* is a desperate search and struggle for America's literal, symbolic, and spiritual home.

Views Cost Extra - L.E. Smith
Views that inspire, that calm, or that terrify—all come at some cost to the viewer. In *Views Cost Extra* you will find a New Jersey high school preppy who wants to inhabit the "perfect" cowboy movie, a rural mailman disgusted with the residents of his town who wants to live with the penguins, an ailing screen-writer who strikes a deal with Johnny Cash to reverse an old man's failures, an old man who ponders a young man's suicide attempt, a one-armed blind blues singer who wants to reunite with the car that took her arm on the assembly line— and more. These stories suggest that we must pay something to live even ordinary lives.

Travers' Inferno - *L.E. Smith*
In the 1970's, churches began to burn in Burlington, Vermont. If it was arson, no one or no reason could be found to blame. This book suggests arson, but makes no claim to historical realism. It claims, instead, to capture the dizzying 70's zeitgeist of aggressive utopian movements, distrust in authority, escapist alternative lifestyles, and a bewildered society of onlookers. In the tradition of John Gardner's *Sunlight Dialogues*, the characters of *Travers' Inferno* are colorful and damaged, sometimes comical, sometimes tragic, looking for meaning through desperate acts. Travers Jones, the protagonist, is grounded in the transcendent—philosophy, epilepsy, arson as purification—and mystified by the opposite sex, haunted by an absent father and directed by an uncle with a grudge. He is seduced by a professor's wife and chased by an endearing if ineffective sergeant of police. There are secessionist Quebecois involved in these church burns who are murdering as well as pilfering and burning. There are changing alliances, violent deaths, lovemaking, and a belligerent cat.

Entanglements - Tony Magistrale
A poet and a painter may employ different mediums to express the same snow-blown afternoon in January, but sometimes they find a way to capture the moment in such a way that their respective visions still manage to stir a reverberation, a connection. In part, that's what *Entanglements* seeks to do. Not so much for the poems and paintings to speak directly to one another, but for them to stir points of similarity.

Fomite
Burlington, VT

The Empty Notebook Interrogates Itself - Susan Thomas

The Empty Notebook began its life as a very literal metaphor for a few weeks of what the poet thought was writer's block, but was really the struggle of an eccentric persona to take over her working life. It won. And for the next three years everything she wrote came to her in the voice of the Empty Notebook, who, as the notebook began to fill itself, became rather opinionated, changed gender, alternately acted as bully and victim, had many bizarre adventures in exotic locales, and developed a somewhat politically incorrect attitude. It then began to steal the voices and forms of other poets and tried to immortalize itself in various poetry reviews. It is now thrilled to collect itself in one slim volume.

My God, What Have We Done? - Susan Weiss

In a world afflicted with war, toxicity, and hunger, does what we do in our private lives really matter? Fifty years after the creation of the atomic bomb at Los Alamos, newlyweds Pauline and Clifford visit that once-secret city on their honeymoon, compelled by Pauline's fascination with Oppenheimer, the soulful scientist. The two stories emerging from this visit reverberate back and forth between the loneliness of a new mother at home in Boston and the isolation of an entire community dedicated to the development of the bomb. While Pauline struggles with unforeseen challenges of family life, Oppenheimer and his crew reckon with forces beyond all imagining. Finally the years of frantic research on the bomb culminate in a stunning test explosion that echoes a rupture in the couple's marriage. Against the backdrop of a civilization that's out of control, Pauline begins to understand the complex, potentially explosive physics of personal relationships. At once funny and dead serious, *My God, What Have We Done?* sifts through the ruins left by the bomb in search of a more worthy human achievement.

As It Is On Earth- Peter M. Wheelwright

Four centuries after the Reformation Pilgrims sailed up the down-flowing watersheds of New England, Taylor Thatcher, irreverent scion of a fallen family of Maine Puritans, is still caught in the turbulence. In his errant attempts to escape from history, the young college professor is further unsettled by his growing attraction to Israeli student Miryam Bluehm as he is swept by Time through the "family thing"—from the tangled genetic and religious history of his New England parents to the redemptive birthday secret of Esther Fleur Noire Bishop, the Cajun-Passamaquoddy woman who raised him and his younger half-cousin/half-brother, Bingham.The landscapes, rivers, and tidal estuaries of Old New England and the Mayan Yucatan are also casualties of history in Thatcher's story of Deep Time and re-discovery of family on Columbus Day at a high-stakes gambling casino, rising in resurrection over the starlit bones of a once-vanquished Pequot Indian tribe.

Signed Confessions - *Tom Walker*

Guilt and a desperate need to repent drive the antiheroes in Tom Walker's dark (and often darkly funny) stories: a gullible journalist falls for the 40-year-old stripper he profiles in a magazine, a faithless husband abandons his family and joins a support group for lost souls, a merciless prosecuting attorney grapples with the suicide of his gay son, an aging misanthrope must make amends to five former victims, an egoistic naval hero is haunted by apparitions of his dead wife and a mysterious little girl. The seven tales in *Signed Confessions* measure how far guilty men will go to obtain a forgiveness no one can grant but themselves.

Fomite
Burlington, VT

Love's Labours - Jack Pulaski

In the four stories and two novellas that comprise *Love's Labors* the protagonists, Ben and Laura, discover in their fervid romance and long marriage their interlocking fates, and the histories that preceded their births. They also learned something of the paradox between love and all the things it brings to its beneficiaries: bliss, disaster, duty, tragedy, comedy, the grotesque, and tenderness. Ben and Laura's story is also the particularly American tale of immigration to a new world. Laura's story begins in Puerto Rico, and Ben's lineage is Russian-Jewish. They meet in City College of New York, a place at least analogous to a melting pot. Laura struggles to rescue her brother from gang life and heroin. She is mother to her younger sister; their mother Consuelo is the financial mainstay of the family and consumed by work. Despite filial obligations, Laura aspires to be a serious painter. Ben writes, cares for, and is caught up in the misadventures and surreal stories of his younger schizophrenic brother. Laura is also a story teller as powerful and enchanting as Scheherazade. Ben struggles to survive such riches, and he and Laura endure.

Suite for Three Voices - *Derek Furr*

Suite for Three Voices is a dance of prose genres, teeming with intense human life in all its humor and sorrow. A son uncovers the horrors of his father's wartime experience, a hitchhiker in a muumuu guards a mysterious parcel, a young man foresees his brother's brush with death on September 11. A Victorian poetess encounters space aliens and digital archives, a runner hears the voice of a dead friend in the song of an indigo bunting, a teacher seeks wisdom from his students' errors and Neil Young. By frozen waterfalls and neglected graveyards, along highways at noon and rivers at dusk, in the sound of bluegrass, Beethoven, and Emily Dickinson, the essays and fiction in this collection offer moments of vision.

The Housing Market - Joseph D. Reich

In Joseph Reich's most recent social and cultural, contemporary satire of suburbia entitled, "The Housing market: a comfortable place to jump off the end of the world," the author addresses the absurd, postmodern elements of what it means, or for that matter not, to try and cope and function, and survive and thrive, or live and die in the repetitive and existential, futile and self-destructive, homogenized, monochromatic landscape of a brutal and bland, collective unconscious, which can spiritually result in a gradual wasting away and erosion of the senses or conflict and crisis of a desperate, disproportionate 'situational depression,' triggering and leading the narrator to feel constantly abandoned and stranded, more concretely or proverbially spoken, "the eternal stranger," where when caught between the fight or flight psychological phenomena, naturally repels him and causes him to flee and return without him even knowing it into the wild, while by sudden circumstance and coincidence discovers it surrounds the illusory-like circumference of these selfsame Monopoly board cul-de-sacs and dead ends. Most specifically, what can happen to a solitary, thoughtful, and independent thinker when being stagnated in the triangulation of a cookie-cutter, oppressive culture of a homeowner's association; a memoir all written in critical and didactic, poetic stanzas and passages, and out of desperation, when freedom and control get taken, what he is forced to do in the illusion of 'free will and volition,' something like the derivative art of a smart and ironic and social and cultural satire.

Fomite
Burlington, VT

Still Time - Michael Cocchiarale

Still Time is a collection of twenty-five short and shorter stories exploring tensions that arise in a variety of contemporary relationships: a young boy must deal with the wrath of his out-of-work father; a woman runs into a man twenty years after an awkward sexual encounter; a wife, unable to conceive, imagines her own murder, as well as the reaction of her emotionally distant husband; a soon-to-be-tenured English professor tries to come to terms with her husband's shocking return to the religion of his youth; an assembly line worker, married for thirty years, discovers the surprising secret life of his recently hospitalized wife.

Whether a few hundred or a few thousand words, these and other stories in the collection depict characters at moments of deep crisis. Some feel powerless, overwhelmed—unable to do much to change the course of their lives. Others rise to the occasion and, for better or for worse, say or do the thing that might transform them for good. Even in stories with the most troubling of endings, there remains the possibility of redemption. For each of the characters, there is still time.

Raven or Crow - Joshua Amses

Marlowe has recently moved back home to Vermont after flunking his first term at a private college in the Midwest, when his sort-of girlfriend, Eleanor, goes missing. The circumstances surrounding Eleanor's disappearance stand to reveal more about Marlowe than he is willing to allow. Rather than report her missing, he resolves to find Eleanor himself. *Raven or Crow* is the story of mistakes rooted in the ambivalence of being young and without direction.

The Good Muslim of Jackson Heights - *Jaysinh Birjépatil*

Jackson Heights in this book is a fictional locale with common features assembled from immigrant-friendly neighborhoods around the world where hard-working honest-to-goodness traders from the Indian subcontinent rub shoulders with ruthless entrepreneurs, reclusive antique-dealers, homeless nobodies, merchant-princes, lawyers, doctors, and IT specialists. But as Siraj and Shabnam, urbane newcomers fleeing religious persecution in their homeland, discover, there is no escape from the past. Weaving together the personal and the political. *The Good Muslim of Jackson Heights* is an ambiguous elegy to a utopian ideal set free from all prejudice.

Meanwell - *Janice Miller Potter*

Meanwell is a twenty-four-poem sequence in which a female servant searches for identity and meaning in the shadow of her mistress, poet Anne Bradstreet. Although Meanwell herself is a fiction, someone like her could easily have existed among Bradstreet's known but unnamed domestic servants. Through Meanwell's eyes, Bradstreet emerges as a human figure during the Great Migration of the 1600s, a period in which the Massachusetts Bay Colony was fraught with physical and political dangers. Through Meanwell, the feelings of women, silenced during the midwife Anne Hutchinson's fiery trial before the Puritan ministers, are finally acknowledged.

In effect, the poems are about the making of an American rebel. Through her conflicted conscience, we witness Meanwell's transformation from a powerless English waif to a mythic American who ultimately chooses wilderness over the civilization she has experienced.

Fomite
Burlington, VT

Body of Work - Andrei Guruianu

Throughout thirteen stories, Body of Work chronicles the physical and emotional toll of characters consumed by the all-too-human need for a connection. Their world is achingly common — beauty and regret, obsession and self-doubt, the seductive charm of loneliness. Often fragmented, whimsical, always on the verge of melancholy, the collection is a sepia-toned portrait of nostalgia — each story like an artifact of our impermanence, an embrace of all that we have lost, of all that we might lose and love again someday.

Four-Way Stop - Sherry Olson

If *Thank You* were the only prayer, as Meister Eckhart has suggested, it would be enough, and Sherry Olson's poetry, in her second book, *Four-Way Stop*, would be one. Radical attention, deep love, and dedication to kindness illuminate these poems and the stories she tells us, which are drawn from her own life: with family, with friends, and wherever she travels, with strangers – who to Olson, never are strangers, but kin. Even at the difficult intersections, as in the title poem, *Four-Way Stop*, Olson experiences – and offers – hope, showing us how, *completely unsupervised*, people take turns, with *kindness waving each other on*. Olson writes, knowing that (to quote Czeslaw Milosz) *What surrounds us, here and now, is not guaranteed*. To this world, with her poems, Olson brings – and teaches – attention, generosity, compassion, and appreciative joy. —Carol Henrikson

Dons of Time - Greg Guma

"Wherever you look…there you are." The next media breakthrough has just happened. They call it Remote Viewing and Tonio Wolfe is at the center of the storm. But the research underway at TELPORT's off-the-books lab is even more radical -- opening a window not only to remote places but completely different times. Now unsolved mysteries are colliding with cutting edge science and altered states of consciousness in a world of corporate gangsters, infamous crimes and top-secret experiments. Based on eyewitness accounts, suppressed documents and the lives of world-changers like Nikola Tesla, Annie Besant and Jack the Ripper, Dons of Time is a speculative adventure, a glimpse of an alternative future and a quantum leap to Gilded Age London at the tipping point of invention, revolution and murder.

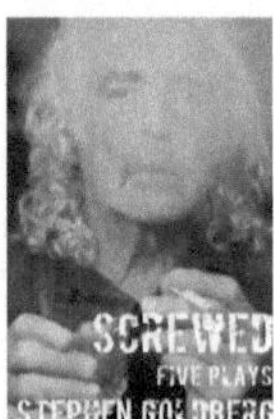

Screwed – Stephen Goldberg

Screwed is a collection of five plays by Stephen Goldberg, who has written over twenty-five produced plays and is co-founder of the Off Center or the Dramatic Arts in Burlington, Vermont.

Visiting Hours, a novel-in-stories, explores the lives of people not normally met on the page——AIDS patients and those who care for them. Set in Baton Rouge, Louisiana, and written with large and frequent dollops of humor, the book is a profound meditation on faith and love in the face of illness and poverty.

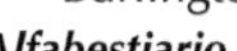

Fomite

Burlington, VT

Alfabestiario
AlphaBetaBestiario - Antonello Borra

Animals have always understood that mankind is not fully at home in the world. Bestiaries, hoping to teach, send out warnings. This one, of course, aims at doing the same.

The Consequence of Gesture - *L.E. Smith*

On a Monday evening in December of 1980, Mark David Chapman murdered John Lennon outside his apartment building in New York City. The Consequence of Gesture brings the reader along a three-day countdown to mayhem. This book inserts Chapman into the weekend plans of a group of friends sympathetic with his obsession to shatter a cultural icon and determined to perform their own iconoclastic gestures. John Lennon's life is not the only one that hangs in the balance. No one will emerge the same.

Unfinished Stories of Girls – Catherine Zobal Dent

The sixteen stories in this debut collection set on the Eastern Shore of Maryland feature powerfully drawn characters with troubles and subjects such as communal guilt over a drunk-driving car accident that kills a young girl, the doomed marriage of a jewelry clerk and an undercover cop, the obsessions of a housecleaner jailed for forging her employers' signatures, the heart-breaking closeness of a family stuck in the snow. Each of Unfinished Stories of Girls' richly textured tales is embedded in the quiet and sometimes violent fields, towns, and riverbeds that are the backdrop for life in tidewater Maryland. Dent's deep love for her region shines through, but so does her melancholic thoughtfulness about its challenges and problems. The reader is invited inside the lives of characters trying to figure out the marshy world around them, when that world leaves much up to the imagination.

Writing a review on Amazon, Good Reads, Shelfari, Library Thing or other social media sites for readers will help the progress of independent publishing. To submit a review, go to the book page on any of the sites and follow the links for reviews. Books from independent presses rely on reader to reader communications.***Visiting Hours*** - Jennifer Anne Moses

9 781937 677459